THE
DIABOLIQUES

BLUE
JADE
LIBRARY

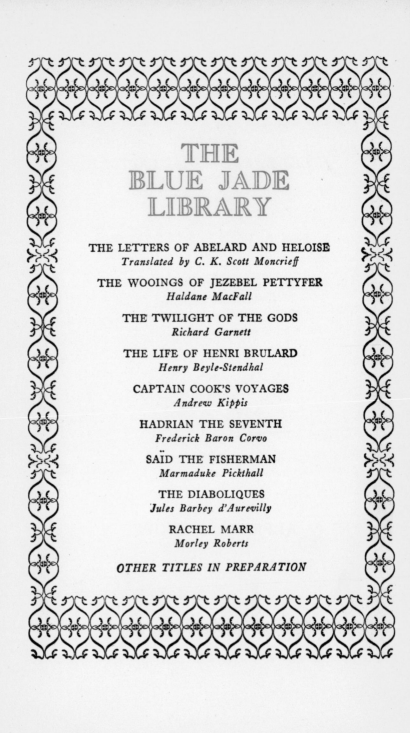

THE
BLUE JADE
LIBRARY

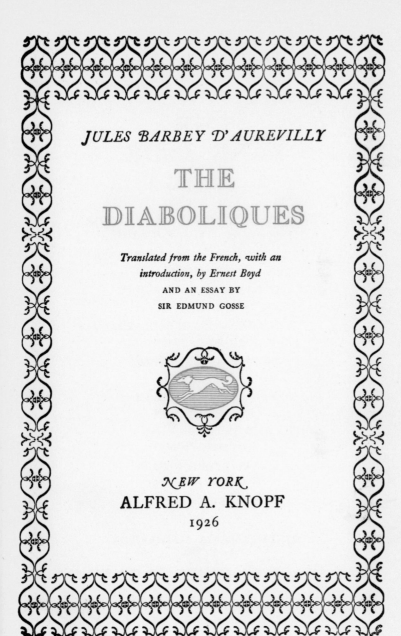

JULES BARBEY D'AUREVILLY

THE
DIABOLIQUES

*Translated from the French, with an
introduction, by Ernest Boyd*
AND AN ESSAY BY
SIR EDMUND GOSSE

NEW YORK
ALFRED A. KNOPF
1926

CONTENTS

INTRODUCTION

BY ERNEST BOYD

Jules Amédée Barbey d'Aurevilly was born at Saint-Sauveur-le-vicomte, in that Norman peninsula of La Manche whose claim upon the attention of the modern world lies rather in the fact that it serves as a background for the peculiar beauties of Cherbourg. That sonorous string of vocables appears in somewhat truncated form in the parish register, which says: "On Wednesday, this second day of November, 1808, Julle-Amédez Barbey, born yesterday, the legitimate offspring of Monsieur André-Marie-Théophile Barbey and Dame Ernestine-Eulalie-Théose Ango, his wife, was baptised by M. Dubost," who did not, as the record shows, foresee that this infant would find Barbey inadequate until, in his twenty-fifth year, he added the d'Aurevilly title which one of his uncles had borne, although by this time the lands of Aureville had passed out of the possession of the family. However, when Barbey d'Aurevilly died in Paris, at the age of eighty-one, that genealogical inexactitude was the least of the legends connected with this almost mythological figure.

During his long life, which actually embraced in its span the First Empire, the Restoration of the Bourbons, Louis Philippe, the Second Republic, the Second Empire, and the Third Republic, Barbey d'Aurevilly produced a very considerable amount of literature; forty-one volumes of poetry, fiction, criticism and biography which, with posthumous publications amounting to nearly half as many again, brings the complete bibliography of his writings to the total of sixty-three volumes. His verse is of little importance, but as a critic he presents a phenomenon of some interest. He was the rival and adversary of Sainte-Beuve, and during the same years both men necessarily commented upon the same publications as they appeared. As the one was the antithesis of the other, the divergence of their views makes comparison between them rather amusing for those interested in literary history. Barbey d'Aurevilly is impetuous, extravagant, impressionistic and inconsistent. His opponent was subtle, malicious, learned and authoritative. D'Aurevilly called Victor Hugo "an imbecile of genius"; the salon of Louise Colet was an "academic oyster bed"; Corneille was a "hydrocephalic hunchback," and the activities of George Sand were compared to those of a mother stork bringing innumerable little adulteries into the home. He had no sense of logic, consistency or proportion, and reviled the same authors for the same works which he had already praised. His own stories were anathema to all moralists, and blasphemous in the eyes of good Catholics, but he never ceased to declare himself a militant and pious child of the Church, and was loud in his denunciations of the immorality of all writers whom he did not like, from the author of *Manon Lescaut* to *Elle et lui*. Yet, to his credit stands his immediate appreciation of Baudelaire, Becque, Huysmans, Mendès, Bourget and Richepin, when he was often alone in his recognition of their potentialities.

The qualities which still lend a flavor to his criticism, however wrong-headed,—his mastery of striking epithet, his superb courage and imagination—find their supreme expression in his fiction. After writing, at the age of sixteen, an *Ode to the Heroes of Thermopylæ*, inspired by the Greek war of independence, and dedicated to Casimir Delavigne, he began his literary career proper, in 1834, with his first book of fiction, *Amaïdée*, which was not published until after his death, in 1890. To the same period belongs the story *Germaine*, written in 1835, but published forty-nine years later under the title of *Ce qui ne meurt pas*, which is known to English-speaking readers in the translation, "What Never Dies," attributed to Oscar Wilde. After two books of minor merit, there began to appear those works upon which he

established the fame that slowly accumulated during his lifetime: *Une vieille maîtresse, L'Ensorcelée, Le Chevalier des
Touches, Un prêtre marié, Les diaboliques,* and *Une histoire sans
nom,* which happens to have been his first book to appear in
English, when Edgar Saltus published *A Story without a Name,*
in 1891.

The trait common to all these stories, and the characteristic
mark of Barbey d'Aurevilly's peculiar talent, is their Satanic
mysticism, their preoccupation with what is diabolical, in the
literal and original sense of that word. The title, *Les diaboliques,*
describes not only the six women of this book, but the central
figures in all the others, for all Barbey's characters are possessed by the devil. In *L'ensorcelée,* the Abbé Croix-Jugan, his
face seared by the pistol shot with which he tried to commit
suicide, looked "like a demon in priestly garb, who came to defy
God in His own Church, in the shadow of the crucifix." He was
shot at the altar by a jealous husband, and his spectre haunts
the church of Blanchelande at midnight, when the clock always
strikes nine (the hour at which the mass was interrupted), trying to celebrate a phantom mass to the end. It is significant that
this same volume contained *Le dessous de cartes d'une partie de
whist,* which was included in *Les diaboliques,* twenty years later,
and which made "the dowagers cry out against the corruption of
their daughters" and the author's "devilish writings." *La vieille
maîtresse,* which is the other novel belonging to the period when
Barbey's Catholicism was most intransigeant, is as Satanic as
any of the works which followed his break with the pious friend
of his youth and his publisher, Trébutien, who acted as a check
upon Barbey's instinctive Romantic æstheticism. That element
warred incessantly with his Christian moralism, but neither
Trébutien nor any other orthodox believer could reconcile
d'Aurevilly's stern theories with his immoral practice. La Vellini
was "a feminine trilogy, composed of woman, demon and animal,"
and even this most Balzacian of his novels was never accepted,
as Barbey wished *La Vieille maîtresse* to be accepted, as a work

of lofty Catholic morality. So much the worse, said he, for the "bloodless of good taste," which became his favourite expression of contempt.

The Chevalier des Touches, as a layman, is lacking in that flavour of sacrilege and blasphemy in which Barbey d'Aurevilly's Catholic soul found its shuddering delight, but he is an enigmatic, cruel, androgynous figure, of the authentic diabolonian lineage. The Abbé Sombreval in *Un prêtre marié* is the perfect devil's disciple, this priest who has broken his vows, and whose daughter has the mark of the cross upon her forehead, who loves her to a point at which no crime nor blasphemy can stop him, but who loses her to God and ends by disinterring her corpse and disappearing for ever from mortal sight by jumping into a pond with the girl clasped in his arms. No trace of them is ever found. His reverend brother in evil is the Capuchin father Riculf in *Une histoire sans nom,* whose mission to the little village in the Cevennes includes the rape of Lasthénie de Ferjol while she is lying in a somnambulistic sleep on the staircase, with mysterious consequences which are explained only after the broken-hearted girl is dead. Léon Bloy, in many ways the unique successor to Barbey's disquieting tradition of Catholicism in French literature, declared that *Un prêtre marié* was "the only Christian novel which a human being could read," but the Archbishop of Paris ordered every copy of it to be destroyed. Like Jules Lemaître, that prelate apparently thought that there was "nothing less Christian than the Catholicism of M. d'Aurevilly. It looks like the feather in a musketeer's cap. . . . M. d'Aurevilly wears his God in his hat." The damned have an irresistible attraction for him. "He cannot admit that they could ever be flat-footed or poor devils . . . Almost all the heroes of the novels written by this Christian are atheists, and atheists of genius—with tender hearts. He regards them with a terror full of secret tenderness. He is deliciously fascinated by the devil."

Jules Lemaître, it is clear, was not very sympathetic to Barbey, and saw the ludicrous rather than the weirdly imaginative side of him. Sadistic Catholicism had no attraction for the French critic, either in his sceptical youth, when he wrote his *Contemporains*, or in the later period of his patriotic and right-thinking royalism, although never was there a more vociferous monarchist, aristocrat and champion of law and order than Barbey d'Aurevilly. Yet, one will search in vain for his name even in a footnote to any of the standard histories of French literature by Brunetière, Faguet, Doumic, and Lanson—not to mention their imitators and echoes in America and England. George Saintsbury and Edmund Gosse have rushed in where the Professors Nitze and Dargan and the rest fear to tread. But appreciation of Barbey d'Aurevilly has been restricted to the "happy few" of Stendhal, who was with Byron and Balzac the master of the author of *Les diaboliques*. These three are a strange but happy combination, the more so perhaps because Barbey, with characteristic perversity, realized without disapprobation the incest motive in Byron's life, and actually related a complaisant story of the same kind, founded upon historical fact, in *Une page d'histoire*, his last work of narrative prose, but denounced Edgar Allan Poe, whose power he recognized, as a reprehensible influence!

His style has been described as "brutal and exquisite, violent and delicate, bitter and sweet. It is like a witches' brew composed of flowers and serpents, tigers' blood and honey,"—a compliment decidedly in his own style. Readers of *The Pleasant Memoirs of the Marquis of Bradomín* will find in *Les diaboliques* the source of Ramón del Valle-Inclán's inspiration, for Barbey d'Aurevilly, like the Marquis, was "ugly, Catholic and sentimental." The story of *The Crimson Curtain* is in essence the fourth *Sonata* of the *Memoirs*, and the Spanish novelist's first book was palpably patterned on *Les diaboliques*. *Femeninas* was also a series of six studies of women, with La Niña Chole so typical a figure out of Barbey d'Aurevilly that the stories were later republished as *Historias perversas*, and served in part to make the *Sonata of Summer* in the *Memoirs*, which is, in turn, essentially a work after Barbey's own heart, in its mixture of perversity, romanticism, blasphemy and sentimentality. Ramón del Valle-Inclán learned also from his French predecessor the value of creating a personal legend and dressing one's part in literature. Barbey d'Aurevilly, as became a dandy of 1840, who had written a book on Beau Brummel and *dandyisme,* preserved to the end of his life the corset and the costume of the period. Eye-witnesses report that he looked like Mesnilgrand, the hero of *Un dîner d'athées.*

He wore what he himself would call "a love of a frock coat," with flowing skirts and broad lapels. His waistcoat was of velvet or black cashmere, and his white cravat had the tint of old ivory, dotted with imperceptible little hand-embroidered stars. He wore lace cuffs fastened with diamond studs, and plum-coloured trousers with mauve tints, strapped under his boots. His long hair, beneath a huge wideawake hat, was dyed, and, as his nails were long, they were usually black, because he would run his fingers wildly through his mane. Such was the figure whom Anatole France remembered when, as a child of nine, he went out with his grandmother, who pointed out the gentleman with the hat whose brim was of crimson velvet, and who slapped his tight, gold braided trousers with his riding-whip. It was the same figure upon whom France and Paul Bourget used to call later on, when he lived in his bare little room in the Rue Rousselet, concealing his poverty with his accustomed magnificence: "I have sent my furniture and my tapestries to my estate in the country." He was one of Anatole France's earliest memories and one of the most enduring, and so he will be for those who once submit to his violent enchantment. Who could forget the man who said to Baudelaire: "I have always put my passions above my convictions"? It would be difficult to find a better summary of Barbey d'Aurevilly, the man and his work.

JULES BARBEY D'AUREVILLY *

BY SIR EDMUND GOSSE

Those who can endure an excursion into the backwaters of literature may contemplate, neither too seriously nor too lengthily, the career and writings of Barbey d'Aurevilly. Very obscure in his youth, he lived so long, and preserved his force so consistently, that in his old age he became, if not quite a celebrity, most certainly a notoriety. At the close of his life—he reached his eighty-first year—he was still to be seen walking the streets or haunting the churches of Paris, his long, sparse hair flying in the wind, his fierce eyes flashing about him, his hat poised on the side of his head, his famous lace frills turned back over the cuff of his coat, his attitude always erect, defiant, and formidable. Down to the winter of 1888 he preserved the dandy dress of 1840, and never appeared but as M. de Pontmartin has described him, in black satin trousers, which fitted his old legs like a glove, in a flapping, brigand wide-awake, in a velvet waistcoat, which revealed diamond studs and a lace cravat, and in a wonderful shirt that covered the most artful pair of stays. In every action, in every glance, he seemed to be defying the natural decay of years, and to be forcing old age to forget him by dint of spirited and ceaseless self-assertion. He was himself the prototype of all the Brassards and Misnilgrands of his stories, the dandy of dandies, the mummied and immortal beau.

His intellectual condition was not unlike his physical one. He was a survival—of the most persistent. The last, by far the last, of the *Romantiques* of 1835, Barbey d'Aurevilly lived on into an

* Reprinted by permission of the publishers, Messrs. Charles Scribners' Sons, from *French Profiles*.

age wholly given over to other aims and ambitions, without
changing his own ideals by an iota. He was to the great man
who began the revival, to figures like Alfred de Vigny, as Shirley
was to the early Elizabethans. He continued the old tradition,
without resigning a single habit or prejudice, until his mind was
not a whit less old-fashioned than his garments. Victor Hugo,
who hated him, is said to have dedicated an unpublished verse
to his portrait:

> *"Barbey d'Aurevilly, formidable imbécile."*

But *imbécile* was not at all the right word. He was absurd; he
was outrageous; he had, perhaps, by dint of resisting the de-
crepitude of his natural powers, become a little crazy. But im-
becility is the very last word to use of this mutinous, dogged,
implacable old pirate of letters.

Jules Barbey d'Aurevilly was born near Valognes (the "V——"
which figures in several of his stories) on the 2nd of November,
1808. He liked to represent himself as a scion of the bluest nobility of Normandy, and he communicated to the makers of dic-
tionaries the fact that the name of his direct ancestor is engraved
on the tomb of William the Conqueror. But some have said that
the names of his father and mother were never known, and
others (poor d'Aurevilly!) have set him down as the son of a
butcher in the village of Saint-Sauveur-le-Vicomte. While yet a
school-boy, in 1825, he published an elegy *Aux héros des
Thermopyles,* and dedicated it to Casimir Delavigne. He was
at college with Maurice de Guérin, and quite early he became
personally acquainted with Chateaubriand. His youth seems to
be wrapped up in mystery; according to one of the best-informed
of his biographers, he vanished in 1831, and was not heard of
again until 1851. To these twenty years of alleged disappearance,
one or two remarkable books of his are, however, ascribed. So
characteristic a novel as *L'Amour Impossible* saw the light in
1841, and it appears that what is perhaps the most characteristic of all his writings, *Du Dandyisme et de Georges Brummell,*

was written as early as 1842. In 1845 a very small edition of it was printed by an admirer of the name of Trebutien, to whose affection d'Aurevilly seems to have owed his very existence. It is strange that so little is distinctly known about a man who, late in life, attracted much curiosity and attention. He was a consummate romancer, and he liked to hint that he was engaged during early life in intrigues of a corsair description. The truth seems to be that he lived, in great obscurity, in the neighbourhood of Caen, probably by the aid of journalism.

Of all the productions of his youth, the only one which can now be met with is the prose poem of *Amaïdée,* written, I suppose, about 1835; this was published by M. Paul Bourget as a curiosity immediately after Barbey d'Aurevilly's death. Judged as a story, *Amaïdée* is puerile; it describes how to a certain poet, called Somegod, who dwelt on a lonely cliff, there came a young man altogether wise and stately named Altaï, and a frail daughter of passion, who gives her name to the book. These three personages converse in magnificent language, and, the visitors presently departing, the volume closes. But an interest attaches to the fact that in Somegod (*Quelque Dieu!*) the author was painting a portrait of Maurice de Guérin, while the majestic Altaï is himself. The conception of this book is Ossianic; but the style is often singularly beautiful, with a marmoreal splendour founded on a study of Chateaubriand and, perhaps, of Goethe, and not without relation to that of Guérin himself.

The earliest surviving production of d'Aurevilly, if we except *Amaïdée,* is *L'Amour Impossible,* a novel published with the object of correcting the effects of the poisonous *Lélia* of George Sand. Already, in the crude book, we see something of the Barbey d'Aurevilly of the future, the Dandy-Paladin, the Catholic Sensualist or Diavolist, the author of the few poor thoughts and the sonorous, paroxysmal, abundant style. I forget whether it is here or in a slightly later novel that, in hastily turning the pages, I detect the sentiment, "Our forefathers were wise to cut the throats of the Huguenots, and very stupid not to burn Luther."

The late Master of Balliol is said to have asked a reactionary undergraduate: "What, sir! would you burn, would you burn?" If he had put the question to Barbey d'Aurevilly, the scented hand would have been laid on the cambric bosom, and the answer would have been: "Certainly I should." In the midst of the infidel society and literature of the Second Empire, d'Aurevilly persisted in the most noisy profession of his entire loyalty to Rome, but his methods of proclaiming his attachment were so violent and outrageous that the Church showed no gratitude to her volunteer defender. This was a source of much bitterness and recrimination, but it is difficult to see how the author of *Le Prêtre Marié* (1864) and *Une Histoire sans Nom* (1882) could expect pious Catholics to smile on his very peculiar treatment of ecclesiastical life.

Barbey d'Aurevilly undertook to continue the work of Chateaubriand, and he gave his full attention to a development of the monarchical neo-catholicism which that great inaugurator had sketched out. He was impressed by the beauty of the Roman ceremonial, and he determined to express with poetic emotion the mystical majesty of the symbol. It must be admitted that, although his work never suggests any knowledge of or sympathy with the spiritual part of religion, he has a genuine appreciation of its externals. It would be difficult to point to a more delicate and full impression of the solemnity which attends the crepuscular light of a church at vespers than is given in the opening pages of *A un Dîner d'Athées*. In *L'Ensorcelée* (1854), too, we find the author piously following a chanting procession round a church, and ejaculating: "*Rien n'est beau comme cet instant solennel des cérémonies catholiques.*" Almost every one of his novels deals by preference with ecclesiastical subjects, or introduces some powerful figure of a priest. But it is very difficult to believe that his interest in it all is other than histrionic or phenomenal. He likes the business of a priest, he likes the furniture of a church, but there, in spite of his vehement protestations, his piety seems to a candid reader to have begun and ended.

For a humble and reverent child of the Catholic Church, it must be confessed that Barbey d'Aurevilly takes strange liberties. The mother would seem to have had little control over the caprices of her extremely unruly son. There is scarcely one of these ultra-Catholic novels of his which it is conceivable that a pious family would like to see lying upon its parlour table. The Devil takes a prominent part in many of them, for d'Aurevilly's whim is to see Satanism everywhere, and to consider it matter of mirth; he is like a naughty boy, giggling when a rude man breaks his mother's crockery. He loves to play with dangerous and forbidden notions. In *Le Prêtre Marié* (which, to his lofty indignation, was forbidden to be sold in Catholic shops) the hero is a renegade and incestuous priest, who loves his own daughter, and makes a hypocritical confession of error in order that, by that act of perjury, he may save her life, as she is dying of the agony of knowing him to be an atheist. This man, the Abbé Sombreval, is bewitched, is possessed of the Devil, and so is Ryno de Marigny in *Une Vieille Maîtresse,* and Lasthénie de Ferjol in *Une Histoire sans Nom.* This is one of Barbey d'Aurevilly's favourite tricks, to paint an extraordinary, an abnormal condition of spirit, and to avoid the psychological difficulty by simply attributing it to sorcery. But he is all the time rather amused by the wickedness than shocked at it. In *Le Bonheur dans le Crime*—the moral of which is that people of a certain grandeur of temperament can be absolutely wicked with impunity—he frankly confesses his partiality for *"la plaisanterie légèrement sacrilège,"* and all the philosophy of d'Aurevilly is revealed in that rash phrase. It is not a matter of a wounded conscience expressing itself with a brutal fervour, but the gusto of conscious wickedness. His mind is intimately akin with that of the Neapolitan lady, whose story he was perhaps the first to tell, who wished that it only were a sin to drink iced sherbet. Barbey d'Aurevilly is a devil who may or may not believe, but who always makes a point of trembling.

The most interesting feature of Barbey d'Aurevilly's temperament, as revealed in his imaginative work, is, however, his pre-occupation with his own physical life. In his youth, Byron and Alfieri were the objects of his deepest idolatry; he envied their disdainful splendour of passion; and he fashioned his dream in poverty and obscurity so as to make himself believe that he was of their race. He was a Disraeli—with whom, indeed, he has certain relations of style—but with none of Disraeli's social advantages, and with a more inconsequent and violent habit of imagination. Unable, from want of wealth and position, to carry his dreams into effect, they became exasperated and intensified, and at an age when the real dandy is settling down into a man of the world, Barbey d'Aurevilly was spreading the wings of his fancy into the infinite azure of imaginary experience. He had convinced himself that he was a Lovelace, a Lauzun, a Brummell, and the philosophy of dandyism filled his thoughts far more than if he had really been able to spend a stormy youth among marchionesses who carried, set in diamonds in a bracelet, the ends of the moustaches of viscounts. In the novels of his maturity and his old age, therefore, Barbey d'Aurevilly loved to introduce magnificent aged dandies, whose fatuity he dwelt upon with ecstasy, and in whom there is no question that he saw reflections of his imaginary self. No better type of this can be found than that Vicomte de Brassard, an elaborate, almost enamoured, portrait of whom fills the earlier pages of what is else a rather dull story, *Le Rideau Cramoisi*. The very clever, very immoral tale called *Le Plus Bel Amour de Don Juan*—which relates how a super-annuated but still incredibly vigorous old beau gives a supper to the beautiful women of quality whom he has known, and recounts to them the most piquant adventure of his life—is redolent of this intense delight in the prolongation of enjoyment by sheer refusal to admit the ravages of age. Although my space forbids quotation, I cannot resist repeating a passage which illustrates this horrible fear of the loss of youth and the struggle against it, more especially as it is a good example of d'Aurevilly's surcharged and intrepid style:

"Il n'y avait pas là de ces jeunesses vert tendre, de ces petites demoiselles qu'exécrait Byron, qui sentent la tartelette et qui, par la tournure, ne sont encore que des épluchettes, mais tous étés splendides et savoureux, plantureux automnes, épanouissements et plénitudes, seins éblouissants battant leur plein majestueux au bord découvert des corsages, et, sous les camées de l'épaule nue, des bras de tout galbe, mais surtout des bras puissants, de ces biceps de Sabines qui ont lutté avec les Romains, et qui seraient capables de s'entrelacer, pour l'arrêter, dans les rayons de la roue du char de la vie."

This obsession of vanishing youth, this intense determination to preserve the semblance and colour of vitality, in spite of the passage of years, is however, seen to greatest advantage in a very curious book of Barbey d'Aurevilly's, in some aspects, indeed, the most curious which he has left behind him, *Du Dandyisme et de Georges Brummell.* This is really a work of his early maturity, for, as I have said, it was printed so long ago as 1845. It was not published, however, until 1861, when it may be said to have introduced its author to the world of France. Later on he wrote a curious study of the fascination exercised over *La Grande Mademoiselle* by Lauzun, *Un Dandy d'avant les Dandys,* and these two are now published in one volume, which forms that section of the immense work of d'Aurevilly which best rewards the curious reader.

Many writers in England, from Thomas Carlyle in *Sartor Resartus* to our ingenious young forger of paradoxes, Mr. Max Beerbohm, have dealt upon that semi-feminine passion in fatuity, that sublime attention to costume and deportment, which marks the dandy. The type has been, as d'Aurevilly does not fail to observe, mainly an English one. We point to Beau Nash, to Byron, to Lord Yarmouth, to Sheridan, and, above all, *"à ce Dandy royal, S. M. Georges IV";* but the star of each of these must pale before that of Brummell. These others, as was said in a different matter, had "other preoccupations," but Brummell was entirely absorbed, as by a solemn mission, by the conduct of his person and his clothes. So far, in the portraiture of such a figure, there is nothing very singular in what the French novelist has skilfully and nimbly done, but it is his own attitude which is so original. All other writers on the dandies have had their tongues in their cheeks. If they have commended, it is because to be preposterous is to be amusing. When we read that "dandyism is the least selfish of all the arts," we smile, for we know that the author's design is to be entertaining. But Barbey d'Aurevilly is doggedly in earnest. He loves the great dandies of the past as other men contemplate with ardour dead poets and dead musicians. He is seriously enamoured of their mode of life. He sees nothing ridiculous, nothing even limited, in their self-concentration. It reminds him of the tiger and of the condor; it recalls to his imagination the vast, solitary forces of Nature; and when he contemplates Beau Brummell, his eyes fill with tears of nostalgia. So would he have desired to live; thus, and not otherwise, would he fain have strutted and trampled through that eighteenth century to which he is for ever gazing back with a fond regret. "To dress one's self," he says, "should be the main business of life," and with great ingenuity he dwells upon the latent but positive influence which dress has had on men of a nature apparently furthest removed from its trivialities; upon Pascal, for instance, upon Buffon, upon Wagner.

It was natural that a writer who delighted in this patrician ideal of conquering man should have a limited conception of life. Women to Barbey d'Aurevilly were of two varieties—either nuns or amorous tigresses; they were sometimes both in one. He had no idea of soft gradations in society: there were the tempestuous marchioness and her intriguing maid on one side; on the other, emptiness, the sordid hovels of the bourgeoisie. This absence of observation or recognition of life d'Aurevilly shared with the other *Romantiques,* but in his sinister and contemptuous aristocracy he passed beyond them all. Had he lived to become acquainted with the writings of Nietzsche, he would have hailed a brother-spirit, one who loathed democracy and the humanitarian temper as much as he did himself. But there is no philosophy in

Barbey d'Aurevilly, nothing but a prejudice fostered and a sentiment indulged.

In referring to *Nicholas Nickleby*, a novel which he vainly endeavoured to get through, d'Aurevilly remarks: "I wish to write
an essay on Dickens, and at present I have read only one hundred
pages of his writings. But I consider that if *one hundred pages*
do not give the talent of a man, they give his spirit, and the spirit
of Dickens is odious to me." "The vulgar Dickens," he calmly
remarks in *Journalistes et Polémistes,* and we laugh at the idea
of sweeping away such a record of genius on the strength of a
chapter or two misread in *Nicholas Nickleby.* But Barbey
d'Aurevilly was not Dickens, and it really is not necessary to
study closely the vast body of his writings. The same charac-
teristics recur in them all, and the impression may easily be
weakened by vain repetition. In particular, a great part of the
later life of d'Aurevilly was occupied in writing critical notices
and studies for newspapers and reviews. He made this, I suppose, his principal source of income; and from the moment when,
in 1851, he became literary critic to *Le Pays* to that of his death,
nearly forty years later, he was incessantly dogmatizing about
literature and art. He never became a critical force, he was too
violent and, indeed, too empty for that; but a pen so brilliant as
his is always welcome with editors whose design is not to be true,
but to be noticeable, and to escape "the obvious." The most cruel
of Barbey d'Aurevilly's enemies could not charge his criticism
with being obvious. It is intensely contentious and contradictory.
It treats all writers and artists on the accepted nursery principle
of "Go and see what baby's doing, and tell him not to." This
is entertaining for a moment; and if the shower of abuse is spread
broadly enough, some of it must come down on shoulders that
deserve it. But the "slashing" review of yester-year is dismal
reading, and it cannot be said that the library of reprinted criticism to which d'Aurevilly gave the general title of *Les Œuvres
et les Hommes* (1861–65) is very enticing.

He had a great contempt for Goethe and for Sainte-Beuve, in whom he saw false priests constantly leading the public away from the true principle of literary expression, *"le couronnement, la gloire et la force de toute critique, que je cherche en vain."* A very ingenious writer, M. Ernest Tissot, has paid Barbey d'Aurevilly the compliment of taking him seriously in this matter, and has written an elaborate study on what his *criterium* was. But this is, perhaps, to inquire too kindly. I doubt whether he sought with any very sincere expectation of finding; like the Persian sage, "he swore, but was he sober when he swore?" Was he not rather intoxicated with his self-encouraged romantic exasperation, and determined to be fierce, independent, and uncompromising at all hazards? Such are, at all events, the doubts awakened by his indignant diatribes, which once amused Paris so much, and now influence no living creature. Some of his dicta, in their showy way, are forcible. *"La critique a pour blason la croix, la balance et la glaive";* that is a capital phrase on the lips of a reviewer, who makes himself the appointed Catholic censor of worldly letters, and is willing to assume at once the cross, the scales, and the sword. More of the hoof peeps out in this: *"La critique, c'est une intrépidité de l'esprit et du caractère."* To a nature like that of d'Aurevilly, the distinction between intrepidity and arrogance is never clearly defined.

It is, after all, in his novels that Barbey d'Aurevilly displays his talent in its most interesting form. His powers developed late; and perhaps the best-constructed of all his tales is *Une Histoire sans Nom,* which dates from 1882, when he was quite an old man. In this, as in all the rest, a surprising narrative is well, although extremely leisurely, told, but without a trace of psychology. It was impossible for d'Aurevilly to close his stories effectively; in almost every case, the futility and extravagance of the last few pages destroys the effect of the rest. Like the Fat Boy, he wanted to make your flesh creep, to leave you cataleptic with horror at the end, but he had none of Poe's skill in producing an effect of terror. In *Le Rideau Cramoisi* (which is considered,

I cannot tell why, one of his successes), the heroine dies at an embarrassing moment, without any disease or cause of death being suggested—she simply dies. But he is generally much more violent than this; at the close of *A un Dîner d'Athées,* which up to a certain point is an extremely fine piece of writing, the angry parents pelt one another with the mummied heart of their only child; in *Le Dessous des Cartes,* the key of all the intrigue is discovered at last in the skeleton of an infant buried in a box of mignonette. If it is not by a monstrous fact, it is by an audacious feat of anti-morality, that Barbey d'Aurevilly seeks to harrow and terrify our imaginations. In *Le Bonheur dans le Crime,* Hauteclaire Stassin, the woman-fencer, and the Count of Savigny pursue their wild intrigue and murder the Countess slowly, and then marry each other, and live, with youth far prolonged (d'Aurevilly's special idea of divine blessing), without a pang of remorse, without a crumpled rose-leaf in their felicity, like two magnificent plants spreading in the violent moisture of a tropical forest.

On the whole, it is as a writer, pure and simple, that Barbey d'Aurevilly claims most attention. His style, which Paul de Saint-Victor (quite in his own spirit) described as a mixture of tiger's blood and honey, is full of extravagant beauty. He has a strange intensity, a sensual and fantastic force, in his torrent of intertwined sentences and preposterous exclamations. The volume called *Les Diaboliques,* which contains a group of his most characteristic stories, published in 1874, may be recommended to those who wish, in a single example, compendiously to test the quality of Barbey d'Aurevilly. He has a curious love of punning, not for purposes of humour, but to intensify his style: *"Quel oubli et quelle oubliette"* (*Le Dessous des Cartes*), *"boudoir fleur de pêcher ou de péché"* (*Le Plus bel Amour*), *"renoncer à l'amour malpropre, mais jamais à l'amour propre"* (*A un Dîner d'Athées*). He has audacious phrases which linger in the memory: *"Le Profil, c'est l'écueil de la beauté"* (*Le Bonheur dans le Crime*); *"Les verres à champagne de France, un lotus qui faisait [les Anglais] oublier les sombres et religieuses habitudes de la patrie";*

"Elle avait l'air de monter vers Dieu, las mains toutes pleines de bonnes œuvres" (*Memoranda*).

That Barbey d'Aurevilly will take any prominent place in the history of literature is improbable. He was a curiosity, a droll, obstinate survival. We like to think of him in his incredible dress, strolling through the streets of Paris, with his clouded cane like a sceptre in one hand, and in the other that small mirror by which every few minutes he adjusted the poise of his cravat, or the studious tempest of his hair. He was a wonderful old fop or beau of the forties handed down to the eighties in perfect preservation. As a writer he was fervid, sumptuous, magnificently puerile; I have been told that he was a superb talker, that his conversation was like his books, a flood of paradoxical, flamboyant rhetoric. He made a gallant stand against old age, he defied it long with success, and when it conquered him at last, he retired to his hole like a rat, and died with stoic fortitude, alone, without a friend to close his eyelids. It was in a wretched lodging high up in a house in the Rue Rousselet, all his finery cast aside, and three melancholy cats the sole mourners by his body, that they found, on an April morning of 1889, the ruins of what had once been Barbey d'Aurevilly.

THE CRIMSON CURTAIN

THE CRIMSON CURTAIN

A CONSIDERABLE number of years ago I went to shoot waterfowl in the western marshes, and, as there was no railway then, I took the diligence, which passed the cross-roads near the Château de Rueil, and which at that precise moment contained only one passenger inside. This person, a very remarkable man in every respect, and whom I knew by having often met him in society, I will ask your permission to introduce as the Vicomte de Brassard. The precaution is probably useless! The few hundred people who constitute Parisian society are, no doubt, able to supply the real name. It was about five o'clock in the evening. The sun shed its slanting rays on a dusty road, edged with poplar-trees and fields, through which we rattled, drawn by four stout horses, whose strong flanks rolled heavily at each crack of the postilion's whip—a postilion always reminds me of life, there is a great deal too much whip-cracking at the outset.

Vicomte de Brassard was at that time of life when he was no longer disposed to crack his whip. But he was one of those men worthy of being an Englishman (he was educated in England), who, if he had been mortally wounded, would have died declaring he was alive. In the world, and even in books, we are used to laugh at the pretensions to youth of those who have passed the happy age of inexperience and foolishness—and the custom is not a bad one when the pretensions take a ridiculous form; but when they do not, but on the contrary assume a pride that will not confess defeat, I do not say they are not senseless, for they are useless, but they deserve respect, like many other senseless things. If it was heroic of the Guards at Waterloo to die and not surrender, it is the same when we are face to face with old age, which is not so romantic as bayonets. Some heads

are built in a military manner, never to surrender, and that is
the whole question, as it was at Waterloo.

Vicomte de Brassard, who has not surrendered—he is still
alive, and I will tell you about him later, for it is worth knowing
—Vicomte de Brassard was then, at the time when I travelled
with him in the diligence, what the world, which is as spiteful as
an old woman, rudely calls "an old beau." For those who care
little for words or figures, and who deem that in the matter of
age a man is only as old as he appears to be, Vicomte de Brassard might have passed for a "beau" without any qualification.
At least, at that very time the Marquise de V . . . —who was an
expert judge of young men, and who had shaved a dozen men
as clean as Delilah shaved Samson—wore, with much pride in
an enamelled gold bracelet, one of the ends of the Vicomte's
moustache, of which time, or the devil, had not changed the
colour. Only, whether old or not, do not attach to the expression
"beau," as the world has done, an idea of someone frivolous, lean,
and cadaverous, for you would not have a proper idea of Vicomte
de Brassard, in whom everything—intellect, manners, physiognomy—was large, opulent, redolent of patrician calmness, as
befitted the most magnificent dandy I have ever known—I, who
have seen Brummell go mad, and d'Orsay die.

For he was really a true dandy. If he had been less so, he
would certainly have become Marshal of France. He had been
in his youth one of the most brilliant officers of the latter days
of the First Empire. I have heard it said many times by his
regimental comrades that he was distinguished by the bravery
of Murat added to that of Marmont, and that as he was cool
and level-headed when the drums were not beating, he might in
a short time have attained to the highest rank of the military
hierarchy if it had not been for dandyism. If you combine
dandyism with the qualities which go to make up an officer—
discipline, regularity, etc.—you will see how much of the officer
will remain in the combination, and whether he does not blow
up like a powder-magazine. If the Vicomte de Brassard had

never exploded, it was because, like all dandies, he was happy. Mazarin would have employed him—and so would Mazarin's nieces, but for another reason. He was superb.

He had had that beauty which is necessary to a soldier more than to anyone else, for there is no youth without beauty, and the army is the youth of France! It was that beauty, moreover, which not only seduces women; but circumstances themselves— the rascals—had not been the only protection spread over the head of Captain de Brassard. He was, I believe, of Norman family, of the race of William the Conqueror, and he had, it is said, conquered a good deal himself. After the abdication of the Emperor, he had naturally gone over to the Bourbons, and, during the Hundred Days, had remained supernaturally faithful to them. So, when the Bourbons came back for the second time, the Vicomte was made a Chevalier of Saint-Louis and decorated by Charles X (then Monsieur) with his own royal hand. During the whole time of the Restoration, the handsome de Brassard never once mounted Guard at the Tuileries without the Duchesse of Angoulême addressing a few gracious words to him as she passed. She in whom misfortune had slain graciousness, managed to find some for him. The Minister, seeing this favour, would have done all he could to advance the man whom Madame thus singled out; but, with the best will in the world, what could be done for this terrible dandy who, at a review, had drawn his sword on the inspecting general for having made some remarks about his military duties? It was quite enough to save him from a court martial. This careless disdain of discipline always distinguished Vicomte de Brassard.

Except when on a campaign, when he was a thorough officer, he was never amenable to discipline. Many times he had been known—at the risk of being imprisoned for an indefinite period— to have secretly left a garrison, to go and amuse himself in some neighbouring town, and only to return when there was a review or a parade—warned by one of the soldiers, who loved him, for if his superiors scarcely cared to have under their orders a man to whom were repugnant all routine and discipline, the soldiers, on the other hand, adored him. To them he was an excellent officer. He only required that they should be brave, punctilious, and careful in their persons and dress, and thus realize the old type of the French soldier, as he is depicted in *La Permission de dix heures,* and in two or three old songs which are masterpieces in their way. He was, perhaps, too fond of making them fight duels, but he asserted that it was the best means he knew to develop the military spirit. "I am not the government," he said, "and I have no medals to give them when they fight bravely amongst themselves, but the Orders of which I am the grand-master (he had a considerable private fortune) are gloves, spare cross-belts, and whatever may spruce them up—so far as the regulations will allow."

So the company which he commanded eclipsed, in the matter of equipment, all the other companies of the Grenadiers of the Guard, brilliant as they were. Thus he flattered to excess the soldiers, who in France are always prone to fatuity and coquetry, two permanent provocations, the one because of its tone, the other because of the envy it excites. It will easily be understood, after this, that all the other companies were jealous of his. The men would fight to get into it, and then had to fight not to get out of it.

Such had been, during the Restoration, the exceptional position of Captain Vicomte de Brassard. And as he had not then every day, as he had during the Empire, the resource of doing brave deeds which would have caused all to be forgiven, no one could have foreseen or guessed how long this insubordination which astonished his comrades, would have lasted, but the Revolution of 1830 happened just in time to prevent him from being cashiered. He was badly wounded during the Three Days, and disdained to take service under the new dynasty of the Orleans, for whom he had contempt. When the Revolution of July made them masters of a country they did not know how to keep, it found the Captain in bed, laid up with an injury to his foot which he had received in

dancing—as he would have charged—at the last ball of the
Duchesse de Berry.

But at the first roll of the drum he, nevertheless, rose and
joined his company, and as he would not put on his boots on
account of his wound, he went to the rioting as he would have
gone to a ball, in varnished shoes and silk socks, and it was thus
he led his grenadiers to the Place de la Bastille, with instructions
to clear the whole length of the Boulevards.

Paris, in which no barricades had yet been erected, had a
gloomy and terrible appearance. It was deserted. The sun
glared down, and seemed a fiery rain, soon to be followed by
another, when from behind the closed shutters of every window
there should pour a deadly storm.

Captain de Brassard drew up his men in two lines, as close as
possible to each row of houses so that each file of soldiers was
exposed only to the fire from the houses opposite, whilst he, more
dandified than ever, walked down the middle of the road.
Aimed at from both sides by thousands of guns, pistols, and
carbines, all the way from the Bastille to the Rue de Richelieu,
he was not hit, in spite of the breadth of his chest, of which he
was perhaps a little too proud—for Captain de Brassard swelled
out his chest in a fight, as a pretty woman who wants to show
off her charms does at a ball—when, just as he arrived in front
of Frascati's, at the corner of the Rue de Richelieu, and at the
moment when he commanded the troops to mass together in
order to carry the first barricade which he had found on his road,
he received a ball in this magnificent chest, which was doubly
tempting, both on account of its size and the long silver braid
which went from one shoulder to the other, and he had also his
arm broken by a stone—which did not prevent him from carrying the barricade, and proceeding as far as the Madeleine at the
head of his excited soldiers.

There, two ladies in a carriage, who were fleeing from the in-
surrection in Paris, seeing an officer of the Guards wounded, covered with blood, and lying on the blocks of stone which at that

time surrounded the Madeleine, which was still in course of
construction, placed their carriage at his disposal, and he was
taken by them to Gros Caillou, where the Marshal de Raguse
was, to whom he said, in military fashion: "Marshal, I have
not, perhaps, more than two hours to live, but during those two
hours put me wherever you like."

Only he was wrong. He was good for more than two hours.
The ball which passed through his body did not kill him. It was
more than fifteen years later when I knew him, and he declared
then that in defiance of all the doctors, who had expressly forbidden him to drink as long as the fever caused by his wound
continued, he had been saved from a certain death only by Bordeaux wine.

And how he did drink!—for, dandy as he was, he drank as he
did everything else—he drank like a trooper. He had made for
him a splendid goblet of Bohemian glass, which held a whole
bottle of Bordeaux, by God, and he would drain it off at a
draught. He would say, after he had drunk it, that he always
drank like that—and it was true. But in these days, when
strength of every kind is continually diminishing and is no
longer thought much of, it may seem that this feat is nothing
to boast about. He was like Bassompierre, and could take his
wine as he did. I have seen him toss off his Bohemian glass a
dozen times without seeming any the worse for it. I have often
seen him also on those occasions which respectable people call
"orgies," and never, after even the most inordinate bouts, did
he appear to be more than what he called a "little tight." I
—who wish to make you understand what sort of man he was, in
order that you may follow my story—may as well tell you that
I have known him to keep seven mistresses at the same time.
He entitled them, poetically, "the seven strings of his lyre"—
and I must say that I disapprove of his speaking in this jesting
and musical way of his immorality. But what would you have?
If Captain Vicomte de Brassard had not been all that I have had
the honour to tell you, my story would have been less sensational,

and probably I should not have thought it worth while to relate it
to you.

It is quite certain that I did not expect to find him there when
I got into the diligence at the Château de Rueil cross-roads. It
was a long time since I had seen him, and I took much pleasure
in the prospect of spending several hours in the company of a
man who belonged to our time, and yet differed so much from the
men of our day.

The Vicomte de Brassard, who could have worn the armour of
Francis I as easily as he did the officer's tunic of the Royal
Guards, resembled neither in his proportions nor his appearance
the young men of the present time. This setting sun, so grand
and radiant, made the rising crescent moons look very pale and
poor. He had the beauty of the Emperor Nicholas, whom he
resembled in body, but his face was less ideal and Greek, and he
wore a short beard, which, like his hair, had remained black in
some mysterious way, and this beard grew high on his cheeks
which had a manly ruddy tinge. His forehead was high, projecting, unwrinkled, and as white as a woman's arm, and beneath
it were two dark-blue eyes, sparkling like cut emeralds. Those
eyes never glanced; they penetrated.

We shook hands, and talked. Captain de Brassard spoke
slowly, with a resonant voice that was capable of filling the Champ
de Mars when he gave the word of command. Having been
brought up from infancy in England, as I have already said, perhaps he thought in English, but this slowness, which was devoid
of embarrassment by the way, gave a distinction to what he said,
even when he joked, for the Captain loved to joke, and his jokes
were sometimes rather broad. Captain de Brassard always went
too far, as the Comtesse de F . . . used to say, that pretty widow
who since her husband's death had worn only three colours—
black, violet, and white. He must have been very good company,
or people would have thought him impossible, and when that is
the case, you know that much will be forgiven in the Faubourg
Saint-Germain.

One of the advantages of talking in a carriage is that you can leave off when you have nothing more to say, without troubling anybody. In a drawing-room that liberty does not exist. Politeness compels you to talk, and this innocent hypocrisy is often punished by the hollowness and boredom of the conversation, in which the fools, even those born silent (and there are such), do their best to say something and be very amiable. In a public conveyance you are as much at home as anyone else is—and you may without rudeness lapse into the silence and reverie which follows a conversation. Unfortunately, the chances are against you in this life, and formerly (for there is a "formerly" already) you rode twenty times in a public conveyence—as you may now twenty times in a railway carriage—without meeting a man whose conversation was animated and interesting.

Vicomte de Brassard and I talked, at first, about the journey, the landscape, and old memories of the fashionable world which cropped up in the course of conversation—then the sun declined, and we both fell into the twilight silence. Night, which in autumn seems to fall from the sky at once, it comes so quickly, chilled us, and we rolled ourselves in our cloaks, resting our heads against the hard corner which is the traveller's pillow.

I do not know whether my companion slept in his corner, but I was wide awake in mine: I was so well acquainted with the route we were travelling, which I had gone over often, that I hardly noticed the external objects which disappeared as the diligence rolled on, and which seemed travelling through the night in an opposite direction to us. We passed through several small towns dotted here and there along the long road. The night became as black as an extinguished stove; and, in this obscurity, the unknown towns through which we passed took on a strange appearance, and made us think we were at the world's end. In most of these little towns gas-lamps were rare, and there was less light than on the country roads behind us. In the country the sky was broader and there was a kind of dim light, but it was blotted out in the narrow streets of the towns, and only a star or two was to be seen between the roofs, adding to the mysterious air of these sleepy towns, where the only person we saw was the ostler with his lantern, at the door of some inn, as he brought out the fresh horses and buckled the straps of the harness, whistling meanwhile, or swearing at some obstinate or skittish horse.

Except for that, and the eternal question, always the same, of some traveller awakened from sleep, who lowered the window and cried in a voice which the silence of the night rendered louder: "Where are we now, postilion?" no sign of life was heard. Nothing was seen but the carriage full of sleeping people, in a sleeping town; though perhaps some dreamer like myself would try to discern through the window the fronts of the houses, or fix his attention and thoughts on some casement still lighted up at this late hour, even in those towns where early and regular hours are the rule, and the night is specially devoted to sleep. A human being watching—even if it be a sentinel—when all others are plunged in that rest which comes from physical fatigue, is always an affecting sight. But ignorance as to who is watching behind the curtains of a window, where the light gleaming betokens life and thought, adds poetry—the poetry of reality—to the dream. At least, for my part, I can never see a window lighted up in the night, in a sleeping town through which I am passing, without attaching a whole crowd of fancies to that light; without imagining behind those curtains all kinds of domestic affairs or dramas. Even now, after all these years, I can still think of those windows with their eternal and melancholy light, and I often say to myself, fancying I see them again in my dreams:

"What can there be behind those curtains?"

Well, one of those which has remained longest in my memory (you will know the reason presently) was a window in one of the streets of the town of ****, which we passed that night. It was in the third house—you see how exact my memory is— beyond the inn at which we changed horses; but this window

I had leisure to examine for longer than a mere change of horses would have necessitated. An accident had happened to one of the wheels of our coach, and they had to send and wake up the wheelwright. Now to wake up a wheelwright in a sleeping town, and get him to come and tighten up a nut on a diligence, when there is no competition on that line, is not a trifling affair of a few minutes.

In the first place, if the wheelwright was as fast asleep as everybody in our coach, it could not have been easy to wake him. I could hear, through the partition, the snores of the inside passengers, and not one of the outside passengers, who, as you know, have a mania for getting down whenever the coach stops, probably —for vanity is found everywhere in France, even on the outside of coaches—in order to show their agility in getting up again, had descended from his seat.

It is true that the inn at which we were, was shut up. We did not sup there. We had supped at the last stage. The inn was sleeping like the rest of us. Nothing betrayed a sign of life. Not a sound disturbed the profound silence—unless it was the wearisome, monotonous sound of a broom wielded by someone (man or woman—we knew not, and it was too dark to ascertain) who was sweeping out the court-yard of this silent inn, the yard-gates of which were usually open. Even the broom dragged as though the sweeper were asleep, or were devilishly anxious to be. The front of the inn was as black as the other houses in the street, where indeed there was only a light at one window—precisely that window which is still fixed in my memory. The house, in which you could not exactly say that this light shone, for it was screened by a double crimson curtain, through whose thicknesses the light filtered mysteriously, was a large building with only one upper story, but that placed very high.

"It is very singular," said Vicomte de Brassard, as though he were talking to himself; "one would think it was still the same curtain!"

I turned towards him to look at him, but the lamp which was by the coachman's box, and which is intended to show the horses the road, had just gone out. I thought he was asleep, but he was not, and he had been struck, like me, by the appearance of the window; but he knew more than I, because he knew why it was lighted up.

But the tone in which he had said that—though it was a simple remark—was so unlike the voice of the worldly Vicomte de Brassard, and astonished me so much, that I was overcome by curiosity to see his face, and I struck a match, as though I had wanted to light a cigar. The blue flame of the match lit up the gloom.

He was pale—not pale as a dead man, but as pale as Death itself.

Why should he turn pale? This window, with its peculiar appearance, the remark, and the pallor of a man who very rarely turned pale, for he was full-blooded, and emotion, when he was moved, made him turn scarlet up to the crown of his head, the shiver that I felt run down the muscles of his powerful biceps, which, as we were sitting close together, was against my arm—all gave me the impression that there was something hidden that I, the seeker after stories, might perhaps learn with a little pains.

"You were looking then at that window, Captain, and even seemed to recognize it," I said in that tone which does not seem to court a reply, and is the hypocrisy of curiosity.

"*Parbleu!* I do recognize it," he replied in his rich, deep voice, seeming to dwell on every word.

Calmness had again resumed its sway over this dandy, the most stolid and majestic of all dandies, who—as you know—scorn all emotions as being beneath them, and do not believe, like that idiot Goethe, that astonishment can ever be a proper feeling for the human mind.

"I do not come by here often," continued the Vicomte de Brassard quietly; "I even avoid passing by here. But there are some

things one never forgets. There are not many, but there are
some. I know of three: the first uniform one puts on, the first
battle one was in, the first woman one ever slept with. Well, for
me that window is the fourth thing I cannot forget."

He stopped and lowered the window which was in front of him.
Was it that he might the better see the window of which we
spoke?

The conductor had gone for the wheelwright, and had not returned. The fresh horses were late, and had not yet come.
Those which had brought us were motionless from fatigue, worn
out, and not unharnessed, and, with their heads between their
legs, they did not even stamp on the silent pavement with impatience to return to their stable. Our sleepy diligence resembled
an enchanted coach, fixed by some fairy's wand in some open
glade in the forest of the Sleeping Beauty.

"The fact is," I said, "that for any man with imagination, that
window possesses a certain character."

"I don't know what it has for you," replied Vicomte de Brassard, "but I know what it has for me. That is the window of
the room in which I lived when I was first in garrison. Confound
it! that is fully thirty-five years ago!

"Behind that curtain—which does not seem to have changed in
all those years—and which is now lighted as it was when——"

He stopped and left his thought unexpressed, but I was determined to make him speak out.

"When you were studying tactics, Captain; in those early days
when you were a second lieutenant."

"You give me more than my due," he replied. "I was, it is
true, a second lieutenant at that time, but I did not spend my
nights in studying tactics, and if my light was burning at unaccustomed hours, as respectable people say, it was not to read
Marshal Saxe."

"But," I said—quick as a ball from a racket—"it was perhaps
to imitate him."

He returned the ball as promptly.

"Oh," he said, "it was not then that I imitated Marshal Saxe in the way you mean. That was not till much later. Then I was merely a brat of a second lieutenant, very stiff and prim in my uniform, but very awkward and timid with women, though they would never believe it—probably on account of my confounded face. I never got the full benefit of my timidity from them. Moreover, I was but seventeen in those happy days. I had just left the military college. We left in those days at the age at which you enter nowadays, for if the Emperor, that terrible consumer of men, had lasted longer, he would have ended by having soldiers twelve years of age, as some of the Asiatic sultans have concubines nine years of age."

"If he goes on talking about the Emperor and concubines," I thought to myself, "I shall not learn what I want to know."

"Yet, Vicomte," I replied, "I would wager that you would never have preserved the memory of that window which is shining there unless there had been a woman behind the curtain."

"And you would have won your bet, sir," he said, gravely.

"Ah, *parbleu!*" I replied. "I was sure of it. For a man like you, in a little provincial town that you have not perhaps passed through ten times since you were first in garrison there, it must be some siege you have sustained, or some woman you took by storm, that could make you remember so vividly the window of a house that is now lighted up amidst the general gloom."

"Yet I did not, however, sustain any siege—at least in the military sense," he replied, still gravely, but gravity was sometimes his way of joking; "and, on the other hand, when one surrenders so quickly, can it be called a siege? But as to taking a woman, by storm or otherwise, I have told you that in those days I was quite incapable of it. So it was not a woman who was taken here—it was I."

I bowed; did he see it in the dark carriage?

"Berg op Zoom was taken," I said.

"And subalterns of seventeen," he replied, "are not generally Berg op Zooms of impregnable wisdom and chastity."

"So," I said gaily, "it was some Madame or Mademoiselle Potiphar."

"It was a demoiselle," he interrupted with a frankness that was almost comic.

"To add to the sum of all the others, Captain. Only in this case the Joseph was a soldier—a Joseph not likely to run away."

"But who certainly did run away, on the contrary," he replied with the greatest coolness; "although too late, and very much afraid!!! With a fright which made me understand the expression used by Marshal Ney, which I heard with my own ears, and which, coming from such a man, I must own somewhat comforted me, I should like to see the b——[only he gave the words in full] who has never been afraid!"

"The story of how *you* came to feel that sensation must be interesting, Captain."

"*Pardieu!*" he said quickly; "I can, if you are curious, tell you the story of an event which bit into my life as acid bites into steel, and which has left a dark stain on the page of my libertine pleasures.—Ah, it is not always profitable to be a rake," he added in a melancholy voice, which struck me as rather strange coming from one I had always regarded as a regular hardened rogue.

He pulled up the glass he had lowered, as though he feared the sound of his voice might be heard outside, though there was no one near the coach, which was motionless as though deserted— or else he thought the regular beat of the broom would interrupt his story. I listened attentively to his voice—to the slightest expression of his voice—for I could not see his face in the dark— and with my eyes fixed more than ever on the window with the crimson curtain, behind which the light still burned with such fascinating power, and about which he was ready to speak.

"I was then seventeen," he continued, "and had just left the military college. I had been appointed ensign in a regiment of the line, which was then impatiently awaiting orders to leave for Germany, where the Emperor was conducting that campaign which history has named the campaign of 1813. I had just time to kiss my old father before joining, in this town, the battalion of which I formed part—for in this little town of some few thousands of inhabitants at most, the garrison consisted of only our two first battalions. The two other battalions were in some neighbouring town.

"You, who have probably seen this town only when you were travelling towards the West, cannot imagine what it is—or at least what it was thirty years ago—when you are obliged, as I was then, to live in it. It was certainly the worst garrison to which chance—which I believe to be the devil, at that time represented by the Minister of War—could have sent me as a starting-place for my military career. What an infernally dull hole it was! I do not remember ever having been in a more wearisome place. But, at my age, and in the first intoxication of the uniform—a feeling you do not know, but which all who have worn it have experienced—I scarcely suffered from what at a later time would have seemed insupportable.

"After all, how could this dull provincial town affect me? I lived in it much less than I did in my uniform—a masterpiece of sartorial art which delighted me. My uniform, of which I was madly fond, hid or adorned everything, and it was—though this may appear an exaggeration, but it is the truth—the uniform which was, strictly speaking, my garrison. When I was too much bored by this uninteresting and lifeless town, I put on full uniform, and boredom fled. I was like those women who give extra attention to their *toilette* when they are alone and expect no one. I dressed myself *for* myself. I enjoyed in solitude my epaulets and the clank of my sabre, as I promenaded the lonely streets in the afternoons, and I felt as puffed up with pride as I have done since in Paris when I have heard people say behind me: 'There is a really fine-looking officer.'

"In the town, which was not a rich one, and had no commerce or activity of any kind, there were only a few old and almost ruined families who grumbled at the Emperor, because he had not, as they said, made the robbers of the Revolution yield up their booty, and who for that reason paid no great heed to the officers. Therefore there were no parties, or balls, or soirées, or dances. At the best there was but the Promenade, where on Sunday, after church, the mothers came to show off their daughters until two o'clock in the afternoon—and when the first bell rang for Vespers all the petticoats disappeared, and the Promenade was deserted.

"This midday Mass, to which we never go, became, by the way, a military Mass during the Restoration, and all the officers were obliged to attend it, and that was quite an event in this dead-alive town. For young fellows like us, who were at a time of life when we care greatly for love or women, this military Mass was quite a pleasure. All the officers, except those on duty, were scattered about the nave of the church. We nearly always contrived to sit behind the prettiest women who came to Mass, because they were sure to be looked at, and whom we delighted by talking between ourselves, loud enough for them to hear, about their charms or appearance. Ah, that military Mass, what romances have I seen begin there! I have seen many love-letters slipped into the muffs which the girls left on their chairs when they knelt by the side of their mothers—letters to which they brought the reply on the following Sunday, also in their muffs.

"But in the days of the Emperor there was no military Mass, and consequently no means of approaching the 'respectable' girls of the little town. Nor were there any compensations. Those establishments which are never mentioned in good society were simply horrible. The cafés, in which so much home-sickness is drowned during the long idlenesses of garrison life, it was impossible for anyone who respected his epaulets to enter.

"Luxury is now found here, as elsewhere, but there was not then a single hotel where the officers could dine together without being horribly swindled, so we were forced to give up all ideas of a mess-table, and we were scattered about various boarding-houses, amongst households that were not over-rich—people who let their apartments as dearly as they could, and so added a little to their skimpy revenues.

"I lived in lodgings. One of my comrades lived at the *Poste aux Chevaux,* which was in this street at that time—there! a few houses behind us, and if it were daylight you could see on the house an old golden sun emerging from a cherry-coloured cloud, with the inscription, 'The Rising Sun.' This comrade found an apartment for me close to his own—where that window is perched up there, and which seems to me this evening to belong to me still, as it did then. I let him find my lodgings for me. He was older than I was, had been longer in the regiment, and he liked to give advice to one who was inexperienced and careless.

"I have already said that except for the uniform—a point on which I lay stress, because that is a feeling of which your generation, with your Peace Congresses, and philosophical and humanitarian clowning, will soon have no idea—and the hope of hearing the cannon in my first battle, in which I was to lose my military maidenhead—excuse the expression—it was all much alike to me. I lived only in those two ideas—in the second especially, for it was a hope, and we always care more for what we have not than for that which we have.

"This is how I spent my life. Except during meal-times—and I took my meals with the people of the house, and about whom I will tell you presently—and the time devoted daily to military duties, I lived nearly always in my own room, lying on a huge dark-blue sofa, which was so cool that it seemed to me like a cold bath after the hot parade-ground, and I scarcely ever left this sofa except to take a fencing-lesson, or have a game of cards with my neighbour opposite, Louis de Meung, who was not so lazy as I was, for he had picked up, amongst the *grisettes* of the town, a rather pretty girl, whom he had taken for his mistress and who served, as he said, to kill time.

"But what I knew of women did not tempt me to imitate my friend Louis. What little I knew of them I had picked up where the cadets of Saint-Cyr acquire that information when they are

out on leave. Besides, some phases of character are late in developing. Did you know Saint-Rémy, one of the greatest rakes of
his day, and who was called by the other libertines 'the Minotaur';
not because of his horns, although he wore them, for he had killed
his wife's lover, but because of the number of virgins he had
destroyed?"

"Yes, I knew him," I replied, "but when he was old and incor-
rigible, and becoming more of a debauchee each year that passed
over his head; of course I knew that *rompu*, as Brantôme would
have called him."

"He was, in fact, like one of Brantôme's men," replied the
Vicomte. "But, at any rate, Saint-Rémy, when he was twenty-
seven, had never touched a glass or a petticoat. He will tell you
the same thing if you ask him. At twenty-seven years of age,
he was, in the matter of women, as innocent as a new-born babe,
and though his nurse no longer suckled him, he had never drunk
anything but milk or water."

"He made up well for lost time," I remarked.

"Yes," said the Vicomte, "and so did I. But I had less lost
time to make up. My first period of prudence hardly exceeded
the time that I spent in this town, and although I was not so
absolutely chaste as Saint-Rémy, I lived like a Knight of Malta
—and indeed I was one, by birth.—Did you know that? I
should even have succeeded one of my uncles as a 'Master' if the
Revolution had not abolished the Order, the ribbon of which—
though the Order is abolished—I sometimes wear—foolishly perhaps.—As to the people who had let me their apartment," continued Vicomte de Brassard, "they were, as you may imagine,
thoroughly bourgeois. They were only two—husband and wife;
both old, and well-behaved. In their relations with me, they even
displayed that politeness you never find in these days—especially
in their class—and which is like the scent of a bygone period.
I was not of an age to observe, and they interested me so little
that I never cared to penetrate the past of these two old people,

into whose life I entered only in the most superficial way, two hours a day—noon and evening—when I dined or supped with them. Nothing concerning this past transpired in their conversation before me, for this conversation generally turned on persons or matters relating to the town, of which they informed me —the husband in a spirit of humorous backbiting, and his wife, who was very pious, with more reserve, but certainly with no less pleasure.

"I think, however, I have heard it said that the husband travelled in his youth, but for whom or what I know not, and that when he returned, he married—the girl having waited for him. They were good, honest people, calm and quiet. The wife spent her time in knitting socks for her husband, and he, being music-mad, scraped old airs on his violin in a garret over my room. Perhaps they had once been better off. Perhaps some loss of fortune (which they concealed) had obliged them to take a lodger; but, except for that, they showed no sign of poverty. Everything in the house breathed an air of comfort, as is the case in old-fashioned houses, which abound with linen that smells fresh and good, heavy silver plate, and movables which seem to be immovable, they are so seldom renewed. I was very comfortable there. The table was good, and I had full permission to quit it as soon as I had 'wiped my beard'—as old Olive, the servant who waited on us, called it, though she did me too much honour in dignifying by the name of a beard the cat's whiskers which constituted the moustache of an ensign who was still a growing lad.

"I had been there about six months, living as quietly as my hosts, and I had never heard a single word of the existence of the person I was about to meet at their house, when one day, in going down to dinner at the accustomed hour, I saw, in a corner of the dining-room, a tall young woman standing on tiptoe and hanging her hat by its ribbons on a hat-rack, like a woman who feels herself quite at home, and has just come in from a walk. Her body was stretched to reach the peg, which was placed

high, and she displayed a figure as graceful as an opera-dancer.
She was dressed in a tight-fitting bodice and a narrow skirt, which
revealed the shape of her hips.

"With the arms still raised, she turned her head when she heard
me enter, and thus I was enabled to see her face; but she finished
what she was about as though I had not been there, and looked
to see whether the ribbons of her bonnet had not crumpled in
hanging it up, and she did all this slowly, carefully, and almost
impertinently—for, after all, I was standing waiting to bow to
her—before she took any notice of me, and did me the honour to
regard me with two very cold, black eyes, to which her hair,
which was done in wavy curls massed on the forehead, gave that
deep expression which is peculiar to that kind of *coiffure*.

"I could not imagine who she could be at that hour, and in
that place. No one ever came to dine with my hosts—yet she
had certainly come to dine, for the table was prepared, and four
covers were laid. But my astonishment to see her there was
greatly surpassed by my astonishment to learn who she was; as
I did when my hosts entered the room and presented her to me
as their daughter, who had just left boarding-school, and who
was going in future to live with them.

"Their daughter! It was impossible for anyone to be more
unlike the daughter of people like them! Not but what the
prettiest girls are the daughters of all sorts of people. I have
known many such, and you also, no doubt. Physiologically speaking, the ugliest being may produce the most beautiful. But there
was the chasm of a whole race between her and them! Moreover, physiologically, if I may employ that pedantic word, which
belongs to your days and not to mine, one could not help remark-
ing her air, which was very singular in a girl as young as she
was, for it was a kind of impassive air very difficult to describe.
If she had not had it, one would have said: 'That is a pretty
girl,' without thinking any more of her than of all the pretty
girls one meets by chance, and about whom one has said that
and never thought any more about it. But this air—which dis-

tinguished her not only from her parents, but from everyone else, amazed you and petrified you; for she appeared to have neither passions nor feelings. 'The Infanta with the Spaniel,' by Velasquez, may, if you know the picture, give you an idea of that air, which was neither proud, nor scornful, nor disdainful, but simply impassive; for a proud, scornful, or contemptuous air informs people that they do exist, since one takes the trouble to despise or contemn them, whilst this air said coolly: 'For me, you do not even exist.'

"I own that her appearance made me put to myself on that first day and many others, a question which is still unsolved: how that tall, slim girl could be the offspring of the little, stout man in a greenish-yellow coat and a white waistcoat, who had a complexion the colour of his wife's jam, and a wen on the back of his fat neck, and stuttered in his speech. And if the husband did not trouble me much, for the husband may be eliminated from questions of this sort—the wife appeared quite impossible to explain. Mademoiselle Albertine (that was the name of this archduchess who had fallen from heaven into this bourgeois family, as though heaven had tried to play a joke upon them) was called Alberte by her parents, because her name was too long. The name suited her face and figure, but she did not appear to be the daughter of either of her parents.

"At this first dinner, and those which followed, she appeared to me to be a young girl very well brought up, with no affectation, and habitually silent, but who, when she did speak, said clearly and sensibly what she had to say, and never exceeded those limits. Besides, if she had had more wit than I knew of, she would hardly have found an opportunity to show it at the dinner-table. The presence of their daughter necessarily had some effect on the gossip of the two old people. All the little scandals about the townsfolk were suppressed. As a matter of course, we never talked about anything more interesting than the weather. There was only the impassive air of Mademoiselle Albertine or Alberte, which had so much struck me at first, and I soon wearied of that. If I had met her in that society for which I was intended, her impassiveness would have aroused my curiosity. But to me she was not a girl to whom I could make love—even with the eyes. My position in respect to her—as I was living with her parents—was delicate, and a mere trifle might have made it much worse. She was neither sufficiently near nor sufficiently remote to be anything in my life, and I soon fell naturally, and quite unintentionally, into the most complete indifference to her impassiveness.

"Nor was this disturbed either on her part or on mine. There was nothing between us but the merest politeness, and the most indifferent speeches. To me she was just a figure that I scarcely saw—and what was I to her? At table—we never met elsewhere —she looked more at the stopper of the decanter or the sugar-basin than she did at me. All that she said was correct, and very well expressed, but signified little or nothing, and gave me no clue to her character. Besides, what did that matter to me? I should have passed my whole life without dreaming of even looking at that quiet and insolent girl, had it not been for a circumstance about which I will tell you, and which struck me like a thunderbolt—a bolt from the blue, indeed.

"One evening, nearly a month after Mademoiselle Alberte had come home, we were sitting down to supper. She was seated next to me, and I really paid so little attention to her that I had never noticed that she had changed her place, and was next to me instead of sitting between her father and mother as usual. I was unfolding my napkin on my knees when—I shall never be able to express my feeling of astonishment—I felt a hand boldly press mine under the table. I thought I was dreaming—or, rather, I could think of nothing at all. I could only feel the touch of that hand, boldly seeking mine under the napkin. It was so extraordinary and unexpected. All my blood, set aglow by that touch, rushed from my heart to my hand, as though attracted by her, and then returned violently as though driven by a pump to my heart. Everything swam before my eyes—my ears tingled.

I must have turned deadly pale. I thought I was going to faint —that I should melt away in the inexpressible pleasure caused by the pressure of that hand,—which was rather large and strong, like that of a boy—when it closed upon mine.

"When you are young, you know, pleasure always brings with it a sense of shame, and I tried to withdraw my hand, but hers seemed aware of the pleasure it had caused me, and compelled mine to remain by a deliciously warm squeeze. . . . That is thirty-five years ago, and, as you may believe, I have touched many a woman's hand since, but I still feel, when I think of it, the sensation of that hand pressing mine with despotic passion.

"The thousand tremors which that hand caused to shoot through my whole body made me fear to betray what I felt to the father and mother whose daughter, before their eyes, dared to . . . Ashamed, however, to prove myself less of a man than this bold girl who risked her reputation, and whose incredible coolness concealed her follies, I bit my lips till they bled, in a superhuman effort to stop the tremors of desire which might have told these poor people so much, and then my eyes sought her other hand, which I had not yet looked at, and which at this dangerous moment was calmly turning up the wick of a lamp which had just been placed on the table, for the evening was beginning to grow dark. I looked at it. It was the fellow of the hand whose touch was thrilling me, and sending long tongues of fire as from a furnace through my veins! The hand was rather thick, but the fingers were long and well-shaped, and looked transparently rosy in the light which fell full upon them, but they never trembled, and performed the little operation on which they were engaged with firmness, ease, and an incomparable, graceful languor.

"We could not stop like that for ever! We needed our hands to eat with. Mademoiselle Alberte's hand dropped mine, but at the same moment her foot, which was quite as expressive as her hand, placed itself on mine in the same despotic manner during all this too brief dinner, and reminded me of one of those baths which are insufferably hot to begin with, but to which you get

accustomed, and end by thinking so comfortable that you willingly
believe that the damned in their cauldron must be as cool and as
much at home as fish in water.

"You may fancy whether I dined that day, or if I took much
part in the chatter of my worthy hosts, who were far from suspecting the mysterious and terrible drama which was going on
under the table. They saw nothing, but they easily might have
seen, and really I was more disturbed on their account than I was
for myself, or for her. I had all the frankness and sympathy of
seventeen. I said to myself: 'Is she quite shameless? Is she
mad?' And I looked out of the corner of my eye at her, but she
did not lose for a single second, during the whole of the dinner,
her air of a princess at a state ceremony, and her face remained
as calm as ever, though her foot was saying and doing all the
foolish things which a foot can say or do—to mine. I must confess that I was more surprised at her coolness than at her imprudence. I had read a good deal of light literature, in which
women were not spared. I had been educated at a military
school. I considered myself quite a Lovelace, like every lad who
has kissed his mother's chambermaid behind the door or on the
staircase. But my experience as a Lovelace of seventeen was
upset. This appeared to me worse than anything I had ever
heard or read about the deceit of women, and how they could
conceal their deepest or most violent emotions. Only fancy!
she was but eighteen! Was she even as much? She had just
left a school which I had no reason to suspect, considering the
morality and the piety of her mother, who had selected it for
her daughter. This absence of all constraint, or, to speak plainly,
this absolute want of modesty, this perfect control over herself
whilst doing the most imprudent things that could be done by a
young girl who had never by a sign or a glance forewarned the
man to whom she made such an advance—all this rose clearly
to my mind, despite my confusion.

"But neither then nor later did I stop to philosophize about it.
I had no sham horror for the conduct of this girl who had shown

such terribly precocious depravity. Besides, at the age I was then, or even much later, you do not consider a girl depraved because she throws herself into your arms. On the contrary, you are almost inclined to regard it as a matter of course, and if you say 'Poor girl,' it is more out of modesty than pity. But though I was shy, I did not want to be taken for a ninny—the good old French reason for doing a bad deed without any remorse. I knew without doubt that it was not love the girl felt for me. Love does not act in that shameless, impudent way; and I also knew well enough that what she had caused me to feel was not love either. But, love or not—whatever it was, I wanted it. When I rose from the table, my mind was made up. Alberte's hand, of which I had not thought for a moment before it seized mine, had stirred in my soul a desire to embrace her whole body as her hand had embraced mine!

"I went up to my room like a madman, and when I was a little bit calmed by reflection, I asked myself what I should do to clinch this 'intrigue'—as they call it in the country—with a girl who was so devilishly tempting. I knew pretty well—like one who has never tried to know more—that she never left her mother, and that the two worked side by side all day in the window-seat of the dining-room, which also served as their drawing-room; that she had no lady-friend who came to see her, and that she hardly ever went out except to Mass or Vespers on Sunday, with her parents.

"That was not very encouraging, was it? I began to regret that I had not seen more of these worthy people; for though I had not held aloof from them, I had treated them with that distant or somewhat listless politeness you show to people in whom you take only a remote interest; but I reflected that I could not very well change my attitude towards them without exposing myself to the chance of revealing to them, or making them suspect, that which I wished to conceal.

"The only opportunities I had to speak to Mademoiselle Alberte in secret were meetings on the staircase, as I went up or came down from my room—but on the staircase we might be seen and heard. The best resource open to me—in that small and well-regulated house where everybody was close to everybody else's elbow—was to write; and since the hand of that brazen hussy knew so well how to find mine under the table, it would perhaps not make much ado about taking a note that was slipped into it; and so I wrote.

"It was a letter suited to the circumstances—supplicatory, commanding, and delirious—of a man who has drunk his first draught of happiness and asks for a second.

"Only, in order to give it to her, I must wait till dinner-time the next day, and that seemed a long time; but at last dinner-time came! The incentive hand, whose touch I had felt for twenty-four hours, did not fail to seek mine under the table as on the previous evening. Mademoiselle Alberte felt my letter, and took it, as I foresaw. But what I did not foresee was, that with that Infanta-like air of sublime indifference, she should slip it into her breast, under the pretence of arranging a bit of lace that was doubled down, and perform the act so naturally and so quickly that her mother, who was engaged in serving the soup, saw nothing; and whilst her old idiot of a father, who was always humming something, and thinking of his violin when he was not playing, was gazing into the fire."

"Oh, that is done every day, Captain," I interrupted gaily, for his story appeared to me to be likely to turn soon into a mere history of a garrison love-affair—for I did not suspect what was to follow. "Why, only a few days ago there was at the opera, in the box next to mine, a lady of probably the same sort as your Mademoiselle Alberte. She was more than eighteen, certainly; but, I give you my word of honour, I have rarely seen more majestic modesty in any woman. During the whole performance she sat as motionless as though she had been on a granite pedestal. She did not turn once, either to the right or left, but no doubt she saw with her shoulders, which were very bare and very beautiful, for there was in the same box with me, and consequently behind us both, a young man who appeared quite as indifferent as she was to everything but the opera that was being sung. I can certify that this young man had not made one of those grimaces which men make to women in public places, and which you may call declarations from a distance. Only, when the piece was over, and amid the general confusion as the boxes emptied, the lady rose and buttoned her cloak, and I heard her say to her husband in a clear and conjugally imperious voice, 'Henri, pick up my hood!' and then over his back, as he was stooping down, she extended her hand and arm, and took a note the young man handed her, just as though she had been taking her fan or her bouquet from her husband's hand. He rose up, poor man! holding the hood—a scarlet satin hood, but not so scarlet as his face, for which he had, at the risk of apoplexy, dived under the seats as he best could. Upon my word, when I saw that, I went away thinking that, instead of giving it to his wife, he ought to have kept that hood to hide his own head in, for the horns were about to sprout."

"Your story is a good one," said Vicomte de Brassard calmly, and at another time I should have enjoyed it more—but allow me to finish my tale. I confess that with a girl of that sort I was not for a moment doubtful of the fate of my letter. She might be tied to her mother's apron-strings, but she would find means to read my letter and reply to it. I even expected a long correspondence, carried on under the table as we had begun, and when the next day I entered the dining-room, firmly convinced in my own mind that I was about to have a reply to my letter of the previous evening, I thought my eyes must have played me a trick when I saw that the covers had been changed, and that Mademoiselle Alberte was placed, where she always ought to have been, between her father and mother.

"What was the meaning of this change? Did her father and mother suspect anything? Mademoiselle Alberte was opposite to me, and I looked at her with that fixed expression which demands an answer. There were twenty-five notes of interrogation in my eyes; but hers were as calm, as silent, as indifferent as usual. They looked at me as though they did not see me. I have never seen a look more annoying than that long calm gaze, which fell on you as though you were an inanimate object. I boiled with curiosity, vexation, impatience, and many other emotions—and I could not understand how it was that this girl, who was so sure of herself, did not dare to give me a sign which would warn me, or make me guess, or tell me, that we understood each other, and that we were conniving or conspiring together in the same mystery, whether it was love or something else.

"I asked myself if it could be really the same girl who had touched my hand and foot under the table; who had received the letter the previous evening and had slipped it so cleverly into her breast, before her parents, as she would have placed a flower there. She had done so much already that she need not have been embarrassed to give me a glance. But no! I had nothing. The dinner passed without that glance for which I was watching and waiting. 'She must have found some means to reply to me,' I said to myself as I left the table and went up to my room, not believing that such a woman would retreat after such an incredible advance—not admitting that fear or prudence could stand between her and her fancies, and *parbleu!* frankly refusing to acknowledge that she had not a fancy for me.

" 'If her parents have no suspicion,' I said to myself, 'if it is by chance that she has changed her place at the table, to-morrow I shall find her by my side again.'—But on the morrow, and on the following days, I was not seated near Mademoiselle Alberte, who continued to wear the same incomprehensible look, and to say the same ordinary phrases in the same impassive way.

"You may well imagine that I observed her with much interest. She appeared as undisturbed as possible, whilst I was horribly annoyed, even to anger—an anger that I was forced to conceal! This air, which she never lost, made me seem farther away from her than ever. I was so exasperated that in the end I did not fear to compromise her by looking at her, and fixing on her im-

penetrable eyes the earnest, burning gaze of mine. Was it a
clever manœuvre on her part? Was it coquetry? Was it but one
caprice following another—or simply stupidity? 'If one knew the
right moment!' as Ninon used to say. Had the right moment
already passed?

"However, I still waited—for what?—a word, a sign—so easily
given as we pushed the chairs back when we rose from dinner—
and as that did not come, all the most foolish and absurd ideas
began to fill my head. I imagined that because of the difficulties
which surrounded us in the house, she would write to me by post
—she was quite cunning enough to slip a letter into the box when
she was out with her mother—and impressed by that idea, my
blood boiled twice a day, an hour before the postman passed.
Ten times a day did I ask the old servant, in a voice choked with
emotion: 'Are there any letters for me, Olive?' to which she replied imperturbably: 'No, sir, there are not.'

"Finally the anxiety grew too intense. Desire deceived turned
to hate. I began to hate Alberte, and to explain to myself her
conduct towards me by motives which would cause me to despise
her, for hate needs scorn. 'Cowardly little wretch, she is afraid
to write,' I said to myself. I endeavoured not to think of her,
and I heaped abuse upon her when I spoke of her, to Louis de
Meung—for I did tell him about her, for she had extinguished all
my sense of chivalry, and I related the whole adventure to my
friend, who twisted his long fair moustache whilst he listened to
me, and who frankly replied—for we were not moralists in
the 27th:

"'Do as I do. One nail drives out another. Take one of the
little sempstresses of the town for a mistress, and think no more
about the young devil.'

"But I did not follow his advice. I had too much at stake. If
I had taken a mistress, and she had known of it, I might have
aroused her vanity or her jealousy. But she would not know it.
How should she? If I had brought home some woman to my
lodgings, as Louis did, I should have embroiled myself with the

worthy people of the house, who would at once have requested
me to look out for other apartments, and I was not willing to
give up the chance of again meeting the hand or the foot of that
confounded Alberte, who, after all she had dared to do, still remained 'Mademoiselle Impassible.'

" 'Call her, rather, impossible,' said Louis, who made fun of me.

"A whole month passed, and in spite of my resolutions to forget
Alberte, and to seem as indifferent as she was—to oppose marble
to marble, and coldness to coldness—my whole life was passed
on the watch—which I detest, even when I am shooting. Yes,
sir, my days were spent on the watch. I was on the watch when
I went down to dinner, and hoped to find her alone in the dining-
room as on the first occasion. On the watch during dinner, when
she met my eyes with a calm cold gaze which did not avoid mine,
or reply to it either. On the watch after dinner, when I remained
a little time to see the two women resume their work in the
window-seat; hoping that she would drop something—her thimble,
or scissors, or a bit of work—that I could pick up, and in restor-
ing touch her hand—that hand which burned into my brain! On
the watch when I had regained my own room, and thought I
heard in the corridor the foot which had pressed on mine so firmly.
On the watch on the staircase, where I hoped I might meet her,
and where old Olive discovered me one day, to my great confusion.
On the watch at my window—the window you see—where I
planted myself when she was going out with her mother, and
from which I did not budge until she returned; but which was as
useless as all the rest. When she went out—wearing a shawl with
red and white stripes, printed with black and yellow flowers—
she never once turned; and when she returned, still by her
mother's side, she never raised her head or her eyes to the window
where I was awaiting her.

"Such were the miserable practices to which she had condemned
me. Of course I know that women make lackeys of us—but not
to that extent. Ah, I no longer took pleasure in my uniform!
When the duties of the day were over—after the drill or the

parade—I returned home quickly, but not to read a pile of memoirs or novels, my sole reading at that time. I never went to see Louis de Meung. I never touched the foils. I had not even the resource of tobacco which deadens the nerves, and which you young men of the present day use. We did not smoke then in the 27th, or only the privates did in the guard-room, when they played cards on the head of the drum. The only exercise I took was to tramp up and down the six feet of clear space in my room, like a caged lioness that smells raw meat.

"And if it were so in the day, it was also the same for a great part of the night. I went to bed late. I did not sleep. That infernal Alberte kept me awake. She had kindled a fire in my veins, and then gone away—like an incendiary who does not even turn his head to see the flames burst forth behind him. In the evening, I lowered, as it is now"—here the Vicomte passed his glove over the coach-window, to wipe away the moisture—"the same crimson curtain in front of the same window, and which was better than shutters to prevent inquisitive neighbours from seeing into the room.

"The room was furnished in the style of the period—the Empire—with a parquetry floor, no carpet, and a bed all bronze and cherry-wood, with a sphinx at each corner, and lion's paws for the feet. There was also on each drawer of the writing-table a lion's head with a ring in its mouth, by which ring you pulled the drawer open. A square table, also in cherry-wood, but of a rather pinker shade than the rest of the furniture, and having a grey marble top and copper ornaments, stood opposite the bed against the wall, between the window and the door of a dressing-room; and opposite the fire-place was the large blue morocco sofa of which I have already spoken. High up in each corner stood a bracket of imitation lacquer, and upon one of them was a statuette of Niobe—rather an astonishing ornament to find in a bourgeois family. But wasn't this incomprehensible Alberte even more astonishing? The walls were painted a whitish yellow, and were devoid of pictures and engravings. I hung up my arms, suspended on gilt copper hooks. When I hired this great calabash of an apartment—as Louis de Meung, who was not poetical, elegantly called it—I had placed in the centre a large round table, which I covered with military maps, books, and papers. It was my bureau, at which I wrote—whenever I did write.

"Well, one evening, or rather one night, I had wheeled the sofa up to this large table, and I was drawing by the light of the lamp —not to distract my mind from the sole thought which had occupied it for a month, but rather the reverse, for it was the head of that perplexing Alberte which I was sketching—it was the face of that she-devil, who worried me as a devotee is worried by the other devil.

"It was late. The street—through which passed two diligences every night, one each way (as now), one at a quarter to one in the morning, and the other at half past two, and both of which stopped to change horses at the Hotel de la Poste—the street was as silent as the grave. I could have heard a fly, and if by chance there was one in my room, it must have been asleep in a corner of the window-pane, or in one of the pleats of the curtain, which was of heavy stuff, and hung stiff and motionless before the window. The only noise was that which I myself made with my pencil and stump.

"Yes, it was her face I was drawing; God knows with what care and attention! Suddenly, without any sound from the lock to forewarn me, my door opened a little way, giving that squeaky sound which doors make when the hinges are dry, and remained ajar, as though it were frightened by the sound it had made. I raised my eyes, thinking that I could not have closed the door properly that it should have opened in this unexpected way with a plaintive squeak that might frighten all those who were awake, and wake those who were asleep. I rose from the table in order to close it, but the half-opened door opened still wider, and still very gently, but with a repetition of that shrill sound which echoed like a groan through the silent house, and I saw, when it had opened to its full extent—Alberte!

"Alberte, who in spite of all her precautions, and the deadly fear in which she was, could not prevent that cursed door from crying out.

"Ah, *tonnerre de Dieu!* they may talk about visions—but not the most supernatural vision would have surprised me, or made my heart bound as it did when I saw coming towards me Alberte, frightened at the noise the door had made in opening, and which it would repeat when she closed it. Remember that I was but eighteen! Perhaps she saw my terror, and her own, and repressed by a quick sign the cry of surprise which might have escaped me— and certainly would have escaped but for this gesture—then she closed the door; not slowly but rapidly, to prevent the hinges from squeaking. It did not prevent them, and they gave one short shrill cry. The door being closed, she listened with her ear against it, if another sound more terrible might not reply to that of the door. . . . I thought I saw her totter. I sprang towards her, and she was soon in my arms."

"She seems to be getting along very nicely, your Miss Alberte," I said to the Captain.

"You think, perhaps," he continued, as though he had not heard my jesting remark, "that when she fell into my arms she had lost her head through fright, or love—like a girl who is pursued, or may be pursued; who does not know what she is doing when she does the most stupid things, but abandons herself to that devil which is in every woman (they say) and which would always be her master, were it not that she has two others also in her—Cowardice and Shame—to interfere with the first one. Well, no, it was not like that! If you think so, you are wrong. She had no vulgar and shamefaced fears. It was rather she who took me to her arms than I who took her to mine. . . . Her first movement had been to throw her head on my breast, but she raised it again, and looked at me with her great eyes—those wonderful eyes—as if to see if it were really I she held in her arms.

"She was horribly pale—more pale than I had ever seen her— but she had not lost that look of a princess. Her features were still as hard and unimpressionable as a medal. Only on the slightly pouting lips there hovered an expression of I know not what, unless it was passion satisfied, or soon to be satisfied! Yet there was something so sad about this, that, in order not to see it, I impressed on her beautiful pink and pouting lips the kiss of triumphant desire! The mouth was half open, but the dark eyes, whose long lashes almost touched mine, did not close—or even wink—but behind them, as upon her mouth, I saw the same expression of madness.

"As she clung to me in a burning kiss, I carried her to the blue morocco sofa—which had been St. Laurence's grill to me during the month that I had rolled upon it thinking of her—and it creaked voluptuously under her bare back, for she was half naked. She had come from her bed and—would you believe it?—had been obliged to pass through the chamber where her father and mother slept! She had crept groping, with her hands in front of her, in order not to knock against some piece of furniture, and so make a noise which would wake them up."

"Ah!" I said, "one is not braver than that in the trenches. She was worthy to be a soldier's mistress."

"And that she was, the first night," replied the Vicomte.

"She was as violent as I was, and I can swear that I was bad enough. But, in spite of that, there was a drawback. Neither she nor I could forget, in our most delicious transports, the dreadful situation in which we both were. In the midst of the happiness which she came to offer me, she was as though stupefied by the act which she had accomplished with such a firm will and such stubborn obstinacy. I was not astonished at it. I, for my part, was also stupefied. I had—though I did not tell her, or show it—a most terrible anxiety in my heart, whilst she pressed me closely to her own. I listened through her sighs and kisses, and through the terrifying silence which lay on that sleeping and trusting household, for something terrible—for the mother who did not awake, for the father who did not get out of bed! And I looked over her shoulder to see if the door—of which she had not taken out the key for fear of the noise it might make—would not open again, and show me the Medusa heads, pale and indignant, of the two old people whom we were deceiving so boldly and so shamefully—spectres of violated hospitality and justice.

"Even the creaking of the blue sofa, though it sounded the reveille of Love, made me tremble dreadfully. My heart beat against hers, which seemed to re-echo the beatings. It was simultaneously intoxicating and sobering; but it was terrible. Afterwards I did not so much mind. By dint of repeating this incredible imprudence, it ceased to disturb me. I grew accustomed to the danger of being surprised. I did not think of it. I thought only of being happy. At this first critical meeting she decided that she would come to me every other night—since I could not go to her, her room having only one door which led to the room of her parents—and she came every second night, but she never got rid of the sensation—the stupor—of the first night! Time did not produce on her the effect that it did on me. She was never inured to the risk she ran each time. She always lay on my breast, hardly speaking—for, as you may suppose, she was not a great talker—and when later on I grew calmer, seeing the danger always avoided, and spoke to her, as a man speaks to his mistress, of what had already passed between us—of that strange insane coldness which had followed her bold step; when I asked her all those endless questions put by a lover, and which are, after all, nothing but curiosity, her only reply was a long embrace. Her sad mouth was dumb—in all but kisses.

"There are women who tell you: 'I have ruined myself for you'; and there are others who say: 'How you must despise me!' They are different ways of expressing the fatality of love—but she, no! She said nothing! A strange thing! A still stranger personality! She gave me the idea of a thick, hard marble slab which had a fire burning beneath it. I believed there would come a moment when the marble would be cracked by the heat, but the marble continued to be as solid as ever. Night after night saw no change in her, and, if I may be permitted an ecclesiastical expression, she was always as 'difficult to confess' as she had been the first night. I could get nothing out of her. At the most a syllable wrung from those beautiful lips, which I doted on the more because I had seen them cold and indifferent during the day, and this syllable did not give me much insight into the character of a girl who appeared to be more of a sphinx than all the others which adorned the Empire furniture."

"But, Captain," I interrupted, "there must, however, have been an end to all this. You are a sensible man, and the sphinxes are fabulous animals. Devil take it! you must at last have found out what idea had got into the girl's mind."

"An end! Yes, there was an end," said Vicomte de Brassard, suddenly lowering the coach-window, as though the breath had failed in his broad chest, and he needed air before he could finish what he had to say. "But the idea, as you call it, of this singular girl was not discovered, after all. Our love, our relations, our intrigue—call it what you will—gave us, or rather gave *me*, sensations which I do not think I have ever experienced since with women I loved more than Alberte, who, perhaps, did not love me, and whom, perhaps, I did not love! I never fully understood what I was to her, and what she was to me—and this lasted more than six months. During these six months, all that I understood was a kind of happiness of which you have not an idea when you are young. I understood the happiness of those who have something to hide. I understood the enjoyment of complicity in mystery, which, even without the hope of success, is the delight of conspirators. Alberte, at her parents' table and elsewhere, was still always the 'Infanta' who had made such an impression on me the first time I saw her. Her Nero face, beneath the hard curls of the blue-black hair which touched her eyebrows, told nothing of the guilty nights, showed no blush.

"I tried to be as impenetrable as she was, but I am sure I must have betrayed myself ten times if I had been well observed. I flattered myself proudly, and almost sensually, at the bottom of my heart, that all this superb indifference was for me, and that she felt for me all the baseness of passion—if passion can ever be base. No one but ourselves knew that; the thought was delicious. No one—not even my friend, Louis de Meung, with whom I had been discreet since I had become happy! He had guessed all, no doubt, but then he was as discreet as I was. He did not question me. I had, without any effort, resumed my friendly habits with him, the walks on the Promenade, in full uniform or undress, cards, fencing, and punch! *Pardieu!* when you know that happiness will come in the shape of a pretty girl, whose senses are aflame, and visit you regularly every other night at the same hour, that simplifies your existence wonderfully!"

"But the parents of Alberte must have slept like the Seven Sleepers!" I said jokingly, cutting short the reflection of the old dandy by a jest, in order not to appear too much interested in his story, though it did interest me; for with dandies a joke is the only way of making yourself respected.

"You imagine, then, I am romancing, and exaggerating the effects?" said the Viscomte. "But I am not a novelist. Sometimes Alberte did not come. The door—the hinges of which were oiled now and went as soft as wool—sometimes did not open all night—because her mother had heard her, and cried out, or her father had seen her creeping on tiptoe across the room. But Alberte, having a head like iron, had always a pretext ready. She was ill. She was seeking the sugar-basin, and without a light, in order not to awake anyone."

"Those heads of iron are not so rare as you seem to think, Captain," I interrupted again. "Your Alberte, after all, was no cleverer than the girl who received every night, in her grandmother's room—whilst the old lady was asleep behind the curtains—a lover, who came in through the window, and, as they had no blue sofa, they calmly lay down on the carpet. You know the story as well as I do. One night, a sigh louder than usual woke the grandmother, who cried from behind the curtains: 'What is the matter, little one?' and the girl nearly fainted on her lover's breast, but nevertheless recovered herself, and replied: 'The

busk of my stays hurt me whilst I was looking for a needle which
has fallen on the floor, and which I cannot find.'"

"Yes, I know the story," replied the Vicomte. "The young girl
of whom you speak was, if I remember rightly, one of the Guises.
She acted up to her name, but you do not mention that after that
night she never opened her window again to her lover, who was,
I think, M. de Noirmoutier; whereas Alberte came to me the day
after one of these terrible shocks, and exposed herself again to
danger just as though nothing had occurred. I was then only
an ensign, and not very strong in mathematics, with which I did
not trouble myself; but it must have been evident to one who
could calculate chances that some day—or night—there would be
a *dénouement*."

"Ah, yes," I remarked, remembering what he had said before
he began his story, "the *dénouement* which made you acquainted
with the sensation of fear, Captain."

"Precisely," he replied, in a voice so grave that it contrasted
strongly with the flippant tone I had assumed. "You have seen,
have you not? that from the time she seized my hand under the
table, to the moment when she appeared like a ghost framed in
my open doorway, Alberte had made me suffer all kinds of emotion. She had caused to pass through me more than one kind
of shudder, more than one kind of terror; but they had been
merely like the bullets which whistle round you—like the cannon-
balls of which you feel only the wind: you shudder, but you go
on. Well! it was not that. It was fear—thorough and complete
fear, and no longer for Alberte, but for myself; for myself alone.
What I felt was that sensation which makes the heart as pale
as the face—that panic fear which makes whole regiments take to
flight. I have seen the whole Chamboran regiment take to its
heels, carrying with it its colonel and all the officers. But at that
time I had seen nothing of the kind, and I learned—that which
I believed to be impossible.

"Listen! It was one night. In the life we were leading, it
was bound to be at night—a long winter's night. I will not say

it was one of our calmest nights. Our nights were all calm. We were so happy that they became so. We slept over a powder-magazine. We were not disturbed at the thought of making love on a sword-blade over an abyss, like the bridge which leads to the Turkish hell. Alberte had come earlier than usual, in order to stay longer. When she thus came, my first caress, my first attention, was for her feet—those pretty feet, not now encased in green or blue slippers, but bare in order to make no sound—for they were icy from the cold bricks over which she walked the length of the corridor which led from her parents' room to mine, which was at the other side of the house.

"I warmed those icy feet, which for my sake had come out of a warm bed, fearing that she might catch some terrible disease of the lungs. I knew how to warm them, and bring back the pink or red tint to those pale, cold feet; but that night my method failed. My mouth was powerless to bring back the flush of blood.

"Alberte was that night more silently loving than ever.

"Her embraces had that languor and that force which were to me like a language, and a language so expressive that, if I had told her all my mad intoxication of joy, I should have needed no other answer. I understood those embraces.

"But suddenly I felt them no longer. Her arms ceased to press me to her heart. I thought it was one of those swoons such as she often had, though generally in these swoons her embrace never relaxed.—I need not be prudish to you. We are both men, and we can speak as men.

"I had had some experience of the voluptuous spasms of Alberte, and when they seized her, they did not interrupt my embraces.

"I remained as I was, on her breast, waiting till she should return to consciousness, and proud in the certainty she would recover her senses under my embraces, and that the blow which had struck her, by striking again, would revive her.

"But this was the exception to the rule. I gazed at her as she lay close to me on the blue sofa, awaiting the moment when her

eyes, now hidden under the long lids, should again reveal to me
those splendid orbs of black velvet and flame; when those teeth
which clenched almost tight enough to break the enamel at the
least kiss on her neck or shoulders, should reopen and allow her
breath to pass. But the eyes did not reopen, and the teeth did
not unclench.

"The icy chill rose from her feet, and mounted even to her lips.
When I felt that horrible cold, I sat up, in order to look at her the
better; with a bound I tore myself from her arms, one of which
fell back on her body, and the other dropped to the ground by
the side of the sofa on which she lay. Frightened, but having
still my senses about me, I put my hand on her heart. . . . No
sign of life! No sign in the pulse, in the temples, no sign in the
carotid arteries, no sign anywhere.—Death with its terrible rigidity
was everywhere!

"I was sure of her death—and yet I could not believe it.

"The human brain sometimes makes those stupid resolutions
even in the face of clear evidence and destiny. Alberte was dead.
Of what? I did not know; I was not a doctor. But she was dead,
and though I saw as clearly as the sun at noonday that all I
could do would be useless, yet I did everything that I knew would
be absurdly useless. In my absolute ignorance of all knowledge, and want of all instruments and resources, I emptied over
her face all the bottles on my dressing-table. I beat her hand,
in spite of the noise it made in a house where the least sound
made us tremble. I had heard one of my uncles, a captain in
the 4th Dragoons, say that he had once saved one of his friends
from apoplexy by bleeding him with a fleam, such as is used for
bleeding horses. I had plenty of weapons in my room. I picked
up a dagger, and cut Alberte's arm deeply, but no blood flowed.

"At the most a few drops coagulated. Neither kisses nor bites
could galvanize into life that stiff corpse—which had become a
corpse beneath my lips. Not knowing what more to do, I ended
by extending myself on her body—the means employed (according to the old legends) by all the miracle-workers of the past

when they resuscitated dead bodies—not hoping to restore her to life, but acting as though I did so hope. And it was whilst I was lying on this cold body that a thought, which had not before been able to form itself in the mental chaos in which the frightfully sudden death of Alberte had thrown me, appeared clearly, and I was afraid.

"Yes, I was seized by a dread—a terrible dread. Alberte had died in my room, and her death would reveal everything. What would become of me? What should I do?

"At the thought, I seemed to feel a terrible physical dread, and my hair stood on end. My backbone turned to ice, and I tried to struggle—but in vain—against the unmanly feeling. I told myself I must be calm; that I was a man—a soldier. I took my head in my hands, and whilst my brain reeled, I compelled myself to think of the terrible situation in which I was, and consider all the ideas which whipped my brain as though it were a top—and all these ideas centred in the inanimate body of Alberte, and how her mother would find her in the morning in 'the officer's room'—dead and dishonoured!

"The thought of the mother whose daughter I had dishonoured and perhaps killed, weighed more on my mind than even the corpse of Alberte. The death could not be concealed—but was there no means of concealing the dishonour proved by the discovery of the body in my room? That was the question I asked myself; the point on which I fixed all my attention.

"The difficulty increased the more I studied it, until it assumed the proportions of an absolute impossibility. Frightful hallucination! Sometimes the corpse of Alberte seemed to fill the whole room. Ah, if her bedroom had not been placed behind that of her parents, I would have carried her back, at all risks, to her own bed.

"But how could I, with a dead body in my arms, pass through a room with which I was unacquainted, and which I had never entered, and where the father and mother of the unfortunate girl slumbered in the light sleep of old people?

"Yet such was my state of mind, and my fear of the morrow
and of the dead body found in my room galloped so madly through
my brain, that this bold madness of carrying Alberte to her own
room possessed me as the only means of saving the honour of the
poor girl, and sparing me the shame of the reproaches of the
father and mother. Would you believe it?—I can hardly believe it myself when I think of it!—I had the strength to take
Alberte's dead body, raising it by the arms, and place it on my
shoulders. Horrible burden! heavier by far than that of the
damned in Dante's hell. You must have carried, as I did, that
fardel of flesh which but an hour before had made my blood boil
with desire, and which now terrified me! You must have carried
it yourself ere you can know what I felt and suffered.

"Thus laden, I opened the door, and, like her, with bare feet
that I might make no noise, I entered the corridor which led to her
parents' room, the door of which was at the end of the passage,
and, stopping at each step, whilst my legs almost gave way under
me, I listened for the least sound, and could hear nothing but the
beating of my own heart. The moments seemed terribly long.
Nothing moved. One step succeeded another. But when I
arrived in front of that fatal door which I must enter, and which
she had not quite closed, that she might find it still open on her
return—and when I heard the long, quiet breathing of those two
poor old people who were sleeping in such peace and confidence,
I dared go no farther. I dared not pass that doorway, looking so
black and threatening in the darkness.

"I drew back; I almost fled with my burden. I returned to
my room more and more terror-struck. I replaced the body of
Alberte on the sofa, and, on my knees beside her, I repeated
those supplicating questions. What is to be done? What will
be the end? So perturbed was I, that the senseless and atrocious
idea occurred to me to throw the body of this beautiful girl, who
had been my mistress six months, out of the window. Despise
me if you will! I opened the window—I drew aside the curtain

you see there, and I looked into the black hole at the bottom of which was the street, for it was very dark that night. I could not see the pavement. 'They will believe it is a suicide,' I said to myself—and I once more raised Alberte's body. But then a ray of common sense shot across my madness. 'How was she killed? From whence could she have fallen if she is found under my window?'

"I fully realized the impossibility of what I had been about to do. I closed the window, the fastening of which creaked dismally. I drew the curtain again, feeling more dead than alive at each sound I made. Besides, either through the window—on the staircase—in the corridor—wherever I might leave or throw the body, it would be an eternal accuser—the profanation would be useless. An examination of the corpse would reveal everything, and a mother's eyes would see all that the doctor or the judge tried to conceal from her.

"What I suffered was insupportable, and I had a good mind to finish it all with a pistol-shot and in the 'demoralized' (an expression of the Emperor's that I learned to understand later) condition in which I was, I looked at the weapons shining on the walls. But there! I will be frank. I was seventeen, and I loved—my sword. Both by inclination and race, I was a soldier. I had never been under fire, and I wished to be. I had military ambitions. In the regiment we joked about Werther—regarded as a hero at that time—but whom we officers pitied. The thought which prevented me from getting rid, by killing myself, of the ignoble fear which oppressed me, led to another which appeared to be salvation in the strait in which I was.

"If I went and saw the Colonel! I said to myself. The Colonel is the father of the regiment—and I dressed myself as though the call to arms were beating for a surprise attack. I took my pistols as a precaution. Who knew what might happen? I embraced for the last time, with all the affection of seventeen—one is always sentimental at seventeen—the dumb mouth of the poor dead Alberte, which during the last six months had showered upon me such delights. I descended the stair on tiptoe. Breathless as one who is fleeing for his life, I took an hour (it seemed to me an hour) to unbolt the street-door and turn the big key in the enormous lock; and, after having closed the door again with all the precautions of a thief, I ran like one fleeing for his life to the Colonel's house.

"I rang as though the house had been on fire. I shouted as though the enemy had been about to capture the flag of the regiment. I knocked everything over, including the orderly who tried to prevent me from entering his master's room, and when once the Colonel was awake, I told him everything. I made a complete confession rapidly and boldly, for time pressed, and I begged of him to save me.

"The Colonel was a man of action. He saw at a glance in what a horrible gulf I was struggling. He had pity on the youngest of his children, as he called us, and indeed I was in a condition to be pitied. He told me—accentuating the statement with a round oath—that I must begin by clearing out of the town, immediately, and that he would undertake the rest; that he would see the parents as soon as I had gone, but that I must go at once, and take the diligence which would stop in ten minutes' time at the Hotel de la Poste, and go to a town which he named, where he would write. He gave me some money, for I had omitted to put any in my pocket, pressed his old grey moustache to my cheeks, and ten minutes after this interview I had climbed on the roof—it was the only place left—of the diligence which was making the same journey as we are now, and I passed at a gallop under the window (you may guess how I looked at it) of the funeral chamber where I had left Alberte dead, and which was lighted up as it is to-night."

Vicomte de Brassard stopped, his voice quite broken.

I no longer felt inclined to joke. The silence did not last long.

"And after?" I said.

"Well," he replied, "there was no after. For a long time I was tortured by curiosity. I followed faithfully the Colonel's instructions. I impatiently awaited a letter that would inform me of what had happened after my departure. I waited about a month; but at the end of the month it was not a letter from the Colonel I received, for he scarcely ever wrote, except with a sabre on the bodies of his enemies, but an order to join in twenty-four hours the 33rd Regiment, to which I had been appointed. A campaign, and that my first, distracted my thoughts. The battles in which I took part, the hardships, and also some adventures with women, caused me to neglect to write to the Colonel, and turned my thoughts from the sad memory of Alberte, without, however, effacing it. I preserved it still, like a bullet that cannot be extracted. I said to myself that I should some day meet the Colonel, who would inform me of that which I wished to know, but the Colonel was killed at the head of his regiment at Leipsic. Louis de Meung also had been killed about a month before.

"It is shameful, no doubt," added the Captain, "but memories end by dying. The devouring curiosity to know what had happened after my departure no longer disturbed me. I might have come back in after years to this little town—and, changed as I was, I should never have been recognized—and learned what had been the end of my tragic adventure. But something, which was certainly not respect for public opinion, which I have all my life despised, but rather a disinclination to face a second time that which had given me such a deadly fear, always restrained me."

This dandy, who had related without any dandyism such a grim and true story, was silent. I was thinking over his story, and I understood that this fine flower of dandyism had other sides to his character than those which appeared to his acquaintances. I remembered that he had said at the beginning that there was a black blot which had all his life destroyed his pleasures as a libertine—when suddenly he astonished me still more by seizing my arm roughly.

"Look!" he said.   "Look at the curtain!"

The slim shadow of a woman was plainly delineated on the curtain.

"The ghost of Alberte!" said the Captain.   "Fortune is mocking us to-night," he added bitterly.

The shadow passed, and the red bright square was again empty. But the wheelwright, who, whilst the Captain was speaking, had been busy with his screw, had finished his task.   The fresh horses were ready, and were pawing the ground, striking out sparks with their iron shoes.

The driver, his astrakhan cap over his ears, and the way-bill between his teeth, took the reins and climbed to the box, and, when once he was in his seat, cried in a loud clear voice:

"Go on!"

And we went on, and had soon passed the mysterious window with its red curtain—but I still continue to see it in my dreams.

THE GREATEST LOVE OF DON JUAN

THE GREATEST LOVE OF DON JUAN

"The Devil's primest fare is innocence."

I

"He is still alive then, that hoary old reprobate?"

"Still alive! I should rather think he was,—by God's grace," I took care to add, remembering Madame's piety, "and of the most distinguished and aristocratic parish of Sainte-Clotilde.—'*Le roi est mort! vive le roi!*' is what they used to say under the old Monarchy, in the days when that fine old piece of Sèvres porcelain was yet unbroken. But Don Juan, in spite of all your democracies, is a monarch they will never break."

"Yes! yes! no doubt the Devil is in the immortal!" she returned in a self-approving tone.

"As a matter of fact, he . . ."

"Who? . . . the Devil? . . ."

"No! no! Don Juan. He supped, I say, only three days ago in pleasant company. . . . Guess where. . . ."

"At your horrid Maison d'Or, of course. . . ."

"My dear Madame! Don Juan *never* goes there now . . . they've no fish fit to fry for his Highness' palate. The Señor Don Juan has always been a bit like Arnold of Brescia's famous monk who, the Chronicles tell us, lived only on the blood of souls. That is what he loves to colour his champagne with, and it's many a long day since it was to be had at that rendezvous of the commonplace *cocotte!*"

"You'll be telling me next," she interrupted, in the ironic vein, "he supped at the Benedictine nunnery with the holy ladies . . ."

"Yes! ladies of the Perpetual Adoration; why, certainly,

Madam. For indeed I do think the adoration he has once inspired, our redoubtable Lovelace, seems to last for good and all."

"And I think that for a good Catholic you are a trifle profane,
sir!"—this she said slowly, but not without a touch of irritation—
"and I must beg you to spare me the details of your naughty
suppers. I suppose this is a new way of telling me about your
disreputable lady friends, this harping on Don Juan and his
doings to-night."

"I merely state the facts, Madam. The disreputable persons
present at the supper in question, if they *are* disreputable, are
not *my* friends at all . . . unfortunately . . ."

"Enough! enough!"

"Forgive my modest disclaimer. . . . They were . . ."

"The *mille è trè?* . . ." she interrupted again, thinking better
of it and all but recovering her good temper under the stress of
curiosity.

"Oh! not all of them. . . . A round dozen merely. With as
many as that, nothing could be more respectable, you know."

"Or more disreputable," she put in tartly.

"Besides, you know as well as I do the Comtesse de Chiffrevas'
boudoir will not hold a crowd. Everything was done that could be
done; but, after all, it's only a small room, her boudoir."

"What!"—raising her voice in her astonishment. "They had
supper in the boudoir?"

"Yes! in the boudoir. And why not? A battle-field makes a
famous place to dine. They wished to give a very special and
particular supper to Señor Don Juan, and it seemed better worthy
of his exploits to give it on the scene of his former triumphs, where
fond memories bloom instead of orange-blossoms. A pretty notion, at once tender and sad! *'Twas no victims' ball!* it was a
victims' supper-party!"

"And Don Juan?" she asked in the tone of Orgon, in the play,
saying: "And Tartufe?"

"Don Juan took it in excellent part, and made an excellent
supper,

' . . . He, he alone before them all,'

as the poet sings—in the person of someone you know very
well indeed—none other than the Comte Jules-Amédée-Hector de
Ravila de Ravilès."

"Comte de Ravilès! Why, yes! He was a Don Juan. . . ."

So saying, the pious lady, case-hardened in her narrow bigotry
as she was, and long past the age of day-dreams, lapsed then
and there into a fond reverie of which Comte Jules-Amédée was
the theme—that man of the old Don Juan breed, to which God
has not indeed given "all the world and the glory thereof," but
has suffered the Devil to do it for Him.

II

What I had just told the aged Marquise Guy de Ruy was the
unvarnished truth.   Hardly three days had elapsed since a dozen
ladies of the virtuous Faubourg Saint-Germain (rest them easy,
I will never damage their noble names!), who every one, the whole
dozen, if we are to believe the cackling dowagers of the quarter,
had been "on the best of good terms" (a really charming, old-
fashioned locution) with the Comte Ravila de Ravilès, had conceived the singular idea of offering him a supper—he being the
only male guest—in pious memory of . . . well! they did not say
of what.   A bold thing to do, but women, while timid individually,
are as bold as brass when banded together.   Probably not one of
the whole party would have ventured to invite the Comte to a
tête-à-tête supper at her own house; but all together, each back-
ing up the other, they feared not to weave a chain, like mesmerists
round their mystic tub, round this magnetic and most compromis-
ing individual, the Comte de Ravila de Ravilès. . . .

"What a name!"

"A providential name, Madam."

The Comte de Ravila de Ravilès, who, by the by, had always
lived up to his high-sounding and picturesque title, was the

perfect incarnation of all the long line of Lovelaces Romance and History tell of, and even the old Marquise Guy de Ruy—a discontented old lady, with light-blue eyes, cold and keen, but not so cold as her heart or so keen as her tongue—allowed that in these times, when women and women's concerns grow day by day less important, if there *was* anyone who could recall Don Juan, it must surely be he! Unfortunately, it was Don Juan in the Fifth Act. The witty Prince de Ligne said he could *not* make himself believe Alcibiades ever grew to be fifty; and here again the Comte de Ravila was to be a true Alcibiades to the end of the chapter. Like d'Orsay, a dandy hewn out of the marble of Michael Angelo, who was the handsomest of men down to his last hour, Ravila had possessed the good looks specially belonging to the Don Juan breed—that mysterious race which does not proceed from father to son, like other races, but appears here and there, at recurring intervals, in the families of mankind.

His beauty was beyond dispute—of the gay, arrogant, imperial sort, *Juanesque* in fact (the word is a picture and makes description needless); and—had he made an unholy bargain with the Devil?—it was his still. . . . Only, God was beginning to exact His penalty; life's cruel tiger-claws already seamed that "front divine," crowned with the roses of so many kisses, and on his wide and wicked temples appeared the first white hairs that proclaim the impending invasion of the barbarian hosts and the Fall of the Empire. . . . He wore them, it is true, with the calm insouciance of pride surfeited with power; but women who had loved him would sometimes gaze at them with sad eyes. Who knows? perhaps they read what hour of day it was for themselves on that whitening brow? Alas and alas! for them as for him, 'twas the hour for the grim supper with the cold white-marble commendator, after which only Hell is left—first the Hell of old age, then the other! And this perhaps is why, before sharing with him this last, bitter meal, they planned to offer him this supper of their own, and made it the miracle of art it was.

Yes, a miracle of good taste and refinement, of patrician luxury, elegance, and pretty conceits; the most charming, the most delicious, the most toothsome, the most heady, and, above all, the most original of suppers. How original, just think for a moment! Commonly it is love of merriment, the thirst for amusement, that supply motives for a supper-party; but this one was dedicated only to fond memories and soft regrets, we might almost say to despair—but despair in full dress, despair hidden beneath smiles and laughter, despair that craved just one more merry night, one more escapade, one last hour of youth, one last intoxication—and so an end of it all for ever.

The fair Amyphitryons of this incredible supper, so far removed from the timid habits of the society to which they belonged, must surely have experienced something of the feelings of Sardanapalus on his funeral-pyre when he heaped upon it, to perish with him, wives, slaves, horses, jewels, all the splendid trappings of his life. They too collected at this last supper of farewell all the splendours of their past. To it they brought all their stores of beauty, of wit and wisdom, of magnificence and power, to pour them forth once and for all in one supreme and final conflagration.

The hero before whom they wrapped and robed themselves in this garment of consuming fire counted for more in their eyes than all Asia did for Sardanapalus. They flirted with him as never women flirted with any man before, or with any roomful of men; and their keen coquetry was yet further inflamed by jealousy, which is concealed in good society, but which they had no cause to dissemble here, for they all knew that he had been the lover of each and all of them, and shame shared among so many ceases to be shame at all. . . . The sole and only rivalry between them was, Which should carve his epitaph deepest in her heart?

That night he enjoyed the rich, sovereign, nonchalant, ruminating pleasure of a father confessor and a sultan. There he sat, monarch and master, in the centre of the table, facing the Comtesse de Chiffrevas, in her boudoir with its peach-blossom hangings—or was it the fruit of the tree of the knowledge of evil?—

this has always been a moot point. The fiery gaze of his blue eye—heavenly blue many a poor creature has deemed to her cost, to find it later of quite another sort—was fixed on his fair companions. All twelve were beautiful, all were dressed to perfection; and, seated round the festive board, which glistened with crystal lights and flowers, they displayed, from the scarlet of the open rose to the soft gold of the mellow grape, every nuance of ripe and opulent charms.

Only the crude green of extreme youth was absent, the little girls Byron loathed, smelling of bread and butter, thin, weedy, undeveloped creatures. Fine, full-favoured summer, rich and generous autumn, these were the seasons represented—full curves and ample proportions, dazzling bosoms, beating in majestic swell above liberally cut corsages, and below the clear modelling of the naked shoulder, arms of every type of beauty, but mostly powerful arms, Sabine biceps that have struggled against the Roman ravisher, vigorous enough, you would think, to grasp the wheels of the car of life and twine around the spokes and stop its course by sheer force.

I have spoken of happy ideas. One of the happiest at this supper was to have all the waiting done by maidservants, that nothing might disturb the harmony of a celebration where women were the only queens, and did all the honours. . . . Señor Don Juan then was able to bathe his burning gaze in a sea of living and dazzling flesh, such as Rubens delights to flaunt in his strong, fleshy pictures, but, besides, he could plunge his pride in the ether, more or less transparent, more or less turgid, of all these hearts. The fact is, at bottom, and despite all appearances to the contrary, Don Juan is an ardent idealist! He is like the Devil, his master, who loves men's souls better than their bodies, and actually traffics in the former by choice, the hellish slave-driver!

Witty, high-bred, and aristocratic, but for the nonce as recklessly gay as pages of the Household—when there was a King's Household and pages of it—they exhibited a scintillating brilliance, a dash, a verve, a *brio,* that were beyond compare. They

felt themselves in better form than they had ever been in their
most palmy days; they felt a new and mysterious power in their
inmost being which they had never suspected the existence of
before.

Joy at this discovery, a sensation of tripled intensity in the
vital powers, still more the physical incitements, so stimulating
to highly strung temperaments, the flashing lights, the penetrating
odour of many flowers dying in an atmosphere overheated with the
emanations of all these lovely bodies, the sting of heady wines,
all acted together. Then the mere thought of this supper, which
had just that piquancy of naughtiness the fair Neapolitan asked
for in her lemonade to make it perfectly delicious, the intoxicating
notion of complicity in this wild, wicked feast—not that it condescended for an instant to any of the vulgar incidents of the
Regent's Suppers; it remained throughout true to the tone of the
Faubourg Saint-Germain and the nineteenth century, and of all
those lovely bosoms, with hearts beating beneath that had been
under fire and still loved to tempt the fray, not one lost so much
as a pin or a knot of ribbon—all these things together helped to
tune the magic harp which all of them carried within themselves
and to stretch the strings well-nigh to breaking-point, till they
quivered again in passionate octaves and ineffable diapasons of
emotion. . . . A curious page it will make of his Secret Memoirs
this, if Ravila ever writes them! . . . As I told the Marquise Guy
de Ruy, I was not at the supper myself, and if I am able to
report some of its incidents and the narrative with which it con-
cluded, I owe them to no other than Ravila himself, who, faithful to the traditional indiscretion characteristic of all the Don Juan
breed, took the trouble one evening to tell me the whole story.

III

It was getting late—or, rather, early—and dawn was near. On
the ceiling and at one spot in the pink silk curtains of the boudoir,
otherwise hermetically closed, there grew and increased a splash

of opalescent light, like an ever-enlarging eye, the eye of day as
if fain to look in through the crevice and see what was doing in
the brilliantly lighted room. A certain languor was in the air,
assailing these champions of the Round Table, these merry-makers
who had been so animated but a moment ago. The crisis is familiar at every supper-party, the instant when, wearied with the
gaiety and emotional stress of the night, everything seems to
languish at once, drooping heads, burning cheeks, reddened or
paled by excitement, tired eyes under heavy, darkened lids, even
the candles themselves, which seem to quiver and grow larger in
the many-branched candelabra, fiery flowers with stems of chiselled
bronze and gold.

The conversation, hitherto general and vivacious, a game of
shuttlecock where each had put in her stroke, had grown frag-
mentary and broken, and no distinct word was now audible amid
the musical confusion of voices, which, with their aristocratic tones,
mingled in a pretty babble, like birds at break of day on the
confines of a wood, when one of them—a high-pitched voice,
imperious, almost insolent, as a Duchess's should be—cried suddenly above all the rest to the Comte de Ravila what was evidently the conclusion of a previous whispered conversation between the two, which none of the others, each engaged in talk
with her immediate neighbour, had heard.

"You are the reputed Don Juan of our day: well! you should
tell us the history of the conquest of all others which most flattered
your pride as a ladies' man, and which you judge, in the light of
the present moment, the greatest love of your life. . . ."

And the question, no less than the voice in which it was uttered,
instantly cut short all the scattered conversations that were buzz-
ing round the table, and imposed a sudden silence.

The voice was that of the Duchesse de * * * * *—I will not
lift the veil of asterisks, but you will very likely know who it
was when I tell you she is the fairest of all fair women, both
complexion and hair, with the darkest eyes under long golden
eyebrows in all the Faubourg Saint-Germain. She was seated,

like a saint at God's right hand, at the right hand of the Comte
de Ravila, the God of the feast, a God that, for the moment,
waived his right to use his enemies as his footstool; slender and
spiritual, like an arabesque and a fairy, in her dress of green
velvet with glints of silver, the long train twining round her chair,
no bad imitation of the serpent's tail in which the alluring shape
of the sea-nymph Melusina terminates.

"A happy thought!" put in the Comtesse de Chiffrevas, second-
ing as mistress of the house the wish expressed by the Duchess.
"Yes! the love of all loves, inspired or felt, you would most gladly
live again, were such a thing possible."

"Oh, I would be glad to live them all again!" cried Ravila with
the unquenchable gusto of a Roman Emperor, the insatiable crav-
ing your utterly *blasé* man of pleasure sometimes retains. And
he flourished aloft his champagne-glass—not the silly, shallow
cup fashionable in these pagan days, but the true champagne-
glass, the glass our fathers drank from, tall and slender, and called
by them a *flute,* mayhap from the celestial harmonies in which
it often bathes our heart!—Then he embraced in one sweeping
look the whole circle of fair women that wreathed the board so
royally.—"And still," he went on, replacing his glass before him
with a sigh that sounded strange from such a Nebuchadnezzar,
whose only experience as yet of the grass of the field as an article
of diet had been the tarragon salads at the Café Anglais,—"and
still, how true it is there is always *one* among all the emotions of
a lifetime that shines ever in the memory more brightly than the
rest, as life advances—one for which we would gladly exchange
them all."

"The brightest diamond of the casket," murmured the Comtesse
Chiffrevas in a dreamy tone, perhaps looking back at the sparkling facets of her own career.

". . . The legends of my country," broke in the Princess Jable
—who is from the foot-hills of the Ural Mountains—"tell of a
famous and fabulous diamond, rose-coloured at first, but which
turns black presently, yet remains a true diamond all the time,

and sparkles only the more brilliantly for the change. . . ."—She
said it with the strange exotic charm peculiar to her, this Gipsy
Princess.   For a true Gipsy she is, married for love by the handsomest Prince of all the exiled Polish nobility; yet having as much
the air of a high-born Princess as if she had first seen the light
in the palace of the Jagellons.

A regular explosion followed!   "Yes!   yes!" they clamoured
with one voice.   "Tell us, Comte!" they urged in tones already
vibrating with a passionate supplication, curiosity quivering in
the very curls that fringed the back of their necks.   They drew
together, shoulder to shoulder; some with cheek on hand and
elbow on the board, some leaning back in their chairs, with open
fans before their mouths, all challenging him with wide, inquisitive
eyes.

"If you are bent on hearing the story," said the Comte with
the nonchalance of a man well aware how much procrastination
adds to the keenness of desire.

"We are, we are!" cried the Duchesse, gazing, as a Turkish
despot might at his sabre's edge, at the gold dessert-knife she
held in her fingers.

"Well, listen then," he said finally, still with the same fine air
of indifference.

They fell into attitudes of profound attention, and, fixing their
gaze on his face, devoured him with their eyes.   Every love-story
is interesting to a woman; but here, perhaps—who knows?—the
chief charm lay for each one of his audience in the thought that
the tale he was about to unfold might be her own. . . . They
knew him to be too much of a gentleman and too well-bred not
to be sure he would suppress all names and, where necessary, slur
over indiscreet details; and their conviction of this fact made them
so much the more eager to hear the story.   They not only desired,
but, what is more, they hoped—each for a special and particular
sop to her own vanity.

Yet this same vanity was on the *qui vive* to scent a rival in
this reminiscence called up as the tenderest in a life that must

have been so full of them. The old sultan was going once more
to throw the handkerchief . . . that no hand would stoop to pick
up, but which the favoured *one* it should have fallen to would
silently and gratefully receive into her heart.

Knowing what his fair audience expected, you will now be able
to realize the utterly unexpected thunderclap he called down on
all those listening heads.

IV

"I have often heard moralists declare—men who have had deep
experience of life," began the Comte de Ravila, "that the strongest
of all our loves is neither the first nor yet the last, as many think,
but the second. But in these matters everything is uncertain, and
at any rate it was not so with me. . . . What you ask me about,
ladies, the story I am about to tell you to-night, dates from the
best period of my youth. I was not then what is technically
called a 'young man,' but I was young, albeit I had already, as
an old uncle of mine, a Knight of Malta, used to say to describe
this epoch of life, sown my wild oats.[1] I was in the full vigour
of my prime, and I was in full *relations* (to use the pretty Italian
phrase) with a woman you all know well and have all
admired. . . ."

At this the look which each of the group simultaneously cast
at all the rest, one and all eagerly drinking in the old serpent's
honeyed words, was a thing to have seen—for, indeed, it is
indescribable.

"The woman in question," Ravila went on, "had every element
of 'distinction' you can imagine, in every sense of the word. She
was young, rich, of noble name, beautiful, witty and artistic—
simple, too, and unaffected, with the genuine unaffectedness to
be found only in well-bred circles, and not always there—to crown

---

[1] *"J'avais fini mes caravanes"; caravane* was the word used by the
Knights of Malta to designate their periodical filibustering cruises against
the Turks.

all, without another thought or inspiration but to please me, to be my devoted slave, at once the fondest of mistresses and the best of comrades.

"I was not, I have reason to believe, the first man she had loved. . . . She had given her affection once before—and it was not to her husband; but the whole affair had been virtuous, platonic, utopian—the sort of love that practises rather than satisfies a woman's heart, that trains its powers for another and fuller passion, which is bound to supervene ere long. It is prentice love in fact, something like the *messe blanche* young priests repeat by way of rehearsal, that they may not blunder in the genuine, solemn Mass that is to follow. . . . When I came into her life, she was only at the 'white Mass'; I was her genuine Mass—and she went through it with every circumstance of pomp and ceremony, like a very cardinal."

At this the prettiest smile flashed out on the twelve sweet mouths that listened round, like a circling eddy on the limpid surface of a pool. . . . It was gone in an instant, but entrancing while it lasted.

"She was indeed one in a thousand!" the Comte resumed. "Rarely have I known more real good-heartedness, more gentle compassion, more justness of feeling—and this even in love, which is, you know, a passion made up of evil as well as good. . . . Nowhere have I seen less manœuvring, or less prudishness and vanity, two things so often entangled in the web of feminine character, like a skein clawed over by a mischievous cat. . . . The cat had no part in her composition. . . . She was what those confounded romance-writers who poison our minds with phrases would call a 'simple, primitive nature, complicated and embellished by civilization'; but she had borrowed of it only the pretty luxury of her habits, and not one of those little vices that sometimes seem even more alluring than the luxuries."

"Was she dark or fair?" suddenly interrupted the Duchesse, with a startling directness, tired out with so much metaphysics. . . .

"Ah! you miss my point!" exclaimed Ravila keenly. "Well, I will tell you; her hair was dark, black as the blackest jet, the most perfect ebony mirror I have ever seen flash back the light from a woman's head, but her complexion was fair—and it is by complexion, not hair, you should pronounce a woman brunette or blonde," added this student of the sex, who had observed women for something else than just to paint their portraits afterwards. . . . She was blonde with black hair. . . ."

Each blond head around the table (alas, only blond-*haired* they!) betrayed an almost imperceptible movement of disappointment. For them clearly the tale had henceforth lost something of its interest.

"She had the ebony locks of Night," resumed Ravila, "but crowning the face of Aurora, for indeed her face glowed with a rosy freshness of dawn, as dazzling as rare, that had triumphantly resisted years of Paris life with its hot rooms and artificial light, that burns up so many roses in the flames of its candelabra. *Her* roses seemed but to win a richer hue, so brilliant was the carmine that mantled on cheek and lip! Indeed, this twofold radiance accorded well with the ruby she always wore on her forehead (the frontlet was still in fashion in those days), which, in combination with her flashing eyes, whose very brilliancy made it impossible to distinguish their colour, formed a triangle, as it were, of three bright jewels in her face! Tall, but robust and even majestic in figure, cut out for the helpmate of a colonel of dragoons—her husband at that time was only a major in the Light Horse—she enjoyed, for all her fine-ladyhood, a peasant woman's vigorous health, who drinks in the sun at every pore. And she had all the heat and ardour of the sun in her veins, and in her very soul as well—ever present, and ever ready. . . . But—and this was the strange part of it—this being, so strong and simple and unspoiled, as generous and as pure as the red blood that mantled in her cheeks and dyed her rosy arms, was—can you credit it?—maladroit and awkward in a lover's arms. . . ."

Here one or two fair auditors dropped their eyes, only to raise them again directly with a look of demure mischief in their depths. . . .

"Yes! awkward in this respect as she was reckless in her regard for appearances," continued Ravila, and vouchsafed no further information on this delicate point. "In fact, the man who loved her had to be incessantly teaching her two lessons, neither of which she ever really learnt—not to affront needlessly public opinion, a foe that is always under arms and always merciless, and to practise in the intimacy of private life those all-important acts of love that guard passion from dying of satiety. Love she had in abundance, but the art and mystery of its skilled exponents were beyond her ken. . . . She was the antipodes of most women, who possess the latter qualifications to perfection, but of the other not a whit. Now to comprehend and apply the cunning maxims of the *Il Principe,* you must be a Borgia to begin with. Borgia comes first, Machiavelli second; one is the poet, the other the critic. No Borgia was she, but just a good woman in love, as simple-minded, with all her monumental beauty, as the little maid in the rustic picture who tries to take up a handful of spring water from the fountain to quench her thirst, but in her trembing haste lets it trickle away every drop between her fingers, and stands there an image of embarrassment and confusion. . . .

"Yet in a way the contrast was piquant and almost delightful between this embarrassed awkwardness and the grand, passion-fraught personality of the woman, who would have deceived the most acute observer when seen in society—who knew love, and even love's bliss, but had not the faculty to pay back half of what she received. Only, unfortunately, I was not artist enough to be content with this mere delight of contrast; hence now and again displays on her part of disquiet, jealousy, and even violence. But all this, jealousy, disquiet, violence, was swallowed up in the inexhaustible kindness of her heart at the first sign of pain she thought she had inflicted—as awkward at wounding as she was at caressing! Tigress of an unknown species, she fondly imagined she had claws, but lo! when she would show them, none were to be found within the sheath of her beautiful velvet paws. Her very scratches were velvet-soft!"

"What is the man driving at?" whispered the Comtesse de Chiffrevas to her neighbour. "This surely cannot be Don Juan's proudest triumph!"

All these complex natures could not understand such simplicity and remained incredulous.

"Thus we lived," Ravila went on, "on terms of friendship, now and then interrupted by storms, yet never shipwrecked, a friendship that, in the little village they call Paris, was a mystery to none. . . . The Marquise—she was a Marquise . . ."

There were three at table, and raven-locked too. But they made no sign. They knew only too well it was not of them he spoke. . . . The only velvet about the trio was on the upper lip of one of the three—a lip bearing a voluptuous shadowing of down, and for the moment, I can assure you, a well-marked expression of disdain.

". . . And a Marquise three times over, just as Pashas may be Pashas of Three Tails," continued Ravila, who was getting into the swing of his narrative. "The Marquise was one of those women who have no idea of hiding anything and who, if they had, could never do it. Her daughter even, a child of thirteen, for all her youth and innocence, saw only too clearly the nature of the feeling her mother had for me. I know not which of our poets has asked what the girls think of us, the girls whose mothers we have loved. A deep question I often put to myself when I caught the child's inquisitive gaze fixed black and menacing upon me from the ambush of her great, dark eyes. . . . A shy, reserved creature, she would, more often than not, leave the drawing-room when I entered, and, if obliged to remain, would invariably station herself as far away from me as possible; she had an almost convulsive horror of my person—which she strove to hide in her own bosom, but which was too strong for her and betrayed itself against her will by little almost imperceptible signs.—I noticed every one. The Marquise, though anything but an observant

woman, was for ever warning me: 'You must take care, dearest.
I think my girl is jealous of you. . . .'

"But I was taking much better care all the while than she was.

"Had the little girl been the Devil himself, I would have defied
her to decipher my game. . . . But her mother's was as clear as
day.   Everything was visible in the rosy mirror of her beautiful
face, so often troubled by passing clouds!   From the strange dislike the child showed, I could not help thinking she had surprised
her mother's secret through some indiscreet burst of feeling, some
involuntary look fraught with excess of tenderness.   I may tell
you she was a funny-looking child, quite unworthy of the glorious
mould she had issued from, an ugly child, even by her mother's
admission, who only loved her the more for it.   A little rough-
cut topaz—how shall I describe it?—a half-finished sculptor's
study in bronze—but with eyes black as night and having a
strange, uncanny magic of their own.   Later on . . ."

But here he stopped dead as if regretting his burst of confidence
and fearful of having said too much. . . . Every face once more
expressed an open, eager, vivid curiosity, and the Countess, with
a knowing air of pleased expectancy, actually dropped from between her lovely lips an expressive "At last!"

v

"In the earlier days of my liaison with her mother," the Comte
de Ravila resumed, "I had shown the child all the little fondling
familiarities one has with children. . . . I used to bring her bags
of sugared almonds; I used to call her my 'little witch,' and very
often, when talking to her mother, I would amuse myself with
fingering the curls that hung over her temple—thin, sickly-looking
curls, like black tow—but the 'little witch,' whose big mouth had
a pretty smile for everybody else, at once waxed pensive, her
cheerfulness disappeared, and her brows would knit fiercely.   Her
little face grew tense and rigid, the wrinkled mask of an overbur-
dened caryatid, and as my hand brushed her forehead, it looked

for all the world as though it bore the crushing weight of some vast entablature.

"After a while, meeting invariably with the same sullenness and apparent hostility, I took to leaving this sensitive plant alone, which drew in its sad-coloured petals so violently at the least touch of a caress. . . . I even left off speaking to her! 'She feels you are robbing her,' the Marquise would say to me. 'Her instinct tells her you are appropriating a portion of her mother's love.' Sometimes she would add outright: 'The child is my conscience, and her jealousy my remorse.'

"Once the Marquise had tried to question her as to the profound disfavour in which she held me, but she had got nothing out of her but the broken, obstinate, stupid answers you have to drag out with a corkscrew of reiterated questions from a child that prefers not to speak. . . . 'Nothing is the matter . . . I don't know . . .' and so on, and so on. Finally, seeing how hard and obstinate the little image was, she had left off questioning her and turned away in sheer weariness.

"I forgot, by the by, to tell you one thing. The queer child was profoundly religious, in a gloomy, mediæval, Spanish, superstitious sort of way. She twined around her meagre little person all kinds of scapularies and stuck on her bosom, which was as flat as the back of your hand, and round her swarthy throat, a whole heap of crosses, Blessed Virgins and Holy Spirits. 'You are a free-thinker, you know,' the Marquise would say to me, 'worse luck; perhaps you have shocked her feelings some time with your talk. Be very careful of anything you say before her; and do not add to my sins in the eyes of my child, towards whom I already feel myself so guilty!' Then, later on, the girl's behavior showing no change or improvement whatever, 'You will end by hating the child,' the Marquise would complain anxiously, 'and I cannot blame you.' But she was wrong in this; my feeling towards the sullen child was one of simple indifference, when I took the trouble to think of her at all.

"I treated her with the ceremonious politeness usual between grown-up people who do not like each other. I addressed her formally, as Mademoiselle, and she returned the compliment with a freezing Monsieur. . . . She would do nothing when I was there to attract admiration or even notice. . . . Her mother could never persuade her to show me one of her drawings or play a piece on the piano in my presence. If ever I came upon her seated at the instrument practising eagerly and industriously, she would stop dead, get up from the music-stool, and refuse utterly to go on. . . .

"Once only, when there was company and her mother desired her to play, she consented to take her place at the open keyboard, with a look of being victimized that was anything but propitiating, I can tell you, and began some drawing-room piece with abominally difficult fingering. I was standing by the fireplace, and enfiladed her with my gaze. Her back was towards me, and there was no mirror in front of her in which she could see I was looking at her. . . . All of a sudden her back—she always held herself ill, and many a time her mother would tell her: 'If you *will* hold yourself like that, you'll end by getting consumption' —well, all of a sudden her back straightened as if my look had broken her spine like a bullet; and, slamming down the lid of the piano with a resounding crash, she rushed out of the room. . . . They went to look for her, but for that evening, at any rate, nothing would induce her to come back.

"Well, vain as men are, it would seem their vanity is often blind, and, for all her strange behavior (and indeed I gave it very little attention), I had never a suspicion of the true feeling the mysterious creature entertained for me. Nor yet had her mother; jealous as the latter was of every woman who entered her drawing-room, in this case her jealousy was as fast asleep as my own vanity. The truth was eventually revealed in a sufficiently startling fashion. The Marquise, who could keep nothing from her intimates, told me the story, her face still pale with the fright she had had, though bursting with laughter at the notion of having been frightened at all. In doing so, she was ill-advised."

The word "ill-advised" the Count had marked with just that

touch of emphasis a clever actor knows how to throw into his voice when he has a point to make. This was the thread, he was perfectly aware of the fact, on which the whole interest of his story now hung!

The mere hint was enough apparently, for all twelve faces flushed once more with an intensity of emotion comparable only to the cherubim's countenances before the throne of the Almighty! Is not curiosity in a woman's heart as intense an emotion as ever adoration among the angels of God? . . . For his part, he marked them all, those cherub faces (which were a good deal more than mere head and shoulders, though) and, finding them doubtless primed for what he had to say, quickly resumed and went on without further pause.

"Yes, she could not help bursting with laughter, merely to think of it!—so the Marquise told me a while after, when she came to relate the story; but she had been in no laughing mood at first!—'Only picture the scene,' she began (I will endeavour to recall her exact words); 'I was seated just where we are now.'

"This was one of those small double sofas known as a *dos-à-dos*, of all contrivances in the way of furniture surely the best-designed for a pair of lovers to quarrel and make it up again, without leaving their seats.

" 'But you were not where you are now—thank goodness!— when, who do you think was announced?—you would never guess —who but the respected *curé* of Saint-Germain-des-Près? Do you know him? . . . No, you never go to church, you bad man! . . . So how should you know the poor old *curé*, who is a saint, and who never sets foot inside the doors of any woman in his parish unless it is a question of raising money for his poor or his Church? For a moment I thought this was what he had come for now.

" 'He had prepared my daughter at the proper time for her first communion; and as she went regularly to communion, subsequently, she had retained him as her confessor. For this reason, over and over again since then, I had invited the good priest to dine with us, but always in vain. On entering the room, he displayed the greatest agitation, and I read in his usually placid features manifest signs of an embarrassment so extreme and so uncontrollable, I could not set it down to the account of mere shyness. Involuntarily the first words that escaped me were: "Good heavens, Father! What is the matter?"

" ' "The matter, dear Madam," he began, ". . . the matter is, you see before you the most embarrassed man in Europe. For fifty years I have been a minister in God's service, and all that time I have never had a more delicate mission to perform, or one that baffled me more completely to understand. . . ."

" 'Then he sat down, asking me to have the door shut against all comers throughout our interview. As you may suppose, all these solemn preliminaries began rather to frighten me. . . .

" 'Noticing this, he added: "Nay! do not be frightened, I beg of you; you will need all your calmness to attend to my story, and to account, to my satisfaction, for the unheard-of circumstance we have to deal with, and which even now I cannot believe authentic. . . . Your daughter, Madam, on whose behalf I am here, is—you know it as well as I do—an angel of purity and goodness. I know her very soul. I have held it between my two hands since she was a child of seven, and I am convinced she is deceiving herself—through sheer innocence of heart, it may be. . . . But this morning she came to me to avow in confession—you will not believe it, nor can I, but the word must come out—that she was *pregnant!*"

" 'A cry escaped me of wonder and incredulity. . . .

" ' "I did the very same thing this morning in my confessional," the priest declared, "on hearing her make this assertion, accompanied as it was by every mark of the most genuine and terrible despair. I know the child thoroughly; she is absolutely ignorant of the world and its wickedness. . . . Of all the young girls I confess, she is undoubtedly the one I could most unhesitatingly answer for before God.—There is no more to tell! We priests are the surgeons of souls, and it is our duty to deliver them of shameful secrets they would fain conceal, with hands careful neither to wound nor pollute. I therefore proceeded, with all possible guardedness, to interrogate, question, and cross-question the desperate girl. But, the avowal once made, the fault once confessed—she calls it a crime herself, and her eternal damnation, fully believing herself, poor girl, a lost soul—she thenceforth refused to say another word, maintaining an obstinate silence which she broke only to beseech me to come to you, Madam, to inform you of the crime—'for mamma *must* know,' she said, 'and I shall never, never be brave enough to tell her.' "

" 'You may easily imagine with what mingled feelings of amazement and anxiety I listened to the *curé* of Saint-Germain-des-Près. I was just as sure as he was, surer in fact, of my little girl's innocence; but do not the innocent sometimes fall, out of very innocence? . . . And what she had told the confessor was not in the nature of things impossible. . . . I did not believe it! . . . could not believe it! but still it was not in itself impossible! . . . She was only thirteen, but she was a woman, and the very fact of her precocity had startled me before now. . . . A fever, a frenzy of curiosity came over me.

" ' "I must and will know all!" I cried excitedly to the worthy priest as he stood there listening to me with a bewildered air, plucking his hat to pieces in his agitation. "Leave me, Father. She would not speak before you; but I am certain she will tell me everything . . . I am certain I can drag everything out of her. Then we shall understand what is now so utterly incomprehensible."

" 'On this the good priest took his departure. The instant he was gone, I sprang upstairs to my daughter's room, not having patience enough to send for her and wait till she came.

" 'I found her kneeling—no! not kneeling, prostrate—before her crucifix, pale as death, her eyes dry and very red, like eyes that have wept many bitter tears. I took her in my arms, seated her by my side, and presently on my knees, and told her I could not believe what her confessor had just been telling me was true.

" 'But here she interrupted me to assure me with a heart-broken voice and look that it *was* true, what he had said; and at this point, more and more anxious and wondering, I asked her who it was that . . .

" 'I left the sentence unfinished. . . . The terrible moment was come! She had her head and face on my shoulder . . . but I could see the blush of shame burning on her neck behind, and feel her shudder. The same leaden silence she had opposed to her father confessor, she now opposed to me. She was impenetrable.

" ' "It must be someone very much beneath you, since you are so deeply ashamed? . . ." I said, trying to make her speak in self-exculpation, for I knew she had plenty of pride.

" 'But still the same silence, the same burying of her head on my shoulder. This lasted what seemed to me an infinity of time, when suddenly she said, without lifting her head: "Swear you will forgive me, Mother!"

" 'I swore everything she asked me, at the risk of perjuring myself a hundred times over—little I cared! I was boiling with impatience—boiling. . . . I thought my skull would burst and let my brains out. . . .

" ' "Well, then! it was Monsieur de Ravila," she whispered, without changing her position in my arms.

" 'Oh! the shock of hearing that name, Amédée! At one fell swoop I was receiving full and condign punishment for the great fault of my life, and my heart quailed within me! You are so terrible a man where women are concerned, you have made me so fearful of rivals, that those fatal words of doubt, "why not?"— so heart-rending when spoken of the man you love, yet suspect —rose involuntarily to my lips. What I felt, however, I had resolution enough left to hide from the cruel child, who had, it may be, guessed her mother's guilty secret.

" ' "Monsieur de Ravila!" I ejaculated in a tone I feared must betray everything; "why, you never even speak to him!"—"You avoid him," I was going to add, for my anger was rising, I felt it

was. . . . "You are surely very deceitful, the pair of you!"—
But I refrained: was I not bound to learn the details, one by one,
of this vile tale of seduction? . . . I began to question her with
an enforced gentleness I thought would have killed me, when
she released me from the torture of the rack, saying with perfect *naïveté:*

" ' "It was one evening, Mother. He was in the big arm-
chair by the fireside, facing the sofa. . . . He sat there ever so
long, then presently got up, and I—I had the misfortune to go
and sit down in the same chair after him. Oh! mamma . . .
it was just as if I had fallen into a flame of fire. I wanted to
get up, but I could not . . . for my heart had stopped beating!
and I felt . . . Oh! mamma, mamma, I felt . . . that what hurt
me so . . . was a baby! . . ." ' "

The Marquise laughed, Ravila said, when she told him the
story; but not one of the twelve women surrounding the table as
much as thought of laughing—nor Ravila either.

"And this, ladies, believe me or not, as you please," he added
by way of conclusion, "I consider the greatest triumph of my life,
the passion I am proudest of having inspired."

And with this he fell silent—a silence they left unbroken one
and all. His auditors were pensive. . . . Had they understood
his meaning?

What time Joseph was a slave in the Lady Potiphar's household, he was so handsome, says the Koran, that, in their dreamy
state, the women he waited on at table used to cut their fingers
with their knives as they gazed at him. But we have travelled
far since Joseph's time, and the preoccupations we experience at
dessert are not so absorbing nowadays.

"But there, what a consummate idiot, with all her cleverness,
your Marquise was, to have told you about such a thing!" at last
said the Duchesse, who condescended to be cynical, but who cut
neither her fingers nor anything else with the gold dessert-knife
she still held in her hand.

Meantime the Comtesse de Chiffrevas was gazing fixedly into

the depths of a glass of Rhine-wine, a green crystal glass, as profound and mysterious as her own reverie.

"And the little witch?" she asked.

"Oh, she was dead—she died quite young—married to somebody in the country—when her mother told me the story,"
Ravila quietly replied.

"But for that . . ." said the Duchesse thoughtfully.

HAPPINESS IN CRIME

HAPPINESS IN CRIME

"In these pleasant days, when a man relates a true story it is to be supposed that the Devil dictated it."

ONE morning last autumn, I was walking in the zoological gardens with Doctor Torty, one of my oldest friends. When I was still a child, Doctor Torty was practising in the town of V., but after thirty years of that agreeable exercise and when all his old patients were dead—his *tenants,* as he called them, who brought him more than the tenants do to their landlords in the best part of Normandy—he had not cared to look for any others, but, being already old and glad to be independent, like a horse that has always felt the bit, and has ended by breaking it, he came to amuse himself in Paris, and lived in the neighbourhood of the Jardin des Plantes—in the Rue Cuvier, I think. He never practised medicine then, except for his own pleasure, but that was very often, for he was a doctor to the finger-tips, clever in his profession and a great observer in many other cases besides physiological or pathological ones.

Have you ever met Doctor Torty? He was one of those bold and vigorous minds that you might call "unmittened," for the good and proverbial reason that "a cat in mittens catches no mice," and this wary old mouser had caught a good many, and wanted to catch still more. I liked him very much, and, I think, for those sides of his character which most displeased others. In fact, few people did like this brusque and original old doctor when they were well, but, when once they were ill, those who disliked him the most salaamed to him as the savages did to Robinson Crusoe's gun, but not for the same reason—because it could kill them—but quite a contrary reason—because he could cure them.

77

Had it not been for that important consideration, the Doctor would never have made twenty thousand francs a year in a small, devout, and aristocratic town, the chief people of which would have shown him the outside of their carriage-gates if they had been prompted solely by their opinions and antipathies. He reasoned about this very calmly, and even joked about it, during his thirty years' "lease" at V. "They had," he said, "to choose between me and Extreme Unction, and, devout as they were, they preferred me to the sacramental oil."

As you see, the Doctor did not trouble to restrain himself. His wit was rather profane. He was a true disciple of Cabanis in medical philosophy, and, like his old comrade, Chaussier, belonged to that terrible school of materialistic doctors, and, like Dubois—the first one—was distinguished by a cynical contempt for all things, and called duchesses, and the maids of honour of the Empress, "my good woman"—treating them with no more respect than if they had been fishwives.

To give you an idea of his cynical humour, I may mention that he said one night at the club, as he gazed at the table with its snowy white napery, laid with covers for a hundred and twenty guests: "I made them all!"

Moses could not have been prouder when he showed the rod with which he had struck the rock.

But what could you expect, Madame? He had not the bump of respect, and even declared that where that bump existed on other men's heads, there was a hole in his.

He was old, being more than seventy, but square-built, robust, and wiry, with a sarcastic face under his light chestnut, shiny, short wig, and penetrating eyes that never needed glasses. He dressed nearly always in grey, or that shade of brown which was long called "Moscow smoke," and looked very unlike the Paris doctors, stiff in their white cravats like their dead patients in their winding-sheets.

He was quite a different sort of man. His doeskin gloves and thick-soled boots gave him something of the look of a horseman—

as indeed he was, for he had ridden every day for thirty years
over roads which would have broken a centaur in half. His
strong legs, which had never felt a twinge of rheumatism, were
bowed like a postilion's. He might have been called a French
provincial Leatherstocking, and, like Fenimore Cooper's hero,
he laughed at the laws of society and had not replaced them
by the idea of God. Such a close observer could not fail to be
a misanthrope—and he was. But he was not a misanthrope like
Alceste. He never displayed any virtuous indignation, nor was
he ever angry. No, he simply despised man as quietly as he
took a pinch of snuff, and had not even as much pleasure in the
scorn as he had in the pinch. Such was, in short, the character
of Doctor Torty, with whom I was then walking.

The day was one of those bright, clear autumn days which
prevent the swallows from leaving. Noon had just sounded
from Notre-Dame, and the deep boom of the bell sounded in long
thrills over the river. The red foliage of the trees had shaken
off the blue fog which envelops them on October mornings, and
the sun was agreeably warm on our backs, as the Doctor and I
stopped to look at the famous black panther, which died the following winter of lung-disease—just as though it had been a
young girl.

All round us was the usual public of the zoological gardens,
soldiers and nurse-maids, who love to stroll round the cages and
throw nutshells and orange-peel at the sleepy animals. The
panther, before whose cage we had arrived, was of that particular
species which comes from the island of Java, the country where
nature is most luxuriant, and seems itself like some great tigress
untamable by man. In Java the flowers have more brilliancy
and perfume, the fruits more taste, the animals more beauty
and strength, than in any other country in the world.

Lying gracefully with its paws stretched out in front, its head
up, and its emerald eyes motionless, the panther was a splendid
specimen of the savage products of the country. Not a touch
of yellow sullied its black velvet skin—of a blackness so deep

and dull that the sunlight was absorbed by it as water is absorbed by a sponge. When you turned from this ideal form of supple beauty—of terrific force in repose—of silent and royal disdain—to the human creatures who were timidly gazing at it, open-eyed and open-mouthed, it was not the human beings who had the superiority over the animal. The latter was so much the superior that the comparison was humiliating.

I had just whispered this remark to the Doctor, when two persons made their way through the group, and planted themselves just in front of the panther.

"Yes," said the Doctor, "but look now, and you will see that the equilibrium between the species is restored."

They were a man and a woman, both tall, and I guessed at a glance that they both belonged to the upper ranks of society. Neither was young, but both were handsome. The man might have been forty-seven or more, and the woman upwards of forty. They had therefore, as sailors say, "crossed the line"—that fatal line more terrible than the equator. But they appeared to care very little, and showed no signs of melancholy.

The man, in a tightly fitting black coat, resembled, in his haughty but effeminate bearing, one of the *mignons* of Henry III, and, to make the resemblance more complete, he wore his hair short, and in his ears were dark-blue sapphire ear-rings, which reminded one of the two emeralds which Sbogar wore in the same place. Except for this ridiculous detail—as the world would have called it—and which showed a disdain for the tastes and opinions of the time, he was simply a dandy in the sense in which Brummell understood the word, that is to "be not remarkable," and he would have passed unnoticed had it not been for the woman he had on his arm.

In fact, this woman attracted more attention than the man who accompanied her, and held it longer. She was as tall as he was. Her head was nearly on a level with his. And as she was dressed entirely in black, she made one think of the black Isis of the

Egyptian Museum, by her shape, her mysterious pride, and her strength. For, strange to say, in this handsome couple it was the woman who had the muscles, and the man who possessed the nerves.

I could see only her profile, but the profile is either the greatest peril of beauty or its most astonishing manifestation. Never had I seen a purer or more noble outline. Of her eyes I could not judge, fixed as they were upon the panther, which, no doubt, received therefrom a magnetic and disagreeable impression, for, though motionless before, it became yet more rigid, and, without moving its head or even its whiskers, it slowly dropped its eyelids over its emerald eyes—as a cat will do when dazzled by a strong light—and seemed unable to meet the fixed glance of the woman.

"Ah, ah! Panther against panther," the Doctor murmured in my ear; "but the satin is stronger than the velvet."

The satin was the woman, who wore a dress of that gleaming material—a dress with a long train. The Doctor was right. Black, supple, as powerfully muscular, and as royal in bearing— quite as beautiful in her own way, and with a charm still more disquieting—this woman, this unknown person, resembled a human panther opposed to the brute panther whom she had conquered; and the animal no doubt felt it when it had closed its eyes.

But the woman—if she was one—was not content with her triumph. She was wanting in generosity. She wished that her rival should see that it was humiliated, and should open its eyes on purpose to see it. Without saying a word, she undid the twelve buttons of the violet glove which fitted so closely her magnificent arm, took off the glove, and, daringly putting her hand between the bars of the cage, flicked the panther's muzzle with it. The panther made but one movement—but such a movement!—and snapped its teeth like lightning. A cry went up from the little group around. We thought her hand must be bitten off at the wrist. But it was only the glove. The panther had swallowed it. The terrible beast, deeply insulted, had opened its eyes to their full size, and its nostrils quivered with anger.

"Fool!" said the man, seizing the beautiful hand which had just escaped this terrible bite.

You know how that word "fool" is sometimes said. That was how he said it, as he passionately kissed her hand.

And as he was on the same side as we were, she turned slightly to look at him, and I saw her eyes—eyes which fascinated tigers, and were at present fascinated by eyes which were two large black diamonds expressing all the pride of life, and adoration of love.

Those eyes were, and told, a whole poem. The man had not released the arm which had just felt the feverish breath of the panther, and, holding it to his heart, led the woman to the broad walk of the garden, indifferent to the murmurs and exclamations of the people—still somewhat excited by the incident—and walked quietly along it. They passed close to the Doctor and me, but their faces were turned towards each other, and they were pressing so close together that it seemed as though they wished to make one body of the two, and see nothing but themselves. They were both, as one could see when they passed, of those superior beings who do not even perceive that their feet touch the ground, and who pass through the world in a cloud, like the immortals of Homer.

Such people are rare in Paris, and we therefore stopped to watch this splendid couple—the woman allowing the long train to trail in the dust, like a peacock disdainful of its plumage.

They looked superb as they passed along, under the rays of the midday sun, in all the majesty of their mutual embrace. We watched them to the gate, where a carriage, the horses resplendent in plated harness, was waiting for them.

"They forget the universe," I said to the Doctor.

"Oh, a lot they care for the universe!" he replied in his sarcastic voice. "They see nothing in all creation, and, what is worse, they even pass close to their doctor without noticing him."

"What, you, Doctor!" I cried. "Then you can tell me who they are, my dear Doctor."

The Doctor made a long pause, in order to produce an effect—the cunning old man!

"Well!" he said quietly, "they are Philemon and Baucis—that's all."

"Rather a proud-looking Philemon and Baucis," I replied, "and not much resembling those of antiquity. But that is not their name, Doctor. What *is* their name?"

"What!" replied the Doctor; "in the fashionable society in which you mix, you have never heard the Comte and Comtesse Serlon de Savigny held up as the models of conjugal love?"

"No," I replied; "in the fashionable world in which I mix, we do not talk much about conjugal love."

"Hum! Hum! that is very probable," said the Doctor—more in answer to his own thoughts than to mine. "In that society—which you mix, you have never heard the Comte and Comtesse rect happy. But, besides having another reason for not going into society, they live nearly all the year in their old château at Savigny, in the Cotentin. Some reports about them circulated in the Faubourg Saint-Germain, but as the nobility all hang together, they are never mentioned there now."

"What were these reports? You interest me greatly, Doctor. The château of Savigny is not very far from the town of V., where you used to practise, Doctor, so you must know something about them."

"Oh, those reports!" said the Doctor, pensively taking a pinch of snuff. "They were believed to be false. It all passed over. But although marriages of inclination, and the happiness which springs from them, are the ideals of all mothers in the country, who are generally virtuous and romantic, they did not talk very much—at least those I knew—to their daughters about this particular one."

"And yet you called them Philemon and Baucis, Doctor."

"Baucis! Baucis! Hum!" interrupted Doctor Torty, crooking

his first finger and passing it over his long parrot-like nose (one of his gestures); "don't you think that woman looks less like Baucis than Lady Macbeth?"

"Doctor—my dear and adorable Doctor," I continued as coaxingly as I could, "you will tell me all you know about the Comte and Comtesse de Savigny—won't you?"

"The doctor is the confessor in these times," said the Doctor, in a mock-serious manner. "He has replaced the priest, sir, and, like the priest, is obliged to keep the secrets of confession."

He looked at me mischievously, for he knew my respect and regard for the Catholic religion, of which he was the enemy. He winked, and thought he had caught me.

"And he is going to keep it—as the priest does!" he cried with a cynical laugh. "Come along with me where we can talk."

He led me to the broad walk which runs between the zoological gardens and the Boulevard de l'Hôpital; we sat down on one of the benches, and he began.

"My dear fellow, you must search pretty deeply for the beginning of my story, as you would for a bullet over which the flesh has formed; for oblivion is like the flesh of living things which forms over events and prevents you from seeing anything, or even suspecting the place after a certain time.

"It was in the first years after the Restoration. A regiment of the Guards passed through the town of V., and, being obliged, for some military reason or other, to stay there two days, the officers determined to give an assault of arms in honour of the town. As a matter of fact, the town fully deserved that the officers of the Guards should do it that honour. It was, as they said then, more royalist than the King. Considering its size (for it contained barely five or six thousand souls), it teemed with nobility. More than thirty young men belonging to the best families of the place were then serving either in the Life Guards or the Prince's Regiment, and the officers then passing through V. knew them nearly all. But the principal reason which induced the officers to give this assault of arms was the fighting reputation of V. The Revolution of 1789 had taken away from the nobles the right to wear their swords, but at V. they proved that if they no longer wore them, they knew how to use them.

"The assault given by the officers was a brilliant success.

"It brought together all the best swordsmen of the district, and even some amateurs who belonged to a younger generation, and who had not much cultivated, as they did in former days, an art so difficult and complicated as fencing; and all showed such enthusiasm for the glorious weapon of our forefathers that an old fencing-instructor of the regiment, who had served his time three or four times over, and whose arm was covered with good-conduct stripes, thought that it would be a good idea to open a school of arms at V. and end his days there; and the Colonel, to whom he broached the subject, approved of the plan, and gave him his discharge.

"The idea was quite a stroke of genius on the part of the fencing-master, whose name was Stassin, but who was more generally known as 'Old Straight-thrust.'

"For a long time past there had been no properly conducted fencing-school at V. This had long been a subject of regret amongst the nobility, who were obliged to teach their own sons, or else have recourse to some friend who had left the army, and who was perhaps not a good swordsman, or did not know how to teach.

"The inhabitants of V. prided themselves on being very particular. They really possessed the sacred fire. It was not enough to be able to kill their man—they wished to kill him neatly and scientifically according to the principles of art. They were most particular about a graceful attitude, and had a profound contempt for those strong but awkward swordsmen who might be dangerous antagonists in a duel, but who were not fencers in the strict sense of the word.

" 'Old Straight-thrust' had been a good man in his youth, and was so still. When quite a young man, he had beaten all the other instructors in the camp, and had carried off the prize—a pair of silver-mounted foils and masks—and in fact was one of those swordsmen who are exceptionally endowed by nature, and cannot be produced by art. He was, naturally, the admiration of all V., and soon was something more. The sword is a great leveller. In the days of the old monarchy, kings ennobled their fencing-master. Louis XV—if I recollect rightly—gave his master, Danet (who has left us a book on fencing), four of his fleurs-de-lis, between two crossed swords, as his coat of arms. These country gentlemen, who were stuffed full of monarchical ideas, very soon looked upon the old fencing-master as an equal, and as though he had been one of themselves.

"So far, Stassin, otherwise known as 'Old Straight-thrust,' was to be congratulated on his good fortune; but, unfortunately, the red-morocco heart on the white-leather padded jacket, which the old fencing-master put on when he gave a lesson, was not the only one he possessed.

"He had, underneath that one, another heart which sought for an affinity amongst all the young women of V. A soldier's heart is always made of gunpowder, it would seem; and when age has dried the powder, it catches fire all the more readily. Most of the women of V. are pretty, so there were plenty of sparks everywhere, ready for the dry powder of the fencing-master, and his history was that of a great many other old soldiers. After having knocked about in all the countries of Europe, and chucked under the chin, or taken round the waist, all the girls whom the Devil had put in his road, the old soldier of the First Empire committed his last folly by marrying, when he was past fifty, and with all the necessary formalities and sacraments—at the municipality and the church—a working-girl from V. Of course, she—I know the working-girls of that country, I have attended enough of them in childbirth!—presented him at the end of nine months, day for day, with a child; and that child, who was a girl, is no other, my dear fellow, than the woman with the air of a goddess who has just passed, brushing us insolently with her robe, and taking no more notice of us than though we had not been there."

"The Comtesse de Savigny!" I cried.

"Yes, the Comtesse de Savigny herself! Ah, you must not look at the origin of women any more than of nations; you should never look into anyone's cradle. I remember having seen at Stockholm that of Charles XII, which looked like a horse's manger, was roughly coloured in red, and did not stand level on its four legs. Yet that was what that tempest of a man came out of. Besides, all cradles are sewers, of which you are obliged to change the linen several times a day, and that is never poetical for those who believe in poetry, but when the child is no longer there."

And to strengthen his dictum, the Doctor, at this point of his story, struck his thigh with one of his doeskin gloves, which he held by the middle finger, and the noise the doeskin made against his thigh proved to one who knows something about music that the Doctor was not deficient in muscle.

He waited, but I did not contradict his statements, and, seeing that I said nothing, he continued:

"Like all old soldiers, who are even fond of other people's children—'Old Straight-thrust' doted on his. There was nothing astonishing in that. When a man who is already old has a child, he loves it more than though he were young, for vanity, which doubles everything, doubles also the paternal instinct. All the fellows I have known who became fathers late in life, adored their offspring, and were as comically proud of it as though it were a wonderful action. Nature, who was laughing at them, had persuaded them in their hearts that they were young again. I know of only one happiness more intoxicating, one pride more droll; and that is when an old man, instead of one child, makes two at once. 'Old Straight-thrust' had not the paternal pride of being the father of twins, but it is certain that his child was big enough to make two ordinary ones. His daughter—you have seen her, and know whether she turned out as well as she promised—was a wonderful child, both for strength and beauty.

"The first care of the old fencing-master was to look out for a godfather amongst the noblemen who continually haunted his school, and he chose, from amongst them all, the Comte d'Avice, the oldest of all the wielders of the foil, and who, during the emigration, had himself been a fencing-master in London, at ever so many guineas a lesson.

"Comte d'Avice de Sortoville, in Beaumont, who was already a knight of St. Louis and a captain of dragoons before the Revolution—and who was at least seventy years of age—could still 'button' the young fellows in fine style. He was a mischievous old rascal, and some of his jokes were rather ferocious. Thus, for instance, he would pass the blade of his foil through the flame of a candle, and when he had rendered it so hard that it would not bend, and would smash your breastbone or your ribs, he would call it his 'rascal-driver.'

"He was very fond of 'Old Straight-thrust,' and treated him familiarly. 'The daughter of a man like you,' he said, 'should be named after the sword of an illustrious warrior. Call her Haute Claire.'

"And that was the name that was given her. The parish priest of V. made rather a grimace at this unaccustomed name, which had never been heard at the font of his church, but as the sponsor was the Comte d'Avice, and there will always be, in spite of the liberals and their tricks, indestructible ties between the nobility and the clergy, and as, on the other hand, there is a saint named Claire in the Roman calendar, the name of Oliver's sword was given to the child without the town of V. being greatly disturbed thereby.

"Such a name seemed to augur a destiny. The old fencing-master, who loved his profession almost as much as his daughter, resolved to teach her, and to leave her his talent as a marriage portion. But a poor pittance considering modern fashions—which the old instructor could not foresee.

"As soon as the child could stand, he began to teach her exercises, and as the little girl was solidly built, with joints like

thin steel, he developed her in such an amazing manner that at
ten years old she seemed to be fifteen, and could hold her own with
the foils against her father, or the best fencers of the town of
V. Little Hauteclaire Stassin was talked about everywhere, and
later she became Mademoiselle Hauteclaire Stassin. It was more
especially, as you may suppose, amongst the young ladies of the
town—into whose society, however well he might stand with their
fathers, the daughter of Stassin, called 'Old Straight-thrust,' could
not decently enter—that there was an incredible (or rather a perfectly credible) curiosity about her, mixed with spite and envy.
Their fathers and brothers spoke of her with astonishment and
admiration before them, and they wished to inspect closely this
female St. George whose beauty was said to equal her skill in
fencing. They saw her only at a distance. I was then living at
V., and I was often a witness of this burning curiosity. 'Old
Straight-thrust,' who had, during the Empire, served in the Hussars, and who had made a good deal of money with his fencing-
school, had bought a horse in order that he might give lessons
in riding to his daughter, and as all the year round he had young
horses to break in for some of his pupils, he often rode with
Hauteclaire along the roads which surround the town.

"I met them many times when returning from my professional
visits, and in these meetings I was able to judge of the extreme
interest which this fine tall young woman had aroused amongst the
other young women of the district. I was always riding about the
roads at that time, and I frequently saw young ladies in carriages
going to make calls at some of the neighbouring châteaux. Well!
you should have seen with what haste, and I may say with what
imprudence, they rushed to the carriage-windows whenever
Mademoiselle Hauteclaire Stassin was seen on the road, riding
alongside her father. But their trouble was useless, and the next
day when I called on their mothers they would tell me that
they had seen nothing but the figure of the young woman, her
face being more or less concealed beneath a thick, blue veil.

"Mademoiselle Hauteclaire Stassin was known only to the men

of V. Foil in hand, and her face hidden by the mask, which she seldom removed, she hardly ever left the fencing-school, and often gave lessons in place of her father, who was beginning to grow feeble. She rarely showed herself in the street, and though she went to Mass every Sunday, both at church and in the street she was as much masked as she was in the school. Was there conceit or affectation in thus hiding herself from the public gaze? It is very possible; but who knows?—who can say? And was not this young woman, who dropped the mask only for the veil, as impenetrable in character as she was in face?—as events well proved!

"You will understand, my dear fellow, that I am obliged to pass rapidly over the details of this period in order to arrive at the moment when my story really begins. Mademoiselle Hauteclaire was then about seventeen. 'Old Straight-thrust' had become a stout old bourgeois. He had lost his wife, and he himself was morally killed by the Revolution of July, which sent all the nobles grieving off to their châteaux, and emptied the fencing-school. Moreover, the gout, which was not afraid of the old master's challenges, had attacked him, and was taking him as fast as possible to the cemetery. To a doctor knowing anything of diagnosis there was no doubt about that; it was easy enough to see, and I gave him but a short time to live.

"One morning there was brought to the fencing-school—by the Vicomte de Taillebois and Chevalier de Mesnilgrand—a young man who, after being educated in some distant place, had returned to inhabit his ancestral château, his father having recently died. This was the Comte Serlon de Savigny, the suitor (as they said in the town) of Mademoiselle Delphine de Cantor. The Comte de Savigny was certainly one of the most distinguished of the swell youth of the locality. There are none of them left now. He had heard much of the famous Hauteclaire Stassin, and wanted to see this miracle. He found her to be what she was, a beautiful young girl, looking provokingly attractive in her silk hose, which showed off the shape of a form like the Pallas of Velletri, and the black morocco jacket tightly fitting her supple and strong figure —one of those figures which the Circassian women obtain by confining their daughters in a leather belt, which the development of the body breaks.

"Hauteclaire Stassin was as serious as a Clorinda.

"He watched her give her lesson, and asked if he might be permitted to cross swords with her. But the Comte de Savigny was not the Tancred of the situation. Mademoiselle Hauteclaire Stassin bent her foïl into a semicircle ever so many times on the heart of the handsome Serlon, and she was not touched once.

" 'I cannot touch you, Mademoiselle,' he said courteously.

" 'Is that an omen?'

"Was the young man's conceit overcome by love?

"From that time, the Comte de Savigny went every day to the fencing-school of 'Old Straight-thrust' to take a lesson.

"The Comte's château was only a few leagues distant, and he could easily ride or drive into the town without remark, for though the slightest thing was enough to provoke scandal, the love of fencing explained all. Savigny took no one into his confidence. He even avoided taking his lesson at the same time as the other young men of the town. He was a young man who was not wanting in cunning. What passed between him and Hauteclaire, if anything passed at all, no one knew or suspected. His marriage with Mademoiselle Delphine de Cantor had been arranged by the two families years before, and was too far advanced for either party to be able to draw back. They were married three months after his return, and he took the opportunity of spending a month in V. near his fiancée, with whom he passed all his days in the orthodox manner, but whom he left in the evening that he might take his fencing-lesson.

"Like everybody else in the town, Mademoiselle Hauteclaire heard the banns of Comte de Savigny and Mademoiselle de Cantor proclaimed at the parish church of V., but neither her attitude nor her face betrayed that she took any interest whatever in those public declarations. It is true that no one was on the look-out,

no liaison between Savigny and the fair Hauteclaire being suspected. The marriage having been celebrated, the Comtesse went
to live quietly in her château, but her husband did not give up
his usual habits, and came to town every day. Many of the other
gentlemen of the locality did the same, however.

"Time went on. 'Old Straight-thrust' died. The school was
shut for a short time, and then opened again. Mademoiselle
Hauteclaire Stassin announced that she would keep the school
open, and, so far from having fewer pupils than before her father's
death, it had more. Men are all the same. Anything strange
displeases them, if it is done by another man; but if it is done by
anyone in petticoats, they rather like it. A woman who does what
a man does, though she may not do it half so well, will always
have a marked advantage over a man, especially in France. But
what Mademoiselle Hauteclaire Stassin did, she did better than
a man. She was more skilful than her father. As a professor
she could demonstrate admirably, and her sword-play was
splendid. She had coups which were irresistible—those coups
which are not learned any more than the wrist-work of a violin-
player, and cannot be taught to anyone.

"I used to fence a little in those days, as everyone else round
me did, and I must confess that some of her passes were simply
wonderful. Amongst other things, she had a way of disengaging
from carte to tierce, which was like magic. It was not a foil
that hit you, it was a bullet. Parry as rapidly as a man would,
his blade only cut the air, even when she had warned him that
she was about to disengage, and he was infallibly hit on the shoulder or breast, without his blade being able even to meet hers. I
have seen swordsmen become quite wild at this coup, which they
called sleight of hand, and ready to swallow their foil in fury. If
she had not been a woman, they would have tried to pick a quarrel
with her about that coup. A man would have had twenty duels
on his hands.

"But apart from this phenomenal talent, so little suited for a
woman, this poor young girl, who had no resource but her foil,

and mixed with all the rich young men of the town—amongst whom there were some sad scapegraces, and some conceited asses —without her reputation suffering at all, was an interesting person.

"Nothing was said about Mademoiselle Hauteclaire Stassin concerning either Savigny or anyone else. 'It seems that she is an honest woman,' said all the respectable folks—as though they had been talking of an actress.

"I myself—as I have been talking about myself—who prided myself on my powers of observation, was of the same opinion as all the town concerning the virtue of Hauteclaire. I sometimes went to the fencing-school, both before and after the marriage of Monsieur de Savigny, and I never saw anything but a grave young woman performing her business simply. She had, I ought to say, a commanding air, and made everybody treat her with respect, and she was not familiar with anyone. Her face was extremely haughty, and had not then that passionate expression with which you have been so struck, but it showed neither chagrin, nor preoccupation, nor anything of a nature to suggest in the most distant manner the astonishing circumstance which, in the atmosphere of the quiet and plodding little town, had the same effect as the report of a cannon, and broke the windows.

" 'Mademoiselle Hauteclaire Stassin has disappeared!'

"She had disappeared! How? Why? Where had she gone? No one knew; but what was certain was that she had disappeared. First there was an outcry, followed by silence, but the silence did not last long. Tongues began to wag. They had been long kept in—like the water in a mill-stream which, when the flood-gates are opened, rushes out and makes the wheel spin round furiously—and now began to chatter about this unexpected disappearance which nothing could explain, for Mademoiselle Hauteclaire had disappeared without saying a word or leaving a word to or for anybody. She had disappeared as people disappear when they wish really to disappear—not leaving behind them some trifling trace which others can seize to explain their disappearance. She had disappeared in the most complete manner.

She had not done 'a moonlight flit,' as it is termed, for she had not left a single debt behind her.

"The neighbours' tongue-mill had nothing to grind, but it turned all the same, and ground her reputation to bits.

"All that was known about her was told, retold, powdered, and sifted. How, and with whom, had this proud and reserved girl run away? Who had carried her off?—for it was certain that someone had carried her off. No reply could be given. It was enough to drive any little town mad, and V. became mad. There were motives for its indignation. Only fancy what the town had lost. Firstly, it lost its time in guessing about a girl it thought it knew and did not know, because it had not judged her capable of disappearing 'like that.' Then it had lost the girl herself, who ought to have grown old or married, like all the other girls of the town, but never have moved off the chess-board of life in a country town. And finally, in losing Mademoiselle Stassin (who was now spoken of only as 'that Stassin woman'), the town had lost a school of arms, celebrated through all the country round, the ornament and honour of the town, and a feather in its cap.

"All these losses were very hard to bear, and were so many reasons comprised in one for throwing all the mud that supposition would allow upon the irreproachable Hauteclaire. And the mud *was* thrown. Except a few old gentlemen who were too grand to indulge in gossip, and who, like her godfather, the Comte d'Avice, had known her as a child, and who, if they thought about the matter at all, regarded it as very natural that she had found a better shoe for her foot than a fencing-sandal, not a soul defended the disappearance of Hauteclaire Stassin. She had offended the self-conceit of all; and the youngest were the most bitter against her, because she had not run away with one of them.

"That was for a long time their great grief and their great anxiety. With whom had she run away? Many of the young men went every year to spend a month or two of the winter in Paris, and two or three of them declared they had seen and recognized her there—at the theatre—or on horseback in the Champs

Elysées—alone or in company—but they were not quite sure. They could affirm nothing. It might have been she, or it might not have been. But it showed how much she was thought about, this girl they had all so much admired, and who in disappearing had thrown consternation into this sword-loving town, of which she was the leading *artiste*—the *diva*—the star. When that star was extinguished—in other words, after the disapearance of the celebrated Hauteclaire—the town of V. fell into that state of lethargy which is the normal condition of all country towns which have not a centre of activity towards which all castes and passions converge. The love of arms grew weak, and without the youthful swordsmen the town was dull. The young nobles who used to ride into the town every day to fence, exchanged the foil for the gun. They became sportsmen, and remained on their own estates, or in their woods—the Comte de Savigny like all the others. He came to V. less and less frequently, and when I did meet him occasionally, it was at the house of his wife's parents, who were patients of mine.

"Only, as I did not suspect at that time that he was in any way connected with the disappearance of Hauteclaire, I had no reason to speak to him about it—indeed, people had got tired of talking of it by that time—nor did he ever speak to me of Hauteclaire, or the occasions when we had met at the fencing-school, or even make the slightest allusion to her."

"I can hear your little wooden shoes coming," I said to the Doctor, using an expression current in the district about which he was talking, and which is also my native country. "It was he who had abducted her."

"Oh, no! not at all," replied the Doctor. "Better than that. But you would never guess what it was.

"Besides, in the country especially, an elopement is not very easily kept secret, and, moreover, the Comte de Savigny had never since his marriage left the château of Savigny.

"He lived there, as everybody knew, along with his wife, in what appeared to be a perpetual honeymoon—and as everything is remarked and talked about in the country, remarks were made about Savigny, and he was cited as one of those husbands who are so rare that they ought to be burned (provincial humour) and their ashes thrown over the others. Heaven only knows how long I myself should have been duped by this reputation, if it had not happened—more than a year after the disappearance of Hauteclaire Stassin—that I was suddenly called one day to the château of Savigny, the lady of the house having been taken ill.

"I started at once, and on my arrival was taken to the Comtesse, who was in reality suffering from one of those vague and complicated diseases which are more dangerous than a severe attack of some ordinary malady. She was one of those women of good family who are worn out, elegant, distinguished, and proud, and whose pale faces and pinched forms seem to say, 'I am conquered by the era, like all my race. I die, but I despise you,' and, devil take me! plebeian as I am, though it is not very philosophic, if I can helping admiring that spirit!

"The Comtesse was lying on a couch in a kind of parlour with white walls and black beams, very large, very high, and decorated with a profusion of old furniture which did honour to the taste of the old Counts of Savigny. A solitary lamp lighted this vast apartment, and its light, rendered more mysterious by the green shade which veiled it, fell on the Comtesse, whose face was flushed with fever. She had been ill some days, and Savigny—in order to watch her the better—had had a small bed placed by the side of the couch of his well-beloved better half. But the fever was not to be shaken off, and had become worse in spite of all his attention, and therefore he had sent for me. He was standing there, with his back to the fire, looking so gloomy and disturbed as to make me believe that he passionately loved his wife, and believed her to be in danger. But the disturbed expression on his face was not for her, but for another, whom I did not suspect to be at the château de Savigny, and the sight of whom amazed me beyond measure. It was Hauteclaire."

"The devil! That was risky!" I said to the Doctor.

"So risky," he replied, "that I thought I must be dreaming when I saw her. The Comtesse had requested her husband to ring for her maid, who had been told, before my arrival, to prepare a drink I had ordered—and some seconds later the door opened.

" 'Eulalie, where is the tisane I asked for?' said the Comtesse impatiently.

" 'Here it is, Madame,' replied a voice that I seemed to recognize, and it had no sooner struck my ear than I saw emerge from the shadow which enveloped the greater part of the room, and advance into the circle of light thrown by the lamp round the bed, Hauteclaire Stassin—yes, Hauteclaire, herself!—holding in her beautiful hands a silver waiter, on which smoked the bowl for which the Comtesse had asked. Such a sight was enough to take away my breath! Eulalie!

"Fortunately, the name of Eulalie pronounced so naturally, told me all, and was like a blow with a hammer of ice which restored the coolness I had lost, and enabled me to resume my attitude as doctor and observer.

"Hauteclaire had become Eulalie, and lady's maid to the Comtesse de Savigny! Her disguise—if such a woman can be disguised—was complete. She wore the costume of the girls of V. and their head-dress, which resembles a helmet, and their long corkscrew curls falling each side of the cheeks—those corkscrews which the preachers of those days called serpents in order to try and disgust the pretty girls with them—which they never succeeded in doing.

"Her eyes were cast down, and she looked beautiful, reserved, and dignified, which only proves that those vipers of women can do whatever they like with their confounded bodies whenever it is to their interest to do so. Having recovered myself, like a man who bites his lips in order to prevent a cry of surprise escaping him, I had a desire to show this impudent woman that I recognized her, and whilst the Comtesse drank her potion, and her face was hidden by the bowl, I fixed my eyes on Eulalie's eyes, but hers—as mild as a fawn's that evening—were firmer than those of the panther she had just stared down. She never winked.

"The hands which held the platter trembled almost imperceptibly, but that was all. The Comtesse drank very slowly, and when she had finished—

" 'Very good! Take it away,' she said.

"And Hauteclaire-Eulalie walked away with that tournure that I should have recognized amongst all the twenty thousand daughters of Ahasuerus. I will own that I did not look at the Comte de Savigny for a minute, for I felt what a look from one would mean at such an instant; but when I did venture to do so, I found his gaze fixed upon me, and his face turned from an expression of terrible anxiety to one of deliverance.

"He saw that *I knew,* but he saw also that *I did not intend to know,* and he breathed more freely. He was sure of my impenetrable discretion, which he explained probably (but I did not care about that) by my interest as a doctor to retain such a good customer as he was, whilst really it was only the interest I took as an observer, who did not want the doors of a house where such interesting events were going on, to be closed against him.

"So I returned with my finger on my lips, well resolved not to breathe a word to a single person, or give anyone any cause to suspect. Ah, what pleasure it is to be an observer, what impersonal and solitary pleasures one enjoys, and which I promised myself in this quiet corner of the country, in this old château, to which as a doctor I could come whenever I liked!

"Glad to be delivered from his anxiety, Savigny had said to me: 'Come every day, Doctor, until further orders.'

"I could therefore study with as much interest as though it had been a disease, the mystery of a situation which no one would have deemed credible if they had been informed of it. And as, from the very first day, this mystery had aroused my ratiocinative faculties, which are the blind man's stick to the *savant,* and especially to the doctor, in their curious researches. I began immediately to reason out the situation in order that I might understand it. How long had it existed? Did it date from the disappearance of Hauteclaire? That was more than a year ago— had Hauteclaire Stassin been lady's maid to the Comtesse de Savigny all that time? How was it that no one had ever seen what I had seen so easily and so quickly? All these questions jumped on my horse with me, and rode along with me to V., accompanied by many others which I picked up on the road.

"The Comte and Comtesse de Savigny, who were believed to adore each other, lived, it is true, remote from all society. But still a visitor might drop in at the château at any time. It is true that if the visitor were a man, Hauteclaire need not appear; and if the visitor were a lady, the ladies of V. had not seen (sufficiently to be able to recognize) a girl who hardly ventured out of the school of arms, and who, when seen at a distance on horseback or in church, wore purposely a thick veil—for Hauteclaire (as I have said) had always possessed that pride of the very proud, who are offended at too much curiosity, and the more they are gazed at, the more they try to hide themselves. As for the servants of Monsieur de Savigny, with whom she was obliged to live, if they did not come from V. they would not know her—and perhaps not even if they did.

"Thus did I reply, as I trotted along, to the first questions which suggested themselves, and, before I got out of the saddle, I had constructed a whole edifice of suppositions, more or less plausible, to explain what, to anyone but a reasoner like me, would have been inexplicable. Perhaps the only thing that I could not explain well, was that the wonderful beauty of Hauteclaire had not been an obstacle to her entering the service of the Comtesse de Savigny, who loved her husband, and might therefore be jealous. But the patrician ladies of V., quite as proud as the wives of Charlemagne's paladins, could not suppose (a grave mistake, but they had never read *Le Mariage de Figaro*) that the prettiest lady's maid could be for their husbands any more than the handsomest lackey was to them—and so I ended by saying to myself, as I took my foot out of the stirrup, that the Comtesse

de Savigny had every reason to believe that she was loved, and
that rascal Savigny was quite capable of keeping up the illusion."

"Hum!" I said sceptically—for I could not keep from interrupting—"all that is very fine, my dear Doctor, but the situation
was a terribly imprudent one all the same."

"Certainly!" replied this experienced student of human nature;
"but suppose the imprudence made the situation? There are
some passions which are only excited by imprudence, and without
the dangers they provoke they would never exist. In the six-
teenth century, which was about as passionate an age as could
be, the most prolific cause of love was the danger of love. A
man stood a chance of being poniarded as he left the arms of his
mistress, or a husband put poison in his wife's sleeve, which you
kissed and made a fool of yourself over in all the usual ways; and
so far from putting a stop to love, this incessant danger only
rendered it the more irresistible. In our tame modern customs,
where the law has replaced passion, it is evident that the article
of the Code which applies to the husband who is capable of having—as the law coarsely puts it—'introduced a concubine into
the conjugal domicile,' is an ignoble danger enough, but for noble
natures this danger seems all the more grand, and Savigny, in
exposing himself to it, perhaps found the only anxious pleasure
which really intoxicates strong minds.

"The next day, as you may imagine," continued Doctor Torty,
"I was at the château early, but neither that day nor the following
ones did I see anything but what was absolutely normal and regular. Neither on the part of the invalid, nor on that of the Comte,
nor even on that of the false Eulalie, who performed her duties
as naturally as though she had been brought up to them, did I
remark anything which could give me information concerning the
secret I had surprised. What was certain was that the Comte
de Savigny and Hauteclaire Stassin were playing the most
abominably impudent comedy with all the ease of consummate
actors, and that they had agreed together to play it. But that
of which I was not so certain, and which I wanted to know first,

was whether the Comtesse was really their dupe, and, in case she were, whether it were possible that she should long be so.

"It was upon the Comtesse, therefore, that I concentrated my attention. I had no trouble in seeing her, as she was my patient, and therefore, on account of her illness, the focus of my observations. She was, as I have told you, a true lady of V., knowing nothing but this—that she was noble, and that outside the nobility there was nothing worthy of regard. The appreciation of their nobility is the only passion of the women of V., of the upper class—and of all classes that have not deep passions. Mademoiselle Delphine de Cantor had been educated by the Benedictine nuns, and, not being at all inclined to religion, had been horribly bored, and had left the nunnery to bore herself still more at home until she married the Comte de Savigny, whom she loved, or thought she loved, with all the readiness of young girls who are bored to love the first comer presented to them.

"She was one of those pale women with soft flesh but hard bones, of the colour of milk with which bran has been mixed; for the little freckles which covered her skin were certainly darker than her hair, which was a very pale gold. When she stretched out her white arm, veined with opalescent blue, and a small aristocratic wrist, in which the pulse was normally languid, she gave me the idea that she had been created specially to become a victim—to be crushed under the feet of the haughty Hauteclaire, who had bowed herself before her to the extent of becoming her servant.

"But this idea, which arose the first moment you looked at her, was contradicted by the chin which finished off this thin face—a chin like that of Fulvia on the Roman medals, out of place amongst ordinary features—and also by a forehead obstinately projecting under her colourless hair. It was a puzzle to express an opinion about her; but, at any rate, it was impossible that the present situation could last long without an explosion. With a view to that future explosion, I set to work to sound this little woman, who could not long remain a secret to her doctor. He who confesses the body, soon holds the heart. If there were moral or immoral causes for the actual sufferings of the Comtesse, she might try to conceal her impressions and thoughts, but she would have at last to reveal them.

"That is what I said to myself; but I turned and re-turned my medical screws in vain. It was evident to me, after some days, that she had not the least suspicion of the complicity of her husband and Hauteclaire in the domestic crime of which the house was the silent and desired theatre. Was it want of sagacity on her part? or the dumbness of jealousy? With the false Eulalie who waited on her, she was imperious but gentle. That sounds contradictory, but it is not—it is true. She gave her orders briefly, but she never raised her voice, like a woman who was made to be obeyed, and is sure of being obeyed—and she was, admirably. Eulalie slipped noiselessly about the room, and her attentions stopped just short of the point at which they would have become tiresome, and everything was done with a readiness and a knowledge of the character of her mistress which showed goodwill and intelligence.

"I even went so far as to speak to the Comtesse about Eulalie, who was always near her when I paid my visits, and the sight of whom gave me a chill up my back—as though I had seen a serpent stealthily approaching a sleeping woman. One day when the Comtesse had sent her to fetch something or other, and she had stolen out of the room noiselessly, I took advantage of the opportunity to ask a question which might give me some light on the matter.

" 'What a velvety footfall!' I said, as I watched her leave. 'You have a maid, Madame, who does her work well. May I ask where you found her? Does she come from V.?'

" 'Yes, she serves me very well,' replied the Comtesse with indifference, looking at herself in a little hand-mirror framed in green velvet and surrounded by peacock's feathers, and speaking in that impertinent tone which was a proof that she took no interest in the subject. 'I am highly satisfied with her. She did not

come from V., but I could not tell you where she does come from
—I know nothing about her. Ask Monsieur de Savigny if you
want to know, Doctor, for he brought her to me soon after we
were married. She had been in the service, he told me, of an
old lady, a cousin of his, who had died, and she could not find
another place. I trusted in him, and I was not disappointed. She
is perfect as a lady's maid. I do not believe she has a single
fault.'

" 'I know of one,' I said with affected gravity.

" 'Ah! what is that?' she replied languidly, without any interest
in what she was saying, and still attentively studying her pale lips
in the little hand-mirror.

" 'She is pretty,' I said; 'she is really much too pretty to be
a lady's maid. One of these days you will have someone run
away with her.'

" 'Do you think so?' she replied, still looking at herself, and
utterly indifferent to what I said.

" 'And perhaps it will be a man of your own station who will
fall in love with her. She is pretty enough to turn the head of
a duke.'

"I weighed my words before uttering them, for I wanted to
sound her, and see how much she knew—if she knew nothing,
I could do no more.

" 'There is no duke at V.,' replied the Comtesse, and her forehead remained as smooth as the glass she held in her hand. 'Besides, all women of that sort,' she added, raising one eyebrow,
'leave you when they like to suit their own convenience. Eulalie
does her work well, but if I showed any affection for her she
would, no doubt, abuse it, so I do nothing of the sort.'

"There was no further mention made of Eulalie that day. The
Comtesse was completely deceived. Who would not have been,
for that matter? Even I—though I had seen Hauteclaire so many
times at only a sword's length between us, in her father's fencing-
school—was almost tempted at times to believe in Eulalie. Savigny, though he ought to have acted as well as she did, was far less

at home in this acted lie, but she lived and moved in this atmosphere of deceit as easily and naturally as a fish does in the water. She must certainly have been in love, and very deeply in love, to do what she did do, and have given up all the advantages of a life which flattered her vanity by making her the cynosure of all eyes in a little town—for her the whole universe—where sooner or later she might have found amongst the young men, her admirers and adorers, one who would marry her for love, and take her into that good society of which she knew only the men. Her lover certainly staked less than she did. His devotion was less than hers. His pride, as a man, must have suffered greatly at not being able to spare his mistress the indignity of such a humiliating position. It seemed out of keeping with the impetuous character generally ascribed to Savigny. If he loved Hauteclaire enough to sacrifice his young wife for her, he might have gone to live with her in Italy—that was often done at that time—without all the abominations of a shameful and concealed concubinage. Was his love less than hers? Did he suffer Hauteclaire to love him more than he loved her? Was it she who had broken down the guard of the conjugal domicile? And did he, finding the experience hazardous and interesting, allow himself to be tempted by this new kind of Potiphar's wife?

"All that I could see or hear did not teach me much concerning Savigny and Hauteclaire. Accomplices in adultery of some sort they certainly were—but what was behind that? What was the position of these two persons in regard to one another? That was a problem I wanted to solve. Savigny's conduct to his wife was irreproachable, but when Hauteclaire-Eulalie was there, I could see, out of the corner of my eye, certain precautions which denoted that his mind was not at ease. When, in the course of my daily visits, he asked for a book or a paper, or some other article, he had a way of taking it from the hands of the lady's maid which would have revealed his secret to any other woman but this little school-girl, brought up by the Benedictine nuns, whom he had married. You could see that he was afraid lest his hand should touch that of Hauteclaire, as though, if he did touch it by chance, he would be obliged to take it. Hauteclaire did not display this embarrassment and these precautions.

"Women are all temptresses, ready to tempt God or the Devil, and she seemed pleased to risk desire and danger at the same time.

"Once or twice my visit took place at dinner-time, and Savigny always took his dinner by his wife's bed-side.

"Hauteclaire waited at table, the other servants never entering the Comtesse's apartment. In order to place the dishes on the table, she was obliged to lean over Savigny's shoulder, and, in doing so, her dress touched his neck or ears, and I noticed that the Comte turned pale, and glanced at his wife to see if she were looking. By Jove! I was young then, and the disturbance of the molecules in the organization, which is called the violence of emotion, seemed to me the only thing worth living for. I thought to myself that it must be strangely delightful to enjoy a mysterious concubinage with a sham servant, under the eyes of an abused wife who might guess the truth.

"But, except for the paleness and the ill-suppressed emotion of Savigny, I saw nothing of the tragedy they were playing, and the inevitable catastrophe in which it must end. What were they doing? I wanted to learn the secret of their romance. The problem worried me so much that from observing I took to spying, which is only observation at any price. Ah, our tastes soon deprave us. In order to know that of which I was ignorant, I allowed myself to commit meannesses which were unworthy and which I knew to be so, and yet did them. It is the being accustomed to sound, my dear fellow. I tried every means. When, in my visits to the château, I put my horse in the stable, I questioned the servants—without appearing to do so, of course. I spied—oh, I won't spare to use the word—solely for my own curiosity. But the servants were all as much deceived as the Comtesse.

"They honestly took Hauteclaire for one of themselves, and

all my curiosity would have been wasted had it not been for chance, which, as usual, did more than all my schemes, and taught me more than all my spying.

"For more than two months I had been attending the Comtesse, whose health did not improve, for she showed more and more all the symptoms of that debility which is so common now, and which the medical men of this enervated age call anæmia. Savigny and Hauteclaire continued to play with the same consummate art the difficult comedy which my arrival at the château had not disconcerted. Nevertheless, it seemed to me that the actors were getting tired. Savigny had grown thin, and I heard it said at V.: 'What a good husband Monsieur de Savigny is! He has quite changed since his wife's illness. How nice it must be to be loved like that!'

"The impassive beauty of Hauteclaire was spoiled by the weary look in her eyes—not the look caused by weeping, for she had never cried in all her life—but a look as though she had sat up too much. The leanness of Savigny, and the wearied eyes, might have been due to some other cause than the life they were leading. There were many things in that land of subterranean volcanoes which might have caused the symptoms.

"I had remarked these tell-tale signs on their faces, and had asked myself the meaning without being able to give a reply, when one day, returning from my rounds, I passed by Savigny. My intention had been to call as usual, but a difficult accouchement had kept me very late, and when I passed the château it was too late for a visit. I did not even know what time it was. My hunting-watch had stopped. But the moon, which had already begun to descend, marked midnight passed on the vast dial, and its crescent was below the summits of the fir-trees of Savigny, behind which it was about to disappear.

"Have you ever been to Savigny?" asked the Doctor, breaking off his story and turning to me. I nodded.

"Yes? Well, then you know that you are obliged to pass

through the wood, and along the walls of the château, which you must double like a cape, in order to get to the high road which leads directly to V. Suddenly, in this thick wood, in which you could not see a ray of light, nor hear the slightest sound, there fell on my ears a noise which I took to be that of beating clothes —some poor woman, I thought, who was occupied all day in the fields, had taken advantage of the moonlight to wash her clothes at some tank or ditch. It was only as I neared the château that with these regular beats there mingled another sound which enlightened me as to the nature of the first. It was the clashing of crossed swords. You know how plainly you can hear in the night, when the least sounds become distinct, and there was no mistake about its being the sound of iron on iron. An idea crossed my mind, and when I emerged from the pine wood before the château, which was bathed in the moonlight, and one of the windows of which was open, I said:

" 'Hallo! so that is their way of making love!'

"It was evident that Savigny and Hauteclaire were fencing, at that hour of the night. I could hear the foils as plainly as though I had seen them. What I had taken for the noise of beating clothes was the stamping of the feet, or *appels,* of the fencers. The open window was in the pavilion which, of all the four, was the farthest removed from the chamber of the Comtesse. The sleeping château, white and gloomy in the moonlight, looked dead. All the rest of the house was dark, but in this one room the Venetian shutters had been closed, and through them streaks of light came, and it was from this room that the noise of the clashing of foils proceeded. As the night was warm—it was in July—they had opened the window, which led on to the balcony.

"I had drawn up my horse at the edge of the wood, to listen to their combat, which appeared to be a lively one, and I was interested in this assault at arms between lovers who had first loved with weapons in their hands, and who continued to love one another after the click of the foils had ceased.

"The blinds were pushed to one side, and I had only just time to back my horse into the shadow of the trees, when Savigny and Hauteclaire came out and leaned over the iron rail of the balcony. I could see them wonderfully well. The moon had fallen below the wood, but the light of a candelabrum that I could see in the room behind them, showed up their figures. Hauteclaire was dressed—if it may be called dressed—as I had seen her often when giving her lessons at V., in a leather jacket, like a cuirass, and her legs, in the tightly fitting silk hose, showed all their muscular beauty. Savigny wore an almost similar costume. Both were lithe and robust, and they looked, in the lighted square of the window, like two beautiful statues of Youth and Strength. You have just admired, in this garden, the proud beauty of both, which time has not yet destroyed. Well, that will help to give you an idea of the magnificent couple I perceived on the balcony, their tightly fitting clothes making them appear bare. They were leaning on the balcony and talking, but so low that I could not hear what they said, but their attitude told me enough. Savigny had thrown one arm round that Amazonian waist, which seemed well fitted to resist—but did nothing of the kind.

"And at the same instant the proud Hauteclaire threw her arms round Savigny's neck, and they thus formed the celebrated and voluptuous group by Canova, which everyone recollects, and thus they remained mouth to mouth long enough to drink a whole bottleful of kisses. That lasted for quite sixty beats of my pulse, which went faster than at present, and which this sight caused to beat even faster still.

"'Oh! oh!' I said to myself when they had returned into the room and closed the heavy curtains, and I had emerged from my hiding-place. 'One of these days they will have to confide in me. It will not be only themselves they will have to hide!' From the sight of their caresses, and this familiarity, I deduced, as a doctor would, the consequences. But their ardour defeated my prophecy. You know that there are persons who love too

much"—the cynical old doctor used another word—"and consequently never have any children.

"The next morning I went to Savigny. I found Hauteclaire,
now become Eulalie again, seated in the embrasure of one of the
windows of the long corridor which led to her mistress's room,
with a quantity of linen and other stuff before her, and which she
was engaged in cutting and mending—she, the fencer of the previous night. Could anyone suspect it? I thought, as I noticed
that graceful form which I had seen almost bare the previous
night, and which not even the petticoat and the white apron could
altogether hide.

"I passed her without speaking, for I spoke to her as little as
possible, not wishing to seem to know what I did know, and which
might have been remarked in my voice or look. I felt that I was
not such an actor as she was, and I distrusted myself.

"Generally when I passed along this corridor, where she was
always at work when she was not attending to the Comtesse, she
heard me coming, and was so certain as to who it was that she
never raised her head, which remained bowed under the starched
cap, or the Norman head-dress she sometimes wore, and which
resembled that of Isabella of Bavaria—and with her eyes bent on
her work, and her cheeks hidden by the blue-black corkscrew
curls which framed her pale oval face, she offered to my gaze only
a gracefully curved neck, covered by thick curls. In Hauteclaire,
it was the animal which was paramount. No other woman had
the same kind of beauty. Men—who say everything when alone
together—had often remarked it. At V., when she gave her
fencing-lessons, the men used to call her, between themselves,
Mademoiselle Esau. The Devil teaches women what they are
—or they would teach it to the Devil if he did not know.

"Hauteclaire, though not much of a coquette, had a habit, when
she was listening to anyone, of rolling round her fingers the long
curls which adorned her neck, and which had rebelled against the
comb that smoothed her chignon. One of these curls was sufficient to trouble a man's spirit, as the Bible says. She knew well

the effect they caused. But now that she was a lady's maid, I had never once seen her indulge in this gesture, even when looking at Savigny.

"My parenthesis has been rather long, my dear fellow, but anything which enables you to understand Hauteclaire Stassin is of importance to my story. On that day she was obliged to rise and show her face, for the Comtesse rang and ordered her to bring me pen and paper, which I needed to write out a prescription. She came, with a steel thimble still on her finger, for she had not had time to take it off, and she had stuck the threaded needle in her tempting breast, where there were already many others. Even these steel needles suited this confounded girl, who was made for steel, and in the Middle Ages would have worn a cuirass.

"When I had finished, I raised my eyes and looked at her, and saw in her face marks of the fatigue of the previous night.

"Savigny, who was not there when I arrived, suddenly appeared. He looked much more fatigued than she did. He spoke to me about the health of the Comtesse, who was no better. He seemed impatient and annoyed that this was so. His tone was bitter and violent. He walked to and fro as he spoke. I looked at him coolly, thinking that this Napoleonic tone was rather too much. 'But if I should cure your wife,' I thought to myself, 'you would not be able to practise fencing and—love-making— all night with your mistress,' I could have recalled him to the reality and politeness which he had forgotten, by putting under his nose—if I had so liked—the smelling-salts of a sharp reply. I contented myself with looking at him. He was more interesting to me than ever, for it was evident that he was acting a part more than ever."

The Doctor stopped again. He plunged his big finger and thumb into his silver snuff-box, and took a pinch of rappee. He, in his turn, appeared so interesting to me that I made no observation, and he continued his story, after having taken his pinch and passed his bent finger over his hooky nose.

"Oh, he was really impatient—but it was not because the wife to whom he was so persistently faithless, did not get well. Confound it! a man who made a concubine of his servant in his own house, could scarcely be angry that his wife was not cured of an illness. If she had been cured, would not his adultery have been more difficult?

"Did he imagine it would not be such a long affair? And, as I have since thought, the idea of ending it came to him, or her, or both of them—since neither the disease nor the doctor would finish—perhaps, at that moment."

"What, Doctor! Then they——?"

I did not finish my sentence: the idea that the Doctor had suggested cut short my words.

He bent his head and looked at me as tragically as the statue of the Commander when he accepts the supper.

"Yes!" he said slowly in a low voice, in answer to my thought. "At least, some days later, everybody heard with horror that the Comtesse had been poisoned, and was dead."

"Poisoned!" I cried.

"By her lady's maid, Eulalie, who had mistaken one bottle for another, and given her mistress some copying-ink instead of a medicine I had prescribed. After all, such a mistake was possible. But I knew that Eulalie was Hauteclaire. I had seen them both forming Canova's group on the balcony. Society had not seen what I had seen. Society was at first under the impression that a terrible accident had occurred. But when—two years after this catastrophe—they learned that Comte Serlon de Savigny had publicly married Stassin's daughter—for the secret had to come out as to who the sham Eulalie was—and that she occupied the hardly cold bed of the Comte's first wife, Mademoiselle Delphine de Cantor, oh, then no end of suspicions were muttered, as though people were afraid to say what they thought. But, in reality, no one knew. They knew about his marriage, which caused the Comte de Savigny to be pointed at and shunned as though he had the pest. That was quite enough, though. You know what a disgrace it is—or rather it was—for things have much changed in that district—to say of a man: 'He has married his servant!' That disgrace rested on him like a stain. As to the horrible rumours of a suspected crime, they were buzzed about, and died away. But there was one person, however, who knew and was sure."

"And that must have been you, Doctor!" I interrupted.

"It was I, as a matter of fact," he continued, "but not I only. If I alone had known it, I should never have had but vague glimmerings of the truth that would have been worse than ignorance. I should never have been certain, and," he said, laying the stress of absolute certainty on each word, "*I am!*

"And listen to how it is that I am!" he added, pressing my knee between his bony fingers. But his story "nipped" me even more than the crablike claws of his strong hand.

"You may well suppose," he continued, "that I was the first to hear that the Comtesse had been poisoned. Whether they were guilty or not, they were obliged to send for the family doctor. They did not stop to have a horse saddled. A groom came at full gallop on a bare-backed horse to me at V. and I followed him at the same pace to Savigny. When I arrived—had that been calculated?—it was not possible to counteract the effects of the poison. Serlon, his face grief-stricken, met me in the court-yard, and, as I got out of the saddle, said, as though he were frightened at his own words:

" 'A servant made a mistake.' (He took care not to say Eulalie, whom everybody named next day.) 'But, Doctor, can it be possible that copying-ink is a poison?'

" 'That depends entirely on what it is made of,' I replied.

"He took me to the Comtesse, who was worn out with pain, and whose contracted face resembled a ball of white thread that had fallen into some green dye.

"She looked awful. She smiled at me horribly with her black lips, and with that kind of smile which seems to say to a man: 'I know well what you think.' I glanced quickly round the room

to see if Eulalie was there. I should have liked to see her face
at that moment. She was not there.

"Brave as she was, was she afraid of me? Ah, at that time, I
was—certain.

"The Comtesse made an effort when she saw me, and raised
herself on her elbow.

" 'Ah, there you are, Doctor,' she said; 'but you come too late.
I am dying. It is not the doctor you should have sent for, Serlon, but the priest. Send for him at once, and leave me alone for
two minutes with the Doctor. I wish it.'

"She said that 'I wish it' as I had never heard her speak before—but like a woman who had that chin and forehead I have
mentioned.

" 'Even me?' said Savigny, feebly.

" 'Even you,' she replied. And she added almost caressingly:
'You know, my dear, that women are sometimes too modest to
speak before those they love.'

"Hardly had he left than a terrible change came over her.
From mild she became ferocious.

" 'Doctor,' she said in a voice that teemed with hate, "my
death is not an accident, it is a crime! Serlon loves Eulalie, and
she has poisoned me. I did not heed you when you told me
that girl was too pretty to be a lady's maid. I was wrong. He
loves that wretched, that abominable woman, who has killed me.
He is more guilty than she is, for he loves her, and has deceived
me for her sake. For some days past, the looks they exchanged
across my bed have warned me. And then the horrible taste of
that ink with which they poisoned me. But I drank it all to the
last drop, in spite of the horrible taste, because I was glad to die.
Don't talk about antidotes. I want none of your remedies. I
wish to die.'

" 'Then why did you send for me, Madame la Comtesse?'

" 'Well, this is why,' she replied breathlessly. 'To tell you that
they have poisoned me, and that you should give me your word
of honour to keep the secret. It would make a terrible scandal.

That must not be. You are my doctor, and people will believe you when you speak of this mistake they have invented—when you say that I should not have died, but might have been saved, if my health had not been so bad for a long time past. That is what you must swear, Doctor.'

"As I did not reply, she saw what was passing in my mind. I thought she loved her husband to such an extent that she wished to save him. That was the idea that occurred to my mind—a natural and vulgar idea, for there are some women so intended for love and all its self-denials, that they would not return the blow that killed them. But the Comtesse de Savigny had never appeared to me to be a woman of that sort.

" 'Oh, it is not what you imagine that makes me ask you to swear that, Doctor. Oh, no! I hate Serlon so at this moment that I could never love him again. But I am not such a coward as to forgive him. I shall leave this life jealous of him and implacable. But this does not concern Serlon, Doctor,' she continued with energy, showing me a side of her character of which I had already caught a glimpse, but the depths of which I had not penetrated. 'It concerns the Comte de Savigny. I do not want it to be known, when I am dead, that the Comte de Savigny murdered his wife. I do not want him tried at the assizes, and accused of complicity with a servant who is an adulteress and a poisoner. I do not want that stain to rest on the name of Savigny, which I bear. Oh, it is not for his sake, for he is worthy of the scaffold. I should like to torture him. But it concerns all the aristocracy of the country. If we were still what we ought to be, I should have thrown Eulalie into one of the dungeons of the château of Savigny, and there would have been no more said about her. But we are no longer masters in our own houses. We have no longer our expeditious and silent justice, and on no account would I have the scandal and publicity of yours, Doctor; and I prefer to leave them in each other's arms, happy, and freed from me, and for me to die as I am dying, than to think when I

am dying that the nobility of V. should have the disgrace of count-
ing a poisoner in its ranks.'

"She spoke with unaccustomed clearness, although her jaws
chattered as though her teeth would break. It was the aristocrat
that was stronger in her than the jealous wife. She would die
as befitted a daughter of V., the last aristocratic town in France.
And, touched by that—perhaps more than I ought to have been
—I promised and swore to do what she asked.

"And I have done so, my dear fellow. I did not save her.

"I could not save her; she obstinately refused to take any remedy.

"I said what she wished me to when she was dead, and I was
believed.

"That is fully twenty-five years ago. At present everything
concerning the affair is silent and forgotten. Most of her contemporaries are dead. Other generations—ignorant or indifferent
—are drifting towards their tombs, and the first account of this
story that I have ever given is to you.

"And if it had not been for what we have seen, I should not
have told you now. It needed those two beings, unchangeably
beautiful in spite of time, unchangeably happy in spite of their
crime, powerful, passionate, absorbed in each other, passing
through life as they did through this garden, like two angels united
in the golden shadow of their four wings."

I was amazed. "But," I said, "if what you tell me is true, the
happiness of these people is a terrible disorder of nature."

"It is disorder, or it is order, whichever you please," replied
Doctor Torty, a confirmed atheist, and as quiet in mind as the
persons of whom he was speaking, "but it is a fact. They are exceptionally happy; insolently happy. I am an old man, and I
have seen, in the course of my life, much happiness which did not
endure, but I have never seen but that one which was so profound
and yet lasted for ever.

"And yet you may believe that I have well studied and scrutin-

ized it. I have sought for a rift in their happiness. If you will
excuse the expression, I may say that I have loused it. I have
searched the life of those two beings to see if there was not, in
their astonishing and revolting happiness, a fault or crack however small, in some secret place, but I have never found anything
but an excellent and successful joke of the Devil's against God,
if there be a God or a Devil.

"After the death of the Comtesse, I remained, as you may
imagine, on good terms with Savigny. As I had lent the weight
of my authority to the fable they had devised to explain the poisoning, they had no interest in putting me on one side, and I had a
great interest in knowing what would follow, what they would do,
and what would become of them. What followed was the period
of mourning of Savigny, which lasted the customary two years,
and which Savigny performed in a manner to confirm the public
idea that he was the most excellent of husbands, past, present, or
future.

"During these two years, he saw absolutely no one, but buried
himself in his château in such solitude that no one knew that he
had kept at Savigny, Eulalie, the involuntary cause of the death
of the Comtesse, and whom he ought in common decency to have
got rid of, even if he had known she was innocent.

"The imprudence of keeping in his house such a woman after
such a catastrophe, showed the senseless passion that I had always suspected in Serlon. Therefore I was not at all surprised
when one day, on returning from my rounds, I met one of the
servants on the road near Savigny, and on asking what was going
on at the château was told that Eulalie was still there. By the
indifferent tone in which he said that, I saw that none of the
Comte's servants suspected that Eulalie was his mistress. 'They
are playing a close game,' I said to myself. 'But why do they
not leave the country? The Comte is rich. He could live in
good style anywhere. Why not run away with this beautiful
she-devil (in the way of she-devil, I do believe in that one) who,
in order that she might hook him the better, preferred to live in

her lover's house, in spite of the danger, than to be his mistress at
V., in some quiet lodging where he could come and see her secretly?' There was something underneath all this I could not
understand. Their infatuation, their devotion to each other,
was then so great that they forgot all prudence and precaution?
Hauteclaire, whom I supposed to have a stronger character than
Serlon, and to be the man of the couple—did she intend to remain
in the château where she had been a servant, and where she
might become mistress, and, if that caused any scandal, prepare
public opinion for a yet greater scandal—her marriage with the
Comte de Savigny? That idea had not occurred to me, if it had
occurred to her at that period of my story. Hauteclaire Stassin,
the daughter of the fencing-master, 'Old Straight-thrust,' whom we
had all seen giving lessons at V., Comtesse de Savigny! Impossible! The world would come to an end! For my own part, I
believed that the concubinage between these two fierce animals,
who had recognized at the first glance that they were of the same
species, and had dared to commit adultery under the eyes of the
Comtesse, would still continue.

"But a marriage impudently accomplished in the face of God
and man—a challenge and defiance to outraged public opinion—
I was, upon my word, a thousand miles from imagining such a
thing, and when, after the two years' mourning, the event occurred, I was quite as much surprised as any of those fools who
never expect anything, and who howl like a whipped dog when the
unexpected does occur.

"Moreover, during those two years of mourning which Serlon
observed so strictly, and which—when people saw what the end
was—caused him to be so furiously taxed with hypocrisy and
baseness, I did not go much to Savigny. What should I do there?
They were both in good health, and until the moment, perhaps not
so far off, when they would send for me in the night for an accouchement (which would require concealing also), they had no
need of my services. Nevertheless, I now and then paid a visit to
the Comte. Politeness mingled with curiosity. Serlon received

me wherever he might be when I arrived. He did not show the
least embarrassment. His kind manner had returned. He was
grave. I have remarked that happy people are grave. They
carry their heart like a full glass, that the least movement might
cause to overflow or break. In spite of his gravity and his black
clothes, there was in Serlon's eyes an unmistakable expression of
immense happiness. It was no longer an expression of relief and
deliverance, as on the day when he saw that I had recognized
Hauteclaire but had determined *not* to recognize her. No, *parbleu!* it was really and truly happiness. Although in these ceremonious and short visits we talked only about superficial matters,
his voice was not as it had been in the time of his wife. Its intonation seemed to show that he was obliged to restrain the sentiments he really felt.

"As for Hauteclaire (still Eulalie, and at the château, as the
servant had told me), it was a long time before I met her. I no
longer passed her in the corridor, working in the window-seat, as
in the days of the Comtesse. And yet the pile of linen in the
same place, and the scissors, work-box, and thimble on the
window-sill showed that she must work there, on that chair empty
now, and perhaps warm, which she perhaps had left when she
heard me coming. You will remember that I was conceited
enough to believe that she was afraid to meet my eye, but at
present she had nothing to fear. She was not aware that the
Comtesse had related that terrible secret to me. Such was her
bold, proud nature that she would have braved anyone sagacious
enough to divine her secret. And, in fact, when I did see her, her
happiness was written on her face in such a radiant manner that
you could not have effaced it if you had poured over it all the
bottle of copying-ink with which she had poisoned the Comtesse.

"It was on the grand staircase of the château that I met her
the first time. She was coming down as I was going up. She
was gliding along rather quickly, but when she saw me she went
more slowly, no doubt with the intention of showing me her face
and looking me full in the eyes—but if she could make the pan-

ther close its eyes, she could not make me close mine. As she came down the staircase, her skirt floated behind her, owing to her rapid movement, and she seemed to have descended from heaven. She had a sublimely happy air. It was fifteen thousand leagues above that of Serlon. I passed her, nevertheless, without any signs of politeness, for if Louis XIV saluted the maidservants when he met them on the stairs, at least they were not poisoners. She was still dressed as a lady's maid, with a white apron; but the happy appearance of the triumphant and despotic mistress had replaced the impassiveness of the slave. That air she has never lost. You have seen her and can judge. It is more striking even than the beauty of the face upon which it shines. That superhuman air of pride in happy love, she has been able to bestow upon Serlon, who did not have it at first; and she continues after twenty years to have it still, and I have never seen it diminished or veiled for an instant on the faces of these two privileged beings. By that air they have always been able to reply victoriously to neglect, slander, or outraged public opinion, and it has caused all those who have met them to believe that the crime of which they were suspected for a short time, was an atrocious calumny."

"But you, Doctor," I interrupted, "after all that you know, you are not imposed upon by that appearance? You have followed them about everywhere, have you not? You have seen them at all sorts of times?"

"Except in their bedroom at night, and it is not there that they would lose it," replied Doctor Torty, jokingly, but wisely, "I have seen them, I believe, at all times of their life since their marriage —which took place I know not where, in order not to face the rough music which the populace of V., quite as furious in its own way as the nobility in theirs, had promised to give them. When they returned home married, and she was properly and authentically the Comtesse de Savigny, and he absolutely disgraced by marriage with his servant, they settled down in their château at Savigny. People turned their backs on them, but they did not care. But they have never wearied of each other; even now their passion is not appeased. As a doctor, I do not wish to die before I have written a treatise on teratology, and as they interest me—as strange monsters—I have not followed those who avoid them. When I saw the sham Eulalie completely a countess, she received me as though she had been one all her life. She was well aware that I remembered the white apron and the silver platter.

"'I am no longer Eulalie,' she said. 'I am Hauteclaire, happy to have been a servant for his sake.'

"I thought she had been something else as well; but as I was the only person in the district who went to Savigny when they returned there, I swallowed my pride, and ended by going there often. I may say that I continued to strive to pierce the intimacy of these two beings, so completely happy in their love. Well, you may believe me or not, as you like, my dear fellow, but I have never seen the purity of that happiness (though I was sure it was stained by a crime), I will not say dulled, not even shadowed for a single minute in a single day. The stain of a cowardly crime, which had not the courage to be a bloody one, had never sullied the blue horizon of their happiness once, so far as I can see. That is enough to knock over—is it not?—all the moralists on earth, who have invented the fine theory about vice punished and virtue rewarded.

"Neglected and solitary as they were, and seeing no one but me, for whom they did not put themselves out of the way, I being a doctor who was almost a friend, by dint of familiarity they ceased to be on their guard. They forgot me, and lived, when I was present, in the intoxication of a passion to which I have seen nothing to compare in all my life. You were the witness of it a moment ago. They passed, and they did not even perceive me, although I was at their elbow. A good part of the time I spent with them, they never saw me either. Polite and amiable, but often absent-minded, their behaviour to me was such that I should never have returned to Savigny if I had not wanted to study microscopically their incredible happiness, and to discover, for my personal edification, the grain of weariness, of suffering, or—if I must speak plainly—of remorse. But there was nothing! —nothing! Love pervaded everything, and obscured their moral sense and what you call conscience, and when I looked at these happy beings, I understood the seriousness of the joke of my old comrade Broussais when he said about conscience: 'I have been dissecting for thirty years and have never found a trace of that little beast.'

"And do not imagine," continued the sarcastic old doctor, as though he had read my thoughts, "that what I am telling you is a mere theory—the proof of the doctrine which denies the existence of conscience as Broussais denied it, I believe to be true. There is no theory here. I do not pretend to ask your opinion. I relate nothing but facts, which astonished me as much as they do you. It is merely the phenomenon of continued happiness— of a soap-bubble which increased in size and never burst. When happiness lasts like that, it is always surprising, but happiness in crime is astounding, and in twenty years I have never got over my amazement. The old doctor, the old observer, the old moralist—or immoralist (he added, seeing me smile)—is disconcerted by this spectacle which he has beheld so many years, and which he cannot relate in detail, for, as is well said, happiness has no history.

"No description is possible. You can no more paint happiness —that infusion of a higher life into ordinary life—than you can paint the circulation of blood in the veins. You can certify by the beating of the arteries that it *does* circulate; and, by the same reasoning, I can certify to the happiness of those incomprehensible beings, whose pulse I have been feeling for so many years. The Comte and Comtesse de Savigny, without knowing it, re-create every day that splendid chapter of "Love in Marriage" of Madame de Staël, or the still more magnificent verses of Milton's *Paradise Lost*. For my own part, I have never been very sentimental or very poetical, but the ideal which they have realized,

and which I deemed impossible, has disgusted me with the best
marriages I have known, and which the world called charming.
I have always found these so inferior to theirs—so colourless
and cold. Destiny, or their star, or chance—whatever it may be
—has decreed that they shall live for themselves alone. Being
rich, they have that idleness without which love cannot exist, but
which often kills the love from which it necessarily springs. But
their case is an exception, and idleness has not killed theirs.
Love, which simplifies everything, has made their life a sublime
simplification. There are none of those important matters which
are called events in the existence of those two married people,
who have lived, apparently, like most rich people, far from a
world of which they ask nothing, caring nothing for its esteem or
its disdain.

"They have never left one another. Where one goes, the
other goes. The roads round V. again saw Hauteclaire on horseback, as in the time of 'Old Straight-thrust'; but it was the Comte
de Savigny who was with her, and the ladies of the district, when
they passed in their carriages, now stared at her more, perhaps,
than when she was the tall and mysterious young girl in the dark-
blue veil, whom they could not see. Now she had raised her
veil, and boldly showed the face of the servant who had known
how to make a good match, and the ladies returned home indignant, but thoughtful.

"The Comte and Countess de Savigny never travel; they sometimes come to Paris, but they stay only a few days. Their
life is concentrated entirely in the château of Savigny, which
was the theatre of a crime, of which they have perhaps forgotten
the memory in the bottomless abyss of their hearts."

"Have they never had any children, Doctor?" I asked.

"Ah!" said Doctor Torty, "you fancy, perhaps, that that is
their curse—the revenge of Fate—what you call the vengeance
or the justice of God! No, they have never had any children.
I once thought they would never have any. They love one an-

other too much. The fire which devours, consumes and does not produce. One day I said to Hauteclaire:

" 'Are you not sorry not to have any children, Madame la Comtesse?'

" 'I do not want any,' she said proudly. 'I should love Serlon less. Children,' she added with a kind of scorn, 'are good only for women who are unhappy.' "

And Doctor Torty finished his story abruptly with this remark, which he deemed profound.

He had interested me, and I said:

"Criminal as she may be, I am interested in this woman, Hauteclaire. Had it not been for her crime, I should have understood Serlon's love."

"And, perhaps, even with her crime," said the Doctor. "As, indeed, I do," he added boldly.

BENEATH THE CARDS OF
A GAME OF WHIST

BENEATH THE CARDS OF A GAME
OF WHIST

"... It is a tale
... full of sound and fury,
Signifying nothing."

Macbeth.

I

ONE evening last summer I was in the drawing-room of the Baronne de Mascranny, one of the most faithful admirers in all Paris of the now almost lost art of witty conversation, a lady always ready to open her doors wide—though a narrower ingress would have amply sufficed—to the few exponents of it still spared us. The fact is that in these latter days wit has been entirely superseded by a pretentious nondescript called Intelligence. . . . The Baronne de Mascranny is, on her husband's side, of an ancient and illustrious family, originally hailing from the Grisons. She bears for arms, as all the world knows: *or, three bars wavy gules; on a chief gules an eagle displayed argent, dexter a key argent, sinister a helmet of the same; the shield charged with an escutcheon of pretence azure, bearing a fleur-de-lis or;* and this chief as well as the devices it bears were augmentations of honour that had been granted by more than one European sovereign to the family of Mascranny in recompense for services rendered them by its members at different periods of history. Nowadays, unfortunately, the sovereigns of Europe have quite other matters of greater urgency to attend to; else they might do worse than add another ornament to a shield, already so nobly filled, in recognition of the really heroic pains the Baronne lavishes on the expiring art of conversation, that doomed child of aristocratic leisure and monarchical absolutism.

127

With wit and manners to match her high name the Baronne de
Mascranny has made her drawing-room into a kind of delectable
Coblentz, a refuge for the elegant conversation of other days,
where the expiring glories of French wit have found a home, when
forced to emigrate by the busy, utilitarian habits of the age.
There night by night, till it fall silent altogether, it chants its swan-
song with a divine melodiousness. There, and in the few other
Parisian houses where the grand traditions of good talk are still
kept up, pretentious and sententious phrases are eschewed, and
monologue is a thing almost unheard of. There nothing recalls
the leading article or the platform speech, those two most commonplace moulds of thought in the nineteenth century. Wit is content
to coruscate in sentences that may be, and often are, both brilliant
and profound, but never long; often a mere intonation of the
voice suffices, or a trifling gesture, that is a work of genius in itself.
I owe it to this twice-blessed *salon* that I have learnt better to
appreciate a power of which I had hardly suspected the existence
before, that of the monosyllable. How often have I heard one
launched, or merely lightly dropped, into the conversation, with a
skill that far exceeded that of Mademoiselle Mars, the queen of
monosyllable on the boards. But the Faubourg Saint-Germain
could have ousted her from her throne with ease, supposing she
could ever have appeared on that stage; for its denizens possess
far too much of the "great lady," when they indulge in refined
and dainty speech, to "refine refined gold," like an actress in a
piece of Marivaux's.

Well, on this particular evening, by way of exception, the wind,
as we shall see, blew from the opposite quarter. When I entered
the Baronne de Mascranny's drawing-room, I found a considerable
number of people assembled there, those she calls *her familiars*,
and the conversation as animated as it always was. Like the
exotics filling the jasper flower-vases on her tables, the Baronne's
familiars hail from pretty well all parts of the world. Among them
are English, Poles, Russians—though all are French in speech and
by virtue of that quality of mind and manners which is one and

the same in all countries at a certain level in the social scale. I cannot tell what had been the original starting-point; but when I entered, they were discussing romance and romances. For them *to discuss romance* meant only that each was busy dissecting his or her own life. For it is needless to remark that a gathering such as this of men and women of society, did not indulge in the pedantry of dragging in the literary aspect of the question. Matter, not manner, was what concerned them most; and not one of these high-bred moralists, these practical exponents of love and life, whose light words and indifferent air hid many a passionate experience, but saw in romance mainly a question of human nature, of history and manners. This seems little, but is it not in reality everything?

Apparently they must already have talked a great deal about the subject, for they all had that intense expression which denotes an interest long sustained. Under the subtle stimulus of each other's excitement, every temperament was at sparkling-point. Only some intense souls—I could count three or four such in the room —sat silent, some with drooping head, some with eyes fixed dreamily on the rings of a hand that lay extended on their knee. Perhaps they were striving to corporealize their dreams—a task as difficult as to spiritualize one's sensations. Under cover of the discussion, I slipped in unperceived behind the dazzling, velvety back of the beautiful Comtesse de Damnaglia, who was biting between her lips the tip of her closed fan as she listened attentively —as all did in this assemblage, where listening is a fine art. The day was declining, a day of rosy light now verging into darkness, as happy lives do. The company formed a circle, in the twilit room, resembling a garland of men and women, posed in various attitudes of easy attention. They made a sort of living bracelet of which the mistress of the house, with her Egyptian profile and the couch which, like Cleopatra, she always occupied, was the central clasp. An open window showed a bit of sky and the balcony where some of the guests were standing, and the air was so clear and the Quai d'Orsay so profoundly quiet for the moment, that these people did not lose one syllable of what the man in the room was saying, and this in spite of the Venetian draperies of the window that must have deadened a voice less sonorous and smothered some of its vibrations in their folds. Directly I recognized who the speaker was, I ceased to wonder at the attention he commanded—which in this case was no mere piece of politeness—or at the audacity of anyone's holding forth at so much greater length than was usual in this home of exquisite refinement.

He was, in fact, the most brilliantly successful talker in this kingdom of brilliant talk. I will not give his name—but that is his distinctive title! Nay, I have made a mistake: he had another equally distinctive. . . . Scandal and calumny, those twin Menæchmi, are so much alike that they cannot well be distinguished, and scrawl their budget of ill words backwards, as if they were Hebrew (which they are sometimes), wrote in characters of shame that he had been the hero of more than one adventure he would scarce have cared to tell that night.

". . . The finest romances of life," he was saying, when I settled myself among the sofa cushions, behind the shelter of the Comtesse de Damnaglia's white shoulders, "are realities one has touched with the elbow, or even the foot, in passing. We have all of us seen them; romance is commoner than history. I am not now speaking of those which were notorious catastrophes, dramas staged with the fine audacity of much high-flown sentiment and flaunted in the dignified face of Public Opinion. Quite apart from these blazing scandals, which after all are infrequent in a society like our own, which yesterday was hypocritical, though to-day it is only timid, there is not one amongst us but has witnessed those mysterious workings of sentiment or passion that blast a whole career to ruin, breaking hearts that give out only a dull, dead sound, like a corpse dropped into the hidden depths of an *oubliette,* and over which the world goes on its way, many-voiced or merely silent. We may often say of romance what Molière used to say of virtue: 'Where the deuce will it build next?' . . . Where you least expect to find it, lo! there it is. In my own person, I saw when a boy—no! *saw* is not the word!— I guessed, I divined, one of those cruel, terrible dramas, that are never played out in public, though the public sees the actors in them every day—one of those *sanguinary comedies,* as Pascal phrases it, but represented with closed doors, behind a stage-cloth —the curtain of privacy and home life. The catastrophe of these hidden, stifled tragedies, dramas, if I may use the expression, of *checked perspiration,* is more sinister and produces a more poignant effect on the imagination and memory than if the whole action had been unrolled under our very eyes. The unknown multiplies the impressiveness of the known a hundredfold. Am I right in thinking that hell, of which a glimpse is visible through some vent-hole in the earth's crust, would be far more terrifying than if beheld in its entirety in one wide-embracing look?"

Here he made a slight pause. He had enunciated a proposition appealing so directly to the human nature of his audience and so convincing to anyone having a touch of imagination, that no one dreamed of challenging what he said. Every face depicted the liveliest curiosity. Little Sybil, who sat crouched double at the foot of the couch where her mother reclined, drew closer to the latter with a convulsive shudder of apprehension, as if someone had slipt an adder between her flat undeveloped bosom and her frock.

"Stop him, Mother!" she cried, with the confidence of a spoilt child, brought up to be a little despot. "Don't let him tell us these horrid, creepy tales. They make me shiver."

"I will not say another word, if you prefer, Sybil," replied the narrator, whom she had designated merely as *him,* with a childish, almost affectionate familiarity.

He, living as he did in such close intimacy with the child, knew the mingled inquisitiveness and timidity of her excitable nature. For she was one of those individuals who at any unexpected incident experience the same thrill we feel on plunging our feet sud-

denly into a bath colder than the surrounding air, that catches
the breath as the limbs sink deeper in the startling coldness of the
water.

"Sybil can claim no right that I know of to impose silence on my
friends," put in the Baronne, caressing her daughter's head, so
precocious in its pensive gravity. "If she is afraid, she has the resource of the fearful, flight; she can run away."

But the capricious girl, who, it may be, was just as curious as her
mother to hear the story, did not run away, but drew up her little
body all a-tremble with fearful interest, fixing her dark, dreamy
eyes on the narrator, as if she were bending shudderingly over an
abyss.

"Well, then, tell on!" ordered Mademoiselle Sophie de Revistal,
turning on him her great brown orbs, so full of light and even yet
so suffused with limpid moisture, for all the fire that had blazed
in them. "Behold!" she added with a theatrical gesture, so slight
as to be almost imperceptible; "we are all hanging on your lips."

Then he proceeded to relate the following strange tale. But
how can I reproduce, without spoiling half its effect, a narrative
that owed so much to the subtle emphasis of voice and gesture—
how make others feel the same vivid impression it produced on an
audience assembled thus in the sympathetic atmosphere of the
Baronne's drawing-room?

"I was brought up in the country," he began, fairly embark-
ing on his narrative, "and passed my boyhood in the home of my
ancestors. My father lived at a village that stood negligently
bathing its feet in a river, at the foot of a hill. I will not tell you
in what part of the country it lay, but it was near a small provincial town you will recognize when I tell you it is, or rather was in
those days, the most profoundly, ferociously aristocratic in all
France. I have never seen anything like it since. Not our own
Faubourg Saint-Germain, not the Place Bellecour at Lyons, nor
the three or four other big towns generally quoted for their
haughty and exclusive spirit of aristocracy, could give a notion of

this little town of six thousand souls, which before 1789 had fifty coaches bedizened with armorial bearings rolling proudly over its flagstones.

"It seemed as if the old sentiment, gradually disappearing from other parts of the country, which more and more every day was being overwhelmed by the encroaching flood of an insolent bourgeoisie, had concentrated in tenfold strength there, as at the bottom of a crucible, giving out like a ruby under fusion a persistent brilliancy that is inherent in the very substance of the stone and will not vanish till the last atom is destroyed.

"The nobility of this nest of nobles, who will die to a man (or it may be are dead by now) still clinging to these prejudices, which for my own part I call sublime social verities, was as incapable of compromise as God. It knew nothing of what humiliates almost all nobilities, the degradation of misalliances.

"The daughters of these noble houses, ruined as they were by the Revolution, would die old maids without a murmur, supported in their stoicism by the all-sufficing glory of their armorial bearings. My youth was fired by the ardent flame of these fair and charming personalities, who one and all knew only too well how futile their beauty was, and felt instinctively that the rich blood beating in their hearts and dyeing their cheeks scarlet, coursed so hotly through their arteries in vain.

"At thirteen I was full of fond dreams of romantic devotion to these poor girls, whose whole fortune was the close crown on their scutcheon and whose whole life, from its earliest day, was imbued with a majestic melancholy, as befits those condemned by fate. Outside their own caste, this nobility kept itself undefiled as a mountain spring, and would know no one.

" 'Would you wish us,' they would say, 'would you wish us to know these vulgarians, whose fathers handed plates to ours?'

"And they were right; the thing was impossible, for in a town of this size it was true. Equalization of ranks is all very well—at a distance; but in an area about as big as a pocket-handkerchief, races are inevitably divided off by the very fact of their proximity. So they visited each other, and no one else whatever, except a few English residents.

"For the English were drawn to the little place, which reminded them of some of their own quiet County-towns. They liked it for its silence, its stiff propriety and the chill respectability of its ways of life, for the close proximity of the sea that had brought them thither, no less than for the possibility, due to the cheapness of living, of doubling the purchasing power of an income inadequate to support their position at home.

"Offspring of the same pirate breed as the Normans, they looked upon this little Normandy town as a sort of Continental England, and used to take up their residence there for long periods at a time.

"There the young English *misses* learnt French as they drove their hoops under the scraggy lindens in the Place d'Armes; but always, as they approached eighteen, they would take flight for England, the poor ruined nobility of the place being quite unlikely to afford themselves the luxury of marrying girls with the small dowry customary in English families. So they would bid farewell to their old haunts, and another immigration would presently succeed to their abandoned homes, so that the quiet streets, where the grass grows between the stones as it does at Versailles, had always much about the same number of fair promenaders with green veils and checked frocks and Scotch plaids. Except for this temporary residence of English families, lasting on an average from seven to ten years, and their comings and goings at long intervals, nothing broke the monotonous existence of the dull little town. The general stagnation and monotony were awful.

"Enough, and more than enough, abuse has been heaped on provincial life for the narrow circle within which it moves; here, this life, everywhere so poor in events, was doubly so from the fact that all rivalry between class and class, and the social antagonisms and petty vanities it gives rise to, were entirely absent. In most small places this is by no means so, and jealousy, dislike,

wounded self-love, keep up a constant ferment at or below the surface which now and again breaks out into some startling scandal,
some ebullition of spite, one of those downright little social villain-
ies that the law cannot recognize.

"Here the gulf of demarcation was so deep, the dividing line so
wide and impassable, separating what was noble from what was
not, that any struggle between patrician and plebeian was out
of the question. To make a struggle possible, some common
meeting-ground and some mutual interests are indispensable, and
these did not exist.

" 'However, the Devil had his due,' as they say, for all that.
At the bottom of their hearts, in their inmost thoughts, these good
bourgeois, whose fathers had handed plates, these sons of gentlemen's gentlemen, now grown rich and independent, were still evil
cesspools of envy and hatred that not unfrequently would belch out
their foulness and fury against their better-born neighbours—who
for their part had simply erased them from their field of vision,
and paid no more heed to them whatever, now they had ceased to
wear their livery.

"Indeed they were oblivious of all these things, securely en-
trenched within the walls of their family mansions, whose doors
remained closed against all but their so-called equals; for their life
ended where another caste began. What matter if their inferiors
spoke ill of them? . . . They had only to shut their ears. Then
the younger men, who might have bandied insults and picked a
quarrel, never met in public places, where the very air is electrical
with the stimulating presence and bright eyes of women.

"There was no theatre in the place and no theatrical perform-
ances, players never coming that way, for lack of a playhouse.
The cafês, mean and provincial, seldom saw any other customers
round their billiard tables but some of the most degraded section
of the bourgeoisie, a few noisy ne'er-do-weels, and half-pay officers,
worn-out relics of the great wars of the Empire. Yet, angered
as they were by all these wounds to their sense of equality (a
feeling capable by itself of fully accounting for the horrors of the

Revolution), these citizens had retained, in spite of themselves, a certain superstitious reverence for rank and birth they had long ago formally repudiated.

"The reverence of the populace is something like the sacred Ampulla of Rheims, on which so much good wit has been wasted. When it is all gone, there is still some left. The toy-maker's son declaims against the inequalities of rank; but he would never dream of walking alone and in cold blood across the public square of his native town, where everybody knows everybody else, and has lived in the same street from childhood, in order to insult in mere wantonness the son, let us say, of a Clamorgan-Taillefer passing by with his sister on his arm. He would have the whole town up in arms against him. Like everything else that provokes malice and envy, birth exercises over the very people who most bitterly reject its claims a physical ascendancy, which is perhaps the best proof of its rights. In time of Revolution this ascendancy is fiercely combated; it still makes itself felt by virtue of the very reaction it provokes. In more peaceable times it acts with a steady and persistent, though unacknowledged, force.

"Well, 182 . . . was one of these periods of tranquillity. . . . Liberalism, which was growing steadily under the shadow of the Constitutional Charter, as were its champions and watch-dogs in their borrowed kennel, had not as yet crushed the life out of that sentiment of loyalty which the return of the Princes from exile had raised to fever-heat in every heart. Say what you will, it was a proud moment for France, convalescent and once more monarchical; the knife of successive Revolutions had cut her bosom to the quick, but full of hope and energy, she still dreamt she could live on thus mutilated, not as yet feeling in her veins the mysterious germs of the cancer that had long been gnawing at her vitals and must one day kill her.

"For the little town I am describing it was a time of profound and utter quiet. A religious mission, which had just closed, had smothered, so far as aristocratic society was concerned, the last vestiges of liveliness, stir and youthful amusements. Balls and

dances had ceased entirely, being now proscribed as a wile of the
Evil One.   The young ladies wore mission-crosses on their bosoms,
and formed themselves into pious organizations under the direction of a Lady President.   Everything tended towards a certain
solemn gravity of deportment that was most laughable, if only
one had dared to laugh.   When the four whist-tables were laid
ready for the dowagers and old gentlemen, and the two écarté
tables for the younger folk, these young ladies used to take up their
station, as if in Church, in a sanctuary apart, where they were
entirely separated from the men, and formed a silent group in one
corner of the drawing-room—silent—that is to say, considering
their sex—for is not everything relative?   They never spoke
above a whisper, but yawned furtively, fit to yawn their poor
heads off, their rigid attitudes offering a piquant contrast with the
supple grace of their figures, the pink and lilac of their frocks
and the bravery of their fluttering silk furbelows and ribbons.

II

"The one thing," continued the narrator of this history, in which
everything is as true and living as the little town itself where it all
happened, and which he had described in such lifelike terms that
one of the company, less discreet than he, had just uttered its
name, "the one thing that possessed any resemblance, I will not
say to a passion, but to activity, desire, strong sensation, of any
sort, in this strangely constituted society where the young girls
had eighty years of world-weariness weighing on their calm and
innocent hearts, was card-playing, that last resource of exhausted
spirits.

"Play was the one great business of these old aristocrats modelled, as they were, on the pattern of the grand Seigneurs of a
former day, and as idle as a lot of old blind women.   They played
like Normans, the ancestors of the English, the most gambling na-
tion on earth.   Their kinship with this people, their residence in
England during the emigration, the solemnity of the game, secret

and silent as the diplomacy of statesmen, all had combined to make them adopt whist, to fill up the bottomless abyss of their empty days. They used to play the game every evening after dinner up to midnight or even one o'clock in the morning,—which is wild dissipation in the country. To take a hand at the Marquis de Saint-Albans' table was the crowning event of each man's day. The Marquis was in a way the Feudal Lord of all of them, and they all flattered him with that sort of respectful consideration that is an Order of Merit in itself, when those who show it are themselves worthy of consideration.

"The Marquis was very good at whist. He was now seventy-nine, and had· met most of the great men and great players of an earlier generation. . . . He had played with Maurepas, with the Comte d'Artois himself, who was as great at whist as he was at tennis, with the Prince de Polignac, with Bishop Louis de Rohan, with Cagliostro, with the Prince de la Lippe, with Fox, Dundas and Sheridan, with the Prince of Wales, with Talleyrand—with the Arch Fiend himself, they said, when he was going recklessly to the devil in the blackest days of the emigration. He required foemen therefore worthy of his steel. Generally speaking, the English who were on visiting terms with the local magnates supplied their contingent of efficients to the Marquis's table, which was recognized as an established institution and always spoken of as M. de Saint-Albans' game, just as they said the King's game at Court.

"One night at Madame de Beaumont's the green tables stood ready as usual; they were only waiting for Monsieur Hartford, an Englishman, to complete the great Marquis's game. He was a business man of a superior sort, this Monsieur Hartford, who ran a large cotton-mill at Pont-aux-Arches—I may observe parenthetically, one of the first of its kind established in Normandy, a country so slow to adopt improvements, not from ignorance or any dullness of comprehension, but in virtue of that weariness that is the distinctive characteristic of the breed.

"However, to return to our Englishman, Monsieur Hartford.

The young men all called him "Hartford" straight out, without any Monsieur, though fifty had long since struck on the silver timepiece of his head, which I can see now in my mind's eye with its cropped hair, close and shiny as a white silk skull-cap. He was a prime favourite with the Marquis. This was not surprising, as he was a player of the first order, a man whose life, otherwise vain and insignificant, had no meaning or reality whatever except when he was seated at the whist-table. One phrase was for ever in his mouth, that 'the best happiness of life was to win at cards, and the next best to lose'—a sublime axiom he had borrowed from Sheridan, but which he applied in so thorough a fashion as to excuse the plagiarism. For the rest, barring this one vice (in consideration of which the Marquis would have forgiven him the most eminent virtues), Monsieur Hartford was reputed to possess all those Pharisaic and Protestant qualities which English people sum up under the smug word "respectable." He was reckoned a perfect gentleman. The Marquis used to invite him for a week at a time to his country-house, the Château de la Vanillière, and in town he spent every evening in his company.

"All were wondering to-night, the Marquis amongst the rest, at the unpunctuality of the Englishman, usually so precise and exact in all his doings. . . . It was in August; the windows were thrown open on one of those lovely gardens you only see in the country, and their recesses occupied by the young girls of the party, who were talking together as they leant their heads against the draperies. The Marquis, seated at the whist-table, was frowning with his long, white eyebrows, impatiently. His elbows were on the table, and his delicate old hands were clasped under his chin, while the dignified features expressed his royal displeasure at being kept waiting; he looked for all the world like Louis XIV under similar circumstances, and was not a whit less majestic. At last a servant announced Monsieur Hartford, who appeared dressed, as always, to perfection, his linen dazzling in its whiteness, rings on all his fingers, as we have since seen Mr. Bulwer wear them, an Indian handkerchief in his hand, and between his lips (for he had

just dined) the scented pastille that covered the fumes of an-
chovies, Harvey sauce and port-wine.

"But he was not alone. He came forward and greeted the Marquis, introducing to him, as a sufficient shield against all reproof,
one of his friends, a Scotchman, Monsieur Marmor de Karkoel,
who had burst upon him like a bomb-shell in the middle of his
dinner, and who was the best whist-player in the Three Kingdoms.

"This latter circumstance at once brought a smile of welcome
to the nobleman's pale lips. The game was instantly made up.
In his haste to get to work, Monsieur de Karkoel did not wait to
remove his gloves, the perfection of which recalled that of the
great Beau Brummell's; these were cut by three special artists,
two for the hand and another for the thumb. He was Monsieur de
Saint Albans' partner, the Dowager Comtesse de Hautcardon giving up her place to him.

"As to his personal appearance, ladies, Marmor de Karkoel
was a man of not more than twenty-eight or thereabouts; but a
burning sun, and the fatigues, perhaps the stormy passions, of an
unknown past, had engraved on his features all the marks of a
greater age. He looked thirty-five at least. His face was not
handsome, but powerful and full of expression. The hair was
black, coarse, straight and rather short, and his hand was continually pushing it from his temples and throwing it back. This often repeated gesture was full of a genuine but sinister kind of
elegance—as it were, a constant effort to be rid of some remorse-
ful memory. This was what first struck one, and always did so,
like all profound impressions.

"I knew Karkoel for several years, and I am convinced this
sombre gesture, repeated as it was ten times over in an hour, never
failed to be impressive and invariably brought the same thought
to the minds of a hundred different observers. His brow, low but
well-cut, bespoke a bold and resolute spirit. His clean-shaven upper lip (moustaches were not then commonly worn, as they are
now) had a statuesque immobility which would drive Lavater to
despair and disconcert believers in the doctrine that the secret of a

man's nature is more clearly to be read in the mobile lines of the mouth than in the expression of the eyes. These latter took no part in his smile, which showed a row of teeth as white and even as so many pearls, such as these islanders often have—only to blacken and ruin them, like the Chinese, with copious libations of their horrid tea. The face was long and hollow-cheeked; the complexion of a natural olive hue, but heavily sunburnt into the bargain, in some climate where the rays of that luminary beat down with greater power than in dull, foggy Albion, or they could never have scorched him so fiercely. A long, straight nose, though not so straight and upright as the forehead, divided the two eyes. These were not so much black as dark, with a sombre depth that recalled Macbeth's fatal look; they were set close together, which they say is the mark of a wild, ill-regulated character or else of some mental obliquity. He was well and elegantly dressed. Seated, as he now was, in a careless attitude at the whist-table, he seemed taller than he actually was, owing to a slight disproportion of the upper part of the body, for he was really short. Except for this defect, he was well built, his figure suggesting the same potentialities of strength and lithe agility as the tiger hides beneath his velvety skin.

"Did he speak French well or ill? His voice, the golden chisel wherewith we carve our thoughts in the soul of our auditors and win their hearts, was it in harmony with the gesture I have described, and which I cannot even now recall without dreaming of it? This much at any rate is certain, that evening it made no one tremble. He pronounced, and in the most ordinary tones, only the sacramental words of *tricks* and *honours*, the only expressions at whist which interrupt at measured intervals the solemn silence that enwraps the players.

"In the large room, which was full of people, for whom the arrival of an Englishman more or less was a circumstance of great indifference, no one except those at the Marquis's table paid any special heed to the unknown whist-player, towed in by Hartford in his wake. The group of girls did not so much as turn their heads to cast a look at him over their shoulders. They were busy discussing (discussion was then first coming into vogue) the composition of the Committee of their Association and the resignation of one of the Vice-Presidents, who was not present that evening at Madame de Beaumont's. This was surely a more important matter than watching any Englishman or Scotchman alive. Indeed, they were a trifle bored by these everlasting importations from Great Britain. This man would be like the rest of them; the only members of the sex he would waste a thought on would be the Queen of Diamonds and the Queen of Clubs! And a Protestant into the bargain! a heretic! If it had been a Catholic nobleman from Ireland, that would have been a very different thing! As for the older guests, who were already engaged in play at the different tables when Monsieur Hartford was announced, they cast a perfunctory glance at the stranger who followed him in, and, this done, buried themselves once more in their cards, as swans bury their heads deep in the water when they dip their long necks below the surface.

"Monsieur de Karkoel having been chosen as the Marquis de Saint Albans' partner, the player facing Monsieur Hartford was the Comtesse du Tremblay de Stasseville, whose daughter Herminie, the sweetest of all the girls who adorned the recessed windows of the drawing-room, was at the moment in conversation with Mademoiselle Ernestine de Beaumont. By chance her eyes fell in the direction of the table where her mother was playing.

" 'Look, Ernestine,' she exclaimed in a low voice, 'look at the way the Scotchman deals!'

"Monsieur de Karkoel had now taken off his well-fitting gloves of scented kid, showing a pair of white, beautifully shaped hands, that a fashionable beauty would have cherished, if she had possessed them, with religious care, and was now dealing out the cards, one by one as is done at whist, but with a circular sweep of such prodigious rapidity, it was as wonderful in its way as the Abbé Liszt's fingering. A man that could handle the cards like that must needs be their master. . . . Ten years of a gambler's life stood confessed in the sleight of hand of this lightning-flash style of dealing.

" 'A hardly won triumph,' was Ernestine's criticism, delivered with a disdainful curl of the lip, '—of bad form!' A harsh thing for so young a girl to say; but then in that pretty head *good form* counted for more than all the wit and wisdom of a Voltaire. She had missed her vocation, this Mademoiselle Ernestine; she should have been *camerara major* to a Queen of Spain.

"The stranger's style of play matched this extraordinary skill of his. He showed a superiority that intoxicated the old Marquis with delight, for did he not actually improve the game of this old partner of Fox and Sheridan, and lift it to the higher level of his own? Sovereign superiority of every kind has about it a fascination that exerts an irresistible force of attraction and carries you away with it in its course. But this is not all; for it enriches you at the same time. Look at great talkers; repartee inspires repartee, and one witty word provokes another. Directly they cease speaking, fools robbed of the golden ray of inspiration that brightened their wits, gasp dull and helpless on the surface of the conversation, like dead fish floating belly upwards, their scales invisible. But Monsieur de Karkoel did more than merely give a new fillip to a man who had exhausted most emotions; he increased the Marquis's estimate of his own powers and crowned with yet another stone the stately obelisk, that had long stood at the same height, which this King of Whist-players had raised to his own glory in the serene solitudes of his self-esteem.

"Notwithstanding the excitement which made him feel young again, the Marquis kept an observant eye on the stranger during the game from the covert of the network of crow's-feet (by this ugly name we designate Time's signature on our temples, to pay him out for the insolence of writing it there) that fringed his keen eyes. A player such as this could only be relished and properly appreciated by a player possessed of rare powers himself. He wore a look of deep and serious concentration, ready with a new combination to meet each turn of the game, yet veiling it all under a superb air of impassivity. Beside him the Egyptian Sphinx, crouching on her foundations of basaltic rock, would have looked like the genius of open-hearted expansiveness. He played as if his adversaries were simply three pairs of hands holding the cards, and he disdained to inquire whose hands they were. The dying breezes of that August night broke softly in waves of fragrance over the waving locks of the score of girls who were standing bareheaded at the open windows, and came laden with fresh perfumes of maidenhood to break against the stranger's broad, low, sunburnt brow; but it remained as hard and as unruffled as a rock of marble. He did not so much as notice it, this man of iron nerve. At this moment he was, indeed, worthy of the name of Marmor. Needless to say, he won.

"The Marquis withdrew, as was his invariable custom, towards midnight. He was conducted to his carriage by the obsequious Monsieur Hartford, who lent him the support of his arm.

"'This Karkoel is the very God of Good Tricks!' the Marquis said to him, surprised and delighted; 'pray! see that he does not leave us too soon.'

"Hartford promised, and the old Marquis, in spite of his age and sex, was ready to play the part of a Siren of hospitality.

"I have described at some length this first evening of a stay which lasted several years, though I was not present myself on the occasion, but I have heard it all from one of my relatives, who was some years my senior, and who like all the young men in this dull little town, where play was the one and only resource available in the dearth of every germ of excitement, was an ardent whist-player, and readily fell under the ascendancy of the *God of Tricks*. Looking back now from the vantage-ground of later events, with all their magic of association, we may well invest the evening, so commonplace a bit of prose in itself—a game of whist and a winning hand—with an importance some might deem exaggerated.

"The fourth player, the Comtesse de Stasseville, my informant would continue, lost her money with the same aristocratic indiffer-

ence which she displayed under all circumstances. Yet it was perhaps at this very game that her lot was decided by Destiny; for
indeed which of us can understand one word of the mysteries of
life? . . . No one at the time had any particular interest in watching the Countess. There was no sound in the room more striking
than the tinkle of the counters used to mark the play. . . . Nothing could well be less likely than that anyone could have learned
from the voice or appearance of this woman, then judged by one
and all to be a cold and sharp icicle, whether what came subsequently to be believed and repeated from mouth to mouth in awestruck whispers, really and truly dated from this moment.

"The Comtesse du Tremblay de Stasseville was a woman of
forty; her health was poor, and she was pale and thin, but pale
and thin in a way peculiar to herself, which I have never seen in
anybody else. Her Bourbon nose, with its thin nostrils, her au-
burn hair and exquisitely delicate lips proclaimed her a lady of
birth, but one in whom pride might easily degenerate into cruelty.
Her complexion was tinged with yellow and had an unhealthy
look.

"According to Mademoiselle de Beaumont, who ransacked even
Gibbon for an epigram, if her name had been Constance, she
might have been called Constantius Chlorus.

"Anyone who understood the character of Mademoiselle de
Beaumont's wit was free to read a sinister meaning into the phrase.
Yet in spite of her pallor, in spite of the faded colour of her
lips, there was for an educated observer in those same lips of the
Comtesse de Stasseville, thin, tense and vibrant as a stretched
bow-string, an almost terrifying look of repressed eagerness and
power of will. That provincial society did not notice it. She herself saw nothing in the rigidity of that narrow, murderous-looking
lip of hers but the steel spring on which for ever danced the
barbed shaft of epigram. Eyes of bluish-green (*vert, with sparkles, or* was the cognizance the Countess bore beneath her brows,
as on her scutcheon) blazed like two fixed stars in a face they
lighted but left cold. These twin emeralds, with yellow glints, set

under the pale, arched brows, were as cold as if they had been the very jewels recovered from the belly of Polycrates' fish.

"A keen and biting wit, sharp and shining as a Damascus sword-blade, alone lighted up now and again her glassy gaze with flashes of the 'flaming sword which turned every way,' of the Book of Genesis. Women hated the Comtesse du Tremblay for her sharp tongue as much as if she had been beautiful; and indeed it *was* her beauty. Like Mademoiselle de Retz, of whom the Cardinal has left so unflattering a portrait, she had a faulty figure that ill-natured people might fairly have called deformed. Her fortune was considerable. Her husband at his death had left her with the slight responsibility of two children. One was a little boy, as stupid as an owl, at present entrusted to the paternal, but most in-effectual, care of an old Abbé, who never taught him anything; the other was her daughter Herminie, whose beauty would have excited admiration in the most critical artistic circles of Paris. She had brought her up irreproachably, from the conventional point of view; but then with Madame de Stasseville irreproachable always implied something of insolent superiority. Even her vir-tue was made a ground for the same feeling, and it may be this was her strongest, if not her only, motive for preserving it so scrupulously. Virtuous at any rate she was, her good name defy-ing scandal. No serpent's tooth of calumny had ever gnawed at that file. So her critics, bitterly resenting the impossibility of find-ing a flaw in her honour, made up for it by accusing her of cold-ness. This was due no doubt, they said (so learned and scientific were they), to an inherited anæmia. A little judicious pressure, and the best of her friends would have discovered in her the same hereditary obstacle that was invented against a very cele-brated and very charming great lady of the last century to account for the fact of her having had all the fashionable gentlemen of Europe at her knees for ten long years, without suffering one of them to advance a single inch higher."

The last words were a trifle risky, but the light tone in which they were spoken saved the situation, though they *did* occasion a slight ruffle of offended modesty. I say modesty, not prudery, for with well-bred and high-born women, who are absolutely devoid of affectation, modesty is genuine and a very charming thing to see. However the daylight was now so dim that the movement was rather felt than seen.

"Upon my word, she was just as you describe her, the Comtesse de Stasseville," observed the old Vicomte de Rassy, with his customary stammer. He had a humpback as well as a stammer, and wit enough to have been a cripple into the bargain. What Parisian does not know the Vicomte, that living *memorandum* of the little weaknesses of the eighteenth century? With a face as handsome in his young days as that of the Maréchal de Luxembourg himself, there was in his case too a reverse side of the medal —and the reverse was all that was left him now. As for the better side, it has been long ago defaced! . . . When young men found him out in some little anachronism of behaviour, he would observe that at any rate he was not dishonouring his white hairs, for he always wore a chestnut tie-wig, with a false parting down the middle, and the most preposterous and utterly indescribable side-curls.

"Ah! you knew her, then?" the speaker said, interrupting his narrative. "Very well! you can tell us, Vicomte, if I exaggerate in the least."

"Sir! 'tis as faithful as a tracing, your p—p—portrait," returned the Vicomte, hitting himself a little blow on the cheek in impatience at his stammering tongue—at the imminent risk of knocking off some of the rouge they say he wears, as he does everything, with an entire absence of shame. "I knew her p—p— pretty near the date of your story. She was in the habit of visiting Paris every winter for a few days. I used to meet her at the Princess de C—C—Courtenay's, to whom she was related in some way. Her wit was served up on ice; a woman cold enough to set you coughing!"

"Except for those four or five days spent every winter in Paris," resumed this uncompromising historian, who did not leave his characters even the half-mask of Harlequin, "the Comtesse de Stasseville's life was ruled with all the tiresome regularity of that monotonous piece of music, a respectable woman's life in the Provinces. She was buried for six months of the year in her dull town-house in the little place I have described so particularly, exchanging it during the other six for her equally dull château on a fine estate she had a dozen miles away. Every second year she used to take her daughter with her to Paris—leaving her, when she visited the capital alone, under the charge of an old aunt, Mademoiselle de Triflevas—early in the winter; but never a thought of Spa, or Plombières, or the Pyrenees! She was seen at none of the usual watering-places. Was this due to the fear of what spiteful tongues might say? In the country when an unprotected female, in Madame de Stasseville's circumstances, goes so far afield for health and amusement, what will not people imagine—what unworthy motives will they not suspect? This is the way the envy of those left behind takes toll of the pleasure of those who go travelling. The most fantastic winds of gossip breathe over these waters and disturb the placidity of their surface. Is it on the Yellow River or the Blue that they expose the infants in China? . . . Our French watering-places have some resemblance to this river, whatever its name. If not a babe, there is always something, somebody or other's good name being sacrificed there, in the opinion of the stay-at-homes.

"The sarcastic Comtesse de Tremblay was too proud to sacrifice one of her caprices in deference to public opinion. But as a matter of fact she had no great love of watering-places, while her doctor much preferred to have her near him rather than four or five hundred miles away, for at that distance coddling visits, at ten francs each, cannot well be numerous. Moreover, it was a question whether the Countess had any special caprices. Wit is not imagination; and her mind was of so clear-cut, incisive and positive a complexion, even in her least serious moods, that its nature seemed incompatible with the very idea of caprice. In moments of expansion (but these were rare), it gave out so hard a ring, like

ebony castanets or the Basque drum, all tight-stretched parchment
and little metallic bells, that you could never picture that dry,
trenchant spirit as harbouring any element of imagination, any of
those wistful reveries that rouse a longing to quit one's own place
for new surroundings. Any time during the ten years she had
been a rich widow, and therefore mistress of herself and much else,
she could easily enough have transferred her stagnant existence
elsewhere, far from this poor little nest of nobles, where her evenings were wasted at whist or boston, in the company of a lot of
old maids who had seen the Chouan rising, and aged warriors, obscure heroes who had helped to deliver Destouches.

"Like Lord Byron, she might have roamed the world with a
library, a portable kitchen and an aviary in her coach; but she
had never shown the smallest inclination that way. She was
something better than indolent, she was indifferent—as finely indifferent as Marmor de Karkoel at the whist-table. Only Marmor was not really indifferent to whist, and in *her* life there was no
whist—not a single thing to break the even tenor of her days!
Her nature was of the stagnant sort; a woman dandy, the English
would have called her. Except for her epigrams, she existed
merely as a fashionable larva. 'She belongs to the class of cold-
blooded animals,' her doctor used to whisper confidentially to his
intimates, thinking to explain her by a simile, as a disease is diag-
nosed by the symptoms.

"Though she always looked ill, the baffled doctor declared that
there was nothing the matter with her. Was this discretion? or
was he really blind? At any rate she never complained of dis-
comfort, whether physical or mental. She had not even that shade
of melancholy, as much physical as anything else, that usually
broods over the mortified features of women of forty. She knew
the secret of growing old gracefully, without unseemly struggle
and reluctance, watching the years go by with the same mocking
glance (such as Undine might have cast from her sea-green eyes)
as she had for all the circumstances of life.

"She seemed determined to falsify her reputation as a woman

of strong mind by refusing altogether to accentuate her behaviour
with any of those forms of originality we call eccentricities. She
did quite simply and naturally whatever other women in her own
circle did, neither more nor less. She was by way of demonstrat-
ing that equality, of which the common herd dream in vain, is
really only to be found amongst noblemen. There and there only
all are peers, for their birth, the four generations of nobility required to make a gentleman, level all distinctions. 'I am only the
first gentleman of France,' Henri IV used to say, by these words
subordinating the pretensions of each individual to the high status
of all. Like the other ladies of her rank, whom she was too
proud even to wish to excel, the Comtesse fulfilled all the external duties of religion and society with a quiet, sober exactitude that
is the acme of good breeding in circles where enthusiasms of any
kind are strictly barred. She neither lagged behind nor spurred on
in front of her contemporaries. Had she so far subdued her spirit
as to have finally accepted the monotonous existence of this dull
little provincial town, where the remaining vestiges of her youth
had dried up, like a stagnant pool asleep beneath its water-lilies?
The common motives of mankind for action, motives of reason,
conscience, instinct, reflection, temperament, predilection, threw
no light on hers. No glimmer from within ever revealed the woman's outward being; no outward condition ever reacted on her in-
ward nature! Tired out with waiting so long and never discovering anything about the Comtesse de Stasseville, her country
neighbours, for all their patience (and country folk when they
want to find something out, are as patient as a man in prison
planning to get out or a fisherman waiting for a bite), had finally
given up the enigma, as a man pitches a manuscript behind a box,
when he finds it impossible to decipher it.

"'I think we are very stupid,' the Comtesse de Hautcardon
had declared dogmatically one evening—and this was now several
years ago—'to make such a rumpus about discovering what's at
the bottom of the woman's soul. Most likely there's nothing there
at all.'

III

"And this ruling of the Dowager's had been accepted as final, as having all the force of law, by these good people, annoyed and disappointed as they were at the futility of their observations, and only anxious to find a satisfactory reason for putting their wits to sleep again. It was still an article of belief, idly accepted by a heedless public, at the period when Marmor de Karkoel, apparently the very last man likely to come into the Comtesse du Tremblay de Stasseville's life, arrived from the other side of the world to take his seat at the green table where a partner was needed to make up the game. He was a native, so said his guide, philosopher and friend Hartford, of the wild, mist-wrapped Shetland Isles, the scene of Sir Walter Scott's sublime tale of *The Pirate*—a character Marmor was now to reproduce as understudy, with modifications, in an obscure little town on the English Channel. He had been reared by the shores of the stormy sea furrowed by Cleveland's bark; as a youth he had footed the same dances young Mordaunt did in the story with old Irvil's daughter. These he had never forgotten, and more than once I have seen him dance them on the polished oaken floors of our little town, so incongruous in its commonplace respectability with the wild, barbaric poetry of these Northern dances. At fifteen he had been bought a Commission as Lieutenant in an English regiment under orders for India, and for a dozen years had fought in the Mahratta wars. This much was soon found out from himself and his friend Hartford, as well as the fact that he was a gentleman of birth, related to the famous Scotch family of the Douglases, *of the Bleeding Heart*.

"But this was all. The rest lay under a veil of mystery that was never to be lifted. His adventures in India, that great and terrible land where men are giants and catch a trick of deep-breasted breathing for which our Western air will not suffice, these he never told. They were traced in mysterious lettering on his dusky brow, a lid that was never lifted, like those Asiatic

poison-caskets which are guarded against the day of disaster and
defeat in the jewel-house of Indian Rajahs. They stood half revealed in the keen flash of his dark eyes, a flash he could instantly
extinguish under scrutiny, as you blow out a candle to escape being seen, no less than in the quick gesture, already described, with
which he would dash back his hair from his temples a dozen times
in succession during a rubber of whist or a game of écarté. But
apart from these hieroglyphics of gesture and physiognomy, legi-
ble enough to competent observers, and like the language of the
Egyptian hieroglyphics restricted to a very small number of words,
Marmor de Karkoel was as undecipherable in his way as was the
Comtesse du Tremblay in hers. He was a Cleveland, who never
unlocked his lips.

"All the young men of family in the place, and there were several with plenty of wit, inquisitive as women and wily as serpents, were devoured with desire to get him to reveal the unpublished memoirs of his youth over a cigarette. But they had invariably failed to draw him. This sea-lion of the Hebrides browned
by the suns of Lahore, declined to be caught in these petty snares
baited to tickle his vanity, the sort of booby-trap in which a
Frenchman's self-conceit leaves all his peacock feathers behind,
for the mere pleasure of showing off. The difficulty was insur-
mountable. He was as sober as a Turk who obeys the Koran
implicitly—a veritable mute, faithfully guarding the seraglio of
his thoughts. I never saw him drink anything stronger than water
or coffee. Card-playing certainly seemed a passion with him; but
it is open to question whether this was genuine or only assumed,
for a passion like a disease may be brought on artificially. Was
it only a kind of screen which he set up to hide his real soul behind? I could never help thinking this was so, when I saw the
way he played. He developed, cultivated, magnified the passion
for play in the amusement-loving heart of the little town, to such
a degree that, after he was gone, an atrocious spleen, the cruel
spleen of baulked infatuations, fell on it like a sirocco, making the
resemblance more striking than ever to an English city. At his

rooms the whist-table stood ready from an early hour in the morning. His day, when not spent at Vanillère or some other château of the neighbourhood, was as simply ordered as that of men consumed by one fixed idea generally is. He rose at nine, took his cup of tea with some friend who had come to play whist, which began directly afterwards, to end only at five o'clock in the afternoon. As his little parties were always crowded, players were changed after each rubber, and such as were not playing betted on the game of those who were. Then it was by no means only young men who frequented these entertainments, but the most 'reverend signors' of the place. Actually *fathers of families,* as ladies of a certain age observed, spent their days in this gambling-hell; and you may be sure they never let an occasion slip of attributing every possible evil motive to the objectionable Scotchman, and emptying many a phial of gall over his unhappy head, as if he had inoculated the whole country-side with a pestilence in the persons of their husbands. This, though they were quite well used to seeing them play, but never before with this degree of persistent infatuation.

"Towards five o'clock the party would break up, only to reassemble later in the evening at some social gathering. There they would to all appearances conform to the ordinary style of play, such was approved by the hostesses of the houses they frequented, but in reality only to play out surreptitiously the morning's match at what they called 'Karkoel's game.' I leave you to imagine to what a high level of play these enthusiasts attained, seeing this was now become the one and only thing they gave their minds to. They brought their whist to the height of the most difficult and superbly scientific fencing. No doubt considerable losses occurred sometimes; but what prevented anything in the way of catastrophe and ruin, such as high play invariably brings in its trail, was just this—the persistent eagerness and superior skill the players brought to bear. All the different factors ended by cancelling each other; besides, in so narrow a field, partners were necessarily so often interchanged that after a certain time every player was bound, to use the technical phrase, to 'have his revenge.'

"The influence Marmor de Karkoel exercised, an influence right-thinking women abhorred and secretly manœuvred against, far from diminishing, only increased the more. Nor was this to be wondered at. It owed its origin not so much to Marmor's own strong personality as to the existence of a passion for play already flourishing in the soil on his arrival, but which his presence, sharing it and sympathizing with it as he did, roused into far greater activity. The best, perhaps the only means, of governing men, is to rule them through their passions. How, then, could Karkoel have missed his ascendancy? He possessed the main element of the power of governments, and yet he had no ambition to govern. All this enabled him positively to bewitch his willing subjects, and they almost fought for his society. The whole time he remained in the place, he invariably received the same welcome, and the most pressing, feverishly pressing, invitations. The very women who feared him would rather see him at their houses than know their sons or their husbands to be at his, and were always ready to receive him, as women will receive, even against their own inclination, a man who is the centre of attention, the nucleus of interest and action, no matter of what sort.

"In summer, he would go for a fortnight or a month to the country. The Marquis de Saint Albans had made him the object of his special admiration—protection, I was going to say, but that is not a strong enough word. There, as in town, the whist-playing never ceased. I remember being present (I was a school-boy home for the holidays at the time) at a salmon fishing-party, where the company and the sport were both of the best, in the crystal waters of the Douve, and from beginning to end Marmor de Karkoel sat in a boat playing double dummy with a gentleman of the neighbourhood. He would have gone on playing, I verily believe, if the boat had upset and he had been tumbled into the river! . . .

"One member only of this society, and that one a woman, never

invited the Scotchman to her house in the country, and very seldom
to her entertainments in town. This was the Comtesse du Tremblay. And who could wonder at it? She was a widow with a
young and charming daughter. In the petty society of a country
town, so full of envy and narrow-mindedness, and where it is
everyone's business to poke into other people's affairs, too many
precautions cannot be taken to guard against those ill-natured in-
ferences from the known to the unknown which are so easy to
draw. The Comtesse du Tremblay was duly cautious, never once
asking Marmor to the Château de Stasseville, and in town only
receiving him on the most public occasions, when she gathered all
her acquaintances around her. Her manner towards him was
cold, polite and formal, expressing merely the consideration a well-
bred person owes to everyone, not so much for their sake as for
one's own. He responded with the same kind of impersonal politeness; and so natural was this to both, so little a matter of
affectation, that it aroused no suspicion for four years.

"Away from the card-table, as I have already mentioned, Ker-
koel could scarcely be said to have any separate existence, and
rarely opened his mouth. This habitual silence, if he had anything to conceal, formed an excellent screen for the purpose. On
the other hand, the Comtesse, you may remember, was anything
but secretive, and only too ready to express her true sentiments
in some biting phrase. For natures of this kind, expansive, brilliant, aggressive, as they are, self-restraint, self-effacement is always difficult. To hide one's true character, is this not, in a way,
to betray oneself? But then, if she had the fascinating, iridescent
scales and triple tongue of the serpent, she had the cunning too.
There was nothing therefore to modify the usual savage impetu-
osity of her witty onslaughts. Often, when Karkoel was mentioned in her presence, she would fire off one of those phrases that
sting and wound, and which turned Mademoiselle de Beaumont,
her rival in the gentle art of epigram, green with envy. Was it
only another piece of deception?—if so, never was deception better
and bolder! Was this terrible power of dissimulation an integral

part of her dry, warped character? But then, why practise it at all? for was she not the very personification of independence by virtue of her position and proud, sarcastic nature? Why, if she loved the man, and her love was returned, why hide it beneath the cruel gibes she cast at him from time to time, under witticisms, the traitorous, renegade, impious witticisms, that depreciate and degrade the adored image, the vilest sacrilege in love?

"Who can tell? it may be she found some source of happiness in it all. . . . Now, looking at her"—the narrator turned to Doctor Beylasset, who stood leaning one elbow on a Buhl cabinet, and whose fine bald brow reflected back the light of a candelabra the servants had lighted a moment before above his head—"looking at the Comtesse de Stasseville from the sound commonplace *physiological* point of view—as you doctors do, an example our moralists might follow with advantage—you could not help seeing quite plainly that, in this impressionable nature, everything was bound to strike home, to penetrate inwards, like the line of faded rose traced by the strongly retracted lips, like the stiff, unquivering nostrils, that narrowed under excitement instead of dilating, like the eyes, so deeply sunk within their orbits that they seemed sometimes to be retreating backwards into the brain altogether. In spite of her apparent delicacy of constitution and a physical weakness whose effects could be traced through her whole being like the gradual spreading of a crack in a substance splitting from excess of dryness, she bore the most unmistakable signs of a strong will, the Volta battery within us which is the centre of our nerves. Everything about her testified to this more strikingly than in any other living being I have ever seen. This flux and reflux of slumbering will-power, of *potential* energy (forgive the pedantry of the expression), was manifested even in her hands, aristocratic and princely in their whiteness, the opalescent smoothness of the nails, and their general elegance, but which, in their extreme leanness, the complication of swollen veins that marked them with a thousand corded blue lines, and above all, the nervous, furtive way they had of grasping things, resembled those harpy claws which

classic poetry, with its exuberance of fantastic imagery, attributes
to certain fabulous monsters with women's faces and bosoms.
When, after darting out one of her sayings, one of her shafts of
sarcasm, as keen and glittering as the poisoned arrows of the savages, she passed her viperish tongue over her sibilant lips, you
felt instinctively that in a supreme emergency, some fatal moment
of destiny, the woman, at once so frail and so strong, would be
quite capable of adopting the Negro's resource of resolutely swal-
lowing that lambent tongue.   To look at her was to be convinced
she was, among womankind, an example of those organisms to be
found in every domain of nature which, by predilection or instinct,
look to the bottom rather than to the surface of things; one of
those beings predestined for occult associations, plunging into the
depths of life as bold swimmers dive deep, and swim beneath the
surface, or as miners breathe the air of subterranean vaults.   Such
creatures love mystery for its own sake, and out of the very pro-
fundity of their nature, create it around them, loving and pursuing
it even to the extent of downright deception—for, after all, what is
deception but a doubling of mystery, a further darkening of the
curtains of secrecy, a weaving about them of wilful darkness?
It may well be such natures love deception for deception's sake, as
others love art for art's sake, or as the Poles love battle."   Here
the Doctor gravely nodded his head in sign of agreement.   "You
think so! well! so do I.   I am convinced there are souls whose
happiness consists in imposture.   These find a hateful, but intoxicating, bliss in the very notion of falsehood and deceit, in the
thought that *they alone know their true selves,* and they are playing off a Comedy of Errors upon society, reimbursing themselves
for the expense of representation with all the fine contempt they
feel for their poor dupes."

"But what you're saying now is simply atrocious!" suddenly
exclaimed the Baronne de Mascranny, interrupting, in the tone of
one whose belief in her fellow-creatures is scandalized.

Every woman in his audience (and very possibly some amateurs of secret pleasures were amongst the number) had expe-

rienced a certain thrill at the speaker's last words. I knew it by
the Comtesse de Damnaglio's naked back, which at the minute was
in such close proximity to my eyes. The particular sort of nervous thrill I mean is familiar to everybody by experience. It is
sometimes poetically called *the Angel of Death going by.* Was
it this time perhaps the Spirit of Truth going by? . . .

"Why, yes!" returned the narrator, "atrocious enough, no doubt!
Only, is it true? People who *wear their hearts on their sleeve,*
as people say, can form no notion of the furtive joys of systematic
hypocrisy, the solitary gratifications of such as live and breathe
without difficulty under the confinement of a mask. But, if you
come to think of it, it is easy to understand how the satisfactions
they enjoy have actually all the deep intensity of hell's fiery delights. For what *is* hell but a heaven reversed, below instead of
above? The two words *devilish* and *divine,* when applied to ex-
tremes of enjoyment, express one and the same idea, *viz.,* sensations that overpass the bounds of nature and reach the supernatural. Was Madame de Stasseville one of these strange souls?
I would rather not say either yes or no! All I propose to do is
to give her story to the best of my ability. No one really knows
the rights of it, and my only object is to throw what light I may
on the mysterious tale by a naturalistic study of her personality,
such as Cuvier bestowed on the subjects of his science. This and
nothing more.

"I can picture the Comtesse du Tremblay now from memory, in
which her image in all its details stands out as clearly and distinct
as the deep-cut lines of an onyx seal impressed on wax; but such
analysis was far beyond me at the time. If I have read her character aright, this was only possible afterwards. . . . The over-
mastering will-power I recognized in her on mature reflection, when
experience had taught me how truly the body is the mould of the
soul, had as yet no more stirred and widened her narrow life, shut
in between her placid habits, than the ocean-wave disturbs some
Highland sea-loch, close shut in by its environing hills. But for
the arrival of Karkoel, the English infantry officer his countrymen

had sent to eat out his life on half-pay in this petty Norman town, the dull respectablity of which made it worthy to be English, this pale and ailing woman with the mocking tongue, she whom some called the *Lady of the Frost,* in playful derision at her coldness, would never even herself have come to know the imperious will that lay within her bosom of melted snow as Mademoiselle Ernestine de Beaumont called it. On its glassy surface, hard-ribbed as polar ice, no moral scruple availed to make the smallest permanent impression.

"What was the immediate effect of his coming? Did she instantly learn the secret that, for a nature such as hers, to feel strongly is to will inexorably? Did she, by sheer exercise of will, draw to her side a man who seemed to have no passion left for anything but cards? . . . How did she contrive an intimacy, in this country town where the risks of discovery were so many? . . . Mysteries all—and mysteries still. But at the latter end of 182 . . , for all the suspicions arrived later on, no living soul entertained a thought of anything wrong. Yet at that very moment, in one of the most peaceful-looking mansions in the whole town, where whist was the great event of every day, and I had almost said every night, behind the silent shutters and embroidered muslin curtains, the chaste, elegant, half-dropped veils of a quiet life, there must have been developing a tragic romance the world would have sworn to be utterly impossible. Yes! romance was there, in that correct, irreproachable, well-regulated life, a life cold and cynical to a fault, where intellect scorned to count for everything, and soul for nothing, gnawing, under all this outside show of ultra-respectability and good repute, gnawing at its vitals, like worms that have begun to devour a man's body before the breath was out of it."

"Oh! the horrid simile!" again interrupted the Baronne de Mascranny. "My poor Sibyl was partly right in not wishing to hear your story. Your imagination has surely run away with you to-night."

"Shall I stop?" responded the other politely, but with the sly

look and teasing manner of a man who is sure of the interest he
has aroused.

"The idea!" cried the Baronne to this proposal; "as if you *could*
leave off now in the middle of a half-told tale, with us all on the
tiptoe of expectation!"

"That would be too great a strain!" put in Mademoiselle Laure
d'Alzanne, looking as she sat there unwinding one of her fine dark
ringlets in her fingers, the very image of happy idleness, startled
into a graceful protest by the threatened interruption of her quiet
enjoyment of the narrative.

"And most disappointing!" added the Doctor with a laugh.
"Just as if a barber, after shaving one side of your face, were
quietly to shut his razor and tell you he could not possibly do
anything more." . . .

"Well, then! to proceed," resumed the narrator, with the fine
directness of the art that conceals art; "In 182 . . . I was
in the drawing-room of one of my uncles, who was mayor
of the little town which I have described to you as so unlikely a scene for anything like passion or adventure. Although it was a solemn occasion, the *Fête du Roi*, kept on Saint
Louis's Day, and always highly honoured by these aristocrats,
these political quietists who had devised that mystic phrase of
disinterested loyalty, 'No matter what, long live the King!'—still
nothing more was going on in the rooms than what took place
there every day of the week. In other words, the company were
at cards.

"I must ask your pardon for talking about myself; it is bad
taste, but necessary for once. I was still in my teens; but thanks
to an exceptional upbringing, I had more of an inkling of the
secrets of life and love than is generally possessed by lads
of my age then. I was less like a great awkward school-
boy, whose eyes have never looked on anything outside his
text-books, than an inquisitive girl, one of the sort who educate
themselves by listening at keyholes and pondering for hours over
what they have picked up there. The whole town crowded that

evening to my uncle's house, and as always happened—all things were eternal in their sameness in this world of mummies, who only shook loose their wrappings to wield the cards—the company was divided into two sections, those who played and the young ladies who did not. Mummies, too, the poor girls whose only destiny was to take their niche one after another in the catacombs of old-maidenhood, but whose faces, sparkling with ineffectual vitality and breathing a freshness no man would ever enjoy, fascinated my eager gaze.

"Among them all, there was perhaps only one, Mademoiselle Herminie de Stasseville, whose position allowed her to think for a moment of a love-match as anything else than a miracle, impossible of realization without derogation from their proper rank. I was not old enough, or else I was too old, to mingle with this bevy of young beauties, whose whisperings were every now and again interrupted by a frank peal of laughter, a pretty, half-stifled giggle. A prey to a boy's hot self-consciousness, at once a delight and a torment to him, I had taken refuge in a seat near the *God of Tricks,* Marmor de Karkoel, whose fervent admirer I was. Friendship of course was out of the question between us. But sentiment has its secret hierarchy, and it is no uncommon thing to see, in undeveloped natures, occult sympathies existing that nothing definite or demonstrable will account for. Children, like savages, who are only grown-up children, must have a chief to reverence; and Karkoel was my chief.

"He used often to visit at my father's house, a great whist-player like all the men of his circle. Moreover, he had frequently taken part in our athletic recreations, in which he had displayed before my brothers and myself a strength and activity that bordered on the marvellous. Like the Duc d'Enghien, he could clear a seventeen-foot brook and think nothing of it. This alone was bound to exercise an immense fascination over lads like ourselves, who were being brought up to be soldiers; but this was not the mysterious magnet that drew me so irresistibly to the man. It must surely have been that his personality acted on my imagination with all the force exceptional beings exert over others equally exceptional—for a commonplace nature is always a safeguard against higher influences, exactly as a bag of wool serves to stop cannon-balls. I cannot tell what wild dreams were suggested to my fancy by that brow, modelled, you would have said, in the substance water-colour painters call Sienna earth, by those sinister eyes under their narrow lids, by the marks unknown storms of passion had left behind them on the Scotchman's frame like the four bludgeon-strokes of the hangman on a criminal at the wheel. What fascinated me most of all, however, was his hands, in which all signs of savage strength ended at the wrist, and which could deal round the cards with that astounding rapidity that was like a revolving flame and had so impressed Herminie de Stasseville the first time she saw it.

"Well, to-night in the corner where the whist-table stood, the Venetian shutter was half closed, and the players looked as sombre as the sort of half-light that surrounded them. It was a champions' game. The Methuselah of Marquises, Monsieur de Saint Albans, was Marmor's partner, while the Comtesse du Tremblay had for hers the Chevalier de Tharsis, an officer in the Regiment of Provence before the Revolution and a Knight of Saint Louis, one of those veterans who are now extinct, who stood astride of two centuries, so to speak, yet had nothing of the Colossus about them for all that. At one particular moment of the game, in consequence of a movement of Madame du Tremblay's hands to pick up her cards from the table, one of the diamonds that sparkled on her finger, caught in the shadow which the darkened window threw over the green table, making it a heavier green than ever, a sudden glint of light, which, meeting the facets of the stone at some subtle angle no human art is cunning enough to repeat, threw out an electric shaft of white brilliancy so dazzling it almost hurt the eyes like a flash of lightning.

" 'Eh, what! what is it flashes so?' shrilled the Chevalier de Tharsis in a voice thin as his legs.

" 'And who is it coughs so?' chimed in the Marquis de Saint-

Albans simultaneously, disturbed in his wrapped attention to the game by a dreadful, hollow cough, and turning towards Herminie, who was working an embroidered collar for her mother.

" 'My diamond, and my daughter,' responded the Comtesse du Tremblay, a smile on her thin lips, answering both inquiries at once.

" 'How superb your diamond is, Madame!' exclaimed the Chevalier. 'I have never seen it shine so brilliantly as it does to-night; it would force the blindest to notice it.'

"As he said this, they finished the game, and the Chevalier de Tharsis took the Comtesse's hand in his own, with the words, 'Will you let me look?'

"The Comtesse languidly removed her ring, and threw it over to the Chevalier on the card-table.

"The old nobleman examined it with interest, turning it about like a kaleidoscope. But light is often tricky and capricious, and fall as it might on the facets of the stone, it struck out no second flash and sparkle to compare with the sudden, startling gleam of a moment ago.

"Herminie got up and went to the window to push open the shutter, that the daylight might fall better on her mother's ring and bring out its full beauty.

"This done, she resumed her seat and, resting her elbow on the table, fixed her eyes also on the prismatic jewel; but another fit of coughing seized her, a terrible, whistling cough that injected the pearly white of her fine eyes with blood, reddening the normal purity of their pellucid depths.

" 'And where *did* you get that fearful cough, my dear?' asked the Marquis de Saint-Albans, more taken up with the girl than the ring, with the human than the mineral jewel.

" 'I don't know, really,' she answered lightly with the heedlessness of youth, that cannot realize that life is not eternal. 'Perhaps it was walking in the night air by the lake in the park at Stasseville.'

"I was struck at the time by the group the four of them made.

"The red light of the setting sun beat in at the open window. The Chevalier de Tharsis was looking at the diamond; Monsieur de Saint-Albans at Herminie, Madame du Tremblay at Karkoel, who himself was turning a lack-lustre eye on the Queen of Diamonds he held in his hand. But what impressed me most was Herminie. The *Rose of Stasseville* was pale, actually paler than her mother. The purple of the dying day, throwing its transparent reflection over her pallid cheeks, gave her all the look of some doomed victim, the face reflected in a mirror silvered, so it seemed, with blood instead of quicksilver.

"Of a sudden a shiver ran through my nerves, and a lightning-flash of memory startled me with the invincible brutality of those ideas which violate one's mind but fecundate it.

"About a fortnight before, I had gone one morning to Marmor de Karkoel's rooms. It was quite early, and I had found him alone. None of the enthusiasts that came every forenoon to play cards with him had yet arrived. When I entered, he was standing before his writing-desk, engaged apparently in some very delicate operation, requiring extreme attention and great steadiness of hand. His head was bent over his work, so that I could not see his face. In his right hand he held between his fingers a tiny phial of some black, shiny substances (it looked just like the tip of a broken dagger), and from this microscopical phial he was pouring some mysterious liquid into the cavity of a ring.

" 'What on earth are you after there?' I called out to him, coming forward. But he cried in a voice of command: 'Stop where you are! not a step nearer, or you'll make my hand shake, and what I am doing now is more difficult, and far more dangerous, than to break a corkscrew at forty paces with a pistol liable to burst at any moment.'

"He was alluding to a little adventure we had had a while before. We were amusing ourselves by shooting with the worst pistols we could possibly get hold of, so that the marksman's skill might be brought out in a stronger light by the very imperfection of his weapon, and we had precious nearly blown our brains out with one that burst its barrel. . . .

"He succeeded in insinuating a few drops of the unknown liquid into the hollow ring, letting them fall one by one from the pointed tip of the phial. This done, he shut the ring carefully, and tossed it into one of the drawers of his writing-desk as if desirous of hiding it from inspection.

"I then noticed he wore a glass mask.

" 'Since when,' I said in a rallying tone, 'since when have you been dabbling in chemistry? Are you compounding a specific against losing at whist?'

" 'No! I'm compounding nothing,' he replied; 'but what's inside there [pointing to the black phial] is a specific against all the ills of life'—adding with the grim humour of the land of suicides from which he hailed: 'It is the sharper's pack that insures a man against losing his last rubber with Destiny.'

" 'And what poison is it?' I asked him, taking up the phial, the shape of which roused my curiosity.

" 'The most exquisite of all the Indian poisons,' he returned, removing his mask. 'To breathe it is very often death, and, no matter how absorbed into the system, there is no need whatever to be anxious, even if it does not kill right off. You lose nothing by the delay, for its effect is as sure as it is secret; it attacks, slowly indeed, almost languidly, but still infallibly the very sources of life itself, striking inwards and developing deep down in the organs it assails, some disease of the kind everybody is familiar with and the symptoms of which are so well known to physicians that they would quite disarm suspicion and be a sufficient answer to any accusation of poisoning, even supposing such a charge at all likely to be made. They say in India the mendicant fakirs compound the drug with substances of an extreme rarity, known to themselves alone and found only in the remote highlands of Tibet. Its action is rather to dissolve away the cords of life. In this it only conforms to the Indian character, so gentle and apathetic, to which death is but slumber, and a death-bed a soft and restful couch of lotus. It is excessively difficult, in fact next door to impossible, to procure. If you only knew all the risks I ran to get this phial from a woman who professed to love me. . . . I have a friend, an officer like myself in the English service, and like me now home from India, where he has spent seven years of his life. He sought this poison with all the frenzied energy of an Englishman's caprice—and some day, when you have lived longer, you will understand what that is. Well! he could never find the real thing, though he bought more than once wretched imitations at more than their weight in gold. In despair he has lately written to me from England, enclosing me one of his rings and praying me to put into it some drops of this elixir of death. And that is what I was doing, when you came in.'

"What he told me caused me little surprise. Men are so constituted that, without any evil intention or one thought of ill, they take a pleasure in having poison by them, as they do any other deadly weapon. They hoard the means of spreading death and destruction around them, as misers hoard gold. They say to themselves: 'If I *should* wish to kill!' just as the others say: 'If I *should* wish to spend!' The same childish fancy dominates both. I was no more than a child myself at the time, and I found it nothing out of the way that Marmor de Karkoel, the Anglo-Indian, should possess this strange, unique, exotic poison, and among the kandjars and native arrows he had brought from foreign parts in his soldier's chest, should have this phial of black agate, this plaything of death and devastation, to show me. When I had sufficiently turned and twisted about in my fingers the pretty polished toy, that perhaps some dancing-girl had worn suspended between the tiny topaz globes of her bosom, and impregnated its porous substance with the golden sweat of her body, I dropped it into a cup standing on the chimney-piece, and thought no more about the matter.

"Well! you will hardly credit it, but it was the recollection of this very phial that now flashed across my mind! . . . Herminie's

look of suffering, her pallor and the hacking cough that seemed
to issue from lungs all flaccid and spongy with disease, through
whose substance perhaps some of those deep and health-destroy-
ing lesions were even now eating their way, that are known to
medicine—am I not right, Doctor?—under the terribly picturesque
name of *caverns,* the ring which by a strange coincidence suddenly darted out so extraordinary a gleam of vivid brilliance just
as the girl was seized with her fit of coughing, as if the flash of
the fatal stone had been the murderer's start of triumph, the incidents of my morning visit, which had till then entirely slipped
my memory but were now instantly revived in perfect clearness—
all this came rushing in a flood of troublous thought into my
head! But yet between the past and present what real connection could I find? The inference I had drawn involuntarily in
my own mind was manifestly absurd. I was horrified at my
atrocious thoughts and endeavoured to crush them down—to extinguish this misleading dream, this *ignis fatuus* of suspicion, that
had flared up in my brain like the flash of the Countess's diamond
across the green table! . . . To steady my wits, and be done
once and for all with the silly, wicked notion I had for a moment
allowed myself to entertain, I turned a scrutinizing eye on Marmor de Karkoel and the Comtesse du Tremblay.

"Their whole attitude and look gave but one answer—the thing
I had dared to fancy was preposterous! There stood Marmor
the same as ever, his eyes still gazing at his Queen of Diamonds,
as if she, and she only, represented the fixed and final passion of
his life. Madame du Tremblay on her part wore in brow and
lips and countenance the calmness that never deserted her—not
even when she was aiming an epigram, for her sarcasm was like
a bullet, the only instrument of death that kills without a stir of
passion, whereas the sword partakes of the anger and excitement
of the hand that wields it. They were two abysses, face to face;
but while Karkoel was dark and black as night, the other, the
pale-eyed Madame du Tremblay, was clear and inscrutable as
space itself. She held her glittering eyes fixed on her partner

with an indifferent, impassive gaze. But as the Chevalier de
Tharsis seemed as though he would never have done with the
examination of the ring, that enclosed the mystery I so longed
to penetrate, she had taken from her belt a big bouquet of mignonette, and began to inhale its fragrance with an intensity of
sensual satisfaction no one would ever have expected from a
woman so little formed apparently for dreamy delights of any
kind. Presently her steady eyes swerved and dropped under the
stress of some mysterious languorous impulse and the lids closed,
and seizing in her thin colourless lips some stalks of the fragrant
mignonette with a passionate avidity, she gnawed them between
her teeth, her eyes once more wide open, and fixed on Karkoel's
face with a wild look of almost idolatrous self-surrender. Was
it a signal, a token, a something agreed upon between two lovers,
this gnawing and chewing the flowers without a word? . . .
Frankly, I thought it was. She tranquilly restored the ring to
its place on her finger when at last the Chevalier had done admiring it, and the game went on again, discreet, silent and sombre,
as if nothing had interrupted it."

At this point the speaker made yet another pause. Indeed,
there was no need for him to hurry; he held us all spellbound by
his tale. It may be the whole merit of the story lay in his manner of telling it. . . . When the voice stopped, you could plainly
hear the audience breathing in the silence that ensued. With my
own eyes, peeping over my alabaster screen, the Comtesse de
Damnaglia's shoulder, I could discern the marks of excited interest
stamped on every face, though in various degrees and variously
expressed. Involuntarily I looked round for Sibyl to see how she
took it, she who had raised her childish protest at the very start of
the narrative. I should have liked to watch the horror grow and
gleam in her dark eyes—that make you think of the gloomy,
sinister Canal Orfano at Venice, for indeed more hearts than one
will some day drown in their depths. But she was no longer at
her mother's sofa. Uncertain how the tale would end, the care-

ful Baronne had doubtless given her some private signal to slip away unseen, and she had left the room.

"As a matter of fact," the narrator went on again, "what was there after all in anything I had seen to move me so strongly and eat like an acid into the tablets of my memory, for time has not even now effaced a single outline of the scene? I can still see Marmor de Karkoel's face, and the Comtesse's look of stony calm, melting for one emotional instant, when the scent of mignonette was inhaled and the poor flowers were ground between her teeth with something very like a shiver of voluptuous satisfaction.

All this has remained clear-cut in my memory, and I will tell you why. These circumstances, the mutual connection of which I could not then properly understand, half revealed as they were by an intuition I blamed myself for harbouring, a tangled skein of the possible and impossible, the comprehensible and the incomprehensible, received subsequently a spark of light which dissipated their obscurity once for all and brought order out of the chaos of my mind.

"As I think I have already told you, I was sent to college very late. The last two years of my education passed without my coming home at all. Accordingly it was at college I first heard, through letters from my relatives, of Mademoiselle Herminie de Stasseville's death, who had succumbed, they told me, to a wasting disease no one had thought serious till the very end, when cure had become hopeless. The news, which they told me without commentary of any kind, froze my blood with the same chill of horror I had before experienced in my uncle's drawing-room when I first heard that churchyard cough, which had suddenly roused such fearful suspicions in my mind. Any who can enter into the more sacred feelings of the soul will understand me when I say I had not the heart to ask a single question as to the poor girl's death, thus snatched away from her mother's love and life's brightest hopes. My thoughts on the subject were too tragic for me to speak of it to any living being.

"On returning to my father's house later on, I found the town
of —— much altered; for in the course of years towns alter as
much as women, and grow quite unrecognizable. 1830 was past
and over. Since the day when Charles X had passed through the
place on his way to take ship at Cherbourg, the greater part of
the noble families I had known during my boyhood lived in retirement in the surrounding country-houses. The political catastrophe had hit these families the harder from the fact of their
having fully expected their party to be victorious, so that they
now felt all the bitterness of disappointed hopes. In fact, they
had witnessed the moment when the right of primogeniture, restored by the only veritable statesman the Restoration could show,
was to re-establish French society on the only true basis, that of
a great and vigorous monarchy; then by a sudden and unexpected
turn of fortune, they had seen this cherished idea, no less ex-
pedient than it was just, an idea that had flattered the eyes of
these gallant dupes of their own loyal enthusiasm, and had
seemed to offer them a recompense for all their ruin and misfortunes, to give them a last rag of vair and ermine to line their
coffin withal and make their last sleep less hard—they had seen
this idea perish under the stress of public opinion that had proved
itself alike impervious to enlightenment and intractable to discipline. The little town so often referred to in my story had become a mere desert of closed shutters and barred gates. The
Revolution of July had frightened away the English from a town
the habits and customs of which had been so rudely broken in
upon by the force of events.

"My first care was to inquire what had become of Monsieur
Marmor de Karkoel. I was told he had gone back to India by
order of his government. The individual who gave me this information was no other than the same Chevalier de Tharsis, who
did not look a day older. He had been one of the players on the
occasion made memorable—at any rate to me—by the incident of
the diamond ring, and his eye, as he replied, fixed mine with all
the look of a man who is eager and anxious to be questioned.

Almost before I knew it (so quick are men to divine the work-ings of each other's minds, long before the will has had time to act), I found myself asking him the question:

"'And Madame du Tremblay de Stasseville, what of her?'

"'You have heard something?' he cried with an air of mystery, as if we had a hundred pairs of ears round us to hear all we said, instead of being entirely alone, as was the case.

"'Oh, no!' I answered; 'I know nothing.'

"'She is dead,' he then told me; 'dead of a chest complaint, like her daughter. She died a month after that infernal Marmor de Karkoel left the town.'

"'What has that to do with it?' I could not help interrupting him; 'and why mention Marmor de Karkoel's name at all?' . . .

"'It is really true, then, you knew nothing whatever about it!' exclaimed the old man. 'Well, then! my good sir, it appears she was his mistress. At least so it was said, when the affair was dis-cussed at the time in whispers. Now no one dares so much as mention it. But she was a hypocrite of the first water, was your Comtesse! I tell you she was born so, as a woman is born blonde or brunette. Falsehood she raised to a fine art, till it was indistinguishable from truth, so simple and natural was she through it all, so absolutely without effort or affectation of any kind. Her skill in deceiving was so masterly, nobody till quite lately even suspected deception was at work at all—and yet some rumours did leak out, that were promptly hushed up for fear of the very horror they excited. . . . According to these, the Scotch-man, whose sole passion seemed to be card-playing, was not only the lover of the Comtesse, who never received him at her house as everybody else did, and when occasion offered never failed to scarify him with her cruel shafts of epigram, reserving her most impish sarcasm for him in preference to any of her acquaintances. . . . He was her lover, yes; but that was not all! there was some-thing worse behind. The *God of Tricks*, it was darkly whispered, had *tricked* mother and daughter both! The unhappy child Her-minie adored him with a deadly, silent infatuation. Mademoiselle

Ernestine de Beaumont will tell you so, if you ask her. It was a fatality. Did he really love the girl? Did he love the mother? Did he love both? Did he love neither? Did he perhaps only find the mother useful to cloak the game he was playing with the other? . . . Who can tell? this part of the tale is wrapped in mystery. The one thing certain is that the mother, as harsh and hard of soul as of body, conceived a hatred for her daughter that contributed not a little to hasten her untimely death.'

" 'They say that!' I interrupted, more dismayed at my suspicions having proved well founded than I should if they had been entirely unjustified; 'but who can really know? . . . Karkoel was no idle talker to boast of his successes. He was not the man to babble secrets. Nothing could ever be drawn from him about his former life; 'was he likely to have suddenly grown talkative and told all the world of his relations with the Comtesse du Tremblay?'

" 'Certainly not!' replied the Chevalier de Tharsis emphatically; 'they made a pair, the two hypocrites. He went as he came, without giving any of us grounds for saying he was anything but a devoted whist-player. But, perfect as was the Comtesse's discretion, irreproachable the exterior she presented to the world, her maids, in whose eyes no mistress is a heroine, related how she would shut herself up alone with poor Herminie and how, after long hours alone together, they would come out each paler than the other, but the daughter always the more tearful and red-eyed of the two.'

" 'You know no other details, nothing certain, then?' I said, to make him talk and so get more light on these obscurities. 'Yet you know as well as I do what servants' gossip amounts to. . . . We should probably learn more from Mademoiselle de Beaumont.'

" 'Mademoiselle de Beaumont!' cried Tharsis. 'Ah! there was no love lost between those two, the Comtesse and Mademoiselle de Beaumont! they hated each other, because each had the same biting tongue! The survivor you will find never mentions the dead woman but with eyes of menace and a treacherous implication of knowing more than she cares to tell. There can be no doubt she takes a pleasure in insinuating the most abominable atrocities . . . but only really knows of one—and that can hardly be called atrocious—poor Herminie's love for Karkoel.'

" 'And that is not knowing much, Chevalier,' I broke in. 'If we could hear all the secrets young girls tell each other in confidence, we should conclude every child that dreams vaguely of a lover to be head and ears in love. Now you will admit that a man like Karkoel was just the sort of romantic figure to set a girl dreaming.'

" 'True enough!' returned the old Chevalier; 'but we have something more than girls' confidential chatter to go upon. You will remember . . . but no! you were too young at the time! anyhow, it was much remarked upon in our little society . . . that Madame de Stasseville, who had never shown much preference before for anything and certainly not for flowers especially (indeed I defy you or any man to say what the woman's predilections were), began towards the end of life to wear a bouquet of mignonette constantly at her belt, and at the whist-table and indeed on all occasions, was in the habit of breaking off the stalks and chewing them. In fact one fine day Mademoiselle de Beaumont actually asked Herminie, with a tinkling note of mockery in the tone of her voice, how long her mother had been a herbivorous animal. . . .'

" 'Oh, yes! I remember perfectly,' I answered. And truly I had never forgotten the wild-beast way, at once amorous and cruel-looking, in which the Countess had inhaled the fragrance of her bouquet and chewed the flowers during that game of whist which had played so large a part in my boyish recollections.

" 'Well! you must know,' the old fellow went on, 'the mignonette came from a magnificent flower-stand Madame de Stasseville had in her drawing-room. The time was quite gone by when strong scents had made her ill. We had seen the day when she could not bear them and after the last confinement, when she had been nearly killed, she used to tell us in a languid voice, with a bunch of tuberoses. Nowadays she delighted in them with an almost passionate ardour. Her drawing-room was almost as stifling as a conservatory when the windows have been kept down till midday. Indeed two or three delicate ladies of her acquaintance left off visiting her for no other reason. It was a great and sudden change; but it was set down to sickness and nerves. After her death, when the room had to be dismantled—for her son's guardian soon marched off that young scamp, who by the way is as rich as a fool of his sort has every right to be, to a boarding-school—the mignonette was transplanted to the open air, and they found buried beneath the roots, what do you think? . . . the corpse of a baby, that had been born alive. . . .' "

The narrative was cut short at this point by a perfectly genuine cry of horror from two or three of the women present, albeit they were barely on speaking terms as a rule with the simpler and more natural emotions. For many a long day these had been quite out of their line; but I tell you, they had their revenge for once! The rest showed more self-control, and only gave an almost convulsive start.

"A pretty fix, and a pretty fixture!" put in the Baron de Gourdes at this moment, with his usual flippancy, an amiable little rascal, known among his friends as "The last of the Barons"—one of those people who poke fun at every mortal thing, and would crack a joke behind a coffin, or even inside one.

"Where did the infant come from?" added the Chevalier de Tharsis, kneading the contents of his tortoise-shell snuff-box. "Whose child was it? Did it die a natural death? Had it been murdered? Who was the murderer? . . . Questions all equally unanswerable, but giving rise to all sorts of abominable conjectures exchanged in awestruck whispers."

"You are right, Chevalier! they are unanswerable," I responded, more than ever determined to bury within my own bosom any more complete knowledge I believed myself to possess. "It will always remain a mystery—and may it grow more and more impenetrable till the day when it shall be utterly and entirely forgotten."

"As a matter of fact," he returned, "there are but two living creatures in all the world who really know the facts, and," he added with a sly smile, "it is highly improbable either of these will make them public. One is our friend Marmor de Karkoel, now gone back to the East Indies, his chest stuffed with the gold he has won of us. We shall never see *him* any more. The other . . .

"What other?" I asked in astonishment.

"What other?" he resumed, with what he intended for a wink of Machiavellian cunning; "we have still less to fear from the other. This is the Countess's Father Confessor. You know, fat Abbé de Trudaine—who, by the by, has just been nominated for the See of Bayeux."

"Chevalier," I broke in, struck by a thought which threw more light than anything else on the woman's nature, which I now felt convinced was originally secretive rather than hypocritical, as a purblind observer like the Chevalier de Tharsis called her, merely because she had thrown the screen of a strong will over the indulgence of her passions, perhaps to double by that means the stormy satisfactions she enjoyed, "Chevalier, you are mistaken. The approval of death never broke down the wall of reserve that barred in that stern spirit, better worthy of sixteenth-century Italy than of our puny modern days. I tell you the Comtesse de Stasseville died as she had lived. The voice of the priest beat in vain against the granite of her resolution, and she carried her secret with her to the grave. If a death-bed repentance had indeed led her to entrust it to the minister of God's mercy, you may be quite sure nothing would ever have been found in the Comtesse's flower-stand."

So ended the story. The narrator had kept his promise; he had told all he knew, though this was after all only the ravelled ends of the complete romance. A long silence followed. Each member of the audience was wrapped in thought, endeavouring with what power of imagination he possessed, to combine the detached details which were all he had to go upon, and complete this romance of real life. In a place like Paris, where raillery is so quick to turn feeling out of doors, silence, in a roomful of clever people, after a story is the most flattering of all marks of success.

"A very pretty game indeed, especially what lay beneath the cards!" at length remarked the Baronne de Saint-Albin, as inveterate a player as any old diplomat's wife. "What you say is very true! what is half seen makes a far deeper impression than if every card had been faced and every turn of the game exposed."

"Verily, truth is stranger than fiction," observed the Doctor sententiously.

"Ah! yes, and the same thing is so true both in music and life!" cried Mademoiselle Sophie de Revistal eagerly. "The highest expression of both comes far more from the silences than the symphonies."

She turned on her bosom friend, the proud impassive Comtesse de Damnaglia, of the unbending carriage, who sat all the while biting the ivory and gold tip of her fan. What said the steel-blue eyes of the fair Countess? . . . Well! I could not see her face, but her back, which was all studded with little beads of perspiration, had a tale of its own to tell. It is hinted that the Comtesse de Damnaglia is not unlike Madame de Stasseville in this, that she possesses force of character sufficient to hide under an unruffled exterior the fierce emotions and occult satisfaction of an intensely passionate nature.

"You've quite spoilt for me the flowers I was so fond of," said his hostess, the Baronne de Mascranny, half turning round to the romancer. And then, decapitating a poor little rosebud she took from her bosom, she added, as she dreamily pulled the flower to pieces, with a little shudder of horror.

"No! never again! I shall never wear mignonette again!"

AT A DINNER OF ATHEISTS

AT A DINNER OF ATHEISTS

Worthy of men who know no God
ALLEN.

NIGHT was just beginning to fall in the streets of ——, but it was already dark in the church of that little town in Western France. Night always falls earlier in churches than it does elsewhere, on account of the small amount of light which comes through the stained-glass windows, and also on account of the number of pillars, and the shadows thrown by the arches. But the doors are not closed because night has fallen inside the edifice, anticipating the close of day. They generally remain open till the Angelus has rung—and sometimes even very much later, as on the eve of great festivals; for, in pious towns, many people confess before taking the sacrament the next day. At no hour of the day are country churches more frequented by church-goers than at this time in the evening, when work has ceased, daylight has vanished, and the Christian soul prepares for the night—night which resembles death, and during which death may come. At that hour you fully realize that the Christian religion was born in the catacombs and retains somewhat of the sadness of its cradle. Then it is, indeed, that those who believe in prayer like to come and kneel with their faces buried in their hands, in the mystery of the shadow of the empty nave, which responds to the deepest wants of the human soul; for if we worldly and passionate ones feel more emotion when we are alone in the dusk with the woman we love, why should it not be the same with religious souls and God, when the church is hidden in darkness, and they can whisper into His ear in the obscurity?

Thus did the pious souls, who had come to offer up their eve-

181

ning prayer according to custom, seem to be speaking to Him this evening in the church of ——. In the town, still grey in the foggy autumn twilight, the street lamps were not yet lighted. Vespers were over two hours ago, and the cloud of incense smoke which long formed a blue screen in the room over the choir, had evaporated. Deep night already unfolded its mantle of shade over the church, like a sail falling from a mast. Two long thin candles, one on each side of the nave, and the sacristy lamp, like a little fixed star in the darkness of the choir, threw a ghostly glimmer rather than a light. In this dim religious twilight it was possible to see indistinctly, but impossible to recognize anyone. You could see here and there in the shadow, a few black spots, darker than the greyness which surrounded them, in which you could distinguish a few bent forms, the white caps of kneeling women, and one or two hoods—but that was all. You heard rather than saw. All those mouths praying in a low voice in the dim, sonorous silence produced a curious whisper like the murmur of an ant-hill of souls visible only to the eye of God.

Sometimes this murmur would be broken by a sigh, or the noise of one of the side-doors swinging on its hinges to admit a newcomer—the sound of a sabot on the tiles, or a chair knocked over in the darkness—or from time to time there would come a cough—one of those coughs which the devout try to keep in out of respect for the holy echoes of the Lord's house. But these noises were but the rapid passing of so many sounds, and did not interrupt the fervent worshippers in the eternal murmur of their prayers.

The darkness explains why none of the faithful who assembled every evening in the church of —— took any notice of a man whose presence would assuredly have astonished more than one of them if there had been light sufficient to recognize him. For he was no frequenter of the church. He was never seen there. He had never put his foot inside the edifice since he had returned to his native town after years of absence.

Why had he entered this evening? What feeling, or idea, or project, had caused him to cross the threshold of a door before

which he passed several times a day without paying any attention to it? He was a very tall man, and his pride must have
stooped as much as his body when he passed under the little
arched door, weather-stained by the dampness of the rainy climate
of the West of France. There was poetry in that fiery brain!
When he entered this unfamiliar place, was he struck by the almost funereal aspect of the church? which resembles a crypt in
its construction, for it is built below the level of the street, and
you go down several steps on entering, so that the doorway is
higher than the altar. He had never read the story of St. Bridget,
but if he had read it, he would, when he entered that dark atmosphere full of mysterious murmurs, have thought of that sad and
terrible dormitory where sighs and whispers come out of the walls.

Whatever may have been his impressions, it is certain that he
stopped in the midst of the side-aisle as though his memory were
at fault. It was evident that he sought someone or something he
could not find in the deep shadow. However, when his eyes were
accustomed to the darkness, and he could see the shapes of things
around him, he perceived an old beggar woman, crouching rather
than kneeling, at the end of the "paupers' bench," and telling her
beads; and he touched her on the shoulder, and asked her where
was the Virgin's chapel, and the confessional of one of the parish
priests whom he named.

The old beggar woman, who for the last fifty years, had formed
part of the furniture of the church, and belonged to it almost
as much as the gargoyles, gave him the information he required,
and the man threaded his way through the disarranged chairs
which encumbered the aisle, and stood before the confessional
which is at the end of the chapel. He remained there with his
arms crossed—the attitude always adopted by men who do not
come to pray, and who wish to assume a suitably respectful attitude. Several lady members of the Congregation of the Holy
Rosary, who were then praying in the chapel, would, if they had
been able to see this man, have remarked what I will not call the
*im*piety but rather *non*piety of his attitude.

Generally, on evenings when there was confession, there stood
alight, beneath the figure of the Virgin, a twisted candle of yellow
wax, which lighted the chapel; but nearly all the faithful had taken
the Communion that morning, and there was no one in the confessional save the priest, who was meditating on the solitude, and
he had come out, extinguished the yellow wax candle, and returned to his wooden box to resume his meditations in the darkness, which prevents all external influences, and thus aids medita-
tion. Was it intentionally, or by chance, caprice, or economy, that
the priest had performed this simple act? At any rate, it had
saved the man who entered the chapel from being recognized
during the few instants he was there.

The priest saw the new-comer through the little grating in the
door, and threw open the door, but without moving from his seat;
and the man, unfolding his arms, handed the priest a small object
which he drew from his breast.

"There, Father," he said in a low but distinct voice. "I have
carried *it* about me many a long day."

Nothing more was said. The priest, as though he understood
the matter, took the object, and quietly closed the door of the
confession-box. The ladies of the Congregation of the Holy
Rosary imagined that the man who had spoken to the priest was
about to kneel and confess, and were extremely astonished to see
him descend the steps, treading lightly, and regain the aisle by
which he had come.

But if they were surprised, he was still more so when, half-way
towards the door by which he had entered, and by which he had
intended to leave, he was seized suddenly by a pair of strong arms,
and a laugh, which was abominably scandalous in such a holy
place, burst forth within two inches of his face. Happily for the
teeth that laughed, he recognized them, being so close to his face.

"*Sacré nom de Dieu!*" said the laugher in a low voice, but not
so low but what those who were near heard the profanity.
"What the devil are you doing, Mesnil, in a church at this hour?

We are not in Spain now, as we were when we used to rumple the veils of the nuns of Avila."

The person he had called "Mesnil" made an angry gesture.

"Be quiet!" he said in a low but commanding voice. "Are you drunk? You swear in a church as though you were in a guard-room. Go on! no foolery, and let us both get out of here decently."

And he quickened his steps, and passed, closely followed by "the other," the small, low door, and when they were out in the street, and could speak out loud, "the other" said: "May all the lightnings of hell burn you up, Mesnil! Are you going to turn monk? Are you going to believe in their mummeries? You, Mesnilgrand! You!—the captain of the Chamboran regiment! in a church, like a lubberly monk!"

"You were there yourself!" said Mesnil quietly.

"I went to follow you! I saw you enter, and was more as-tonished—I give you my word of honour—than if I had seen my mother violated. I said to myself: 'What is he doing in that nest of priests?' Then I thought there must be some petticoat at the bottom of it, and I wanted to see what *grisette,* or what great lady of the town, you were after."

"No, I was about my own business, my good fellow," replied Mesnil, with the quiet insolence of a supreme contempt that is in-tended to be evident.

"Then I am more devilishly surprised than ever."

"My good fellow," said Mesnil, stopping, "ever since the crea-tion of the world there have been men like me specially intended to astonish—men like you."

And turning his back, and quickening his steps, like a man who does not *mean* to be followed, he ascended the Rue de Gisors to the Place Thurin, in one of the corner houses of which he resided.

He lived with his father, old Monsieur de Mesnilgrand, as he was called in the town when they spoke of him. He was an old

man, rich and miserly (it was asserted), "hard as a stone"—that
was the expression they used—who had for many years lived in
retirement, and saw no company except during the three months
when his son, who resided in Paris, came to stay with him.
Then old Monsieur de Mesnilgrand, who ordinarily did not
see so much as a cat, invited and received all old friends and
regimental comrades of his son, and gave such good dinners
that all the old topers and good livers of the town talked about
them.

He was proud of his son—but the old man was not happy, and
had good reason. His "young man," as he called him—although
he was more than forty—had had his career ended by the same
blow which had reduced the Empire to dust and destroyed the
fortunes of him who was then known simply as The Emperor, as
though his office and glory had obliterated his name. He had left
home at eighteen, but he was of the stuff of which great generals
are made, and he had fought in all of the wars which the Emperor had waged, but Waterloo had ruined all his hopes. He was
one of the men who was not taken into the army at the Restoration, for he had not been able to resist the temptation of joining
his old commander after the return from Elba—an event which
seemed to deprive many able men of their own free will.

Captain Mesnilgrand—of whom the officers of that romantically
brave regiment, Chamboran, said: "A man may be as brave as
Mesnilgrand, but braver he cannot be"—saw many of his regimental comrades, who had not seen nearly so much service as he
had, become colonels in all the crack regiments; and though he
was not jealous, it was a cruel blow to him! He had an intensely
sensitive nature.

Military discipline—at a time when it was nearly as strict as it
was amongst the Romans—was the only thing capable of restrain-
ing his passions, which were so violent that eighteen years before
they had shocked his native town, and nearly killed *him*. For,
before he was eighteen, inordinate excesses with women had

brought on a nervous disease, a kind of *tabes dorsalis,* for which he was obliged to have his spine burned with moxas.[1]

This terrible remedy, which astonished the town as much as his excesses had astonished it, was utilized by some of the fathers in the town to impress their sons, who were taken to see the operation, in order that the spectacle might improve their morals; terror being considered the most adequate way of attaining that end. They were taken to see young Mesnilgrand burnt. He survived the operation, thanks to possessing a constitution like iron. This exceptional constitution withstood the moxas, and, later, withstood fatigue, wounds, and all the hardships which afflict a soldier; and Mesnilgrand was still a strong man and less than middle-aged when he found the military career closed against him, and his sword glued to its scabbard, and that soured his temper and made him furious.

To understand Mesnilgrand, one must search through history for a man to whom he could be compared, and we should be obliged to go back to the famous Charles the Bold, Duke of Burgundy. An ingenious moralist has explained the incongruities of our destinies by the theory that men resemble portraits, wherein some, who have only the head and bust painted, seem too large for their frames, whilst others are dwarfed or disappear entirely, owing to the immense size of their frames. Mesnilgrand, the son of a mere Norman squireen, compelled to live and die in the obscurity of private life, after having missed the great historic glory for which he was intended, experienced all the terrible force of long, continued fury and envenomed rage which devoured the vitals of Charles the Bold, who is also called in history, Charles the Terrible. Waterloo, which had thrown him out of employment, had been at once what Granson and Morat had been for that hu-

---

[1] Moxa is a peculiar form of counter-irritant practised in the East. A small cone of pith, or linen steeped in nitre, is placed on the skin, set alight and allowed to burn gradually down. It is said to be useful in many cases of sciatica, paralysis, etc.

man thunderbolt who found his end in the snows of Nancy.   Only
there was neither snow nor Nancy for Mesnilgrand, a cashiered
captain.   It was believed that he would kill himself or go mad,
but he did not kill himself, and his head was too strong—he did
not go mad.   He was so already, the jokers—who are found everywhere—said.   If he did not kill himself—and considering his
nature his friends could have asked him, but *did not* ask him,
why he did not—he was not a man to let his heart be eaten by
a vulture without an attempt to crush the vulture's beak.   Like
Alfieri, who knew nothing except how to break horses, but learned
Greek when he was forty, and even composed Greek verses, Mesnilgrand threw himself, or rather precipitated himself, into painting, that is to say, *that which was farthest removed from him,*
precisely as a man, in order to make sure of killing himself, will
mount to the seventh floor before throwing himself out of window.

He knew nothing of drawing, but he became a painter, like
Géricault, whom he had, I believe, known in the Musketeers.
He worked as furiously as one flying before the enemy—he said
with a bitter laugh—exhibited, made a sensation, did not exhibit
again, destroyed his canvases after he had painted them, and set
to work again with indefatigable zeal.   This officer, who had lived
sword in hand, and ridden all across Europe, passed his life in
front of an easel, and was so disgusted with war—the disgust of
those who adore—that what he chiefly painted was landscape—
landscapes like those he had ravaged.

Whilst he was painting them he chewed some curious mixture
of opium and tobacco, which he smoked day and night; for he
had had made a hookah of his own invention which he could smoke
even whilst he was asleep.   But neither narcotic, nor drugs, nor
any of the poisons with which men paralyse or slowly kill themselves, could lull to sleep the monster of fury which was never
quieted within him, and which he called the crocodile of his fountain—a phosphorescent crocodile in a fountain of fire.   Others,
who did not know him, long thought that he was one of the Car-
bonari.   But those who knew him better were aware that there

was too much talk and too much stupid liberalism about the Car-
bonari for a man of such strong character, who estimated all the
petty foolishnesses of his time with the shrewd perception which
distinguishes the Normans.

He was never deluded into joining any conspiracy. He fore-
told the fate of General Berton. On the other hand, for the
democratic ideas to which the Imperialists inclined during the
Restoration that they might conspire the better, he had an instinctive loathing. He was profoundly aristocratic, and not so
merely by birth, caste, or social rank—he was so by nature; of
himself, and would have been the same had he been the meanest
cobbler in the town. He was so, as Heine says, "by his manner of
feeling," and not like a bourgeois, like those parvenus who care
only for external distinctions. He never wore any orders or
medals. His father, who saw that he was upon the eve of becoming a colonel when the Empire crumbled to pieces, had bought
for him the reversion of a barony; but he never used the title,
and on his visiting-cards, and for all the world, he was only the
Chevalier de Mesnilgrand. Titles, deprived of all political priv-
ileges, or as a reward for real feats of arms, he valued no more
than the rind of a sucked orange, and he laughed at them, even in
the presence of those for whom they had an importance. He
proved this one day in the little town of ——, which teemed with
nobles, and where the old landed gentry, now ruined and robbed
by the Revolution, had—perhaps to console themselves—the in-
offensive mania of assuming the title of Count or Marquis, which
their families—which were very ancient and did not need them—
had never borne. Mesnilgrand, who thought such claims ridiculous, took a bold method of putting a stop to it. One evening,
at a party given by one of the most aristocratic families in the
town, he said to the servant: "Announce the Duc de Mesnilgrand."

And the servant, much astonished, called out in a stentorian
voice: "The Duc de Mesnilgrand!"

There was a general start throughout the company.

"*Ma foi!*" he said, seeing the effect he had produced, "as every-body takes a title nowadays, I thought I would take that one."

No one said a word; some of the jokers retired into private cor-ners and laughed, but they ceased to use sham titles. There are always knights-errant in the world. They no longer redress wrongs with sword and lance, but they cure ridiculous presump-tions with satire, and Mesnilgrand was one of these knights-errant.

He had a natural gift for sarcasm. But that was not the only gift that God had given him. Although force of character was the most prominent feature in his mental economy, his wit, though it took but second place, was a great source of strength to him against others. No doubt if the Chevalier de Mesnilgrand had been a happy man he would not have been very witty, but being unfortunate he had the opinions of the desperate, and when he was in good spirits, which was rarely, it was with the gaiety of despair; and there is nothing which so fixes the kaleidoscope of wit and prevents it from turning, as the fixed idea of unhappiness.

But that which he most possessed, and was of the greatest use to him, considering the passions that surged within his breast, was eloquence. It has been said of Mirabeau, and may be said of all great orators: "If you had only heard him!"—and the ex-pression seemed specially intended for him. You should have seen, during any discussion, his breast dilate, and his brow, fur-rowed with wrinkles—like a sea, in the hurricane of his wrath—become paler and paler—the pupils of his eyes glaring from their whites, as though they would strike those to whom he spoke, like two burning balls. You should have seen him breathless, gasp-ing, his voice becoming more pathetic the more broken it became, irony making the foam upon his lips tremble long after he had finished speaking; his wrath only to revive again the next day, or hour, or minute like a phœnix arising from its ashes.

In fact, no matter at what moment you touched certain chords in his nature which were ever on the strain, there would escape from them sounds which would overthrow anyone who had the imprudence to strike them.

"He spent the evening at our house," said a young lady to one of her friends, "and, my dear, he roared all the time. He is a demoniac. It will end by Monsieur de Mesnilgrand not being asked out at all."

Had it not been for the "bad form" of these outbreaks, which are not intended for drawing-rooms or the people who inhabit them, he might perhaps have interested young ladies by talking in a tone of mocking raillery. Lord Byron was very fashionable in those days, and, when Mesnilgrand was silent and reserved, he somewhat resembled one of Byron's heroes. It was not the regular beauty which young women of a calm temperament seek. He was extremely ugly, but his pale and care-worn face, under the chestnut hair which still looked youthful, his prematurely wrinkled forehead, like that of Lara or the Corsair, his broad, leopard-like nose, his blue eyes bordered with a thread of blood, like those of fiery racehorses, gave him an appearance which disturbed even the most flighty of the young ladies of ——. When he was present, the most laughter-loving women mocked no more.

Tall, strong, well-made, although he stooped a little, as though the existence he bore were too heavy a burden, the Chevalier de Mesnilgrand wore, under his modern costume, the strange air which you find in some old majestic family portraits. "He is a picture that has walked out of its frame," said a young lady, the first time she saw him enter a drawing-room.

Moreover, Mesnilgrand capped all these advantages by one which was better than all of them, in the eyes of young girls—he was always splendidly dressed. Perhaps it was the last remaining coquetry of his career of woman's man—a remnant which had survived, like the last ray of the setting sun across a bank of clouds behind which it has set. Or it might have been a trace of the Oriental luxury which as an officer of the Chamboran regiment he had formerly displayed, for when he was gazetted to the regiment he had made his miserly old father pay eight hundred pounds, simply for tiger-skin housings and red boots. But the fact remains that no young man of Paris or London displayed more elegance than this misanthrope, who no longer belonged to the world of fashion, and who, during the three months that he spent at ——, paid but very few visits, and did not repeat those.

He lived as he did at Paris, painting all day until nightfall. He walked but little about the neat and charming little town, which has a dreamy aspect, and seems built for dreamers and poets, though it does not contain a single poet. Sometimes, when he passed down a street, a shopkeeper would say to a stranger who remarked his proud bearing: "That is Commandant Mesnilgrand," as though Commandant Mesnilgrand ought to be known to everybody. If you saw him once, you did not forget him. His appearance struck you, as that of a man who asks nothing from the world always does, for if you ask nothing from the world you are above it, and then it will do any baseness for you. He never went to the cafés like the other officers who had been dismissed from the army at the Restoration, and with whom he never failed to shake hands when he met them. Provincial cafés disgusted him. It was contrary to his tastes to enter one. No one was horrified at that. His comrades were sure to find him at his father's house, and the old man, though a miser during his son's absence, became a spendthrift when his son was staying with him, and gave feasts which were likened by the guests to those of Belshazzar, though they had never read the Bible.

At these dinners he sat opposite his son, and though he was old, and looked like a character out of a comedy, you could see that the father had been in his time worthy of procreating the son of whom he was so proud. He was a tall, thin, old man, upright as the mast of a vessel, who proudly resisted the advance of age.

Always clad in a long frock-coat of a dark colour, which made him look taller than he was, he appeared outwardly to have all the severe look of a thinker, or a man who has done with all the pomps and vanities of the world. He wore, and had always worn for many years, a cotton night-cap with a broad lilac band, but no joker had ever dared to laugh at this night-cap, which is the traditional head-dress of the *Malade imaginaire*. There was noth-

ing comic about old Monsieur de Mesnilgrand. He would have
checked the laugh on the lips of Regnard, and made the pensive
look on Molière's face more pensive still. What the youth of
this almost majestic Géronte or Harpagon had been was too remote for anyone to recollect. He had been (it was said) on the
side of the Revolutionary party, although he was related to Vicq
d'Azir, the doctor of Marie-Antoinette, but had soon changed.
The well-to-do man, the landed proprietor, had triumphed over
the man of ideas. But he had come out of the Revolution a
political atheist, and had entered it a religious atheist, and these
two atheisms combined had made him a sort of "arch-denier"
who would have frightened Voltaire.

He said little about his opinions, however, except to the men
whom he invited to dine and meet his son, when he allowed to
escape opinions which justified what was said of him in the town.
The religious people and the nobility, of whom the town was full,
looked upon him as an old reprobate who punished himself very
properly by never visiting anyone. His life was very quiet.

He never went out. The boundaries of his garden and court-
yard were for him the ends of the world. In the winter, he sat
in the ingle-nook of the kitchen fire-place, to which he had wheeled
a huge arm-chair covered in reddish-brown Utrecht velvet, where
he sat silently, much to the annoyance of the servants, who did
not dare to speak out loud before him, and they talked to one another in a low voice, as though they were in church. In the summer they were freed from his presence, for he kept to the dining-
room, which was cool, and sat reading the papers or some old
books which he had bought at an auction, and which had belonged
to the library of some monastery; or he would sit arranging his
receipts, at an old maple writing-table with copper corners, and
which he had brought down in order to save himself the trouble
of going upstairs when his tenants came—although it was not an
article of furniture suitable for a dining-room. Whether aught—
save the calculation of interest—passed through his mind no one
knew. His face, with the short and rather flat nose, white as wax,

had had at each weekly dinner in the Place Thurin. At these feasts, which generally took place every Friday, they had the best fish and shell-fish to be found in the market. They wickedly joined together fish and meat, in order that the rule of abstinence and mortification prescribed by the Church might be the better transgressed.

That was really the intention of old Monsieur de Mesnilgrand and his diabolical associates. It was an extra spice to their food to feast on a fast-day, and add a fast—a real cardinal's fast—to their choice dishes. They were like that Neapolitan who said that an ice was delicious, but it would be much better if it were a sin to eat it. In these impious wretches it would have been better had it been not one sin but many—for all those who sat at this table were impious—mortal enemies of the priesthood, which to them represented the Church—absolute and violent atheists, of which there were many at that time, when a peculiar form of atheism was very prevalent. For there were at that period many men of action, of intense energy, who had passed through the Revolution, and the wars of the Empire, and had indulged in all the excesses of those terrible times. Their atheism was not the atheism of the eighteenth century, from which, however, it had sprung. The atheism of the eighteenth century made some pretensions to truth and thought. It reasoned, was sophistical, declamatory, and, above all, impertinent. But it did not possess the insolence of the weather-beaten veterans of the Empire, and the regicide apostates of '93. We who have come after these men, have also our atheism; absolute, concentrated, wise, icy, and hating with an implacable hate, and having for all religious matters the hate of the insect for the beam it bores into. But neither of these forms of atheism could give an idea of the inveterate atheism of the men of the beginning of the century, who being brought up like dogs by their fathers, the Voltairians, had plunged their hands up to the shoulders in all the horrors of politics and war, and the manifold corruptions which spring from them.

After three or four hours of blasphemous eating and drinking, the dining-room of old Monsieur de Mesnilgrand had quite a different aspect from that miserable little restaurant room in which a few Chinese mandarins of literature recently held a demonstration against God at five francs a head! These were feasts of quite a different kind, and as they are not likely to be repeated, at least under the same conditions, it is both interesting and necessary to describe them here.

All those who took part in these sacrilegious feasts are dead now, but at that time they were in the plenitude of life, which is at its highest when misfortune has amplified it. The friends of Mesnilgrand, the guests at his father's house, still enjoyed all the active strength they had ever possessed, and they had all the more because they had exercised it, and drunk to excess all vices and pleasures. Circumstances and events had torn the breast from their mouth before they had time to suckle it, and left them only the more thirsty. For them, as for Mesnilgrand, it was "the hour of madness." They had not the high soul of Mesnil, that Orlando Furioso, whose Ariosto, if he had an Ariosto, would have needed the tragic genius of Shakespeare. But on their own mental level, and according to their own passions and intelligence, they had, like him, finished their lives before their death—which is not always the end of life, and often comes long before the end. They were disarmed men, yet still with the strength to carry arms. They were not merely officers revoked from the army of the Loire; they had been also revoked from Life and Hope. The Empire was lost and the Revolution crushed by a reaction which could not keep under its foot, as Saint Michael keeps the dragon, all these men who had been turned out of their positions, their employment, and deprived of their ambition and all the benefits of their past life, and had drifted, powerless, defeated, and humiliated, to their native towns, there "to die miserably like dogs," as they bitterly said. In the Middle Ages they would have become shepherds, freebooters, or soldiers of fortune, but you cannot choose the age you will live in, and their feet were entangled in the grooves of an imperious and ordered civilization, and they *beaux,* and they were certainly handsome and elegant, but their good looks were purely physical, and their elegance soldierly. Although dressed as ordinary citizens, they retained the stiffness of the uniform they had worn all their lives. To use one of their own expressions, they were rather too much dressed up. The other guests—men of science, like the doctors, or turncoats, like the old monks, who were concerned about their clothes, though they had trampled underfoot the sacred ornaments of priestly splendour—all looked shabbily dressed. But Mesnilgrand was, as women would say, splendidly "got up." As it was still the morning, he was wearing an adorable black frock-coat, and (as was then the fashion) a white or light cream-coloured necktie, spangled with almost imperceptible gold stars, embroidered by hand. As he was at home, he had not put on boots. His feet, so small and well-shaped that the beggars at the street-corner called him "Prince" when they caught sight of them, were encased in open-work silk socks and high-heeled pumps, such as were affected by Chateaubriand, who thought more of his feet than any man in Europe except the Grand Duke Constantine. His coat, which was cut by Staub, was worn open, showing off his sloe-coloured trousers and a plain black cashmere waistcoat without a watch-chain, for that day he wore no jewellery of any sort, except an old cameo of great price, representing the head of Alexander, on his necktie. You felt from his appearance and the good taste shown, that the artist had surpassed the soldier in him, and that he was not of the same race as the others, although he talked so familiarly with them.

He was but the second master of the house, for his father did the honours—and, unless some discussion called forth his stormy eloquence, he spoke little at these noisy meetings—the tone of which was not quite in accordance with his views—and at which, from the time the oysters appeared, there was such a babel of sounds and ideas that it seemed as if one note more and the ceiling—the cork of the room—would pop off, as so many other corks were doing.

It was at noon precisely that they sat down to table, according to the ironical custom of these irreverent mockers, who took advantage of the least thing to show their contempt for the Church. There is a belief in that pious Western country that the Pope sits down to table at midday, but that before doing so he blesses all the Christian world. Well! this august *Benedicite* appeared comic to these free-thinkers; therefore old Monsieur de Mesnilgrand never failed to say in a jeering way in his resonant voice, when the first stroke of twelve sounded from the church clock—and with that Voltairian smile which sometimes seemed to split in two his motionless moon-like face:

"Sit down, gentlemen! Christians like us ought not to deprive ourselves of the Pope's blessing!"

And this remark, or one equivalent to it, was like a jumping-board for the impieties which sprung up at every turn of conversation at a male dinner-party, especially of such men as they were. As a general rule it may be said that all dinners composed exclusively of men, and not presided over by the harmonizing grace of the lady of the house, or where there is not the peaceful influence of woman to throw her grace, like a caduceus, between the gross vanities, the loud pretensions, and the stupid, angry passions, and the personalities always heard at a dinner of men, seem inclined to end like the feast of the Lapithæ and the Centaurs—at which there were no women either. At all repasts devoid of women's society, even the most refined and best-bred men lose the charm of their politeness and natural distinction—and it is not astonishing that they do so. They have not a gallery to play to, and they immediately adopt a tone of licence which is apt to become rough when wits are jarring. Selfishness—that unbanishable selfishness which it is the art of society to conceal under polite forms—causes elbows to be put on the table, previous to their being stuck into your ribs. And if it is thus with the most refined men, what was it likely to be with the guests of the Mesnilgrands—fire-eaters and warriors, most at home in Jacobin Clubs or around bivouac-fires, who always fancied themselves at the bivouac or the club, or even in worse places?

It would be difficult to imagine, unless you had heard it, the scraps of conversation of these men, all great eaters and drinkers, stuffed with hot meats and heated with strong drinks, and who, before they came to the third course, had given loose rein to their tongues, and metaphorically "put their feet in the trough." Their conversation was not all impiety, but that was what may be called the flower of their conversation. Remember that it was at this time that Paul Louis Courier—who might well have figured at those dinners—wrote this phrase to stir up the blood of France: "The question is, shall we become monks or lackeys?" But that was not all. After politics, hatred of the Bourbons, the dark spectre of Religion, regrets for the past by these broken-down officers, and all the other conversational avalanches which rolled from one end to the other of this steaming table, there were other noisy and tempestuous subjects for talk. For example, there was woman. Woman is the eternal subject of conversation of men between themselves—especially in France, the most conceited country on earth. They talked about women in general, and in particular—of women all over the world, as well as next door—the women of various countries these soldiers had visited, and in which they had victoriously flaunted their uniforms —and those of the town, whom they, perhaps, did not visit, but whom they insolently called by their Christian and surnames as though they knew them intimately, and about whom they spoke without any reserve, stripping off their reputation as they skinned a peach at dessert.

All took part in this abuse of women, even the oldest, the toughest, and those most disgusted with females, as they cynically called women—for a man may give up sex love but he will retain his self-love in talking about women; and though on the edge of the grave, men are always ready to root with their snouts in the garbage of self-conceit.

And on this occasion they had rooted up to their ears, for this dinner was, as regarded unlicensed talk, the hottest that old Monsieur de Mesnilgrand had ever given. In the dining-room, now silent, but the walls of which could have told strange tales if they could have spoken—there had arrived that time which comes in all dinners of men only, when the boasting begins—at first decent —then soon indecent—then unbuttoned—then without a shirt and without shame—and everyone related some anecdote or other.

It was like a confession of demons! All these insolent railers, who could not have scoffed sufficiently at a poor monk confessing aloud his sins at the feet of his abbot, in the presence of all the Brothers of the order—were doing exactly the same thing; not to humiliate themselves as the monk does, but to pride themselves on and boast of their abominable life—and all, more or less, spat out their soul against God, and their spittle fell back in their own faces!

But in the midst of all this flood of boastful romance of all sorts, there was one which seemed more—piquant shall I say? No, piquant is not a word strong enough—but more "spicy," more peppery, more suited to the palates of these frenzied fools, who, in the way of stories, would have swallowed even vitriol. Yet the man who related it was, of all these devils, the coolest. He was like Satan's back: for Satan's back, in spite of the hell which warms it, is quite cold—so say the witches who kiss it in the Black Mass at their Sabbat.

This was a certain ex-Abbé Reniant—an appropriate name— who, in this society on the wrong side of the Revolution, prepared to undo all that was done, had appointed himself of his own accord, to be a priest without faith, and a doctor without science, and who clandestinely carried on practices which were suspicious, and—who knows?—perhaps murderous. Amongst educated people he did not acknowledge his business, but he had persuaded the lower classes in the town and the neighbourhood that he knew more than all the doctors with all their degrees and diplomas.

It was whispered mysteriously that he had *secrets* for curing people. *Secrets*—a fine word, which means everything because it
means nothing; the battle-horse of the quacks, the sole survivors
of the sorcerers who formerly exercised so great an influence on
popular imagination.

This ex-Abbé Reniant—for as he said angrily, "that confounded
title of Abbé was like ringworm on his name, and no resin plasters
would ever remove it!"—did not employ these secret remedies
(which were possibly poisons) for the sake of gain: he had enough
to live on. But he obeyed the dangerous demon of experiment,
which begins by treating human life as a subject for its essays,
and ends by making Sainte Croixs and Brinvilliers!

Not wanting to have anything to do with licensed doctors, as
he scornfully called them, he made up his own medicines, and
sold or gave his mixtures—for he very often gave them away—
on the sole condition that the bottles should be returned. The
rascal was no fool, and he knew how to appeal to his patients.
He gave herbs, of I know not what kinds, infused in white wine,
in cases of dropsy brought on by overdrinking, and to girls
who were "in trouble"—as the peasants said with a wink—and
these drinks removed their trouble.

He was a man of average height, with a cold quiet look, and
was dressed in the same style as old Monsieur de Mesnilgrand
(but in blue), but his face, which was of the colour of unbleached
linen, was surmounted by hair of an ugly towy colour, perfectly
straight, and cut round his head—the only trait of the priest
which remained. He spoke but little, and what he did say
was brief and to the point. Cold and clean as the pot-hook of
a Dutch chimney, at these dinners he sat at the corner of the
table, and affectedly sipped his wine whilst the others took huge
draughts. He was not much liked by these hot-blooded fellows,
who compared him to the sour wine of Saint Nitouche—a vine-
yard of their own creation. But this quiet air only added more
flavour to his story, when he said modestly that for his part

the best thing he had ever done against what Monsieur de Voltaire called "the Infamy," was that once—hang it, you do what you can!—he had given a packet of consecrated wafers to the pigs!

At these words there was a roar of triumphant interjections, but above them all rose the shrill, sarcastic voice of old Monsieur de Mesnilgrand.

"That was, no doubt, Abbé," he said, "the last time that you gave the Communion!" and the malicious old fellow put his white, dry hand above his eyes in order to look at Reniant, who was half hidden behind his glass, between the two stalwart figures of his neighbours, Captain Rançonnet, red and fiery as a torch, and Captain Travers de Mautravers of the 6th cuirassiers, who was as stiff as a limber wagon.

"It was long after that," replied the former priest, "and after I had thrown my gaberdine in the muck. It was during the height of the Revolution; at the time when you had come down here, Citizen Le Carpentier, as representative of the people. Do you remember a young girl of Hémevès whom you caused to be put in prison?—a mad woman!—an epileptic?"

"Ah!" said Mautravers; "so there was a woman mixed up in the affair! Did you give her to the pigs as well?"

"You think yourself funny, Mautravers!" said Rançonnet. "Don't interrupt the Abbé. Finish your story, Abbé!"

"Oh, the story," replied Reniant, "is soon told. I was asking Monsier Le Carpentier if he remembered that girl. She was named Tesson—Josephine Tesson, if I remember rightly—a big, chubby young woman; and she was the cat's-paw of the Chouans and the priests, who had hypnotized her, fanaticized her, and driven her mad. She spent her life in hiding priests. When there was one to be saved, she would have braved thirty guillotines. Ah, she hid the ministers of the Lord, as she called them, in her house, and everywhere else. She would have hidden them under her bed, or under her petticoats; and, if they could have stayed there, she would have stuffed them—devil take me if she would not!—where she put their boxes of consecrated wafers—between her breasts!"

"A thousand cannon-balls!" said Rançonnet, excitedly.

"No, not a thousand, but only two, Monsieur Rançonnet," said the rakish old apostate, laughing at his own joke, "but they were good-sized ones!"

The joke took, and there was a general laugh.

"A strange ciborium, a woman's breast!" said Doctor Bleny, dreamily.

"Oh, the ciborium of necessity," replied Reniant, who had recovered his phlegmatic air. "All the priests whom she concealed, and who were prosecuted, pursued, tracked down, and without a church, or sanctuary, or hiding-place, had given her their holy sacraments to guard, and she had hidden them all in her breast, believing that they would never be looked for there. Oh, they had thorough faith in her. They called her a saint. They made her believe that she was one. They unsettled her mind, and made her long to be a martyr. She was brave, and ardent, and boldly went everywhere with her box of sacramental wafers under her bib. She carried them at night, in all weathers, through rain, wind, snow, or fog, over abominable roads, to the priests who were in hiding who were absolving the dying in *catimini*. One night we took them by surprise at a farm where a Chouan was dying—I and a few good lads of Rossignol's Infernal Column. One of our fellows, tempted by those splendid outposts of warm flesh, tried to take liberties with her, but she was a tough customer, and she printed her ten nails on his face in a way that would leave him marked for the rest of his life. But, bleeding as he was, the rascal would not let go, and he pulled out the box of wafers hidden in her breast. I counted a full dozen of hosts, which, in spite of her cries and struggles, for she rushed on us like a fury, I caused to be at once thrown into the pig-trough."

He stopped—giving himself as many airs, about his feat, as a flea on the top of a boil.

"You well avenged the porkers of the Gospel into whom Christ made the devils enter," said old Monsieur de Mesnilgrand, in his sarcastic head voice. "You put the *bon Dieu* into them instead of the Devil—it was tit for tat."

"Did they have indigestion, Monsieur Reniant?—or was it the people who ate them?" asked seriously a hideous, little old man named Le Hay, who lent money at fifty per cent, and who used to say that "you should always consider whether the end justifies the means."

There was a pause in the flood of blasphemy.

"But you say nothing, Mesnil, about Abbé Reniant's story," remarked Captain Rançonnet, who was watching for an occasion to bring in his account of Mesnilgrand's visit to the church.

In fact, Mesnil had said nothing. He was sitting with his elbow on the table, and his cheek on his hand, listening without any great taste for all these abominations uttered by hardened sinners, and to which he had long been accustomed. He had heard so many in the course of his career. A man's surroundings are almost his destiny. In the Middle Ages, the Chevalier de Mesnilgrand would have been a Crusader, burning with faith. In the nineteenth century, he was a soldier of Bonaparte, to whom his unbelieving father had never spoken about God, and who had lived, particularly in Spain, in the ranks of an army to which everything was permitted, and who had committed as many sacrileges as the soldiers of the Constable of Bourbon did at the taking of Rome. Fortunately, surroundings are not absolutely fatal, except to vulgar souls and minds. With really strong characters there is something, though it be but an atom, which escapes or resists the action. This atom remained invincible in Mesnilgrand.

He would have said nothing that day, and allowed to pass in stony indifference the torrent of blasphemous filth which surged around him, boiling like the pitch of hell, but when he was addressed by Rançonnet, he replied—with a drawl that was almost melancholy:

"What do you want me to say? Monsieur Reniant did not do anything to boast of that you should admire him so much. If he believed that it was really God, the living God, the God of vengeance, whom he had thrown to the pigs, at the risk of being struck by lightning on the spot, on the certainty of hell hereafter, there would at least have been some courage about it—some scorn of *more than death,* since God, if He exists, can torture for eternity.

"That would have been courageous—foolish, no doubt, but still courageous enough to tempt a man like you to imitate it. But it had not that merit, my dear fellow. Monsieur Reniant did not believe that those sacred hosts were God. He had not the least doubt on the subject. To him they were nothing but breadstuff, only made holy by foolish superstition, and for him, or for yourself, my poor Rançonnet, to empty a box of sacramental wafers into the pig-trough was no more heroic than it would have been to empty a snuff-box, or a packet of letter wafers, there."

"Eh! Eh!" said old Monsieur de Mesnilgrand, leaning back in his chair, looking at his son from under his hand, as he would have looked at a target to see where the shot had told. He was always interested in what his son said, even when he did not share his opinions, and in this case he did. So he repeated his "Eh! Eh!"

"In fact, it was nothing, my poor Rançonnet," continued Mesnil, "just merely—I must use the word—swinish. But what I do admire, and admire exceedingly, gentlemen—though I do not believe in much myself—is this girl, Tesson, as you call her, Monsieur Reniant; who carried what she believed to be her God upon her bosom; who of her two virgin breasts made a tabernacle in all purity for this God—and who breathed, and lived, and passed tranquilly through all the dangers of life, with this brave breast bearing the burden of a God—tabernacle and altar at the same time—and an altar on which, at any minute, might have been poured forth its own blood. . . . You, Rançonnet—you, Mautravers—you, Sélune—and myself also; we have all carried the Emperor on our breast, for we had his legion of honour, and it gave us more courage in battle to have it there. But it was not the *image* of her God that she carried on her breast; for her it was the reality. It was a substantial God who could be touched and eaten, and whom she carried at the risk of her life, to those who needed that God. Well! on my word of honour, I call that sublime. I esteem that woman as did the priests who gave her their God to carry.

"I would like to know what became of her. Perhaps she is dead; perhaps she still lives miserably in some corner of the country—but I know that if I were a Marshal of France, and I met her seeking her bread, her naked feet trudging through the mire, I would dismount from my horse and respectfully take off my hat to that noble woman, as though she still really carried God in her breast. Henri IV, when he knelt in the mud before the holy sacrament which was being carried to some poor person, did not feel more respect than I should in kneeling before that woman."

His cheek was no longer leaning on his hand. He had thrown his head back; and when he spoke of kneeling, he seemed to grow bigger and, like the Bride of Corinth in Goethe's poem, to have risen from his chair to the ceiling.

"The world is coming to an end!" growled Mautravers, breaking a peach-stone with his closed fist, as though it had been a hammer. "Here is a captain of hussars talking about going down on his knees to a devotee."

"And suppose," said Rançonnet, "that the cavalry passed over at full gallop to the enemy! After all, they did not make bad mistresses, those nuns who sing the *Oremus*, and eat the *bon*

Dieu, and think themselves damned for every pleasure they bestow upon us, and which we make them share with us. But, Captain Mautravers, there are worse things for a soldier to do than wrong a few pious females; and one of them is to become a devotee himself, like a drowned chicken of a civilian. No longer ago than last Sunday, at nightfall, where do you suppose, gentlemen, that I caught Commandant Mesnilgrand, now present?"

No one replied; and from all parts of the table, eyes were fixed on Captain Rançonnet.

"By my sabre!" said Rançonnet, "I met him—no, not met him, for I have too much respect for my boots to trail them in the filth of their chapels—but I saw his back, slipping into the church, and stooping under the little, low door at the corner of the Place. Was I astonished?—astounded? *Sacrebleu!* I said to myself, my eyes must deceive me. But that is surely Mesnilgrand's figure.—What can Mesnilgrand be going to do in a church? The recollection came into my head of our old love-affairs with those cursed nuns in Spain. What, I said, hasn't he finished yet? Is he still under the influence of some petticoat? May the Devil scratch out my eyes with his claws if I don't see what this one is like! And I entered their Mass shop. . . . Unfortunately, it was as dark there as the jaws of hell. I walked about, and stumbled over the old women who were down on their knees, muttering their paternosters. It was impossible to see, but in groping about in that infernal mixture of darkness and the carcases of old women praying, I caught hold of Mesnil, who was gliding along one of the side-aisles. But, would you believe it? he refused to tell me what he was doing in that confounded church. That is why I denounce him now, gentlemen, that you may oblige him to explain his conduct."

"Go on! speak, Mesnil! justify yourself! Reply to Rançonnet!" they cried from all parts of the room.

"Justify myself!" said Mesnil gaily. "I have no need to justify myself for doing what I please. You, who grumble so much about the Inquisition, are you not at present an inquisi-

tion in another sense? I went into the church, Sunday night, because I chose to do so."

"And why did you choose?" asked Mautravers; "for if the
Devil is a logician, a captain of cuirassiers may well be also."

"Ah, there!" said Mesnilgrand, laughing; "I went there—who
knows?—perhaps to confess. At all events, the door of a confessional was opened for me. But you cannot say, Rançonnet,
that my confession lasted very long!"

They could all see that he was laughing at them—but there
was an air of mystery about the fun which annoyed them.

"Confess! A thousand hells! Have you taken the plunge?"
said Rançonnet sadly, for he took the matter seriously. Then,
throwing himself back like a rearing horse, he cried: "No! by
heavens! it is impossible. Look here, you fellows! can you believe that Captain Mesnilgrand has confessed like some old
granny, kneeling on a stool, with his nose against the grating of
a priest's box? I cannot get the idea of such a spectacle into
my head! Thirty thousand bullets sooner!"

"You are very good—I thank you," said Mesnilgrand, with
comic mildness—the mildness of a lamb.

"Let us talk seriously," said Mautravers. "I am like Rançonnet. I could never believe in a man of your sort doing monk-
ish tricks. Even on their death-beds, men like you don't jump
like a frightened frog into a basin of holy water."

"I do not know what you would do on your death-bed, gentlemen," replied Mesnilgrand slowly; "but as for me, before I left
for the other world, I should like, at all events, to pack up my
portmanteau.

"But let us leave that on one side," continued Mesnilgrand.
"You are, it seems, more brutalized by war and the life we lead
than I am. I have nothing to say about your unbelief, but as
you, Rançonnet, particularly want to know why your comrade,
Mesnilgrand, whom you believe to be as much an atheist as yourself, entered a church, I should like to tell you. There is a story
attached to it. When you have heard it, you will understand per-

haps, even without believing in a God, why I entered that church."

He made a pause, as though to give more solemnity to what he was about to relate, and then began.

"You were speaking about Spain, Rançonnet. It was in Spain that the incidents I am about to relate occurred. Many of you took part in that fatal war of 1808 which began the downfall of the Empire and our misfortunes. Those who were in that war will not have forgotten it—you less than anyone, Commandant Sélune. You have a forcible reminder on your face."

Commandant Sélune was seated near old Monsieur de Mesnilgrand, opposite to Mesnil. He was a man of military appearance and had more right to the nickname of *le Balafré* than the Duke of Guise, for he had received in a skirmish of outposts in Spain, a terrible sabre-cut, which had split his face, nose and all, from the left temple to below the right ear. Under any circumstances this would have been a very severe wound, though one which would have a noble appearance on a soldier's face, but the surgeon who brought together the edges of this gaping wound had been either clumsy or in a hurry, and had joined them badly. The army was on the march, and in order to get the job over, he had cut away part of the flesh with scissors, so that it was not a seam which crossed Sélune's face, but a regular ravine. It was horrible, but after all it was grand. He was passionate, and when the blood rose to his face, the scar became red, and resembled a broad red ribbon across his bronzed face. "You wear," Mesnil had said to him one day, "your Cross of Grand Officer of the Legion of Honour on your face before you have it on your breast—but be easy, it will come down."

It never did come down—the Empire finished first—and Sélune remained a Chevalier only.

"Well, gentlemen," continued Mesnilgrand, "we saw some atrocious deeds committed in Spain, and even did some ourselves, but I do not remember having seen anything more abominable than that which I am about to have the honour to relate."

"For my part," said Sélune, nonchalantly, with the air of an old stager who does not mean to be surprised at anything, "for my part I have seen eighty nuns thrown one on the other, half dead, into a well, after each one had first been violated by two squadrons."

"Mere brutality of soldiers," said Mesnilgrand coolly; "but this was the refined cruelty of an officer."

He sipped his wine, and then glanced round the table.

"Did any of you know Major Ydow?" he asked.

Rançonnet was the only one who replied.

"I did," he said. "Of course I knew Major Ydow. *Parbleu!* he was with me in the 8th Dragoons."

"Then, since you knew him," replied Mesnilgrand, "you must have known someone else. When he joined the 8th Dragoons, he had a woman with him."

"La Rosalba, called la Pudica," said Rançonnet, "his well-known ——," and he used a coarse word.

"Yes," replied Mesnilgrand pensively; "such a woman does not deserve the name of a mistress, even of a man like Ydow. The major had brought her from Italy, where, before he came to Spain, he had served in a reserve corps, with the rank of captain. As you are the only person here, Rançonnet, who knew Major Ydow, you will permit me to introduce to these gentlemen this foreign devil, whose coming made such a stir when he first arrived amongst the 8th Dragoons with this woman on his back.

"He was not a Frenchman, it would seem—which was certainly no great loss to France. He was born I don't know where, and of I don't know whom, in Illyria, or Bohemia—I am not sure which. But, wherever he was born, he was so strange that he seemed a stranger everywhere. He was, you might imagine, the product of a mixture of several races. He said himself that his name ought to be pronounced in the Greek way because he was of Greek origin, and you could believe that from his appearance, for he was handsome—perhaps too handsome for a soldier. A man who has such good looks is apt to take too great care of them, and other persons have the respect for him that

they would have for a masterpiece. Masterpiece as he was, however, he went into battle with the others, but when you have said
that of Major Ydow, you have said all. He did his duty, but
he never did more than his duty. He had not what the Emperor
called the 'sacred fire.' In spite of his beauty, which I willingly
grant him, I considered him ugly, in spite of his handsome
features. I have visited museums—to which you fellows never
go—and found there a resemblance to Major Ydow. He was
strikingly like the busts of Antinous, especially that one in which
the sculptor, by fancy or bad taste, has inserted two emeralds
for the eyeballs. But instead of white marble the Major's sea-
green eyes lighted up an olive face with its faultless facial angle,
but there was something more in those eyes than the melancholy
light of the evening star, or the voluptuousness of idleness, such
as you see in the statues of Antinous—there was a sleeping tiger,
which I one day saw awake!

"Major Ydow was both dark and fair. The curly hair round
his narrow forehead was jet-black, whilst his long and silky
moustache was as brown as a weasel's fur. It is said that that
is a sign of treason, or perfidy, when the beard or moustache is
of a different colour from the hair. Was he a traitor? The major
might have become so later. He would, perhaps, like many
others, have betrayed the Emperor, but he had not at that time.
When he joined the 8th Dragoons, he was probably only false,
and not false enough to avoid having the look of it. Was it this
air which first caused his unpopularity amongst his comrades?
At any rate, it is certain that he was very soon loathed by all
the regiment. Very vain of his beauty—though for my own
part I would rather have resembled many uglier men I knew—
he seemed, as the soldiers said, to be fit for nothing but to be
a mirror for a—what you called Rosalba just now, Rançonnet.

"Major Ydow was thirty-five years of age. You can well understand that with such good looks he pleased all the women, even
the proudest—that is their weakness—and that Major Ydow was

terribly spoiled by them, and learned all the vices one learns from women—but he had also some others they never taught him. We were certainly not monks in those days. We were all vicious enough—gamblers, libertines, seducers, duellists, drunkards, if need be, and spendthrifts in every way. We had no right therefore to be over-particular. Well! bad as we were, he passed for being worse than any of us. For us, there were certain things—not many, but there were one or two—of which, demons as we were, we should not have been capable. But he—it was said—was capable of anything. I was not in the 8th Dragoons, but I knew all the officers, and they spoke of him with much bitterness. They accused him of servility and toadying to his superiors. They suspected him of many things—of being a spy amongst others; and he even fought two duels, courageously enough, because of this half-expressed suspicion; but that did not change the general opinion. There always hung about him a cloud which could not be dissipated.

"Moreover, he was not only both fair and dark—which is rare enough—but he was lucky at cards, and lucky with women— which is not the rule either. But that double good fortune cost him dear, for his success in both fields, and the jealousy inspired by his good looks—for though men pretend to be above, or indifferent to, considerations of ugliness, and repeat the consoling expression they have invented, that 'a man is quite handsome enough when he doesn't frighten his horse,' they are amongst themselves quite as cowardly and petty-minded as women are— no doubt, these advantages explained the antipathy which was felt towards him; an antipathy which affected the form of contempt, for contempt is a deeper insult than hate, and hate knows that well.

"Many times have I heard it half whispered that he was a 'dangerous rascal,' although it would have been difficult to prove that he was one. And, in fact, gentlemen, even at this moment I am uncertain whether Major Ydow was what he was said to be.

But, by God!" continued Mesnilgrand energetically, with a strange horror in his voice, "what they did *not* say of him, and what he was one day, I know, and that is enough for me!"

"It would be enough for us too, probably," said Rançonnet, gaily, "but, *sacrebleu!* what the devil connexion is there between you entering a church, as I saw you enter it last Sunday night, and this damned major of the 8th Dragoons, who would have pillaged all the churches and cathedrals of Spain and the Christian world to make jewellery for his concubine of the gold and precious stones of the sacramental vessels?"

"Keep in the ranks, Rançonnet," said Mesnilgrand, as though he had been commanding his squadron, "and hold your tongue. Are you always going to be as hot-headed and impatient as you are before the enemy? Let me make my story manœuvre as I like."

"Well, then! march!" replied the fiery captain, as he tossed off a glass of Picardy wine to keep himself cool.

And Mesnilgrand continued.

"It is very probable that if it had not been for the woman he had with him, and whom he called his wife, although she was only his mistress, and did not bear his name, Major Ydow would have had some difficulties with the officers of the 8th Dragoons. But this woman, who was all that people called her, or she would never have taken up with such a man, prevented him from being sent to Coventry! I have often seen *that* occur in regiments. A man falls under suspicion or into discredit, and the others hold no communication with him beyond what is required by the interests of the service, and he has no chums; no one shakes hands with him, and even at the café—in the hot and familiar atmosphere of which all coolnesses dissolve—his comrades keep aloof from him with a polite reserve until he goes, when the constraint vanishes. Most probably that is what would have happened to the Major; but a woman is the Devil's loadstone. Those who did not like him for his own sake, liked him for hers. Those who would never have offered the Major a glass of *schnapps* had he been without his 'wife,' offered it when they thought of her, thinking it might prove the means of getting an invitation, and thus meeting her.

"There is a law of moral arithmetic written in every man's breast long before a philosopher put it on paper, and that is, 'that it is farther from a woman to her first lover than the first is from the tenth,' and I believe that axiom was truer of the Major's wife than it was of anyone else. As she had bestowed herself upon him, she might bestow herself on another—and anybody might be that other! And in a very short time it was known throughout the regiment that there was very little presumption in such an aspiration. All who have any skill in reading a woman, and can detect the true odour through the white and scented veils in which they enfold themselves, knew directly that Rosalba was *the* most depraved of all depraved women— the perfection of vice.

"I am not calumniating her—am I, Rançonnet? Perhaps you have made love to her, and, if so, you know that there was never a more fascinating crystallization of every vice. Where did the Major find her? Where did she come from? No one dared ask at first, but the hesitation did not last long. The conflagration she lighted up, not only in the 8th Dragoons, but in my regiment, and also—as you may remember, Rançonnet—throughout all the General Staff of the expedition, soon assumed huge proportions. We had seen plenty of women, mistresses of officers, and following the regiment—if an officer could afford the luxury of a woman amongst his other baggage; the colonels shut their eyes to the abuse, or even permitted it. But we had never seen one like Rosalba, and had no idea of one like her. The ones we were accustomed to were all pretty, if you like, but all of the same type; bold, determined young women, almost masculine, almost impudent; generally pretty brunettes of a more or less passionate temperament, who looked like boys, and were very fascinating and voluptuous in the uniform that their lovers sometimes took the fancy to make them don.

"If the legitimate and honest wives of officers can be distinguished from other women by some subtle characteristic which is common to them all, and which they derive from the military surroundings amidst which they live, the same may be said of the mistresses of officers. But Major Ydow's Rosalba had nothing in common with the adventuresses or camp-followers to whom we had been accustomed. To begin with, she was a tall, pale young girl—but she did not long remain pale, as you will hear —with a mass of fair hair. That was all. Nothing to make a great fuss about. Her skin was not whiter than that of other women who have fresh and healthy blood under their skin. Her fair hair was not of that wonderful colour which has the metallic sheen of gold, or the tender tints of amber, which I have seen in some Swedish women. She had a classical face—what you might call a cameo face—but its passive correctness did not differ from that of many others who are the delight and annoyance of passionate lovers. Whether you cared for her or not, you were bound to confess that she was a pretty woman. But the love philtres she gave men to drink had nothing to do with her beauty. They came from elsewhere. They were where you would never guess in this monster of lubricity who dared to call herself Rosalba—who dared to bear the spotless name of Rosalba, which should only be borne by innocence, and who, not satisfied with being Rosalba—the White Rose—called herself as well, over and above, 'Pudica, the Modest.' "

"Virgil also called himself the modest, and he wrote *Corydon ardebat Alexim,*" remarked Reniant, who had not forgotten his Latin.

"And it was not in irony," continued Mesnilgrand. "The name of Rosalba was not invented by us, but we read it in her face when we first saw her, where Nature had written it with all the roses at her command. La Rosalba was not merely astonishingly modest, she was Modesty itself. If she had been as pure as the virgins in heaven, who, perhaps, blush when the angels look at them, she would not have been more the incarnation of modesty.

Who said—it must have been an Englishman—that the world was the work of a Devil gone mad? It must surely have been that Devil who had created Rosalba to give men pleasure.—A Devil who knew how to mingle voluptuousness with modesty, and modesty with voluptuousness, and spice them with a celestial condiment, and make the most infernal hotch-potch of delights a woman can bestow on mortal man.

"The modesty of Rosalba was not merely in the expression of her face, though that would have upset all Lavater's theories. No; with her, modesty was not only on the surface, it flowed in her blood, and was not only skin-deep. Nor was it assumed out of hypocrisy. The vices of Rosalba had never rendered that homage, or any other, to virtue. It was really a truth. La Rosalba was as modest as she was voluptuous, and strange to say she was both at once. When she said or did the most daring things, she had an adorable way of saying 'I am ashamed,' which I fancy I can still hear. And—an unheard-of phenomenon—in a love-affair with her, you were always at the beginning, even after you had come to the end. She would have left an orgy of bacchantes with the air of a maiden who commits her first sin. Even in the woman steeped, worn out, half dead with vice, there was the troubled confusion, and the blushing charm of the virgin. . . . I could never make you understand the delightful effect of these contrasts on one's heart—language would fail to express that."

He stopped, and thought, and all the others remained lost in thought. It seemed as though his words had transformed into dreamers all these soldiers who had been under fire of every sort, these debauched monks, and old doctors, and brought back to them visions of their old life. Even the impetuous Rançonnet did not speak. He was dreamy.

"You must understand," continued Mesnilgrand, "that this phenomenon was not known at first. When she first came to the 8th Dragoons, we saw nothing but a very pretty girl; of the same kind as Princess Pauline Borghese, the Emperor's sister—whom she greatly resembled, by the way. Princess Pauline had that ideally chaste look, and you know—what she died of. But Pauline had not enough modesty to give a rosy tint to the smallest part of her charming body, whilst La Rosalba had enough to dye scarlet every part of hers. The naïve remark of astonishment of Pauline Borghese when she was asked how she could pose nude before Canova—'But the studio was warm! There was a stove!'—La Rosalba would never have uttered. If you had addressed the same question to her, she would have fled, hiding her face, divinely purple, in hands divinely pink. But be sure that, as she fled, there would have lurked in one of the folds of her robe all the temptations of hell.

"Such was Rosalba, whose virginlike aspect deceived us all when she arrived in the regiment. Major Ydow might have presented her to us as his legitimate wife, or even his daughter, and we should have believed him. Although her limpid blue eyes were beautiful, they were never more beautiful than when they were cast down. The lids were more expressive than the look. To us men—who had spent our time in war, or with women, and what women!—this strange creature caused a new sensation.

"It was vulgarly, but forcibly, said of her that 'she might have gone straight to God without confessing.' 'What a confoundedly pretty girl!' whispered the old stagers; 'but what an affected minx! How does she manage to make the Major happy?' He knew, but he did not tell.

"He drank his happiness in silence, like those true drunkards who drink alone. He never told of the secret happiness which made him faithful and discreet for the first time in his life—him! the Lauzun of the garrison, the most pompous and conceited of men, and who, when at Naples—said officers, who had known him there—was called the drum-major of seduction. The good looks, of which he was so proud, might have brought all the daughters of Spain to his feet, and he would not have raised a single one of them.

"At that time we were on the frontier between Spain and

Portugal, with the English in front of us, and we occupied the
not much less hostile border towns of King Joseph. Major Ydow
and La Rosalba lived together as they would have done in a
garrison town in time of peace. You remember that stubborn
war in Spain, furious yet slow, which was not like any other war,
for we did not fight solely for conquest, but to plant a new
dynasty, and a fresh order of things in a country which must be
first conquered. You all remember that between these stub-
bornly fought fields there were long pauses, and that, in the intervals, we gave, in the part of the country we held, fêtes, to
which we invited all the most *afrancesadas* of the Spanish
women. It was at these fêtes that the wife of Major Ydow, who
had been already much noticed, became celebrated. She shone
amidst the dark daughters of Spain like a diamond on a jet
fringe. It was then she first began to exercise on men all those
fascinations which composed her devilish nature, and made her
the most depraved of courtesans, with the look of the most heavenly Madonna of Raphael.

"The passions she aroused continued to burn and spread. In
a short time everyone was under her thrall, even the generals
who were old enough to be prudent—all were smitten with La
Pudica, as they liked to call her. Everyone had pretensions to
her, and duels were fought about her, as was sure to be the case
amongst high-spirited men who had always their sword in hand.
She was the sultan of these terrible odalisques, and threw her
handkerchief to anyone who pleased her—and many pleased her.

"As for Major Ydow, he let her say and do what she liked.
Was he too conceited to be jealous, or, knowing he was hated and
despised, did he enjoy, in the pride of possession, the passions
which the woman of whom he was the master, inspired in his
enemies? It was hardly possible that he failed to notice anything.
I have sometimes seen his emerald eyes turn dark as carbuncles
when he saw some officer, who was suspected of being the favoured
lover of his better half at the moment—but he restrained himself.
And as everybody always thought the worst possible about him,

his calm indifference, or voluntary blindness, was imputed to the most unworthy motives. It was thought that his wife was not so much a pedestal for his vanity as a ladder for his ambition.

"That was said—as things of that sort are said—but he never heard it. I, who had my reasons for observing him, and who deemed that the hate and scorn which were heaped upon him were unjust, often asked myself whether there were more weakness than strength, or more strength than weakness, about the sombre impassiveness of this man, who was daily betrayed by his mistress, and who never showed the bites of jealousy. By heaven! gentlemen, we have all known men so hypnotized by a woman as still to believe in her when everything accuses her, and who, instead of revenging themselves, when the absolute certainty of treason is brought home to their souls, prefer to hide in the happiness of cowardice, and draw over their head the coverlet of ignominy!

"Was Major Ydow such a man? Perhaps. Certainly La Pudica was capable of having reduced him to that degrading condition of fanaticism. The mythological Circe, who changed men to brutes, was not to be compared to this Virgin-Messalina. With the passions that burned in her heart, she was soon compromised in the eyes of all the officers (who were not very particular about women), but she never compromised herself.

"This distinction must be borne in mind. She never by her conduct gave anyone a hold over her. If she had a lover, it was a secret between her and her alcove. Major Ydow had not the ghost of a chance of making even the pretence of a scandal. Did she love him, perchance? She lived with him, and she could surely, if she had wished, have linked her fortunes to another. I knew a Field Marshal who so doted on her that he had his *baton* made into an umbrella-handle for her. There are women who love—not their lover, though they love him as well. The carp regret their mud, said Madame de Maintenon. La Rosalba did not want to regret hers, so she never came out of it—and I fell into it.

"You all know the song which was sung last century:

> When Boufflers came to Court,
> With love she made all burn.
> And each one had her in his turn.

"And I had her in my turn. I have had women by the gross.

"But I very much doubt if there was one like Rosalba amongst them all. The mud was a paradise. I am going to give you an analysis of my feelings, as a novelist would. I was a man of action, sensual in love-affairs, like Comte Almaviva, and I did not love her in the elevated and romantic sense of the word. Neither soul, intellect, nor vanity counted for anything in the kind of happiness she lavished on one, but the happiness had nothing of the lightness of a passing fancy. I had not supposed sensuality could be so profound. It was the most profound of sensualities. Ah! the body of that woman was her only soul. And with that body she one evening gave me a pleasure that will enable you better to judge of her than anything I can say about her. Yes, one evening she had the boldness and indecency to receive me when her only costume was a thin, transparent Indian muslin—a mist, a vapour, through which you saw her body, the shape of which was its only purity, and which was dyed with the deep vermilion of voluptuousness and modesty. May the Devil take me if she did not resemble a statue of living coral beneath this white mist. Since that time, I do not care *that* for the whiteness of other women."

And Mesnilgrand flicked a bit of orange-peel up to the ceiling over the head of Representative Le Carpentier, who had helped to bring low the head of a king.

"Our amour lasted some time," he continued, "but do not imagine that I wearied of her. I did not weary of her. Into sensation, which is finite, as the philosophers say in their abominable jargon, she imported the infinite. No; if I left her it was for reasons of moral disgust—of pride for myself and scorn for her—for

in her most lascivious embraces I could not believe that she loved
me.

"When I asked her: 'Do you love me?'—that question which
it is impossible not to ask, even with every proof given you that
you are loved—she would reply: 'No,' or shake her head in a
puzzling manner. She wallowed in modesty and shame, and remained beneath them as impenetrable as the Sphinx. Only the
Sphinx was cold, and she was not.

"Well, this impenetrability, which irritated and annoyed me,
followed by the certainty I had that she indulged in as many
amours as Catherine II, formed the double cause why I pulled
myself up short with a strong curb, and tore myself from the
seductive arms of this woman. I left her—or rather I never went
back to her. But I preserved my opinion that there could never
be another woman like her, and that thought made me easy, and
even indifferent to all other women. But she put the finishing
touch to me, as an officer. After I left her, I thought of nothing
but my military duties. She had dipped me in the Styx."

"And you became quite an Achilles," said old Monsieur de
Mesnilgrand, proudly.

"I do not know what I became," continued Mesnilgrand, "but
I know that after our separation, Major Ydow—who was on the
same terms with me that he was with the other officers of the
Division—told us one day at the café that his wife was pregnant,
and that he soon expected the happiness of being a father. At
this unexpected news, some looked at one another, others smiled,
but he noticed nothing, or, if he did, paid no attention, being probably resolved to resent nothing but a direct insult. When he had
left, 'Is the child yours, Mesnil?' whispered a friend in my ear,
and in my conscience a secret voice, better informed than his,
put the same question to me. I did not dare to reply. La
Rosalba, even in our most confidential interviews, had never said
a word to me about this child, which might be mine, or the
Major's, or someone else's."

"The child of the regiment," broke in Mautravers, as though he were delivering point with his cavalry sabre.

"Never," Mesnilgrand went on, "had she made the least allusion to her pregnancy—but what was there astonishing in that? La Pudica was, as I have said, a Sphinx, who devoured pleasure silently, and kept her secret. No heart or affection ever filtered through her corporal frame, which was only open to pleasure, and in whom modesty, no doubt, was the first fear, the first trembling, the first faint spark of pleasure. To learn that she was pregnant had a curious effect upon me. We must agree, gentlemen, now that we are past the bestial period of passion, that there is something terrible about these partnerships in paternity—this shared platter—and that is the loss of all paternal feeling; the terrible anxiety—which prevents you from hearing the voice of nature, and chokes it in a doubt from which there is no escape. You say to yourself: 'Is this child mine?'

"Uncertainty pursues you, as a punishment for your share in the transaction—the shameful partnership in which you are involved! If you had a heart, and you thought for long on this question, you would go mad; but life, with all its powerful interests and frivolities, carries you away on its flood, like the cork float of a broken line.

"When I had heard this statement made by Major Ydow, the paternal instinct I had first felt, died away.—It is true that a few days later I had something else to think of than La Pudica's baby. We fought at Talavera, and Major Litan of the 9th Hussars was killed in the first charge; so I was obliged to take command of the squadron.

"The battle of Talavera only embittered the war. We were more often on the march, more harassed by the enemy, and naturally there was less talk about La Pudica amongst us. She followed the regiment in a wagon, and it was there, it was said, that she was delivered of a child, which Major Ydow, who believed himself to be the father, loved as though it had really been his.

At least, when the child died, for it died some months after its birth, the Major evinced deep grief, and was almost beside himself. He was no longer laughed at in the regiment. For the first time, the antipathy of which he was the object was stilled. He was pitied much more than the mother, who, if she wept for her offspring, still continued to be the Rosalba we all knew, that harlot of the Devil's own make, who had, in spite of her vices, preserved the almost miraculous faculty of being able to blush to her backbone two hundred times a day. Her beauty did not diminish. It resisted all wear and tear. And yet the life she was leading was calculated, if it had lasted, to have made her 'as worn out as an old saddle-cloth,' as they say in the cavalry."

"It didn't last? You know then what became of that —— of a woman?" asked Rançonnet, breathless with excitement, and forgetting for a minute the visit to the church he was so anxious to have explained.

"Yes," said Mesnilgrand, concentrating his voice as though he had reached the climax of his story. "You believed, as everybody else did, that she sunk with Ydow in the storm of war, and those events in which so many of us were scattered and disappeared. I will tell you the fate of Rosalba."

Captain Rançonnet put his elbows on the table, and listened attentively, holding his glass in his big hand as though it had been the hilt of his sabre.

"The war did not cease," continued Mesnilgrand. "The patient fury of the Spaniards, who took five hundred years to drive out the Moors, would have taken as long to drive us out. We could not advance through the country without examining every step we took. Every village we took we fortified, and turned it into a weapon against the enemy. The little town of Alcudia, which we had taken, was our garrison for some time. A large convent there was transformed into a barrack, but the staff was lodged in private houses in the town, and Major Ydow had that of the *alcalde*. As this was the largest house in the town, Major Ydow often received the officers there, for we kept to ourselves

now. We had broken off all relations with the *afrancesados*, mis-
trusting them, as the hatred of the French was on the increase.
At these meetings, which were sometimes interrupted by the fir-
ing of the enemy and a brush with our outposts, La Rosalba did
the honours; always with that incomparably chaste air, that
seemed to me a joke of the Devil.

"She chose her victims, but I never troubled about my succes-
sors. I had torn myself away from her, and I did not drag behind me what someone or other has called the broken chain of
lost hopes. I felt neither spite, jealousy, nor resentment. I was
interested, but as a spectator only, in the doings of this woman,
who concealed the most impudent vices under the most charming affectation of innocence.

"I used to go to her house, and before other people she spoke
to me with the simplicity and almost the innocence of a young
girl you meet by accident at a well or in a wood. She no longer
intoxicated me, turned my head, or set my senses on fire—all those
terrible symptoms had passed. I looked upon them as having
melted away and disappeared. But I could not, whenever I saw
that scarlet flush suffuse her face for a word or a look, help thinking of a man who sees, in his emptied glass, the last drop of the
rosy champagne he has been drinking, and who pours on his
thumb-nail the last forgotten drop.

"One evening, I was alone with her. I had quitted the café
early, and had left all the officers there playing cards or billiards,
and gambling heavily. It was evening, but an evening in Spain,
when the hot sun had scarcely torn itself away from the sky. I
found her hardly clad, with her shoulders and arms bare—those
beautiful arms I had so often bitten, and which under certain
emotions that I had caused sometimes, assumed what artists call
the 'tone' of the inside of a strawberry. Her hair, charmingly
disordered by the heat, fell thickly over her delicately tinted neck,
and this dishevelled, negligent, languorous air made her look
beautiful enough to have tempted Satan and revenged Eve.

"She was half reclining on a couch, and was writing. No

doubt what La Pudica wrote was an assignation for some lover—
some fresh infidelity to Major Ydow, who swallowed them all as
she devoured pleasure—in silence. When I entered, the letter was
written, and she was melting the wax in the flame of a candle—a
blue wax sprinkled with silver, which I seem to see still, and you
will learn directly why that blue wax streaked with silver has
lingered so long in my memory.

" 'Where is the Major?' she asked, when she saw me enter; and
she had already put on a troubled air—but then she always had a
troubled air, this woman who flattered men's conceit by always
appearing to tremble before them.

" 'He is playing heavily this evening,' I replied, laughing and
looking longingly at the pink tint which suffused her face; 'but I
have other desires this evening.'

"She understood me. Nothing surprised her. She lit up the
fires of desire in all men, on every occasion.

" 'Bah!' she said slowly, though the carnation tint I so adored
on her lovely and abominable face grew deeper at the thought
my words occasioned. 'Bah! your desires soon pass away!'
And she pressed the seal on the burning wax—the flame died
out, and the wax hardened.

" 'Look!' she said with provoking insolence; 'that is like you
men. A moment ago it was burning, and now it is cold!'

"As she said this, she turned the letter, and bent over it to
write the address.

"Must I keep on repeating that I was not jealous of this woman?
—but we are all the same. In spite of myself, I wished to see to
whom she was writing, and to do that, as I was still standing, I
leaned over her head, but could not see because of her shoulders,
and that intoxicating velvety space between them which I had so
often kissed; and, magnetized by the sight, I could not help adding one kiss the more, and the sensation prevented her from writing. She raised her head, which was bending over the table, as
though she had been touched with a red-hot iron, and throwing
herself back on the couch, gazed at me with that mixture of desire

and confusion which was her great charm, her eyes raised and turned to me, and as I was standing behind her, I was obliged to bestow upon the moist, pink, half-opened mouth a kiss as warm as that I had just let fall between her shoulders.

"Sensitive as she was, she had the nerves of a tiger.

"Suddenly she sprung to her feet.

" 'The Major is coming upstairs,' she said. 'He must have lost, and he is jealous when he has lost. There will be a terrible scene. Go in here! I will get rid of him!' and she opened the door of a large cupboard in which her dresses hung, and pushed me in. I suppose there are few men who have not some time or other been put in a cupboard, when the husband or protector arrived on the scene."

"You were lucky to have a cupboard," said Sélune. "I had once to get into a coal-sack. That was before my damned wound, of course. I was in the White Hussars then. You may guess what state I was in when I came out of my coal-sack."

"Yes," continued Mesnilgrand bitterly, "that is one of the drawbacks of adultery. At such a time even the most high-spirited man loses his pride, and, in generous consideration for a frightened woman, becomes as cowardly as she is, and commits the cowardice of hiding himself.

"It made me feel sick to find myself in a cupboard, in my uniform, and with my sabre at my side, and covered with ridicule, for a woman who had no honour to lose, and whom I did not love.

"But I had not much time to reflect upon my mean conduct in hiding myself there like a school-boy in a dark cupboard. The touch of her dresses as they brushed against my face seemed to intoxicate me. What I heard was sufficient to dissipate all voluptuous sensations; the Major had come in, and, as she had guessed, was in a very bad humour, and, as she had also said, had a jealous fit, and a jealousy all the more explosive because he concealed it from us. Suspicious and angry as he was, his eye probably fell on the letter which remained on the table, and which my two kisses had prevented La Pudica from addressing.

" 'What is that letter?' he said, roughly.

" 'A letter for Italy,' replied La Pudica quietly.

"He was not deceived by this quiet reply.

" 'That is not true!' he said rudely, for there was no need to scratch the Lauzun in this man to find the free-lance, and I understood at once what kind of life these two led together. From inside the cupboard, I could hear all that went on, though I could fancy their actions from their words, and the intonation of their voices. The Major insisted on seeing this unaddressed letter, and La Pudica, who had possession of it, obstinately refused to show it to him. Then the Major tried to take it by force. I could hear that a struggle was going on between them, but, as you may suppose, the Major was stronger than his wife. He got hold of the letter, and read it. It was to give a rendezvous to one of her lovers—to offer him a happiness he had already enjoyed. But the lover was not named. Absurdly curious, like all jealous men, the Major sought in vain for the name of the man who had deceived him. And La Pudica was revenged for having had the letter taken away from her, and her hand bruised, and perhaps bleeding, for I heard her cry during the struggle: 'You have hurt my hand, you wretch!'

"Mad at not being able to learn the truth, and defied and mocked by this letter, which only told him one thing, that she had a lover—a lover the more—Major Ydow fell into one of those rages which dishonour a man, and loaded La Pudica with insults that a bargee might have used. I thought that he was about to strike her. The blows did indeed come, but a little later. He reproached her—and in what terms!—with being—what she was. He was brutal, vile, revolting, and to all this fury she replied like a woman who cares little or nothing; who understands thoroughly the man to whom she is linked, and knows that their life, in their own lair, must be a continual battle.

"She was not so base, but more atrocious, more insulting, and more cruel in her coolness than he was in his anger.

"She was insolent, ironical, laughing with the hysterical laughter

of hate, at the most acute paroxysms of his wrath, and replying
to the torrent of abuse which the Major vomited forth, with those
remarks which women know how to make when they want to
drive us mad, and which to an angry man are like a hand-
grenade falling into a powder-magazine. Of all her coolly insulting words, the one with which she most often pricked him was
that she did not love him—that she had never loved him.
'Never! never! never!' she repeated with a joyous fury, as though
the declaration made her heart bound with joy.

"Now, nothing could have been more painfully cruel to this
conceited ass, whose good looks had done so much execution
amongst women, and whose affection for her was overtopped by
his vanity, than this idea that she had never loved him. He could
no longer bear the stings of this oft-repeated insult that she had
never loved him, and obstinately refused to believe it.

"'And what about our child?' he foolishly asked, as though he
had reminded her of a convincing proof she was not telling the
truth.

"'Ah, our child!' she replied with a burst of laughter. 'It was
not yours!'

"I can imagine the expression in the Major's green eyes,
when I heard the choked cry like that of a wildcat. He uttered
a terrible oath.

"'Whose was it, then, cursed harlot?' he asked with something
that was no longer a voice.

"But she continued to laugh like a hyena.

"'You shall never know,' she replied teasingly. And she
lashed him with this 'you shall never know,' a thousand times repeated, a thousand times inflicted on his ears, and when she was
tired of saying it, she—would you believe it!—sang it as a refrain.
Then, when she had made him spin like a top in the spirals of
anxiety and uncertainty, under the lash of this word, and the man,
beside himself with wrath, was in her hands but a puppet she was
about to break; when with cynical hate she had named all her
lovers, nearly every officer there was, 'I have had them all,' she

cried, 'but they have none of them had me. And that child you are ass enough to think yours is the child of the only man I ever loved—I ever idolized. You haven't guessed who he is? You cannot guess who he is?'

"She lied. She had never loved any man. But she knew that this lie was a deadly stab, and she cut and slashed him with this lie, till tired of being the executioner of such a victim, she finished by driving into his heart, up to the hilt, this last avowal.

" 'Well, as you can't guess, cudgel your brains no longer, poor fool! It is Captain Mesnilgrand!'

"Probably this was another lie, but my own name struck me like a bullet coming through the door. After she had pronounced my name, there was complete silence. Has he killed her instead of replying? I said to myself, when suddenly I heard the splintering crash of a glass that had been thrown on the floor, and had broken into a thousand pieces.

"I have told you that Major Ydow felt a deep, paternal affection for the child he believed to be his, and his grief at the child's death had been long and lasting. As we were soldiers on a campaign, it was impossible for him to erect to his son a tomb and visit it every day—the idolatry of the grave—but the Major had caused his son's heart to be embalmed, in order that he might carry it about with him everywhere, and had the heart enclosed in a glass vase which generally stood on a bracket in his bedroom. It was this vase which was now shattered in pieces.

" 'Ah, it was not mine, miserable whore!' he cried; and I heard him grind the glass under his feet, and stamp upon the heart he had believed to be that of his son. No doubt she tried to pick it up, to—to save it from his fury—for I heard her throw herself upon him, but with the sound of the struggle there mingled another sound—that of blows.

" 'Well, if you want it, there is your brat's heart, shameless drab!' said the Major. And he beat her face with the heart he had so much adored, and even threw it at her head as a missile. 'Deep calls unto deep,' they say. Sacrilege created sacrilege.

"La Pudica, beside herself with passion, did what the Major had done. She threw back at his head the child's heart, which, perhaps, she would not have done had it been really his—the offspring of the man she execrated, to whom she wished to render torture for torture, ignominy for ignominy. Surely this must have been the first time that such a sight was ever beheld by human eye! a father and a mother throwing in each other's faces the heart of their dead child!

"This impious combat must have lasted some minutes. It was so astonishingly tragic that I was unable to think of putting my shoulder to the door, bursting it open, and interfering, when a cry such as I have never heard, nor you either, gentlemen—and yet we have heard some frightful enough on the field of battle— gave me the strength to break open the door, and I saw—what I shall never see again.

"The Major had pushed down La Pudica on the table where she had been writing, and held her with a grip of iron. All her clothes had been torn off in the struggle, and her beautiful, naked body twisted like a wounded snake beneath his grasp.

"But what do you think he was doing with his other hand, gentlemen? The writing-table, the lighted candle, the wax lying by the side—all these had given the Major an infernal suggestion— that of sealing his wife as she had sealed the letter—and he was steadily carrying out this terrible vengeance of a perversely jealous lover!

" 'Be punished where you have sinned, miserable woman!' he cried.

"He did not see me. He was bending over his victim, who no longer cried out, and it was the pommel of his sabre that he was using as a seal to press the burning wax.

"I rushed towards him: I did not even tell him to defend himself, and I plunged my sabre up to the hilt in his back between the shoulders, and wished I could have plunged my hand and arm as well as my sword through his body that I might have killed him the more surely."

"You did well, Mesnil," said Commandant Sélune; "a scoundrel like that did not deserve to be killed in front, like one of us."

"Why, it was the fate of Abelard—changed to Heloïse," remarked Abbé Reniant.

"A fine surgical case," said Doctor Bleny, "and rare." Mesnilgrand was too excited to notice these remarks.

"He fell dead," he continued, "on the body of his fainting wife. I tore him away, threw down his body, and kicked the carcass. The shriek that La Pudica had given—wild as that of a she-wolf—and which still rings in my ears—brought the maid to the door. 'Run for the surgeon of the 8th Dragoons!' I cried, 'there is some work for him to-night.' But I had no time to wait for the surgeon. At that moment the bugles rang out the alarm, and called us to arms. The enemy had crept up silently and surprised our sentinels. I sprang to my horse, but before I left I threw one last look on the beautiful mutilated body, lying motionless, and, for the first time, pale before a man's eyes. Then I picked up the poor little heart which was lying on the dusty floor, and which they had used to insult and abuse each other, and carried away in my hussar's belt—the heart of the child they said was mine."

Here Chevalier de Mesnilgrand stopped, overcome by an emotion which they all respected, materialists and dare-devils as they were.

"And La Pudica?" asked—almost timidly—Rançonnet, who was no longer toying with his glass.

"I never heard again of La Rosalba, *alias* La Pudica," replied Mesnilgrand. "Is she dead? Is she still alive? Was the surgeon able to go to her? After the surprise of Alcudia, which was so fatal to us, I looked for him. I could not find him. He had disappeared like many others and had not rejoined the remnant of our decimated regiment."

"Is that all?" said Mautravers. "And, if that is all, that's a fine sort of story. You were right, Mesnil, when you told Sélune that you would cap his story of the eight nuns, violated, and thrown into a well. But as Rançonnet is dreaming in his chair, I will take up the question where he left it. What connexion has your story with your devotions in the church the other day?"

"True," said Mesnilgrand. "You were right to remind me of it. This is what remains to be told to you and Rançonnet. For many years I carried about, as a relic, the heart of the child I supposed to be mine; but when, after Waterloo, I was obliged to take off the belt in which I had hoped to die, and when I had carried for some years longer that heart—and I assure you, Mautravers, that it was heavy, though it may seem to you very light—reflection came with age, and I feared to profane, even but a little more, that heart so profaned already, and I decided to place it in Christian ground.

"I spoke, therefore, to one of the priests of this town, without entering into all the details which I have given you to-day, and it was that heart, which had so long weighed on mine, that I had just placed in his hands in the confessional of the chapel, when Rançonnet grabbed me in the aisle."

Captain Rançonnet was probably satisfied. He did not utter a syllable; nor did the others. No remarks were made. A silence, more expressive than any words, sealed the mouths of all.

Did these atheists at last understand that even if the Church had been established for nothing else but to receive those hearts—dead or alive—with which we no longer know what to do, it would be accomplishing a good work?

"Serve up the coffee," said old Monsieur de Mesnilgrand, in his high-pitched voice. "If it is only as strong as your story, Mesnil, it will be good."

A WOMAN'S REVENGE

A WOMAN'S REVENGE

Foriter.

I HAVE often heard of the daring of modern literature, but, for my own part, I have never believed in it. The reproach is merely an idle boast of morality. Literature, which has long been called the expression of society, does not express it at all—quite the reverse; and when some writer, bolder than the others, dares to go a little further than they do, heaven knows what a fuss is made.

If you examine the matter you will find that literature does not relate half the crimes which society commits mysteriously and with impunity every day, with delightful frequency and facility. Ask the confessors—who would be the greatest novelists the world has ever had if they could relate the stories which are whispered into their ears in the confession-box. Inquire how many cases of incest (for example) are committed in the proudest and noblest families, and see if literature, which is so much accused of immoral boldness, has ever dared to relate them, even to terrify the evil-doers. Except for a slight breath—which is but a breath, after all—on the subject in the *René* of Chateaubriand—the religious Chateaubriand—I do not know of a book in which incest, an offence so common in our day, both in the upper and lower ranks of society, and, perhaps, more in the lower than in the upper, has been freely handled, and all the lessons of a truly tragic morality deduced therefrom. Has modern literature—at which hypocrisy throws its little stone—ever *dared* to relate the histories of Myrrha, Agrippina, and Œdipus, which (believe me) are as true to-day as they were then; for I have not lived—at least up to now—in any other hell than the social hell, and I have, for my own part, known and rubbed shoulders with plenty

239

of Myrrhas, Œdipuses, and Agrippinas in private life, and what
is called the best society. *Parbleu!* their stories are not related
as they would be on the stage, or in history. But glimpses may
be seen under the social surface of precautions, fears, and hy-
pocrisies.

I knew—and all Paris knew—a Madame Henri III, who wore
at her girdle a little chaplet of death's-heads, mounted in gold,
and hanging down on her blue velvet dress; and who sometimes
flogged herself, mingling her penance with the other pleasures of
Henri III. Who would write the history of that woman, who
composed pious works, and whom the Jesuits believed to be a
man (a nice detail that) and even a saint?

It is not many years ago since a lady of the Faubourg Saint-
Germain took her mother's lover, and furious at seeing that
lover return to her mother—who, though old, knew better than her
daughter how to make herself loved—stole some of the letters her
mother had addressed to this lover, had them lithographed, and
thrown by thousands from the "Paradise" (well named for
such an action) of the opera on the night of a first performance!
Who has ever written the history of that woman? If poor literature essayed to write such stories it would not know at which
end to begin.

Yet that is what it would relate if it were outspoken.

History has many a Tacitus and Suetonius; Romance has not
—at least among writers who possess both morality and talent.
It is true that the Latin language dares to be honest—like the
pagan that it is—whilst our language was baptized with Clovis
in the font of Saint-Remy, and there contracted an imperishable
modesty, for the old woman still blushes.

Nevertheless if a writer *dared to dare,* a Suetonius or a Tacitus
might exist amongst the novelists, for the Novel is specially the
history of manners put in a dramatic form, and History is often
the same. There is only this difference between them; that the
one (the Novel) describes manners under the cover of fictitious
personages, and the other (History) gives the real names and

addresses. But Romance goes further than History. It has an ideal, whilst History has not, being restrained by reality. Romance, too, holds the stage for a much longer period. Lovelace will live longer in Richardson than Tiberius will in Tacitus.

But if Tiberius in Tacitus was described as fully as Lovelace is in Richardson, do you think that History would lose by that, and Tacitus would be less terrible? But I am not afraid to say that Tacitus, as a painter, is beneath Tiberius as a model, and that in spite of all his genius he is crushed by it.

And that is not all. To this striking but inexplicable failure in literature, when you compare its reality with the reputation it has, must be added the physiognomy that crime has assumed in these times of delightful progress. High civilization deprives crime of its terrible poetry, and does not allow an author to restore it. "That would be too horrible," those people say who like to look on the light side of everything, even crime. One of the advantages of philanthropy! Idiotic criminalists diminish the penalty, and inept moralists the crime, and yet they only diminish the latter in order to reduce the penalty. The crimes of high civilization, however, are certainly worse than those of extreme barbarism, by the very fact of their refinement, the corruption which they indicate, and the higher degree of intelligence of the perpetrators. The Inquisition knew that well. At a time when religious faith and public manners were both strong, the Inquisition, the tribunal which judged thought—that great institution, the very idea of which puckers our weak nerves, and turns our feather-brained heads—the Inquisition knew well that spiritual crimes were the worst, and punished them as such.

And in fact if those crimes appeal less to the senses, they appeal more to the intellect; and the intellect, after all, is the deepest part of us. The novelist, therefore, can draw upon a whole realm of unknown tragic crimes, more intellectual than physical, which seem less criminal to the superficiality of an old, materialistic society because no blood was spilt, and the murder was within the domain of sentiment and custom.

It is of this kind of tragedy that I wish to give a specimen in relating the history of a vengeance of a most terribly original nature, in which no blood flowed, and neither steel nor poison was used; a *civilized* crime, in fact, in which the narrator has invented nothing but his manner of relating the story.

Towards the end of the reign of Louis-Philippe, a young man was one evening strolling along the Rue Basse-du-Rempart, which at that time well deserved its name Basse, for it was lower than the pavement of the Boulevard, and formed an excavation, always sombre and badly lighted, and to which you descended from the Boulevards by two staircases which turned their backs to one another—if you can employ that term about two staircases. This excavation, which no longer exists, ran from the Chaussée d'Antin to the Rue Caumartin, where it again sloped upwards to the level of the Boulevard. This dark valley was not over-safe in the day-time, and few dared to venture into it at night. The Devil is the Prince of Darkness, and this was one of his principalities. Almost in the middle of this excavation, and bordered on one side by the Boulevard, which formed a terrace, and on the other by some large, quiet-looking houses with carriage-entrances, and a few old-furniture shops, there was a narrow, uncovered passage, in which the wind—if there were ever so little wind—whistled down as though it were a flute, and this passage led to the Rue Neuve-des-Mathurins.

The young man in question was well dressed, and he had taken this path, which was certainly not a path of virtue, because he was following a woman, who had entered this suspiciously dark passage without hesitation or embarrassment.

He was evidently a dandy, or, as it was called in those days, "a yellow glove." He had had a good dinner at the Café de Paris, and afterwards had leaned against the low balcony (now removed) at Tortoni's, chewing his tooth-pick and ogling the women who passed along the Boulevard. This particular woman had passed in front of him several times, and although this circumstance, and her loud dress and swaggering walk showed

plainly what she was, and although this young man, who was
called Robert de Fressignies, was horribly blasé, and had returned
from the East (where he had seen every variety and species
of the animal woman), yet, the fifth time this nightwalker had
passed him, he had followed her—*currishly*, as he said of himself—for he possessed the faculty of examining and judging his
own acts, though his judgment did not prevent the acts, even
when they were contrary to it—a terrible asymptote!

Fressignies was more than thirty years of age. He had out-
lived that first youth of folly which makes a man the buffoon
of his own senses, and during which any woman exerts a magnetic influence over him. He was long past that. He was a
libertine of the cold and calculating sort of that positive age—
an intellectual libertine who had thought about those feelings of
which he was no longer the dupe, and was neither afraid nor
ashamed of any of them.

What he had seen, or what he thought he had seen, had aroused
a curiosity to analyse a new sensation. He had therefore left his
balcony and followed her—resolved to see to its end this vulgar
adventure he had undertaken. For him, the woman who was
gliding gracefully in front of him was only one of the lower sort
of prostitutes, but she was so beautiful that he could not help
wondering her beauty had not obtained her a higher position, and
that she had not found someone who would save her from the
miseries of the streets, for in Paris, whenever God places a pretty
woman there, the Devil in reply immediately puts a fool to keep
her.

And then Robert de Fressignies had another reason for following her, besides her wondrous beauty (which perhaps the
Parisians did not see, for they know very little about true beauty,
their æsthetic standard being low). She resembled someone he
had seen. She was the mocking-bird which imitates the night-
ingale, of which Byron speaks so sadly in his memoirs. She reminded him of another woman. He was certain, absolutely certain, that it was not she, but she resembled her enough to deceive

anybody, if deceit had not been impossible. He was, moreover, more attracted than surprised by this, for he had enough experience as an observer to know that, in the long run, there is much less variety than is imagined in human faces, the features of which are ruled by hard and fast geometrical laws, and are easily classified in a few types. Beauty is single. Only ugliness is multiple, and even then its multiplicity is soon exhausted. God has decreed that infinite variety should exist only in the physiognomy, because the physiognomy is the reflection of the soul across the lines—straight or erratic, natural or contorted—of the face.

Fressignies said all this confusedly to himself as he followed along the Boulevard the sinuous steps of this woman, who looked prouder than Tintoretto's Queen of Sheba, in her dress of saffron satin with gold shades—that colour which is so much esteemed by the young Roman women—and the shiny folds as she walked rustled and shone and seemed a call to arms. She threw back her figure to an extent rarely seen in France, and she wore a magnificent Turkish shawl with stripes of white, scarlet, and gold, and the red feather of her white bonnet—splendid in its bad taste—hung down to her shoulder. At that period, women wore long drooping feathers which they called "weeping willows."

But there was nothing weeping about this woman, and her feather expressed something else rather than melancholy.

Fressignies thought she would take the Rue de la Chaussée d'Antin, then sparkling with its thousand lamps, and saw with surprise all the showy finery of the courtesan, all the impudent pride of the harlot disappear into the Rue Basse du Rempart—the disgrace of the Boulevard at that time.

The dandy, less brave than she, hesitated to risk his varnished boots in such a street. It was but for a second. The gold robe, lost sight of for an instant in the shadows of this dark hole, reappeared beyond the spot where the solitary lamp shed its flicker, and he hastened to it. He had not much difficulty in overtaking the woman—she was waiting for him, sure that he would come,

and as he came up to her she looked him full in the face, meeting
his glance with all the effrontery of her calling. He was literally blinded by the beauty of the face, which, though plastered
with rouge, was of a golden brown, like the wings of certain
insects, and which the dim light falling from the lamp could not
pale.

"You are Spanish!" said Fressignies, who saw that she was one
of the purest types of that race.

"*Si,*" she replied.

To be a Spaniard meant something at that time, something
highly quoted in the market. The novels of those days, the plays
of Clara Gazul, the poetry of Alfred de Musset, the dances of
Mariano Camprubi and Dolores Serral, had caused the daughters
of Spain to be popular favourites, and many women claimed to be
Spanish who had no right to the title. But this woman appeared
to take no special pride in her nationality.

"Will you come?" she said brusquely, with all the familiarity of
the low-class prostitute.

The tone, the harsh, hoarse voice, the sudden familiarity of the
tutoiement, so heavenly upon the lips of a woman you love, and
so horribly insolent in the mouth of a creature to whom you are
a stranger, would have sufficed to disgust Fressignies, but the
Devil tempted him. Curiosity, spiced with desire, seized him, and
for this woman, who was more to him than a superb animal in
satin, and for her sake he would not only have swallowed Eve's
apple, but all the toads in a marsh.

"By Jove! of course I will," he replied. As though she could
doubt it! "I will take precautions to-morrow," he thought.

They entered the passage which leads to the Rue des Mathurins.
Amidst the huge blocks of stone which lay about, and the build-
ings which were being erected, there stood one house alone, narrow, ugly, grim, which must have seen much vice and much crime
on every floor of its old crumbling walls, and which perhaps had
been left there that it might see more still. A blind-looking
house, for not one of its windows (and windows are the

eyes of a house) was lighted—a house that seemed to cling
to you as you groped in the dark night. This horrible house
had the sort of entrance usual to such places, and, at the end
of a miserable corridor, was the staircase, the first few steps of
which were lighted by a dim flicker from a dirty lamp.

The woman entered a narrow passage which was filled by her
shoulders, and her sweeping, rustling dress, and with a step evidently accustomed to the place, slowly ascended the winding staircase, appropriately snail-like in this case, for the walls were
slimy.

But, what was rather unusual in such a den, the dirty staircase
grew lighter as you ascended, and at the first floor it was no longer
the feeble glimmer from the stinking oil-lamp, but a strong light,
which became splendid when the second floor was reached. Two
bronze griffins, fastened to the wall, bore a number of candles,
and illuminated with strange luxury a common-looking door, on
which was pasted the card which women of that sort use as the
sign of their calling.

Surprised at this unexpected magnificence in such a place,
Fressignies paid more attention to these candelabra, which had
evidently been wrought by the hand of a skilful artist, than to the
card which bore the woman's name, which he did not need to
know, since he accompanied her. As he looked at them, whilst
she turned the key in the lock of the door so curiously ornamented
and flooded with light, he remembered the *surprises* which were
often found in the houses of prostitutes in the days of Louis XV.
"This woman," he thought to himself, "has read some novel or
some memoirs of those times, and has had a whim to fill her apartment with all sorts of voluptuous coquetries where you would
never have expected to find them."

But what he saw when the door was opened, redoubled his
astonishment—but in a very different manner.

It was in fact only the ordinary, untidy room of the common
prostitute. Dresses thrown about on every article of furniture,
a big bed—the field of her manœuvres—with those immoral

looking-glasses at the end and on the ceiling, showed well what sort of an occupant the apartment had. On the mantelpiece were bottles of perfume, carelessly left uncorked by the woman when she started out on her evening prowl, and the odours, mingling with the warm air of the room, formed an atmosphere in which a man's energy would melt away at the third breath he took. Two candelabra, similar to those at the door, burned on either side of the chimney. Skins of various animals were thrown down over the carpet. Through a half-open door could be seen a mysterious dressing-room—the vestry of the priestess.

All these details Fressignies did not notice till later. He saw nothing at first but the woman. Knowing where he was, he did as he liked. He threw himself on the sofa, and made the woman —who had taken off her bonnet and shawl and thrown them on an arm-chair—stand between his knees. He took her by the waist, as though he would have spanned it with his two hands, and looked at her from head to feet, like a toper who raises his glass to the light before sipping the wine. The impression he had formed on the Boulevard had not deceived him. Blasé and accustomed to women as he was, he could not help owning she was splendid. The resemblance, which had struck him so much in the broken light and shade, this woman still preserved in the full light of the room. But the person of whom she made him think, though her features were so like that they seemed identical, had not that expression of resolute and almost terrible pride which the Devil, the father of all anarchy, had refused to a duchess, and had given —for what purpose?—to a street-walker of the Boulevards. When she had bared her head, her black hair, yellow dress, and her broad shoulders, which were surpassed in breadth by her hips, she reminded you of the Judith by Vernet (a picture of that period), but her body was more suited for the sports of love, and the face was even more ferocious.

This grim ferocity was perhaps due to a wrinkle which divided her beautiful eyebrows, and extended to her temple: Fressignies had seen the same thing in some Asiatic women in Turkey. It seemed a striking contrast that this woman had the figure of her profession, but not the face. The harlot's body seemed to say eloquently: "Take me"—yet this rounded cup of love which invited both the hands and lips, was surmounted by a face the haughty pride of which would have arrested desire, and petrified the hottest lust into respect.

Happily the ready smile of the courtesan with which she was able to disguise the scornful curl of her lips, attracted to her those whom the cruel pride of her face would have repelled. On the Boulevard she had displayed this set smile, but now, when she was standing in front of Fressignies and between his knees, she was serious, and her face wore such a stern implacable look that if she had had a curved sabre in her hands, the dandy, Fressignies, could, without conceit, have imagined himself Holophernes.

He took hold of her unarmed hands, and remarked how beautifully formed they were. She silently allowed him to examine her, and she also looked at him, not with the sordid interested curiosity of women of her sort, who look at you as you would look at a doubtful coin. Evidently there was something beyond the gain she was about to make or the pleasure she was about to give. There was in the open nostrils, which were quite as expressive as the eyes, and seemed to dart forth flames as the eyes did, a stern decision, as of that of some crime to be committed. "If the implacable look of that face were due to love, what a piece of good fortune for me in these empty, hollow-hearted days!" thought Fressignies, who before he got rid of a whim, examined it as though it were an English horse.

He, the experienced, the critical in the matter of women, who had bought pretty girls in the market at Adrianople, and who knew the price of human flesh of that colour and firmness, threw, as the price of a couple of hours with this woman, a handful of louis into a blue glass cup which was placed on a level with his hand on a console table, and which cup had probably never received so much gold.

"Ah, you like me, then?" she cried impudently, and perhaps impatient at the long examination, in which curiosity had seemed more powerful than desire, and which had been either a loss of time for her or an impertinence. "Let me take off all this," she added, as though her dress weighed heavily upon her, as she pulled open the buttons.

She sprang from his knees and hurried into the dressing-room. A prosaic detail! did she want to "spare" her dress? The dress is the most useful tool of these workwomen. Fressignies, who thought he had detected in her face the unquenchable lust of a Messalina, was brought face to face with the commonplace. He felt once more that he was in the chamber of a prostitute—a common prostitute of Paris, in spite of a face so out of keeping with the destiny of her to whom it belonged. "Bah!" he thought, "romance is never but skin-deep with these women; you must take it where you can find it."

In following this woman, he had but obeyed an irresistible curiosity, and a vulgar whim, but when she who had inspired these feelings came out of her dressing-room, where she had taken off her habiliments, and came towards him in the costume, which was not one, of a gladiatrix about to fight, he was literally thunderstruck by a beauty which his experienced eye—the sculptor's eye of the real lover of woman—had not entirely divined on the Boulevard, in spite of the whispered revelations of the dress and the walk. If the lightning had entered by the door in place of her, he could not have been more profoundly struck.

She was not quite naked—but she was worse. She was much more indecent than if she had been honestly naked. Statues are naked, and their nakedness is chaste. It is even a boasted chastity. But this woman, who was wickedly immodest, who would have lighted herself, like one of the living torches of the garden of Nero, that she might better incite the passions of men, and who had, no doubt, been taught by her profession all the common tricks of depravity, had combined the insidious, trans-

parency of gauze and the daring of bare flesh, with the bad taste
of abominable libertinism—for who does not know that in libertinism bad taste is powerful?

Her monstrously provoking appearance reminded Fressignies
of that undesirable statuette before which he had often stopped,
for it was on view then at every shop where bronzes were sold,
and upon the pedestal of which you read nothing but the mysterious inscription: "Madame Husson." A dangerous obscene
dream! The dream here was a reality. Before that irritating
reality, that perfect beauty which had not the coldness perfect
beauty too often has, Fressignies, who had been in Turkey, had
he been the most blasé Pasha of Three Tails, would have recovered the emotion of a Christian, or even of an anchorite.

So, when—certain of the effect she would produce—she came
hurriedly towards him, and placed, almost against his mouth, the
magnificent charms of her bosom, with a movement like that of
the courtesan who tempts the Saint in the picture by Paul Ver-
onese, Robert de Fressignies, who was not a saint, yearned for
what she offered him, and took the temptress to his arms with a
passion which she reciprocated, for she threw herself into his
arms. Did she throw herself like that into the arms of everyone
who embraced her? However skilful she might be in the arts and
profession of the prostitute, she could not always have been as
furious and ardent as she was that night, and which not even
exceptional excitement or morbid desire would explain. Had she
only just embraced the horrible profession, that she exercised it
with so much ardour? There seemed so much of the wild beast
about her, that one would have thought she either wished to lose
her own life or take that of the other in each of her caresses. At
that time the Parisian prostitutes, who did not think the pretty
name of *lorette,* which literature had bestowed upon them, and
which Gavarni had immortalized, was sufficiently serious, had
adopted the Oriental soubriquet of "panthers." Not one of them
had a better right to be called a panther. She had all the sup-
pleness, the activity, the bounds, the scratches, and the bites.

Fressignies could testify that no woman who had ever been in his arms up to then had given him such indescribable sensations as this woman gave him in a delirium of lust which was contagious; yet he had been in love.

Yet—must it be said to the glory or to the shame of human nature?—there are in what we call (with an excess of scorn, perhaps) pleasure, abysses as deep as those of love. Was it in these abysses that she overwhelmed him, as the sea overwhelms a strong swimmer in its depths? She greatly surpassed the most guilty souvenirs of this hardened libertine, and soared even to the limits of his imagination, violent and depraved as it was. He forgot everything—both what she was, and why he had come into that house, and into that room, which, when he had entered it, had almost sickened him. She had positively drawn his soul into her own body. She rendered him delirious, though his senses were not easily intoxicated. She satiated him with such voluptuous delights that at one time this atheist in love, this sceptic in all things, had the foolish thought that he had taken the fancy of this woman who bartered her body. Yes, Robert de Fressignies, who had almost the same steel-like character as his model, Robert Lovelace, believed that he must have inspired a caprice, at least, in the heart of this prostitute, who could not behave like that with everybody without being soon consumed by her own lust.

He thought this for two minutes—like a fool—he, the clever man! But the vanity which she had lighted at the fire of a pleasure as burning as that of love, experienced between two caresses the shiver of a sudden doubt. A voice cried to him from the depths of his soul: "It is not yourself she loves in you," for he had noticed that when she was the most pantherish, and was clinging to him the most lovingly, she was absorbed in the contemplation of a bracelet she wore on her arm, and which Fressignies saw contained the portrait of a man. Some words in Spanish, which Fressignies, who did not know the language, did not understand, mingled with the cries of the bacchante, and seemed to him to be addressed to this portrait.

Then the idea that he was *passing for someone else*—that he was there on account of another—flashed across his mind, and chilled his passion to ferocity. In one of those fits of absurd jealousy, and tigerish vanity, when a man is not the master of himself, he seized her arm roughly, and demanded to see this bracelet which she regarded with an ardour which was certainly not intended for him at such a moment, when all of this woman ought to belong to him.

"Show me that portrait!" he said in a voice that was even harder than his hand.

She understood, but showed no indignation.

"Surely you cannot be jealous of a girl like me," she said. But it was not the word "girl" that she employed. To the surprise of Fressignies, it was the coarsest epithet ever applied as an insult to a woman that she used.

"Do you want to see it?" she added. "Well! look!" And she placed before his eyes her beautiful arm, still reeking with the intoxicating sweat of the pleasure in which they had been indulging.

It was the portrait of an ugly, lean man, with an olive complexion, and yellowish-black eyes, very gloomy-looking, but not without an air of nobility; the air of a bandit or a Spanish grandee. And he must have been a Spanish grandee, for round his neck was the ribbon of the Golden Fleece.

"Where did you get that?" said Fressignies—who thought to himself: She will spin me a yarn about how she was seduced; the story of the "first one"—the regular story all these women tell.

"Get!" she replied indignantly. *"Por dios,* it was he himself who gave it to me!"

"He! who? your lover, no doubt?" said Fressignies. "You deceived him. He drove you away, and you have come down to this."

"It is not my lover," she replied coldly, as insensible to the insult of such a supposition as though she had been of bronze.

"Perhaps he is not any longer," said Fressignies. "But you love him still—I saw it just now in your eyes."

She laughed bitterly.

"Ah, don't you know the difference between love and hate?" she cried. "Love that man! Why, I detest him! It is my husband!"

"Your husband!"

"Yes, my husband," she said; "the greatest noble in all Spain; thrice a duke, four times a marquis, five times a count, grandee of Spain, and many other titles, knight of the Golden Fleece. I am the Duchess of Arcos de Sierra Leone."

Fressignies, almost thunder-struck by these incredible words, had not the slightest doubt as to the truth of this astounding statement. He was sure the woman did not lie. He had recognized her. The likeness which had so much struck him on the Boulevards proved it.

He had met her before, and not so very long ago either.

It was at Saint-Jean de Luz, where he had gone for the bathing-season. That year, it happened that all the best Spanish society had visited this little town on the coast of France, which is so close to Spain that you may still imagine yourself in Spain, and to which even the most patriotic Spaniards could resort without treason to their country. The Duchess of Sierra Leone had resided all that summer in that little town so profoundly Spanish in its manners, character, appearance, and historical associations, for—it may be remembered—it was there that were celebrated the marriage festivities of Louis XIV—the only king of France, by the way, who resembled a Spanish king.

The Duchess of Sierra Leone was then, it was said, on her honeymoon, after her marriage to the greatest and richest noble-man in Spain. When Fressignies arrived in this fishing-village, the birth-place of some of the most terrible filibusters the world has ever known, she was displaying a luxury and extravagance such as the place had never known since the days of Louis XIV; and her beauty even surpassed that of the Basque women, though they, with their beautiful antique figures, and ultramarine eyes, need fear few rivals.

Attracted by her beauty, and being, by birth and fortune, able to enter any society, Robert de Fressignies had endeavoured to get an introduction to her, but the little circle of Spanish society of which the duchess was the centre, was strictly closed that year to all the French who were passing the season at Saint-Jean de Luz. The duchess, seen from afar, either on the beach, or at church, left without his being able to make her acquaintance, and for that reason she had remained in his memory like one of those meteors which pass and are never seen again. He had travelled in Greece and part of Asia, but of all the most beautiful women of those countries in which beauty holds such a high place that the inhabitants of the country cannot conceive a heaven without it, he had seen no one who could efface the remembrance of the duchess.

And now, by a strange and incomprehensible chance, this duchess, admired for an instant and then gone, had returned into his life by the most incredible means. She was leading an infamous life—he had bought her. She had belonged to him. She was nothing more than a prostitute, and a prostitute of the lowest class; for there are ranks even in infamy. The superb Duchess of Sierra Leone, of whom he had dreamed, and whom he had, perhaps, loved—a dream is so near love in our souls!—was no other—could it be really possible?—than a street-walker in Paris!!! It was she who had been in his arms but a few moments before, as she had been in the arms of another—any comer, like himself—the previous night, and as she would be in the arms of a third to-morrow, or—who knows?—perhaps in another hour. This terrible discovery struck him as with a hammer of ice.

The man in him, which had burned so hotly but a minute before, was now sobered, chilled, crushed. The idea—the certainty —that she was really the Duchess of Sierra Leone, had not revived his desires, which had been extinguished as suddenly as a candle that is blown out, and his mouth no longer sought to take long draughts of the delights of which he had drunk. By revealing herself, the duchess had caused the courtesan to disappear. To him, she was now only the duchess—but in what a condition! soiled, ruined, lost, fallen from a greater height than the Leucadian rock into a filthy and disgusting sea of mud, from which no power could rescue her.

He looked at her with a haggard eye, as she sat there, upright and grim, metamorphosed and tragical, at the extremity of the couch on which they were lying—a Messalina changed at once into some mysterious Agrippina. He no longer cared to touch, even with the tip of his finger, that creature who had made his blood boil, and prove that she was an illusion—that he did not dream—that he was not mad! The duchess had emerged from the harlot, and the phenomenon had stunned him.

"Yes," he said with an effort, for his voice stuck in his throat and choked him. "I believe you [he no longer addressed her familiarly] for I recognize you. I saw you at Saint-Jean de Luz three years ago."

At the name, her face lighted up for a moment.

"Ah," she said, "I was then enjoying all the intoxications of life—and now!"

The light died out of her eyes, but she did not lower her head.

"And now?" echoed Fressignies.

"Now," she said, "it is the intoxication of vengeance. But I will make it so deep," she added with concentrated violence, "that I will die in that vengeance; like the mosquitoes in my country, which die, gorged with blood, in the wound they have made."

She gazed into the face of Fressignies.

"You do not understand," she said, "but I will make you understand. You know what I am, but you do not know all that I am. Would you like to know? Would you like to learn my history? Shall I tell it to you?" she went on with excited persistence. "I like to tell it to all who come here. I would like to tell it to all the world. I should be more degraded, but I should be the better revenged."

"Tell me!" said Fressignies, moved by a curiosity and interest such as he had never felt to a like degree, neither in his life, nor in novels, nor at the theatre; for it seemed to him that she must needs relate a story such as he had never heard. He thought no more of her beauty. He looked at her as though he were about to assist at the autopsy on her dead body. Was she about to revive it for him?

"Yes," she continued, "I have often wished to relate my history to those who come up here; but they say they didn't come here to hear stories. When I begin, they interrupt me or they go away—brutes gorged with what they have obtained. Either indifferent, or mocking, or insulting, they call me a liar or a mad woman. They do not believe me, but you will believe me. You have seen me at Saint-Jean de Luz in all the glory of a happy woman, in the highest position, and wearing as a diadem that name of Sierra Leone which I now trail at the skirt of my dress through all the filth, as they used in old days to drag at a horse's tail the shield of a dishonoured knight.

"That name, which I hate, and only bear that I may degrade it, is still borne by the greatest lord of all Spain, and the proudest of all those who have the privilege to remain covered before His Majesty the King; for he thinks himself ten times more noble than the king. What are the most illustrious houses which have reigned over Spain—Castile, Aragon, Transtamare, Austria, and Bourbon—to the Duke of Arcos de Sierra Leone? He is, he says, of older family than they. He is descended from the old Gothic kings, and is allied by Brunehild to the Merovingians of France. He prides himself on having nothing but 'blue blood' in his veins, whilst even the oldest families, degraded by misalliances, have now only a few drops.

"Don Christoval d'Arcos, Duke of Sierra Leone, and *otros ducados*, made no misalliance in marrying me. I am a Turre-Cremata, of the old family of the Turre-Crematas of Italy—

the last of the Turre-Crematas, for the race ends with me, who
am well fitted to bear the name of Turre-Cremata [burnt tower]
for I have been burnt with all the fires of hell. The Grand In-
quisitor, Torquemada, who was descended from the Turre-
Crematas, inflicted fewer tortures in all his life than there are in
my accursed breast.

"I must tell you that the Turre-Crematas were not less proud
than the Sierra Leones. Divided into two branches, both equally
illustrious, they were for centuries all-powerful in Italy and Spain.
In the fifteenth century, during the pontificate of Alexander VI,
the Borgias, who in the intoxication of their good fortune wished
to appear connected with all the royal families of Europe, gave
out that they were connected with us, but the Turre-Crematas
scornfully denied the assertion, and two of them paid with their
lives for their proud audacity. They were, it is said, poisoned
by Cæsar Borgia.

"My marriage with the Duke of Sierra Leone was a match between two families. Neither on his side nor on mine was there
any feeling in the matter. It was quite natural that a Turre-
Cremata should marry a Sierra Leone. It was quite natural,
even to one brought up in the terrible etiquette of the old Spanish
families, which reflected that of the Escurial—that hard and
stifling etiquette which prevented hearts from beating—unless
the hearts were stronger than the iron corsets.

"I was one of those hearts. I loved Don Esteban. Before I
met him, my married life was without happiness—the grave affair
that it was formerly in ceremonious and Catholic Spain, though
it is not the rule now, except in a few aristocratic families which
preserve the old customs. The Duke of Sierra Leone was too
much of a Spaniard not to keep up the old customs. All that
you have heard in France about Spanish gravity, and the manners
of that proud, silent, and moody race, was true and more than
true of the Duke.

"Too proud to live elsewhere than on his own estates, he in-
habited a feudal castle on the Portuguese frontier, and his

habits were more feudal than his castle. I lived there with him, and divided my time between my confessor and my waiting-women—a sumptuous, monotonous, and sad life, which would have killed with boredom a weaker mind than mine. But I had been brought up for what I was—the wife of a great Spanish nobleman. Then I had the religious sentiment of a woman of my rank, and was nearly as passionless as the portraits of my an-cestresses which hung in the galleries of the castle of Sierra Leone. I should have added a generation the more to this row of irre-proachable majestic women whose virtue was guarded by their pride as a fountain is guarded by a lion.

"The solitude in which I lived did not weigh upon my soul, which was as peaceful as those mountains of red marble which surround Sierra Leone. I did not suspect that under that mar-ble slept a volcano. I was in a limbo, like an unborn child, but I was about to be born, and receive, by one look from a man, the baptism of fire.

"Don Esteban, Marquis of Vasconcellos, of a Portuguese family, and cousin to the Duke, came to Sierra Leone, and love, of which I had no idea beyond what I had gleaned from a few books, swooped down upon my heart as an eagle swoops down on and carries off a child who cries out. I cried out also. I was a Spanish woman of old family. My pride revolted when I felt myself in the presence of this dangerous man, Esteban, who ex-ercised such a terrible influence over me. I told the Duke to make some pretext to get rid of him, but he must leave the castle at once—that I saw he was in love with me, and I was offended by it as by an insult. But Don Christoval replied to me in the words of the Duke of Guise when he was warned that Henri III would assassinate him: 'He would not dare!' It was the dis-dain of Destiny—which avenged itself by accomplishing itself. That reply threw me into the arms of Esteban."

She paused for an instant; he listened to her and would have known, by her words and expressions, that she was, without any doubt, who she said she was—the Duchess of Sierra Leone. Ah!

the street-walker of the Boulevard was entirely obliterated. You would have declared that a mask had fallen, and that the real face, the real person, had reappeared. Even her attitudes had become chaste. Whilst she was speaking, she had taken from the sofa behind her a shawl, and wrapped it round that "cursed" breast—as she had called it—which prostitution had not been able to rob of its perfect form and virgin freshness. Even her voice had lost the hoarseness it had when she was in the street. Was the illusion produced by what she said?—at any rate, it seemed to Fressignies that her voice sounded purer and clearer—that she had recovered her nobility.

"I do not know," she continued, "whether other women are like me. But that incredulous pride of Don Christoval—that disdainful and calm 'He would not dare,' in speaking of the man I loved, seemed to me, in the bottom of my soul, like an insult to the man I reverenced as a God. 'Prove to him that you can dare,' I said to him that same evening when I told him of my love. There was no need to tell him. Esteban had loved me from the first day he saw me. Our love had been like two pistol-shots fired together, and which both kill.

"I had done my duty as a Spanish woman in warning Don Christoval. I now owed him nothing but my life, as I was his wife, for the heart is not free to love where it likes; and my life he would certainly have taken had he driven away Don Esteban as I wished. My heart had so overflowed that it would have driven me mad not to see him again, and I exposed myself to that terrible chance. But as the Duke, my husband, had not understood that—since he thought himself so superior that he deemed it impossible that de Vasconcellos could lift his eyes or pay court to me, I was not going to push my conjugal heroism too far, in opposition to a love which ruled me.

"I will not endeavour to give you an exact idea of that love.

"Perhaps you would not believe me if I did.—But, after all, what does it matter what you would believe? You may believe me, or not believe me! it was a love at once both burning and chaste—a chivalric, romantic, almost ideal, almost mystic love. It is true that we were both hardly twenty years old, and that we belonged to the same race as Bivar, Ignatius Loyola, and Saint Theresa. Ignatius, the knight of the Virgin, did not love the Queen of Heaven more purely than Vasconcellos loved me; and I, for my part, feel for him somewhat of that ecstatic love which Saint Theresa had for her divine Spouse.

"Adultery? bah! Did it even enter our minds to be adulterous? Our hearts beat too high, we lived in an atmosphere of sentiments so transcendent and elevated that we felt nothing of the evil lusts of sensuality and vulgar love. We lived under a clear, blue sky; but the sky was African, and the blue was a fire. Could souls exist under such conditions? Was it possible for it to last? Were we not playing, without knowing or suspecting it, at the most dangerous game in which weak mortals could indulge, and were we not bound to be precipitated sooner or later from this stainless height?

"Esteban was as pious as a priest, or as a Portuguese knight of the time of Albuquerque; and assuredly I was no worse than he, for I had in him, and his love for me, a faith which kindled the purity of my love. I lived in his heart like a Madonna in its niche of gold, with a lamp at her feet—an unextinguishable lamp! He loved my soul for my soul. He was one of those few lovers who wish to ennoble the woman they adore. He wanted me to be noble, devoted, heroic—one of the great women of those times when Spain was great. He would rather have seen me do a good action than waltz with me mouth to mouth. If the angels before the throne of God love one another, they must love as we loved.

"We were so much to each other that we passed long hours together and alone, hand in hand, eyes meeting eyes; able to do all we would, for we were alone, but so happy that neither desired more. Sometimes this immense happiness which filled us, pained us by its very intensity, and we wished to die—but with each other and for each other, and we understood then the say-

ing of Saint Theresa, 'I die of being unable to die!'—that desire
of the finite creature succumbing under an infinite love, and thinking to give more scope to the torrent of infinite love by the an-
nihilation of life. I am now the lowest of soiled creatures, but
believe me, at that time the lips of Esteban had never touched
mine, but if he kissed a rose and I kissed it after him, it made me
swoon. In this sea of horror in which I plunged voluntarily, I
remember each instant, as my punishment, the divine joys of
the pure love in which we lived, lost, absorbed, and so openly,
no doubt, in the innocence of our sublime affection, that Don
Christoval had not much difficulty in seeing that we adored each
other. We lived with our heads in the skies. How could we
perceive that he was jealous, and with such a kind of jealousy?
The only one of which he was capable—the jealousy of pride.

"He did not take us by surprise—only those who conceal themselves can be surprised. We did not conceal ourselves. Why
should we? Our love was like the flame burning in open day,
which can be perceived even in the daylight, and, besides, our
happiness was so great that it could not fail to be seen, and the
Duke saw it. Blinded as he was with pride, the splendour of
our love dazzled his eyes. Ah! Esteban had *dared*. I also!
One evening we were, as usual, gazing at one another, and he was
at my feet before me, as before the Virgin Mary, in a contemplation so profound that we needed no caress. Suddenly, the Duke
entered with two Negroes whom he had brought back from the
Spanish colonies, of which he was for a long time Governor.

"We did not see them—lost as we were in the heavenly contemplation which elevated our souls whilst uniting them—when
Esteban's head fell heavily on my knees. He was strangled!
The Negroes had thrown round his neck that terrible lasso with
which in Mexico they strangle the wild cattle. It was done with
the rapidity of lightning. But it was lightning which did not
kill me. I did not faint, I did not cry out. No tears came to
my eyes. I remained silent and rigid, in a nameless state of
horror, from which I could not escape without a violent wrench

to my soul. I felt as though my breast had been opened, and my heart torn out. Alas! it was not mine that was torn out—it was Esteban's. The corpse of Esteban, which lay at my feet strangled, was cut open, and the hands of these monsters groped in it as though it had been a sack!

"My love caused me to feel as much as Esteban would have himself felt had he been alive. I felt the pain his corpse could not feel, and it was that which released me from the horror which had seized me when they strangled him. I threw myself upon them. 'Kill me also!' I cried. 'I wish to die the same death!' and I stretched forth my neck for the cord. They were about to put it round.

" 'Touch not the queen!' said the Duke, that proud Duke who thought himself greater than the king, and he drove away the Negroes with his riding-whip.

" 'No! you shall live, Madame,' he said, 'in order that you may remember always that which you are about to see.'

"He whistled. Two enormous savage dogs rushed in.

" 'Give the heart of the traitor,' he said, 'to these dogs.'

"At that, a feeling—I know not of what—overcame me.

" 'Seek a better revenge than that!' I cried. 'It is I you should make eat it.'

"He seemed astounded at the idea.

" 'You love him, then, so wonderfully?' he said.

"Ah! I loved him with a love my husband had rendered boundless. I loved him so that I should have felt neither fear nor disgust at that bleeding heart, filled with me, and still warm with me—and I wished to join that heart to mine. I prayed for it on my knees with joined hands.

"I wished to spare that noble, adored heart that impious, sacrilegious profanation.

"I would have communed with that heart as with a Host.

"Was he not my God? The resolution of Gabrielle de Vergy, whose story Esteban and I had so often read together, came to my mind. I deemed her happy to have made her breast the living tomb of the man she loved. But the sight of such a love made the Duke fiercely implacable.

"His dogs devoured Esteban's heart before me. I fought with them for it, but I could not snatch it from them.

"They covered me with fearful bites, and tore my dress with their bloody jaws."

She paused. These memories had made her face become livid —and she arose breathlessly, and, opening a drawer, took from it, and showed to Fressignies, a dress, torn to tatters, and stained with blood in many places.

"Look!" she said; "that is the heart's blood of the man I loved—the heart I could not save from the dogs. When the thought of the accursed life I am leading occurs to me; when I am filled with disgust; when the filth rises to my mouth and chokes me; when the spirit of vengeance is weak within me; when the former duchess returns and the life of the harlot shocks me, I wrap myself in this robe, my soiled body wallows in its red folds that still burn me, and my vengeance revives. There is a talisman in these bloody rags! When they are around my body the rage for vengeance burns within me, and I recover strength that, it seems to me, will last for an eternity."

Fressignies shuddered as he heard this terrible woman.

He shuddered at her gestures, her words, her face, which was like that of a Gorgon; he seemed to see round her head the snakes this woman had in her heart.

He began to understand—the curtain was drawn!—the word "vengeance" which was ever on her lips.

"Vengeance! yes," she continued; "you understand now what my vengeance is. Ah! I have chosen it amongst all others, as you choose amongst all kinds of daggers that which will create the most suffering—the toothed blade which will best tear the flesh of the hated being you kill. I did not wish to kill that man at a blow.

"Had he killed Vasconcellos with his sword, like a gentleman? No, he had had him killed by his varlets. He had thrown his

heart to the dogs, and his body on the dunghill, perhaps. I did
not know. I have never known. Kill him, for that? No! that
would have been too gentle, too speedy! I needed a vengeance
that was slower and more cruel. Besides, the Duke was brave.
He did not fear death. Every generation of the Sierra Leones
had faced it courageously. But his pride, his enormous pride,
was cowardly when it concerned dishonour. I must torture him
in his pride therefore. I would dishonour the name of which he
was so proud. I swore to myself that I would drag that name
through the most stinking mire—that I would cover it with shameful and nameless filth!—and for that I have become what I am—
a common harlot—the public prostitute Sierra Leone, whom you
have 'picked up' to-night!"

As she said these last words her eyes sparkled as though with
the joy of a well-struck blow.

"But," said Fressignies, "does the Duke know what you have
become?"

"If he does not know it now, he will know it some day," she
replied with the absolute confidence of a woman who has thought
of and calculated every chance, and who is sure of the future.
"The stain of my shame is sure to reach him some day or other.
One of the men who has come here will spit in his face his wife's
dishonour, and that spittle will be never wiped off; but that is
only a chance, and I would not leave my vengeance to chance.
That I may be quite sure, I have resolved to die, and my death
will assure my revenge."

Fressignies could not guess the meaning of these last words,
but her next sentence threw a hideous light upon them.

"I wish to die as the prostitutes like me do die," she continued.
"Do you not know that there was a man in the time of Francis
I who caught, from a woman like me, a terrible and shameful
disease, that he might give it to his wife to poison the king, whose
mistress she was, and thus he might be revenged on both? I
would do no less than that man did. The shameful life I lead
will some day cause the putrefaction of debauchery to gnaw the

prostitute, and then I shall rot away and die in some hospital. Oh, then I shall have paid the debt I owe," she added with the enthusiasm of this most terrible hope; "then it will be time enough for the Duke of Sierra Leone to learn how his wife, the Duchess of Sierra Leone, has lived and died."

Fressignies had not imagined the depth of her vengeance, which exceeded aught that he had ever read in history. Neither in Italy in the fifteenth century, nor in Corsica at any time, though both countries were renowned for implacable revenge, did he remember to have heard of such a deeply calculated and terrible vengeance as that of this woman, who sacrificed to her revenge both her body and soul. He was terrified at its horrible sublimity, for intensity in any passion, carried to such a point, is sublime. But it is the sublimity of hell.

"And even if he did not know it," she continued again, "I, at least, should know it. I should know what I do every night— that I drink this filth and find it nectar because it is my revenge. Do I not rejoice every minute at the thought of what I am? Have I not, each time that I dishonour this haughty duke, the delirious joy of knowing that I dishonour him? Do I not see clearly in my own mind all that he would if he knew it? Ah, feelings like mine may be insane, but it is their madness which makes their happiness. When I escaped from Sierra Leone, I brought with me the Duke's portrait, that I might show this portrait, as though it were himself, the shameful life I lead! How many times have I said to him, as though he could see and hear me: 'Look! Look!' And when I feel the horror of being in the arms of you men—for I always do feel it: I can never get accustomed to the taste of this filth—I have for a resource this bracelet"—and she raised her superb arm with a tragic movement.

"I have this ring of fire which burns me to the marrow; and which I keep on my arm, despite the torture of wearing it, that I may never forget the executioner of Esteban; that his image may excite my transports—those transports of vengeful hate which men are stupid enough and conceited enough to believe are due to the pleasures they create in me! I do not know who you are, but you are certainly more than a mere chance-comer; and yet you thought, but a moment ago, that I was still a human creature—that there was still a fibre of humanity which vibrated in me; and yet there was in me but the idea of revenging Esteban on the monster whose portrait is here. Ah! his portrait was for me like the spur, broad as a sword, which the Arab horseman drives into his horse's flank to make it cross the desert.

"I had even a wider expanse of shame to cross, and I buried that abominable portrait in my eyes and in my heart, that I might the better bound under you when you held me in your arms. This portrait was as though it were himself; as though he saw us with his painted eyes!

"How well I understand the spell of the waxen image in those days of sorcery! How I should have enjoyed the senseless happiness of planting a dagger in the heart of the image of the man I wished to kill! In those days when I was religious—before I loved Esteban, who took the place of God for me—I had need of a crucifix that I might the better think of the Crucified: but if, instead of loving Him, I had hated Him, I should have been an impious wretch had I needed a crucifix that I might the better blaspheme and insult.

"Alas!" she added, changing her tone, and passing from the harshness of the most cruel feeling to the deep sweetness of the most surprising melancholy, "I have no portrait of Esteban. I only see him in my mind's eye—and that is, perhaps, fortunate. If he were before my eyes, he would lift up my poor heart; he would make me blush at the unworthy humiliation of my life. I should repent, and then I could no longer avenge him!"

The Gorgon had become tender, but her eyes remained dry. Fressignies, moved by quite another sentiment than those which she had excited in him, took her hand, and kissed it with a respect mingled with pity. So much misfortune and energy had made her seem great in his eyes. "What a woman!" he thought to himself. "If instead of being the Duchess of Sierra Leone, she had been the Marquise de Vasconcellos, she would, by the purity and warmth of her love for Esteban, have offered to human admiration something akin and equal to the great Marquise de Pescaire.—Only," he added to himself, "she would not have shown it, and no one would ever have known the depth and force of her character."

Despite the scepticism of the period, and his habit of watching the world only that he might laugh at it, Robert de Fressignies did not feel it absurd for him to kiss the hand of this fallen woman; but he did not know what to say to her. By throwing her story between him and her, she had cut, as though with an ax, those transient ties which bound them together. He felt an inexpressible mixture of admiration, horror, and scorn; but he would have deemed it very bad taste to have preached sentiment or morality to this woman. He had often laughed at those moralists who had neither warrant nor authority, and who pullulate in these days, and who, under the influence of certain dramas or novels, think it their bounden duty to pick up fallen women as though they were flower-pots that had been knocked over. Sceptic as he was, he was endowed with sufficient good sense to know that it is only the priest—the priest of redeeming God— who can raise such fallen creatures—and he believed that even the priest would be powerless against the soul of this woman. All kinds of sad thoughts weighed upon his heart, and he preserved a silence that was more embarrassing to him than to her. She, carried away by the violence of her ideas and her memories, continued:

"The idea of dishonouring instead of killing this man, for whom honour—as the world understands it—was more than life, did not occur to me at once. It was long before I thought of that. After the death of Vasconcellos, whose presence in the castle was, perhaps, not known, and whose body had probably been thrown into some cell with those of the Negroes who had assassinated him, the Duke never addressed a word to me, except briefly and ceremoniously before people, for Cæsar's wife should be above suspicion—and I should have remained in the eyes of all, the immaculate Duchess d'Arcos de Sierra Leone. But when alone with me, never a single word or allusion passed; only silence —the silence of the hate which feeds itself, and has no need of speech. Don Christoval and I fought each other with the weapons of resolution and pride. I kept back my tears. I am a Turre-Cremata. I have all the potent dissimulation of my race, which is Italian, and I turned to bronze, so that he should not suspect the idea of vengeance which lurked beneath that face of bronze. I was absolutely impenetrable. Thanks to that dissimulation, which closed every opening though which my secret might filter, I prepared my flight from the castle, the walls of which crushed me, and where I could not accomplish my vengeance, for the Duke would have prevented me. I trusted no one. Had any of my duennas or waiting-women ever dared to lift their eyes to mine to learn my thoughts?

"At first I thought of going to Madrid; but at Madrid the Duke was all-powerful, and the police would have arrested me at once. I should have been sent back to him, and once sent back, I should have been thrown into the *in pace* of some convent, and buried there between four walls, out of the world—the world I so needed for my vengeance. Paris was safer. I preferred Paris. It was a better stage for the display of my infamy and my revenge; and as I wished that it should one day burst like a thunder-clap, what better place than this city, the centre of all echoes, and through which pass all the nations of the world! I resolved to live there the life of a prostitute, and boldly to descend to the lowest ranks of those fallen women who sell themselves for a piece of money, even to the lowest ruffians.

"I was pious before I knew Esteban, who tore God from my heart to put himself in the place, and often rose in the night and went, without my women, to say my prayers before the Virgin in the chapel. It was from there one night that I made my escape, and boldly gained the gorges of the Sierras. I carried with me all the jewellery I could, and all the money in my cash-box. I hid myself for some time, amongst the peasants, who conducted me to the frontier. I came to Paris, and fearlessly began this vengeance which is my life. I thirst so for revenge that I have sometimes thought of fascinating some energetic young man, and then sending him to the Duke to tell him my ignominy, but I have always ended by dismissing that idea, for it is not merely a few feet of filth that I wish to pile on *his* name and my memory—it is a whole pyramid of dung. The later I am avenged, the better I shall be avenged."

She stopped. She had turned from a livid hue to purple. The sweat ran down her forehead, and she became hoarse. She fever-ishly seized a water-bottle that stood on a side-table, poured herself out a large glass, and drained it at a draught.

"It is hard to get used to shame," she said, "but I must get used to it. I have swallowed enough of it during these three months to be used to it."

"Has it lasted three months?" (he did not dare to say what) asked Fressignies with a vagueness that was more horrible than precision.

"Yes," she replied, "three months. But what is three months?" she added. "It needs time to cook and recook the dish of ven-geance I prepare for him, and which will repay for refusing me Esteban's heart that he would not let me eat."

She said this with terrible passion and a wild sadness. Fres-signies did not suspect that there could exist in a woman such a mixture of idolatrous love and cruelty. He had never gazed with more concentrated attention on any work of art than he did at this singular and most powerful *artiste* of vengeance who stood before him.

But something that he was astonished to feel, mingled with his contemplation as an observer. He thought he was free from in-voluntary sensations, but he felt that in the same atmosphere as this woman he was breathing a dangerous air. The room, so full of physical and savage passion, choked the civilization within him.

He needed fresh air, and he thought he would go, even if he should return.

She believed that he was about to leave. But there was still one side of her character she had to reveal to him.

"And that?" she said with one of the disdainful gestures of the former Duchess, and pointing with her finger to the blue glass cup that he had filled with gold.

"Take back that money," she said. "Who knows? Perhaps I am richer than you. No gold enters here. I accept it from no one." And with the pride of a degradation which was her revenge, she added: "I am only a five-franc girl!"

The sentence was said as it was thought. It was the last trait of that reversed and infernal sublimity which had been spread before him, and which certainly the great Corneille had never imagined in the depths of his tragic soul. The horror of this last sentence gave Fressignies the strength to go away. He emptied the gold out of the cup, and only left what she had asked. "Since she wishes it," he said, "I will press upon the dagger she has driven in, and I will add my stain of mire, since it is that she requires."

He left, much excited and agitated. The candelabras still shed their flood of light over the common-looking door through which he had passed. He understood now why they were put there when he saw, pasted on the door, the card which was the sign of this mart of human flesh. There was written on the card, in large letters:

THE DUCHESS D'ARCOS
DE SIERRA LEONE

and underneath was a horrible word, to tell what her calling was.

Fressignies returned home that night, after this adventure, so troubled in mind that he was almost ashamed. Fools—that is to say, nearly all the world—believe that it would be a charming invention if we could grow young again, but those who know life well know it would be an unprofitable transaction. Fressignies owned to himself that perhaps he felt too young—and he therefore vowed never to see the Duchess again, in spite of the interest, or rather because of the interest, the woman created in him.

"Why," he said, "return to that infected place into which a woman of high rank has wilfully precipitated herself?

"She has told me all about her life, and I can easily imagine the horrible details of her present existence, which never change."

Such was the resolution which Fressignies made when he was sitting by the fire in the solitude of his own room. For some time he did not indulge in any amusements out of his own house, but remained thinking over the impressions and memories of an evening on which his mind could not help but linger, as on a strange and powerful poem, the like of which he had never read either in Byron or Shakespeare, his two favourite poets.

Thus he passed many hours, with his elbow on the arm of his chair, dreamily turning over in his mind the ever-open pages of this hideously powerful poem. It was to him a lotus which made him forget the *salons* of Paris—his country. It required a strong effort of will to make him return there. The irreproachable duchesses he met there seemed colourless.

Though Fressignies was not prudish, or his friends either, he never said a word about his adventure, through a feeling of delicacy which he deemed absurd—for had not the Duchess asked him to tell her story to all comers, and spread it abroad as much as he could? On the contrary, he kept it to himself. He put it under seal in the most mysterious corner of his soul, as you cork a bottle of very rare perfume which loses somewhat of its scent each time you smell it. Considering what sort of man he was, it was astonishing that neither at the Café de Paris, nor the club, nor in the stalls at the theatre, nor anywhere else where men talk unreservedly, did he speak to any of his friends without being afraid to hear related the counterpart of his own adventure; and he trembled during the first ten minutes of a conversation lest that chance should arrive.

Nevertheless, he kept his word, and revisited neither the Rue Basse du Rempart nor the Boulevard. He no longer leaned, like the yellow-gloved dandies of his day, against the balcony at Tortoni's. "If I were to see that confounded yellow dress flaunting before me," he said to himself, "I should perhaps be fool enough to follow her again."

He loved yellow dresses now, though he had always detested them. "She has spoiled my taste," he said; thus did the dandy in him make fun of the man. But what Madame de Staël, who knew them, calls somewhere or other "the Devil's thoughts," were stronger than the man or the dandy. Fressignies became moody. He had been lively in society, and well known for his gaiety. His spirits were gone. "Is he in love?" the gossips asked. The old Marquise de Clérembault, who thought that he was in love with her grand-daughter, then just fresh from the Sacré Cœur, and romantic, as people were then, said to him crossly: "I cannot bear you when you put on those Hamlet airs." First he was sad and then he became ill. His complexion grew leaden. "What is the matter with Monsieur de Fressignies?" they asked, and perhaps they would have discovered that he had a cancer in his stomach, like Bonaparte; but one fine day he put an end to all questions and inquiries concerning him, by packing up his portmanteau, and disappearing as suddenly as though he had gone down a trap.

Where had he gone? What was he doing? He was away more than a year, and then he returned to Paris and took his usual place in society. One night he was at the Spanish Embassy —where all the best society in Paris had congregated on that occasion. It was late. Supper had been announced, and the *salons* had emptied, everyone crowding round the buffet. In the card-room a few men were lingering over a game of whist. All at once Fressignies's partner, who was turning over the pages of a little tortoise-shell note-book in which he wrote down the bets that were made over each rubber, saw something which made him say: "Ah!"—as a man does when he finds something he has forgotten.

"May I ask your Excellency," he said, addressing the Spanish Ambassador, who was standing with his hands behind his back, watching the game, "if there are any of the Sierra Leone family still at Madrid?"

"Certainly there are," replied the Ambassador. "In the first place, there is the Duke, who is the peer of the highest grandees in the realm."

"Who, then, is this Duchess of Sierra Leone who has just died in Paris—and what relation is she to the Duke?" continued the questioner.

"That must be his wife," quietly replied the Ambassador. "But for nearly two years the Duchess has been looked upon as dead. She disappeared; and no one knew why or how she disappeared—it has always been a profound mystery. You must know that the splendid Duchess d'Arcos de Sierra Leone was not like a woman of the present day—one of those silly girls that any lover can carry off. She was quite as haughty as the Duke, her husband, who is certainly the proudest of the *Ricos hombres* of all Spain. Moreover, she was pious—of an almost monastic piety. She lived always at Sierra Leone, a desert of red marble, where the eagles, if there are any there, must die of boredom amongst the peaks. One day she disappeared, and no one has ever found a trace of her. Since that time, the Duke—who is quite a man of the time of Charles V, and to whom no one has ever dared to put the least question—has lived in Madrid, and has never said any more about his wife and her disappearance than though she had never existed. She was a Turre-Cremata—the last of the Turre-Crematas of the Italian branch of the family."

"Exactly," interrupted the player, and he looked at the page of his note-book. "Well, then," he added solemnly, "I have the honour to inform your Excellency that the Duchess of Sierra

Leone was buried this morning and—what you would assuredly never suspect—she was buried at the church of the Salpêtrière, of which hospital she was an inmate."

At these words, the players laid their cards down on the table and gazed at the speaker in amazement.

"Yes," said the player, who saw he was "making a hit"—a thing so delightful to every Frenchman, "I was passing by there this morning, and I heard such beautiful sacred music that I entered the church—such events being rare there—and I nearly tumbled backwards when I passed the portal—which was draped with black, in the centre of which was a coat of arms with many quarterings, to see in the choir the most magnificent catafalque. The church was almost empty. There were a few beggars in the poor seats, and one or two women—some of the horrible lepers from the hospital near by, who were not insane, and could stand. Surprised at seeing such an assemblage round such a catafalque, I approached, and read this inscription, which was written in large silver letters on a black ground, and which so astonished me that I copied it in order that I might not forget it:

HERE LIES

SANZIA FLORINDA CONCEPTION

DE TURRE-CREMATA

DUCHESS D'ARCOS DE SIERRA LEONE,

A REPENTANT HARLOT.

DIED AT THE SALPÊTRIÈRE THE — — 18—

Requiescat in pace."

The players thought no more about the game. As for the Ambassador, although a diplomatist ought no more to show surprise than an officer ought to show fear, he felt that his astonishment might compromise him in the eyes of his guests.

"And you asked for no information?" he cried, as though he had been speaking to one of his inferiors.

"No, your Excellency," replied the player. "There were only a few poor people there—and the priests, who perhaps might have informed me, were chanting the Mass. Besides, I remembered that I should have the honour to see you this evening."

"I shall have the information to-morrow," said the Ambassador.

The game finished, but was broken by so many exclamations, and everyone was so preoccupied with his own thoughts, that even the best whist-players made mistakes, and no one perceived that Fressignies had turned pale, seized his hat, and left suddenly, without taking leave of anyone.

The next morning he was at the Salpêtrière early. He questioned the chaplain—a good old priest—who gave him all the information he asked concerning "No. 119," otherwise the Duchess of Sierra Leone. The wretched woman had ended as she had foreseen she would end. At the terrible game she had played, she had gained a most frightful disease. "In a few months," said the old priest, "she was rotten to the bones. She had died—stoically—in intolerable sufferings. She was still rich, and had much money and jewels which she had bequeathed to other patients in the hospital, and she had ordered a grand funeral.

"Only, to punish herself for her disorderly life," said the old priest, who knew nothing about this woman's life, "she insisted, in her penitence and humility, that it should be put after her titles, both on her coffin and on her tomb, that she was a *Repentant Harlot*.

"And even," added the old chaplain, who had been deceived by her confession, "so great was her humility that she did not wish the word 'repentant' to be written."

Fressignies smiled bitterly, but he took care not to undeceive the simple, good old priest.

For he knew that she had not repented, and that this touching humility was a further vengeance after her death.

A NOTE ON THE TYPE IN
WHICH THIS BOOK IS SET

• •
•

*The type in which this book has been set (on the Lino-
type) is Caslon Old Face, a faithful and authentic re-
production from the original patterns of William
Caslon I. Historically considered, Caslon's old face
types are the most important contribution the English
speaking world has ever made to the art of typography.
No other face has ever attained to so lasting and
general a popularity. Caslon's types were made to
read. Even their apparent imperfections contribute to
this effect being, in fact, the result of a deliberate
artistry which sought above all else for legibility in the
printed page.*

SET UP, ELECTROTYPED AND PRINTED BY
THE VAIL-BALLOU PRESS, INC., BING-
HAMTON, N. Y. · PAPER MANUFAC-
TURED BY THE TICONDEROGA PULP
AND PAPER CO., TICONDEROGA,
N. Y. AND FURNISHED BY W. F.
ETHERINGTON & CO., NEW
YORK · BOUND BY THE H.
WOLFF ESTATE, NEW
YORK. ·